Praise for

BRAVE

"Delving into the depths of adolescence, Corbo's debut novel weaves a suspenseful, heart-tugging tale where secrets lurk in every shadow. A coming-of-age thriller, where the intertwined journeys of twins, brother and sister, unfold and survival skews the lines of right and wrong, *Brave* is the perfect blend of suspense and horror, promising an unforgettable ride through the complexities of youth and the darkness that lies inside one's soul."

—*Tina Carreiro, author of* Power of the Moon *Series*

BRAVE

A Novel

◆

Nancy P. Corbo

LUCID
DREAM
PUBLISHING

Cover design by Leon N. Kellar
Author photograph by Paj Crank
Published by Lucid Dream Publishing
nancypcorbo.com
E-book ISBN: 979-8-9935360-1-9
Paperback ISBN: 979-8-9935360-0-2
First Edition
Printed in USA

BRAVE

*In memory of Uncle Billy, who wrote that letter to
Mom and Dad. If not, this book would not exist*

*And my late friend and poet, Allison Rice.
You left us way too soon.*

"The future doesn't belong to the fainthearted; it belongs to the brave."

RONALD REAGAN

Ramapo State Forest

Prologue

Prologue

She wants to go home, but nobody's home.
That's where she lies, broken inside.
With no place to go, no place to go.
To dry her eyes, broken inside.

- "Nobody's Home," Avril Lavigne

THE GIRL

THE GIRL

April 1

I'm twelve years old. I'm not ready to die.

Beth's gaze swept the room, her heart pounding at the bits of skull and brain smeared across the wall. She clamped a trembling hand over her mouth, stifling a scream. If anyone discovered their whereabouts, they were dead.

The boards had been scrubbed clean, yet her eyes still caught slivers of gray-white bone and streaks of heavy, leaden matter clinging to the wood's grooves. Patches of blood, now dried to deep brown, mottled the wall and floor.

Flat, pale light bathed the room, mingling with the acrid tang of lingering gunfire. Pressed into the corner, Beth sat cross-legged on a urine-stained mattress, patting a hunter's knife with one hand, a shaky hand gripping a pen with her left.

She didn't realize how hard she'd been trembling until the blanket slipped from her shoulders. With a huff, she tore her gaze from the wall, set her pen aside, and wrapped the blanket around herself again. She had refused to wear the driver's leather jacket; the blanket was her only shield.

Hunted by state police, the FBI, and members of a proud community, you became a virus—buzzing, vile, marked for eradication. Society moved like white blood cells, ruthless and fast. Escape wasn't possible. Not by diving off a ledge. Not by flying into a burning building with explosives strapped to your chest. Beth told herself one day she'd laugh at all this—if she lived long enough to look back. Maybe then her situation would seem absurd. Senseless.

Chris had stormed into the trees. With him gone, Beth had space to gather her thoughts before they scattered. That urge to document everything built inside her, like steam under a rattling lid. It was good that Chris left—better to write before the weight of unnamed casualties bent her into someone else.

Journaling offered solace, a way out of her own head. Unlike the kids at school, fading into a blur of faces and quiet judgment, the journal never mocked her. It kept her secrets. But now it was gone, discarded like a dirty sock, replaced by a magazine stuffed with condom ads and essays on sex and pumping iron.

Before the fire, life was rough but predictable. Beth worried about wrong answers, being disliked. Boys looked past her. She hated her clothes, hadn't developed breasts, wore her hair shorter than the other girls.

Then everything changed. Whatever concerns once came with being an ordinary girl no longer mattered.

Since the first killing, Beth felt herself growing numb. Most things passed through her untouched. Emotions once close to the surface now filtered through a thick mesh of grief and resistance. Cutting herself off became a kind of armor—a way to survive. Anger and sorrow pushed her forward. Hope barely clung on.

Wait, hold on. Feeling guilty doesn't help. You didn't cause all of this. If anything, you're the victim here.

Set to retort, Beth opened her mouth.

Then wind pressed against the plywood walls. It slipped through cracked glass and rattled the windowpane as it curled into the room. Beth looked back at the smeared ichor on the wall. She shivered, pulling deeper into the corner. A squeal nearly escaped, but her throat, raw from dehydration, refused to cooperate. It was always dry now. Outside, sweet alyssum drifted in, cutting through the stale, damp air. Even Beth couldn't deny the pleasant scent. Still, the air was stinging, like acid vapors on skin.

Heightened awareness became instinct. Before the nightmare, Beth never noticed her surroundings. Now, that choice was gone. She heard wind murmurs, rustling bushes, insect chants. She smelled the bosky scent of wood. Even the air had flavor—thick and musky today. Earthy, like moist clay.

Dad spoke up. *Mother Nature doesn't care how we feel about her. So why waste energy feeling anything back?*

Beth cracked a smile.

Dad.

The smile vanished. Brief, but it felt good while it lasted. Her lips throbbed, as if a lit match had skimmed them. She barely noticed. According to Chris, focusing on pain would mean giving it satisfaction. That was dangerous.

Chris.

He'll come back, she thought, *and then curse me for not going with him.*

Cue the snarky, survival voice.

Hold on a second. You're protecting your base. You need to guard the food and weapons. And your leg needs time to heal.

Beth nodded.

Minutes passed before sharp fragments of memory pierced her consciousness. A sinking weight swamped her gut.

Pen hovering over an ad for men's custom suits, her eyes snapped to the wall across the room. Jaw clenched, she tightened her grip, and scribbled.

People are dead, and it was all my fault.

Those men were horrible. And they tried to kill Chris.

That was true. Self-protection might have justified the killings, but it didn't make them easier.

Whenever Beth tried to rehash the events, the present pulled her in. Short-term memory was fractured—a symptom of trauma. So how could she trust any of it? Hand resting on the knife, she stared down at the forest of letters on her lap.

Beth's left hand lingered until something brushed her face.

She blinked.

Droplets of water trickled down her cheek onto the magazine, smearing the black ink. It had rained last night, and the roof still needed repair. She wiped her cheek with the back of her hand, leaving a black smudge on her right cheekbone.

A drop glided to the corner of her mouth, and she licked it away. It tasted salty.

Well, damn.

Alarm poured through her. Tears welled as the muddiness in her mind cleared. Numbness faded, and Beth found herself in a different world. Questions and gaps remained, but she remembered how the nightmare began. Her stomach felt like a lead balloon.

Had she forgotten everything or numbed herself to the truth?

Relax. Freaking out isn't going to help.

Beth shook her head. Resisting the inevitable felt like stopping a speeding truck with outstretched arms.

She looked up. "Mom...?"

The pen slipped through her fingers and clinked on the hardwood floor. She buried her face in her hands. Abandoning concerns about what—or who—might be near, Beth screamed her pain into the silence of the hut.

If only she'd found the words for Chris back in his bedroom, would things have turned out differently?

Could her words have stopped the cruel chain of events that followed?

Maybe then, no one would have died.

○   ○   ○

This is my life.
It's not what it was before.

-"So Far Away," Staind

THE BOY

THE BOY

He hitched the pack higher on his back and followed the weedy game trail. Pausing, he squinted at the trees, judging the light's angle. Forgetting to slap on his watch was careless, but he'd learned to gauge time without it.

Chris nodded, wincing at a beating headache, a stale taste of bourbon in his mouth. He changed direction and headed east, kicking away broken pieces of deadwood.

With the pack strapped to his back and the revolver tucked into his jeans, he gripped the bolt cutter. The firearm was a last resort; drawing attention was dangerous. Yet he relished its weight, the cool smooth metal pressing against his skin, And the steel blades of the bolt cutter had already served as a cunning and unexpected defense.

Chris narrowed his eyes at the broken sneaker prints pressed into the earth and scowled. He should have brushed them away, but his rush to return two days ago caused an oversight. Counting on the rain to erase them was foolish. He cursed his carelessness and made a fierce mental note to cover his tracks on the way back.

With scabbed knuckles and dirt-caked hands, Chris tightened his hold on the jaws and neck of the bolt cutter, nearly losing his balance as he swung at the swarm of flies and gnats clogging his path. The tool was eighteen inches long and weighed nearly four pounds. Cumbersome—nothing like a baseball bat, and impossible to wield with the same leverage.

His hands and wrists ached from yesterday's battle, arms stinging with puffy red scratches. They looked as if scraped countless times with a dull knife. A sea of dark bruises mottled his chest and neck.

Chris secretly enjoyed the trips to the stream. He liked watching the sunlight pierce the canopy, diagonal beams lighting the ground as if guiding the way. The greenery had shifted to a livelier, verdant hue; the rain left white pines and softened wood to release a fresh, intoxicating scent.

But things had changed.

There was no joy in today's mission.

Spring took its time this year. Shady patches still carried a wintry chill. With effort, Chris had recovered his Islanders jacket. It was still damp from the ravine, mud crusted along the orange sleeves. But it kept him warm. He left the driver's jacket for Beth, knowing she wouldn't use it.

As his sneakers smacked against the muddy ground, an unexpected breeze tore through the greenery. His dark, greasy hair fluttered around his ears, nearly blowing off his Yankees hat. The wind whipped through his clothes, jacket billowing like a cape, carrying a sour smell with it. He couldn't deny that he stank. The air hung thick and sticky from last night's rain, and he'd been moving nonstop for days.

Chris stuck his nose in his armpit and sniffed. "Damn," he winced. "My pits reek." Cleanliness was never a priority, but he figured he should wash up after finishing. He shivered, imagining the water's icy temperature, a million needles stabbing his skin.

Soon, he heard the faint, familiar hiss of the creek.

Chris clenched the bolt cutter, tensing his muscles and slowing his breath.

This was the place to stay sharp. Black bears, coyotes, timber rattlesnakes, and copperheads prowled these woods. Any of them would welcome a small boy for breakfast.

He felt unwelcome here, an uninvited guest at a party.

Chris reached the narrow stretch of stream, where rock-strewn shoals pushed the water north, downhill through a long, winding channel. Insects buzzed in the weedy grass along the banks. He followed the stream another fifty yards until it widened. To bathe, he needed to find a waist-deep section. He remembered a cut where the stream deepened as it flowed downhill.

He paused to inspect the area, then knelt on the floodplain. Setting the bolt cutter aside, Chris fished the bottles from his pack, the flimsy plastic crackling in his grip. In his rush to leave the clearing, he'd forgotten the canteen, so the bottles would have to do. He uncapped one and pushed it into the water. Surprisingly, his hands had grown used to the biting cold and no longer flinched.

As the bottle filled, Chris' eyes drifted to the bolt cutter. He smirked. Dried, crimson stains and gummy hair glazed the rusty bolts and blades.

His left hand traveled to the raw skin below his Adam's apple, then slid down to his damp groin.

The smile dropped.

With no mirror between them, Beth gave an update on the wound's healing. What was once an inflamed red blotch was now mustard-colored, with deep plum, finger-length welts tracing his neck.

Keep your eyes open. Be ready for anything that tries to attack you, Dad said. *Otherwise, when something happens, you'll have no one to blame but yourself.*

Dad.

Chris shook his head, casting out the unwelcome thoughts.

Time in the woods had hardened him. His old carefree self was fading, giving way to instinct and reflex, and it sharpened every day. He'd grown more alert, quick-witted. Smells intensified, tastes fine-tuned, sounds unmistakable. What was once a cavalier kid was now a stony, astute young man.

A soldier.

Beth was a different story.

Chris often wondered what she did in her room for hours, shut off from the world. He knew she liked writing in that diary of hers. Sometimes on the school bus, he'd catch her cowering alone, scribbling in her little purple book. Hanging in the rear seats with the popular kids, he'd peer over a few heads, curious. He never understood how she found pleasure in writing things no one else read.

At any rate, call it furious curiosity, but Chris once peeked. The book sat on her desk, practically begging to be read.

He cringed.

Chris had convinced himself they were just words on paper. And still, they stung—more than anything else he'd seen or read.

Girls can be so freaking cruel, he thought.

A knot tightened in Chris's chest. His eyes burned, and he drew in a sharp breath. He yanked off his cap and plunged his sweat-soaked head into the cool, glassy pool, letting the cold swallow him whole.

Part 1

There is no greater agony than bearing
an untold story inside you.

- Maya Angelou (1928-2014)

Instinct and common sense
they come in different quantities.

-"Sally's Pigeons," Cyndi Lauper

1

January, 20 years ago...

SANDERS

SANDERS

The morning was cool and sticky. A thin ray of light beamed through the window, casting a strip of daylight across his back.

By the time he woke, face pressed against the pillow, she was already up, a mug of coffee cradled in both hands. He could feel her at the foot of the bed, staring at his ass on display over the bedraggled comforter. He didn't have to turn his head to know she looked incredible in his bathrobe.

The smell in the room was intoxicating. Freshly brewed coffee from the kitchen, strips of swine blistering in the oven, traces of sex. Sanders blinked an eye open, puzzled at first by the sight of the bedroom door, not the usual sea-green wall bedecked in artwork.

Christ, the bed had ended up on the other side of the room.

It had been a fine evening, bursting with proud colleagues, a boatload of friends eager to offer the next round of drinks, and, more importantly, a wonderful woman who was more than happy to give her private, lavish congratulations. To his surprise, Sanders transformed into a leopard last night: dark, unblinking eyes studying his mate's every move while she stripped for him, clawed paws gripping her hips and swollen breasts, grunts and snarls shooting from his mouth in breathless, fiery gusts. He had been hard as steel. And the woman took it all with uncontrolled abandon.

God, he loved her.

It had been a beautiful ceremony. Excited murmurs from friends and family flooded the packed theater, though dead silent whenever a speaker rose to take the podium.

Members of the US Army, Air Force, Coast Guard, Navy, and Marine Corps came to witness over five hundred officers, ready for the pressures of their new careers, swear in. A thousand officers had recently retired or resigned; the new crew faced a demanding period ahead.

Packed with rigorous physical and tactical training, Sanders acquired six months of knowledge and experience, testing his limits and introducing him to an intense world of academic instruction. The new officer's determined efforts proved worthwhile when he received formal recognition from the mayor and police commissioner.

He'd left the theater carrying three shield-shaped mahogany plaques and gold citation chords draped over his shoulder, proclaiming his outstanding status in the graduating class. He earned the Mayor's Award as the graduate with the highest overall average of 99.38% and the Chief of Departments Award for achieving the highest physical fitness runoff score. The mayor and commissioner were too proud to hand Sanders his third plaque for Class Valedictorian. Pipes and drums proudly echoed the space after Sanders' acceptance speech—the speech his wife, who had a better way with words, helped him write.

The man was now a part and keeper of a living legacy of service and sacrifice.

With his work ethic and determination, Sanders would soon develop into a commanding officer. Or even deputy commissioner of the city. Hell, why not mayor while he was at it?

Assistant Chief Harris, known to the congregation as Reverend Monsieur Harold Martinez, offered a prayer of benediction for the graduates. The mayor had given them a mission, one Sanders, like hundreds of eager recruits, was proud to accept. Hungry to fight crime and help build a city rooted in peace and respect. Ready for a lifetime of service. Ready to protect and serve. Ready to uphold the constitution of the United States—and of New York state—just as the mayor had said.

And now, the plaques and chords lay across the living room floor, long-forgotten courtesies of the burlesque-style dance last night.

The couple had just purchased their first home but lacked the funds to buy furniture. A chipped, weathered TV stand tossed away on the sidewalk, a pair of gilt wood candlestick lamps, and dining chairs with a matching (unremarkable) kitchen table decked the rest of the house.

The midnight show was his wife's idea. Sanders had half expected to head home, maybe enjoy one last glass of champagne, then collapse into bed with her legs wrapped around him like thirsty ivy.

"Time to get up, officer," she whispered behind his ear. "Don't act like you're still asleep. You have to move this bed before heading off to save the world."

Sanders drew in a breath of her and grinned. He was ready for the new day—his first day.

But first, breakfast with his wife.

"Mom thinks Dad may have found a couch and bassinet. She said a TV is up to us." She took a sip of juice, snatching the last piece of bacon from the plate between them.

Sanders had no qualms about accepting help from his in-laws. Help was help, and he appreciated it more than he led on. "You'll pay for that, you know," he warned, smirking.

"Oh yeah?" She nibbled the meat. "Well, my actions are defensible, officer."

"And how long do you plan on using that excuse?"

A growing grin carved a playful dimple into her right cheek, disarming Sanders.

Then her smile dropped, replaced by a grimace, and she lifted in her chair an inch before settling back down again. Sanders knew that look. She'd spent part of last night and, no doubt, the morning throwing up in the bathroom.

"You okay, baby?"

She offered a heartfelt nod.

"Don't worry." He gave her a wink. "I'll hold off punishing you for the bacon." He rose with his plate in hand and stood awhile. Her face, bare of the day's stressors or fancy cosmetics, hypnotized him. "But when I get home, that's a different story."

"We'll see about that, officer." She looked up at him with those eyes, pledging tonight's disobedience. "Just don't forget your handcuffs."

God, he freaking loved this woman.

He had to pull his eyes away and get on with the rest of his day. Today began a new and brilliant chapter in the young officer's life. The life he'd pictured and planned since spotting that little girl looking up adoringly at what must have been her daddy in his shiny uniform along 125th Street, holding his hand, and as young as she was, she seemed to understand the massive undertaking the man took on for her and his family.

Watching them, Sanders—for the first time—wanted to be someone else. He longed to know what it felt like to be looked at that way. The vision of the little girl and her daddy's proud smile would haunt him forever.

2

BETH and CHRIS

BETH and CHRIS

March 28

Today, I hated! I went to school, and I got nothin' but homework. I will ask my dad for some help (with my Math because I'm not good with word problems).

Since there is nothing much to say about today, I'll say that I always wanted a diary, and I'm glad I got one. This is good because, in this part of my life, I don't expect to have many friends.

Anyhow, last night I attended my Girl Scouts meeting. My mother couldn't record my favorite show because she was watching something.

I was disappointed.

She dropped her pen. It toppled against the shag lavender carpet just as a knock hit the door. Any concerns about getting on the honor roll and Mom's disapproval would have to wait.

Chris pushed the door open just as Beth slapped her journal shut. She tucked it under a pillow. About a year ago, he busted the lock, and privacy was now a thing of the past. Since then, Beth had developed an intuition whenever bodies drew near her room.

Chris stepped in, eyes straying to the floor. "You gonna throw more stuff against my wall today?"

Trying to look distracted, Beth flicked her head around the room and shrugged. "Depends. If he does twisted stuff again."

She referred to the main character in a book lying open on her desk—a story about a successful young man who committed unthinkable acts of violence for pleasure. While the other girls gossiped about older siblings, relationships, and sex, Beth was drawn to what real life couldn't offer.

Dark stories.

Difficult truths.

Experiences beyond reach.

They stirred something in her that ordinary life never could.

Lately, whenever she reached a shocking passages, her blood surged. Hurling paperweights, books, and pens at the wall felt like the fastest release. Above the dresser, gray smudges and pinprick holes bore silent witness to her wrath.

"Hey," she said, straightening the pillows on her bed, "it's not just *your* wall."

Chris rolled his eyes, stepping further into the lavender space. "Whatever, same difference."

It was an average-sized room, bright and chilly from the ceiling fan and opened blinds on the windows flanking the twin-sized bed. A chipped white dresser stood against the wall, matching the wooden desk next to the bed; framed photos of bears, kittens, and teen heartthrobs covered the walls.

"I'm in trouble, man," he mumbled.

"You're never in trouble. Well, never in *big* trouble."

"Yeah, but—"

"—and even if you are—" Beth shot her brother a steely look— "you always talk your way out of it."

The remark pulled Chris' lips into a smile. "It's big trouble this time," he said after a while. Eyes on the books covering the desk, he cocked his head. He couldn't understand how his twin could work so hard on her studies and for what—ordinary grades?

"Wait!" Beth sat up. "You couldn't be flunking out. Did you get into another fight? Did you get caught fooling around with a girl?"

Chris forced out a hard laugh. He snapped his head up, making eye contact. "Yeah, right! Do I look freaking stupid?"

"Then what is it? Did you crap your shorts or something? Don't forget, I'm the one who folds the laundry, and it ain't pretty."

"Yeah, right, idiot."

A breeze slipped through the window, rustling papers on the desk. Silence followed.

"I got caught shoplifting and—" Chris sighed— "so far, only Mom knows. She picked me up from the store and begged the cops to go easy on me."

Beth's hand flew to her mouth. "Wow…"

"Yeah."

In the middle of a strip mall, Wanapatchee harbored one of the last music stores in a twenty-mile radius. While other kids stayed home glued to computer screens, downloading music and videos, Chris set out to own the real thing. Some teased him for it. But what did he care? Other kids' parents took away gadgets as punishment. Chris, buried in bedsheets, was all smiles—secretly rocking out with his Discman.

But he had no money, so he and some friends would pickpocket video games and CDs whenever they felt their collections running dry. It had been going on for months; only now, the owner caught them and contacted the police.

As Chris replayed the events, he saw his sister freeze. He knew she was thinking about the time when she'd shoplifted that fancy pen from the drugstore. In her early grade school days, quarreling with boys had been routine. Teachers often caught her and sent her to the principal's office. Over the years, scuffles during recess gave way to chatting during class.

But Principal Edmund didn't intimidate anyone. A lowly middle-aged man with a receding hairline, thick glasses, and ties too short for his broad frame, he was more tired than threatening. For Beth, the peeved, weary look in Mom's eyes terrified her most—especially when she came to collect her from detention.

A brief spark of relief lit up his sister's face; she wasn't the one in trouble this time. Yet Chris noticed guilt creeping in, silent and weighty, as if she carried every misstep that did not belong to her.

○   ○   ○

Beth's eyes traveled across the room, chewing her lip. She hated this feeling; it felt dirty, like mud oozing through her veins. She thought of Dad, imagining his reaction.

Dad was a hard-working, short-tempered man with thick brown hair and tired hazel eyes. "He has two emotions," Chris would say, "angry and pissed off." At five feet eight, Dad's larger-than-life personality made him seem seven feet tall. An Irish Catholic upbringing and Navy service had to have hardened him.

"So Dad doesn't know yet?"

Chris shook his head and glanced at the clock on the wall. The garage door would soon open below Beth's bedroom, signaling Dad's return.

Beth's eyes narrowed. "Mom's gonna tell him, right?"

Chris shot a look at his sister. "Why?"

Eager to retort, Beth's mouth snapped open, but no words came out. Unnerved by another feeling of shame, she dropped her head. "No reason."

Another long silence.

"What am I gonna do?"

3

THE GIRL

THE GIRL

Mom and Dad met at a party. Dad's friend enlisted in the Marines; the event was his final farewell before leaving for boot camp.

Wearing a sapphire evening dress, Mom's manicured hands curled around a glass of white wine. Her silky hair and slender frame stood out in the room. She spotted Dad shadowed in the corner with a friend, dressed in pressed slacks and a crisp white shirt. Clean-shaven, with brown hair parted neatly on the side, he wore a smile that softened even the nuns at his Catholic school. Reserved as he was, Dad wasn't the most exciting boy in class. But he was the most handsome and respectable.

Swallowing the last of her wine, Mom nudged her girlfriend and whispered, "I'm going to marry him."

Then she wandered over, her brown hair bouncing on her shoulders, long neck arched high. Smitten at first glance, she dropped onto his lap.

At first, Dad resented Mom's boorish display of affection. But when she slid his car keys down her bra and said, "You want them, come and get them," he realized his taciturn nature had backfired.

For months, Mom pushed herself on him, undeterred. It wasn't until he saw her on the arm of another man that something shifted. Jealousy took root, and this time, he didn't resist. Mom was a woman of many phobias—water, heights, cats, small spaces, highway driving—but with Dad, she was fearless.

Raised in an Italian home in Brooklyn, Mom was the only child to marry and have children. Beth's grandmother, an outspoken Italian woman with impeccable taste in soft furnishings, worked in a clothing factory before motherhood. The twins never met her because she died from a brain aneurysm before they were born.

Grandpa, an Italian from Naples, spent his early years in New York cutting headstones and repairing shoes, like many other Italians of the time, before retiring after fifteen years as a costume jeweler.

After high school, Mom's two brothers and sister left New York, scattering across the country. It didn't take long for them to get swept up in their new, liberated lives. Mom stayed behind. The house grew quiet, as were the dinners and evenings in front of the television.

Dad, the oldest of three boys and a younger sister, grew up in an Italian-Irish Catholic home in Brooklyn. Granddad was a hard nut to crack. A retired New York City fire lieutenant with thirty years on the job, he stayed active at the firehouse and spent weekends selling or boxing books.

Grammy, fierce and no-nonsense, didn't believe in coddling her kids and managed them largely on her own. At times, to keep Nicolas—her youngest, barely three—from wandering off while she cleaned, she'd tie him to the garage door.

"Thank God your grandparents didn't have an automatic garage door!" Mom joked. "His brothers would've dipped him like a tea bag!"

Sitting at the head of the kitchen table, Dad often shared witty stories from his childhood—like how his father poured homemade red wine for the kids before their milk, or how his oldest brother used their little brother as a human football.

But the tension in Dad's house was thick. Dad was a proud man of finance, and his lack of interest in Granddad's trade fostered distance between them. He even passed the firefighter's test but later turned down the position. Dad sensed his father's disappointment, and the lack of genuine interest in him, and still refused to yield to the man's expectations.

Despite his need for acceptance, Dad launched a career as a

mechanical technician with an esteemed multinational computer company, deepening the divide. In college, he seized the chance to move out and enlisted in the Navy Reserves. He trained in Pensacola, then deployed to Guam for eight months.

But the Navy wouldn't let him return to the States to marry Mom—until Grammy wrote a firm letter to her congressman, insisting they allow it. After coming home for good, he and Mom found their first apartment in New York and soon began building a family of their own.

Years later, Dad clung to the nightly rituals of his childhood: dinners without distractions, then homework. Meanwhile, Mom, indifferent by his routines, would vanish into the living room, leaving Beth to tackle the dishes. There, she lost herself in a haze of soap operas and shopping channels, humming along to Barbra Streisand and Air Supply, a cigarette smoldering between her fingers and a diluted glass of Zinfandel always within reach.

As time passed, whatever gusto Beth had left seemed to drain at the dinner table. Gazing at her plate, she could feel Mom and Dad watching her, irritated by her silence—just like the teachers at school when she couldn't answer a hard question.

They resent me, she'd think.

Sometimes, she would catch glimpses of Mom and Dad together and imagine them as happy teenagers. She'd sneak into their old photo albums, picturing them as a young couple in New York, surrounded by friends.

She loved the wedding photos most. Dad dressed in a sleek black tuxedo, Mom wrapped in a mile-long shimmery gown with a sparkling veil. The images looked forged, like something from a movie set or a world that never truly existed. Beth loved seeing their young, almost saintly faces inches apart, hypnotized by emotion. She doubted she'd ever feel that kind of joy.

"Daddy's almost home," said Mom. She leaned against the stove, stirring a pot of boiling macaroni. A rich smell of garlic and chicken filled the kitchen, masked by the acrid fumes of a cigarette sloped along a nearby ashtray. "Get your brother."

Beth set the last of the silverware on the kitchen table, and coughed, waving her hand to clear the smoke. Driven by duty more than desire, she walked down the hall and stopped at Chris' closed door. At eye level, a wooden Islanders sign read: *Don't Bother Me, I'm Watching Hockey.*

Beth tapped on the door. "Chris, it's dinner."

No answer.

She waited a minute, then braced herself before turning the knob. A second later, she stepped inside.

The room had one window, a twin-sized bed, a walnut-colored desk, and a twenty-inch television perched atop a stereo in the corner. Against the far wall, Chris crouched inside the closet, digging through a shin-deep pile of sports gear, comic books, old toys, and boxes of baseball cards.

"Mom said—"

Chris lifted his head, eyes wide. "Sshh! Don't say anything! Close the door!" He wore his puffy orange and blue Islanders jacket, a backpack slung over his right shoulder, and a Yankees cap perched high on his head.

Beth closed the door behind her. "What are you doing?"

"I'm getting out of here until it's safe to come back."

"What? Wait…"

Chris peeked over his shoulder. "What? Wait for what?"

Beth stared blankly at her brother.

Lately, Chris and Dad clashed more than ever. After dinner, Dad would summon Beth to the kitchen table, scrutinizing every page of her schoolwork. Beth, tangled in the frustrations of remedial math and English, fought to make sense of her assignments. Night after night, she burned the midnight oil, longing to retreat to her room and sink into her bed. One evening, her silence and soft sniffles finally snapped Dad's patience. With a burst of anger, he struck Beth across the face and kicked her as she huddled on the cold kitchen floor.

Chris jumped to her defense and thoughtlessly muttered, "Dad's a fucking asshole."

Mom overheard Chris' show of foolish regard for his sister and didn't hesitate to tattle to Dad. Enter Dad, towering over Chris with dark, dense eyes. *"What did you say?"*

Disgusted, Chris dragged out the kitchen chair and sat down with both arms crossed indignantly over his chest. "Go ahead," he dared. "Do your worst."

Just one hit knocked Chris out cold. An hour later, he woke on his bed with wet, crusted eyes, breathing in painful gasps. The room was dark except for a Yankees' nightlight glowing its faint white light from across the room.

Chris shook his head, shifting his attention to the closet. "I'm not being stupid this time. I'm not waiting for things to happen. I'm going to *make* them—yes!" From the heap, he pulled out a signed baseball from Frank Eufemia. "Here it is." He dropped the ball into his pack.

"So you're just gonna leave—"

"Yes." He snatched a shirt off the bed. "I'm outta here."

—us here alone?

Chris stopped and looked at his sister for the first time since she'd entered the room. His expression fell.

The room went quiet, followed by a grainy voice calling out from the kitchen. "Daddy's home! Let's go! You want an invitation?"

Wrapped in thought, the twins didn't notice the rumble of the garage door or the thump as it struck the concrete floor beneath their feet.

Beth broke eye contact, then glanced over her shoulder. "Well, you're not missing out on much. It's leftovers tonight."

"You better go," Chris warned, stuffing another T-shirt into his backpack. "And *eat* for once. Stop giving her such a hard time."

Figures he'd take her side.

Beth's eyes narrowed, close to tears. Her gaze drifted to the wall behind the unmade bed, where dust caked over a dozen trophies, lined haphazardly on box shelves Chris had built in shop class.

Jesus, he has to dust those, she thought—anything to distract her from being left alone.

Whispered words finally sprang from her mouth. "I can't stand living under the same roof with them another minute."

Chris stopped and looked at her. More silence hung between them before he spoke, his voice thickened. "Okay. You coming or not?"

Skeptical, Beth's eyes flipped over to her brother.

Chris arched a brow. His mouth formed a straight line.

Bobbing her head, she smiled.

"Grab your stuff, and hurry up," he said. "Meet me out back. I have to grab one more thing first."

4

THE BOY

THE BOY

"Remember when you and Dad drove home from the Mets game, and you crapped your pants? What was it, a bad hot dog? Too many peanuts?"

Chris slowly shook his head. "I had four hot dogs. And figures you'd remember that."

The twins sat on a concrete wall beneath a low, white sky, legs dangling nine feet above a sea of gray boughs tipped with amber leaves. The air was still, dewy.

"Of course, it was hilarious! You were stuck in bumper-to-bumper traffic and couldn't get out of the car!"

A smile lined Chris' cheek. "I had to use the scarves I bought for you and Mom—"

"—to wipe your butt!" Beth threw her head back and burst into laughter.

To his surprise, Chris caught himself laughing, too.

Hours earlier, after sneaking out the back door, Chris led Beth several miles east into the next county, to Fox Mountain at the remains of a swimming pool connected to the famed Van Slyke Castle. He and his friends discovered the site last fall. The neighborhood lake had not frozen, so, awaiting the season's first hockey game, the boys journeyed to Ramapo State Forest. They came across the mysterious ruins inside a mass of bare trees and thick underbrush.

The twins gazed down at a space once filled with thousands of gallons of water. Six concrete steps, an iron railing, and rusty diving board pegs were all that remained of a once-alluring pool. Loud graffiti marked the inside of the four walls.

"Wh-what the heck made you think of *that*?" asked Chris, fighting a grin. He appreciated Beth's attempt to break the silence.

"I dunno," Beth shrugged.

"Weirdo." He caught a glimpse of Beth's shoes, suddenly hit by a memory of her limp legs high off the ground seconds before crumpling against the dining room floor. Foolishly, one summer evening, she'd missed curfew and didn't arrive home until an hour past dinnertime. Chris, playing street hockey in front of the house while Mom and Dad paced inside, didn't know what happened until days later. Moments after Beth came home, he tossed his stick on the front lawn and raced inside, only to see his sister drop against the shag carpet, Dad storming away in a blind rage.

No one believed Beth's excuse, not even Chris. But seeing her that night, sitting cross-legged on her bed with a flushed face and frazzled hair slipping from drooping elastics, was enough to keep his snide remarks to himself.

Eager for answers, he peeked into Beth's backyard hideaway after school the next day. It wasn't much, just a few thick trees with overlapping branches, their trunks wrapped in dense juniper. A rocky patch of earth, about eight feet wide and three feet deep, covered the floor. The canopy hung low enough that you had to crouch to move around inside. Four large stones sat about a foot and a half apart, each marked with a letter in black marker. The taupe-colored one in the center had a *B*—Beth's, as Chris would later learn. The space felt less like a hideout and more like a place to be alone with bad thoughts.

His stomach rumbled. Having missed dinner, Chris felt drained, legs heavy from the hike. He wondered what Mom made (or reheated) for dinner, cursing himself for not grabbing something before taking off.

Steller's Jays called out from tree limbs, as if warning him of the threats waiting at home. His pulse quickened.

Dad's going to kill me, he thought.

"We can't stay, Chris. Mom and Dad must be going crazy."

His eyes refocused.

"I know you're, like, scared. I am too, but—"

Chris shot Beth a pointed look. "I'm not scared." He scratched the back of his neck, shifting against the unforgiving concrete. "I just don't feel like being punished again, that's all," he mumbled, eyes traveling back to the pool.

THE GIRL

THE GIRL

She followed Chris' gaze, slowly nodding. Things fell silent as a gust of air picked up and whistled through the sea of silvery branches.

Chris had introduced the ruins to Beth. Seeing them was like discovering a mysterious, underground place—like being awake in a dream. The following day, she fired up Dad's computer to investigate the castle, saddened to discover its popularity.

A century ago, a New York City nurse's second husband started constructing the enormous stone building; her third husband completed it. After the woman died, subsequent owners moved in, then abandoned the castle. Beth was disheartened to learn vandals had burned the house down, leaving what remained of the structure, the pool, and the water tower to Ramapo State Forest.

The woods extended nearly 5,000 acres, bordering the Ramapo Valley County Reservation, a part of the county's park system. Beth had a poor sense of direction with no internal map of the area. When Chris led her to the spot, she hadn't bothered to pay attention. She relied on Chris to take command, something she often took for granted since they were small.

Several times, she urged him to return with her. But he grew obsessed with sports and had no time or interest. After a few failed attempts, Beth's passion for the place faded, and she returned to journaling and daydreaming.

The woods offered its share of discomforts, but not without

restitution. Kids at school taunted Beth for being different, but she rejected their pressure to conform, like the trees that refused to change despite the turning seasons. The forest was never without some green.

A chill raced through her body. It was getting late, the temperature biting her skin. In their haste to leave home, Beth avoided taking a jacket but grabbed her journal, slipping it into her back pocket. It pressed up against her bottom like a blister.

"C'mon, let's go," said Chris after another awkward silence. "You're shaking. You should have brought a jacket."

He led her downhill to the park's entrance. Rush hour traffic came and went as cars flew by at high speeds. The dirt parking lanes lining the street were empty. It would be a few weeks before peak touring season—too chilly for hikers, fishers, mountain bikers, and those wanting to explore views of the New York skyline.

The twins continued home in silence, deep in thought.

THE BOY

His breathing sped up the moment they entered the development. His guts stirred, and his heart raced so fast he thought it might pop a rib and burst through his chest. Chris looked over at his sister to see if she could hear it. But she was distracted, eyes locked on her feet, mouth twisted into a frown.

Nightfall arrived, cold and damp. Streetlights lined the streets, spilling tawny rays across the asphalt. Strangely, the sky had turned murky gray. Like smoke from a chimney, dark billows drifted in a definite space five hundred feet ahead.

Steep roads and cul-de-sacs shaped the neighborhood; the houses were all split-level, following just six basic designs. Chris always imagined an invisible mirror between his home and the house across the street. But instead of rustic brown shingles with white and red accents and the number 13 above the front door, the neighbor's shingles were painted yellow, the number 16 above theirs. The twins often joked about that house, branding it the "Ronald McDonald House." All it was missing were the golden arches.

Mom grew unnerved by the carbon copy patterns, and one night at dinner, remarked, "This place looks like Stepford town." Chris later discovered she was referring to an old movie about free-spirited housewives transformed into obedient robots.

Chris thought to sneak up to the back of the house. That way, Mom and Dad wouldn't run out into the street in hysterics and embarrass them in front of the neighborhood. But it wouldn't be easy because they had to cut through Mark Bellini's backyard, which sat on a road behind Schicara Drive, their street.

As the twins crept past Mark's house, a drone of sirens and voices echoed ahead. A gray and black cloud spread across the overcast sky, carrying the sharp scent of wood chips searing in a frying pan. It was hard to take a deep breath without coughing.

Beth was the first to hop on the first landing. Chris watched her, ready to offer a boost. The noises grew as they touched the third and final landing. The twins headed uphill through the brush and slowed when pieces of home became visible through the foliage.

"Something's happening," mused Chris. Fighting the urge to rest, he rushed up the hill.

Beth struggled to keep up and slipped on a large rock, stumbling on one knee, grating it against the ground. "Jesus, Chris!" she panted. "What's your hurry?"

A few yards ahead, Chris stopped, his face tightening in alarm.

Wincing, Beth glared at her knee. She rubbed it briskly. "What's your problem?"

Chris inched back and set a heavy hand on her shoulder. His fingers curled around her skin like a claw in department store machines.

"Ouch, Chris!"

He lifted his hand, slapping it again on the same spot. Beth sprung her head up. "What—?" She followed his gaze, her expression dropping. "Chris...?"

Twelve yards ahead were pieces of Schicara Drive. Police

cruisers, a fire truck, a van from Action News Eight, and two ambulances with lights flashing packed the street. Bright lights rotated intensely on the roof of the cars and vans. Yellow tape with black lettering surrounded the house. Eager for a better view, neighbors crowded in to get a closer look. Mrs. Calmin was among them.

Beth shot up, planting both feet on the ground before Chris seized her arm and pulled her down behind a thick bush.

Every muscle in Chris' body locked. From the corner of his eye, he saw Beth's mouth moving, but all he could hear was the thump of his heartbeat. Then everything fell silent.

A few seconds passed. Or had it been an hour? Chris couldn't tell. Red and orange flames sprouted from what had once been home, leaving him stupefied.

A second news van arrived. A reporter with long blonde hair rushed out with a microphone. A lean man holding a large camera followed.

"Whose house is that?" a voice in the crowd shouted.

"It's Alessandro and Rosa's!" called out another.

Flames towered, crackling inside the house. Firefighters shot thick jets of water at the blaze. A loud sound, like a car crashing off a roof, thundered from the front of the house. The sound echoed faintly in Chris' ears, and he wondered if the awning over the front porch collapsed. Pulling heavy, thick hoses over their shoulders, the men quickly changed course and charged an attack from the rear.

Chris regained control of his mind and slipped behind another patch of dense scrub, pulling Beth close. His ears popped, and sounds returned to normal. He recalled friends' stories about traveling on airplanes. Glancing at Beth, he saw her eyes fixed on the burning house—still and silent as a sea sponge.

THE GIRL

The police captain struggled to calm the swelling crowd. "Get those folks back," he ordered one of his deputies. "Folks, *please stay back.*"

"What in God's name happened, Douglas?" asked Mrs. Calmin after brushing through the crowd. "Is the family alright?" She was a tall lady with short, curly red hair, large brown eyes, and bright red lips.

Forty-four years old, Mrs. Calmin was a lonely but feisty woman with a shrilling laugh. Beth wondered why the woman never had children and then overheard Mom and Dad once saying something about a hysterectomy. Most neighbors politely ignored the woman because talking with her meant setting aside at least an hour for conversation. Even Mom avoided Mrs. Calmin; she hated phony small talk and neighborhood coffee klatches.

On warm days, Beth would step off the school bus and spot the woman in her chair on the front porch, a book resting on her lap. Mrs. Calmin's husband had been on the force, fatally stabbed on duty years ago. After his death, she often sat outside, eager for a friendly exchange with Beth.

Captain Ramsey regarded the neighbor with tired eyes. "We don't know yet, Ruth. We only just arrived a short time ago. We're doing what we can to stop it from spreading."

"Please, Douglas," she said. "They're children in there!"

Chris loosened his grip on Beth's shoulder. Much like a jack-in-the-box with its lid sprung open, Beth bounced to her feet. He yanked her back with brute force.

"No, Chris! Mom and Dad are in there!"

He tightened his grip on Beth's arm, gaze flicking between the neighbor and the officer. He looked confused. Overwhelmed.

Beth's adrenaline ignited. Frantic, she grappled against Chris' hold, nearly breaking free before he yanked her back, shooting her a hardened look. Defeated, she cried, "We can't just stand here and watch. We can't—"

"What do you want to do, Beth—run inside? It's insane out there. You'll get hurt."

Beth dropped her voice. "They have to know we're here, Chris. We have to see if Mom and Dad are okay. We have to..." Her voice trailed off.

Soon, the fire abated. Smoke and ash floated across the sky, casting a heavy pall over the neighborhood. Beth stared at the blackened frame of what used to be their house. It didn't look real. It didn't even look familiar. Just bones now, burned-out and broken.

A firefighter dashed from the rear of the house, hollering for assistance. Seconds later, four paramedics pulled out two stretchers and hurried inside a cloud of smoke. It felt like hours before they reemerged with bodies on the gurneys hidden in ashen-covered sheaths. The attendants pushed them through the back doors of the ambulance.

Mrs. Calmin's hand flew to her mouth.

Tears flooded Beth's eyes, but she fought to keep them contained. She was too shocked to grieve. "That's our home."

Mrs. Calmin and Ramsey continued talking. After a minute, horror flashed across on Mrs. Calmin's face then gave way to relief. The twins caught a few scattered words.

"…in there?" Mrs. Calmin asked.

Ramsey shook his head.

"…what will happen to the children?"

Ramsey looked at the burning house before returning to Ruth. He palmed the back of his neck and cleared his throat before speaking. "Do you…they can be…?"

Mrs. Calmin nodded.

"…turn them over to the state," said Ramsey.

The twins turned to each other, eyes locked. Beth felt Chris' heart falter, just like hers. His eyes burned, but he didn't cry. Neither did she.

"Chris," said Beth, her voice trembling. "What are we—?"

Before she could finish, Chris yanked her down the hill.

5

THE BOY

THE BOY

The twins rushed along the jagged rim of Skyway Drive, a winding road snaking north towards the interstate away from town. Panic and adrenaline thundered in their veins, propelling them forward.

Chris clung to Beth's wrist, certain she would float away into the clouds if he let go.

Entering the neighboring town of Rookwood, Beth pulled back her arm and fell to her knees on the side of the road, gasping for air. "W-W-Wait, Chris. Gimme a sec!"

Chris took deep breaths, hands pressed to his knees for balance. Sweat slid down his face. His stomach churned, threatening to spill on the blacktop.

A few minutes passed before his breathing slowed. By now, the smoke from the fire had diffused, leaving behind a dark, flat sky.

"C'mon," he said, grabbing her hand. "We have to move."

Rookwood, a humble town of nearly ten thousand, nestled among rolling hills and mountain forests thirty miles from New York City. Its streets buzzed with blue-collar workers and small business owners, the air thick with the scent of summer barbecues and the sound of winter karaoke. The twins longed for Rookwood's simple luxuries: convenience stores, restaurants, glowing stoplights, and fast-food spots—things Wanapatchee lacked.

The twins reached the area drolly labeled "downtown." A row of unremarkable mom-and-pop shops stretched along the street, their windows dusty and storefronts made of clapboard. Among the shops were a couple of diners, two bars, a church, and a grade school.

Walking along the uneven sidewalk, Chris wondered if he'd imagined the events in the last hour. He came close to asking Beth but, not wanting to appear crazy, stopped himself.

A group of glowing television screens caught his attention. Chris turned to the town's family-owned electronic store, struck by a memory of standing in the exact spot with Dad, pleading for a sporty, black and yellow portable CD player. His insides dropped like a roller coaster cage down a steep track.

THE GIRL

Six large TVs sat in glass cases on either side of the door. On one, a female reporter interviewed a Wanapatchee police officer, a man in his mid-thirties with thinning hair, a round face, and dark glasses. Beth instantly recognized him from a photo on Mrs. Calmin's mantel.

The woman told many stories, usually sparked by a question or comment Beth made about one picture or another in the house. Mrs. Calmin took great pride in her photo collection; it dated back to her engagement with her late husband. She loved hearing the stories, mostly because Mrs. Calmin seemed eager to share them, and she told them with genuine enthusiasm. But Beth liked it best when Mrs. Calmin imitated her husband and a few of his old friends from the force.

"...we were called out on a house fire at approximately six o'clock this evening," reported Officer Wade Castaneda. The man's brow was covered with deep creases, beaded with sweat. He looked flustered, tired. "Upon our arrival, we saw the building consumed in flames. At that point, firefighters initiated an exterior attack from the front and sides of the house. They went into transitional attack mode, entering from the back of the house for an interior attack..."

No sound came through the glass, so Beth focused on the closed captions flashing at the bottom of the screen. All six screens showed different reports of the incident. One set displayed a photo of Chris, wearing his white and blue baseball uniform, a confident smirk on his face and a bat perched on his shoulder. Beside it stood a school photo of Beth with a short, lopsided haircut and a crooked smile. She scowled. She hated that picture. It looked like a mug shot with a pastel backcloth.

"Have you determined the cause of the fire?" asked a reporter.

Castaneda shook his head. "Not yet, but our investigators are looking into it and probably will for some time. If they have to take things to testing laboratories, it could be a couple of weeks before they get any answers. Beyond that, we'll continue our interviews, talking to whoever may have witnessed the fire."

The reporter nodded. "We saw paramedics taking stretchers out of the house. Can you tell us who they are and what their condition is?"

Beth's body tightened.

"I'm afraid I am not at liberty to disclose information about that right now."

Beth glanced to her left. Chris bit his upper lip, eyes shut. When he opened them again, they were wet.

It felt like a slow-motion scene from the creepiest movie she'd ever seen, filled with moments pulled straight from her worst nightmares. "Oh my God…"

"There's been talk of children living there. Were they harmed?"

Beth directed her gaze to another screen, then gasped.

THE BOY
THE BOY

He thought he was going to faint. He pressed a hand over the glass to steady himself and turned over to Beth, who was too absorbed with the interview to notice.

"There were no children in the house when we arrived," said Castaneda, "and we've already begun taking action to locate them. We're interviewing the neighbors and checking if they have camera footage that may help the investigators see what was going on before our arrival."

Chris' tears dried, and he shook his head. "C'mon, let's get moving. I have to piss." He walked ahead, avoiding eye contact with everyone in his path while Beth hurried at his heels.

It would be easy to disappear behind a large tree—hell, he'd done it a million times on the field—but he thought of something better. Risky, yes, but it would ease another pressing concern.

About a hundred feet down the walkway stood one of the town's bars, Lion's Lair. A large awning lit by yellow and green fluorescents cast beams of light several yards from the entrance. The wooden sign hanging over the front door was splintered and faded. Chris had heard stories about the place at school. Drunk middle-aged people gathered there. Fights were common, and some said rapes had happened too.

True or not, it was the last place a kid thought to enter. But Chris could take what he needed, and no one would recognize him.

"Hang here for a sec," he said. Sucking in a deep breath, he yanked open the wooden door and marched in.

The space was small, the lighting pale and dim. A faint smell of timber filled the room. Bob Seger's song "Roll Me Away" pulsed from an old, fuzzy-sounding jukebox in the far right corner.

Three heavyset men and an older woman sat at the long oak bar that extended down a narrow space to Chris' left. They turned towards the door as it opened. Chris' heart rocked against his chest.

"What happened," one of the men yelled, "school bus break down?"

The men dropped their heads back and laughed. Uncapping a beer, the bartender smirked.

As scared as he was, Chris refused to show tension. He nodded, a shaky grin stretching his cheeks. "Gentlemen." Craning his neck, he spotted the restrooms at the far end of the bar.

He took a deep breath and crossed the room, eyes fixed on the handwritten *Men* sign on the door. Snickering came from the left, eyes burning into him like lasers. Aside from dragging himself home after a long hike from the castle, it was the longest walk of his life.

Moments later, he flung the front doors open, rushing out.

"C'mon, we're outta here," he said, grabbing his sister's hand.

6

THE DEPARTMENT

THE DEPARTMENT

Wanapatchee was a small town with six policemen: Captain Ramsey and five deputies. Preceding the last few hours, the station led a quotidian schedule monitoring traffic and handling domestic disputes and bar fights. Now, a suspicious fire had landed in their laps, drawing significant attention.

The department took full responsibility for reporting and investigating the disappearance of the Pacelli twins. Most likely, family or friends had taken the children in. But at less than thirteen years old, Beth and Chris were at risk—too young to be independent or possess the survival skills needed to avoid exploitation on the streets. Time was critical. Especially since, in most cases of pedophilia, victims died within six hours. Yet twenty-four hours had not passed, and with no signs of harm, Ramsey delayed calling for backup from other departments.

After the press conference, the captain assembled his team and launched a discreet search and rescue operation. He appointed Barry Warsoff, recently promoted to detective sergeant, as the search operation coordinator. His job was to help manage the investigation and handle the debriefing.

The officers raced to collect information about the twins: friends, hobbies, anything, from neighbors and the school. Strangely, neither Beth nor Chris had social media accounts. Warsoff appointed his partner, David Powell, to prepare their findings and share them with broadcasters tomorrow. The header would read:

Police seek twelve-year-old youth siblings missing in Wanapatchee.

Ramsey hoped they wouldn't have to deliver it.

He felt uneasy about the case. Something didn't feel right. He'd been in this job long enough to trust his hunches. But a hunch wasn't proof.

All the captain could do now was wait. Wait for a call. Wait for news from his team.

7

THE GIRL
THE GIRL

Chris glanced at his Islanders watch; the hockey sticks hovered near twelve and ten.

The sky's deep indigo melted into pitch black, and the air pressed in, heavy and close. The moon spilled pale shadows over the asphalt as they walked. Mosquitoes buzzed around them. Their arms were like inoperative windshield wipers, slicing through the haze of tiny, hungry bodies.

The night was grimly quiet as Chris trudged several miles through town with Beth shadowing behind. Her feet and legs throbbed, but she said nothing. Watching the report had crushed any urge she had to speak out.

She couldn't stop thinking about the news. Nothing about this made sense. House fires happened to other people you read about in the papers. People you didn't know.

The twins' steps were sluggish, lacking the vitality they had when leaving the bar. Beth imagined them like zombies slogging through the empty streets. Heading west, they reached Ditchburn Street, a road cutting between the north and south ends of Ramapo Forest. They followed it for half a mile before stepping off. A field of grass sprinkled with shrubs and small trees stretched a mile long and fifteen yards deep, bordering the forest. It sloped down towards the treeline, thick with pine, spruce, and maple.

Unable to bear the sound of her thoughts, Beth spoke up. "I'm tired, Chris. What are we doing here?"

Chris turned to her. His eyes softened for the first time since they left home. He pulled off his hat, raked his fingers through a mess of greasy hair, then set the hat back in place. "We need a place to rest. The park isn't a good idea. They'd find us there."

Beth nodded towards the forest. "Stay in there? Are you crazy? We can't stay out here alone!"

"Yes, we can. I did before."

"Huh?"

"Remember a few months ago when I stayed at George's?"

Beth reflected for a moment, then shrugged. Chris slept at his friend's house at least twice a month.

"Well, we were out here. We got lost. George had his cell phone, so he called his folks. He told them he was staying with me. I called Mom and said I was staying with him."

Beth's eyes widened. "Why…?"

"We didn't want to admit we were lost. We found our way out the next day anyway." Chris cracked a smile. "We even gathered leaves for toilet paper in case one of us had to go."

Beth turned towards the trees, shaking her head. "I dunno, Chris…"

Chris shut his eyes and rubbed them with a sweaty thumb and index finger. "I don't know what else to do. It's either stay here tonight or turn ourselves in."

Beth shot a look at her brother. "What do you mean, turn ourselves in? We didn't do anything wrong!"

"I know that. It's not what I meant…Grammy and Granddad are dead. And there's no family I can think to go to, can you?"

He's right.

Beth scowled. "Shut up," she muttered.

"What?"

Shaking her head, she said, "Nothing."

They stood looking at each other. "Do you wanna live in some orphanage, like Annie? You want other parents? A foster home?"

Watching the classic film on the family room couch, Beth secretly wondered what it would be like to be a girl like Annie. Or Pepper. Pepper was a girl she could relate to—cranky, antagonistic, misunderstood. No one seemed to like Pepper or care if someone took her away.

He's right. Chill here for the night, and figure everything out tomorrow.

Beth opened her mouth but said nothing. It occurred to her to be grateful to her brother. If he hadn't taken her, she might have burned in the fire—left behind as charred bones and stinky flesh. Maybe Chris was right, and turning themselves in was a bad idea. What if they got split up and sent to different homes? Could she survive alone?

She remembered a documentary she'd seen on TV, *Kids in Crisis*. One story stuck with her for months, even bled into her nightmares. A girl from Detroit, Jasmine, reminded Beth of herself. Jasmine's parents had cooked meth in a storage shed, and the state took her away. Her foster parents chained her to a basement pipe by her neck, like a dog. She slept on cold concrete, ate dog food—sometimes worse. They kept her locked up most of the summer, until neighbors dropped by, asking if the couple could watch their house during vacation.

Jasmine's breath was a whisper when the police lifted her from the shadows. The sight of her pale, limp body in tattered clothes, cradled in the officer's sturdy arms, etched itself into Beth's memory. Starved and silenced by the savagery, Jasmine never spoke another word.

Beth was exhausted. "Chris," she mumbled, "I feel awful. Even though I said all those terrible things about Mom and Dad, I didn't mean it. They were never *that* bad."

Chris looked at his sister askance.

"Okay, I may not have *said* anything, but I…thought it."

Chris' brow relaxed. He nodded, then looked back at the forest.

"I thought it…*a lot*," she added.

He crouched and grabbed a stone near his shoe, fingering its coarse edges. He sprang up, drew back his arm, pitching it into the woods. The stone shot through the green. The twins listened for the sound of its landing.

Nothing. A silent arc, proof of Chris' impressive drive from years of baseball training.

"C'mon, Beth. We can do this." The corner of his mouth rose. "Remember playing Manhunt with us guys about, what...a year ago? You were good. You held your own."

Beth smiled and nodded. "Yeah," she said. "That was fun. We had fun, didn't we?"

Chris nodded, his eyes hardening. "We can do this. We're not as helpless as people think. Staying together is the least we can do for Mom and Dad."

O   O   O

They stepped into an endless sea of black.

Crossing the opening, a blast of wind tore through the trees, slicing the air with needle-sharp cold. Beth shivered as the chill crept down her spine.

She gripped the back of Chris' jacket and kept her head low, eyes fixed on the heel of his sneakers. They needed to stick together and stay out of sight. Chris was right. Mom and Dad would have insisted, even if it meant spending the night in a cold, dark place.

Crossing the opening, she stole a glance back through the first interlacing branches of the woodlands. They sprang back to their usual position, closing them in.

The moon hung low, casting thin, scattered beams of gray through the thickening canopy. She could barely see ten feet ahead.

A twig snapped under Chris' weight. Beth tightened her grip on the cuff of his jacket. It was dark, and she had no idea which way to go or what parts of the ground to avoid. Boys were better at that. Maybe that's why Dad was always in the driver's seat on those Sunday trips to visit Grammy and Granddad.

Chris led the way as they zigzagged through nettles and roots jutting from the dirt. Beth's foot caught on one, and she stumbled into him, sending him forward through a patch of low-hanging branches. They scraped his face and arms, and brambles snagged his jeans. "Watch it, moron!"

"Sorry."

Spaces between towering maples, Scotch pines, and sparse undergrowth guided Chris north along the path. About two hundred yards in, he spotted a clearing and stopped. They were far enough from the edge of the woods to avoid detection, yet close enough to find their way back.

He insisted they collect leaves and small shrubs, anything that could offer support and shield them from the cold forest floor. They collected enough brushwood to form a few inches of suitable cushion. But it would only blanket a few feet of earth, so they had to lay close together.

With lengthy sighs, they collapsed on their makeshift beds. Leaves rustled under their weight, the crown of their heads inches apart.

Crickets stirred the stillness with their nighttime mating calls, breaking the sea of silence. Beth knew Chris couldn't stand the quiet. Back home, he always turned on the TV before falling asleep. Something about those late-night reruns and infomercials never failed to lull him.

Beth liked the silence. If Mom wasn't hollering at Dad for working late or yelling Beth's name in frustration, that meant things were peaceful. But tonight, the quiet wanted Beth to believe everything was safe and sound when it wasn't. She could no longer hear the craziness along Schicara Drive, yet piercing sirens and disorder echoed in her ears.

A gust of wind whistled, sending a stinging chill through her body. "Chris?"

A long pause. "Yeah?"

In the terrifying blackness, his voice comforted her. He was listening, and he was alive. Not like the voice inside her head. "What are we going to do?"

Chris sighed, his breath hovering over her like a ghostly shield. "Are you asleep? I mean, are you tired? I can't sleep. I'm cold."

"Try," he slurred. "Close your eyes, and you'll fall asleep.

We're okay for now."

Beth wrapped her bare arms around herself and squeezed. "I don't want other parents, Chris. I just wanted to say that."

Chris waited a moment before responding. "I know you don't."

"Chris?"

"…hmm?"

"Thanks. For saving my life."

Silence stretched between them, deafening.

Had he fallen asleep? "Chris…?"

Hey, I'm still with you. Just try to sleep. Try.

8

THE GIRL

THE GIRL

She glares at the chicken on her plate. The stringy meat splinters her tongue, so she douses it with vinegar. But the texture stays awful, now sharpened by a tang that assaults her taste buds like rotten lemon. A yellow iceberg salad, soaked in oil and vinegar, sits untouched at the center of the round table.

Silverware clanking against ceramic plates pierces her ears. It's the most grating, alienating sound in the world.

Mom and Dad are alive, the fire nothing more than a twelve-year-old's supercharged imagination at play. Beth can hear them chewing away without a care in the world and feels ashamed because she, too, sits in silence. She imagines shooting up from her chair and flipping the table upside down, plates and glasses shattering against the walls like jagged bullets, and grins.

Her eyes peek up and travel to the dark, empty chair next to Mom. She wants to slap herself hard, as she often does when feeling ashamed. How can she, even for a minute, fantasize about what it would feel like to be an only child? Here she is, her fantasy come true, and nothing has changed. The grass is not greener—and stupid her for thinking it would be. Better to remain in quicksand where she belongs than dream of a life on flourished ground.

Then anger flushes away the shame. How can Chris leave her alone like this? What was he thinking, stealing a police car and speeding it into a burning building packed with police officers? Chris was a boy of few words, and even if he had survived the crash, he never would have felt the need to justify himself. It was one of the *qualities Beth secretly admired most. But how selfish, leaving her all alone.*

Beth shifts in the wooden chair, wondering what Chris is up to, flattering herself into thinking he is watching over her. But he's probably floating around in some other dimension, having adventures on white-winged horses, conversing with great minds of the past like Einstein, Mozart, and Shakespeare.

The stillness in the air feels unbearable; no more hearing her twin gab about school or baseball practice. He was always telling some funny story—how the boys jam chewing gum in each other's locker doors or crack each other in the balls on the baseball field. Beth always looked forward to the stories because they distracted Mom and Dad from focusing on her.

She envies boys and silently curses God for making her a girl. Adults expect boys to be wild, unruly, and free. They can get dirty, say the wrong things, and still be forgiven. But whenever Beth dares to step outside what parents and peers consider acceptable, they shut her down and leave her feeling bitter and bruised.

"Eat!"

Beth flinches, her eyes springing with tears.

After a moment, a squeak springs across the tile floor. It's Mom rising from her seat. She circles the table and crouches down beside Beth's chair. Her index finger, stacked with many sharp rings that you can only see the tip of her taupe-painted nail, reaches up to brush a few strands of hair from Beth's eyes. She wraps an arm around Beth's shoulder. Beth cries harder; Mom's arm stiffens, then shakes. "Wake up! Open your eyes!"

She jolted awake, a cold rush flooding her body, reaching even her shoulders. She cried out.

"Relax," said Chris, pulling away. "It's only me."

Beth rubbed her eyes with icy fists. For the next few moments, she couldn't place where she was. Then it hit her.

To her surprise, she'd fallen asleep, rankled from an abrupt transition into reality, but still smiled. Chris was alive, with his bloodshot eyes and unkempt hair sticking up from his head.

"What are you grinning at?"

Beth blinked her eyes into focus. A gray haze bellied over the clearing. Thick branches obscured large chunks of the sky, the visible patches the color of skim milk. The air felt damp and sticky, her skin clammy, as if submerged in gel. Hidden birds chirped from all directions.

"You okay?"

Beth looked down to meet her brother's eyes and nodded.

He smiled. "I thought you said you couldn't sleep?"

She shrugged, a yawn fleeing from her mouth. She stretched her arms up high, and something dropped in her lap. It was Chris' Islanders jacket. She looked at him.

"I woke up and saw you shaking."

"Thanks."

Chris nodded and looked away, surveying the area.

Beth thought about her dream. Was Mom delivering a message, as Beth felt spirits often did in dreams? "So last night…it wasn't a dream."

She didn't say anything for a while. "Mom and Dad are gone, aren't they?"

THE BOY

THE BOY

He glanced over his shoulder just as Beth stared down at the damp earth, a blank look in her eyes. For a moment, he forgot about the fire. They were camping, roughing it in the woods—that's the simple truth he'd convinced himself of until now. Seeing Beth so lost and still, Chris felt compelled to console her.

But how does he respond to a question like that?

He felt like a gorilla trying to soothe a baby. His mind jumped to King Kong and how the giant held that tiny woman in his massive hand, earning her trust and love.

"How long have you been awake?"

Chris didn't want to admit it, but he had no idea where they were. Every angle looked the same: rows of trees, bristly undergrowth, and dead pine needles blanketing the forest floor. He had a remarkable sense of direction but hadn't spent enough time in these woods to get familiar with the trails. "Don't know," he said. "A while, I guess."

"What have you been doing?"

"Thinking." He had his back to Beth but felt her eyes on him. She expected more. "Listen," he said, "I don't think I should have brought you out here."

"What?"

Chris turned to his sister. Her eyes were bulging. She squeezed his jacket against her body. "It's not safe for you to be out here."

A heavy silence fell between them.

"I mean, look at you. You're shaking. You can't handle this."

Beth scrambled to her feet and met her brother's gaze. "And you are? Why? Because you were a stupid Boy Scout?"

Chris frowned, shifting his weight to one leg.

"I'm not helpless, you know," she continued. "I can handle whatever you can."

Chris' eyebrows rose high on his forehead. He tilted his head upward and squinted, as if studying a batter at home plate. "Really?"

"Yes."

"Yeah?"

Beth took a second, pressed her lips together, and nodded.

He grinned.

Beth matched her twin's smile.

"Then what are we arguing for?" he said, shrugging. "I'm starving. Let's get some food."

9

THE BOY

Wolves clawed at his stomach. It had been eighteen hours since his last meal. He wondered how long a kid his size could last before hunger finally did him in. Times like this, he envied Beth. She could go all day, probably longer, without as much as a piece of lettuce and not miss a beat.

On the trips to the city to visit Grammy and Granddad, Chris had learned to endure Dad's self-produced oldies mix. Secretly, he looked forward to hearing the Carpenters and that haunting, frail voice. The lyrics felt girlish, but that didn't matter. The words told a story, the melodies hypnotic. He learned the singers were siblings, and the sister died from being too skinny because she refused to eat. He wondered why Beth sat sulking at the kitchen table hours after everyone else had left, her plate of cold meat and wilted greens untouched.

They lumbered down a dusty trail winding through thick trees and wilting branches. Chris led, brushing aside twigs. Retracing last night's hike was impossible, but he pressed on, confident the trail would lead out. Showing doubt around Beth wasn't an option. If she sensed uncertainty, she'd grow anxious and likely demand heading to the nearest police station. Complaining and fasting was what girls did best.

It wasn't long before Beth spotted a pair of faded ruts and suggested they leave the path to follow them out of the forest. He hated to admit it, but it made sense. Though not a service road, the ruts promised less resistance than the path they'd been on.

As they changed course, methods of finding food filled Chris' brain. For about two seconds, he considered begging on the street. Then Dad spoke up: *I'm raising you so that you never have to rely on anyone.*

Chris considered trapping a squirrel or rabbit. But beyond a bundle of T-shirts, a pair of jeans, and some socks, his only possessions were an autographed baseball and a penknife—useless to stop even a small animal's beating heart.

Then a clever idea struck him, one he couldn't dismiss. Beth wouldn't like it. It wasn't the safest or most practical plan, but it beat standing by the roadside, hat dangling in hand, flagging down drivers for money.

The ruts led them to the mouth of the woods, about a hundred yards west of where they entered last night. Chris peeked out from the greenery to see if anyone was near. He looked up at the open sky, frowning at the gray clouds drifting across a sea of white.

There was no movement other than the occasional bird humming inside the trees. "It's recon time." Stepping out, he signaled Beth to follow.

A distant rumble roared overhead.

Beyond the field stood the two-lane road polished with bright mustard-yellow pavement markings. It curved into obscurity around the east bend before running south towards the heart of Wanapatchee. A street sign read Ditchburn Street.

The twins hurried across the field, their muddied sneakers pressing into the soft turf. There was no sidewalk, just pebbly trails bordering the road.

It was a quiet street. Since exiting the forest, only three cars had passed. Chris figured they'd avoid attracting attention if they acted normal and kept their heads down.

He could hear his sister breathing over his shoulder. She was itching to speak up, probably to ask a load of questions that had no answers. But focusing on ways to present his plan took precedence.

A mile down, a new road branched off to the west, cutting

across their path. A large stone sign read Dominion Gardens.

Chris stopped, craned his neck past the sign, and smirked. He pulled the brim of his Yankees cap to veil his eyes. "Let's go," he said.

Finally, Beth spoke up. "What are we doing, Chris?"

"Busting into a house and taking some food," he said.

Beth stopped short. She blinked and shook her head. "Are you crazy? We can't do that! What if we get caught?"

Chris stopped suddenly and turned around. "I don't know about you, but my stomach is *eating* itself. Besides, do you have a better idea?" He spun around and marched on, not offering her a chance to respond. "Try not to look so guilty."

Split-level homes lined the street, spaced about twenty yards apart. They wore brilliant colors and boasted dark, smooth driveways, budding lawns, and flower beds. No one was around, but Chris felt eyes on him, like the road was a trap waiting for him to step into it.

A Mercedes, a Lexus, a Range Rover, and an Audi gleamed on driveways up the road. The twins passed two houses before stopping at one with an empty drive. Its freshly mown lawn glowed green, and manicured shrubs and trees framed the house, offering privacy from the neighbors. Chris nodded towards it. "That one."

"You sure we should do this?"

It was chilly, but sweat clung to his skin, his palms slick. "Sshhh, just act normal." The front door and street-facing windows were risky, so he darted to the side of the house, heart pounding, eyes searching for a way in.

Beth snatched his arm. "Chris," she warned, "I hear a kid!"

Chris tilted his head and listened. Voices came from the backyard thirty feet ahead. "Hang here a sec," he said.

Before she could object, he edged closer to the house and peered his head around the side. Then he rushed back, wearing a wide grin. "Okay, here's the plan," he said. "You may not like this, but believe me…it's the best way."

THE GIRL

THE GIRL

A teetotum spun in her gut, just like when she'd show Dad her report card. To her surprise, Chris looked calm.

Frozen, Beth heard the mother call out playfully from the backyard, "I'm gonna getcha! Where could Missy be?" She pressed an arm to her stomach, trying to keep the bile down.

Chris pointed to an open side-hinged window leading into the kitchen. "Here's the part you may not like, Beth," he said, eyes narrowing. "I can force the pane and pull out the glass with this." He pulled a penknife from his pocket and held it up. "But I'm too big to fit through."

The knot in Beth's stomach tightened. "You want *me* to go in?"

Chris nodded, his eyes softening. "It's the only way."

A child's giggle rose from behind the house. Beth flinched, her eyes zipping across the street to check for onlookers. She wanted to glance at Chris for reassurance but dreaded the look he'd give once he saw how scared she was.

Push aside that stuff they jammed down your throat since you were crapping in your diapers, and do it. It may be wrong, but you have to do it.

Beth turned back to her brother and nodded.

He led her to the side of the house.

"I'm gonna getcha!"

Another flinch.

Chris told her to stand guard while he raised his hands to remove the glass from the window frame.

With shaking hands, he pried the beading off the windowpane, pulled it free, and dropped it to the ground. Inserting the knife between the glass and frame, he eased it loose. The glass slid out effortlessly, nearly slipping from his grip. "Shit!" he hissed, signaling Beth for help.

She rushed over and helped him set the glass down on the grass.

Chris pulled off his pack and shoved it towards her to put on. He held up a hand, signaling her to freeze.

"I can't believe I'm doing this," she hissed.

"Shut up. Keep quiet."

Grunting, Chris lifted her several feet off the ground until she hooked a firm grip on the windowsill. She pulled herself up and through the window, their combined effort nearly sending her face smacking into the granite countertop. She swung her legs through and lowered them to the floor.

Chris rushed to sneak a peek in the backyard as Beth skimmed the room, her heart pumping fast and hard.

The kitchen stretched twenty feet and opened to a formal dining room. Six large windows, draped in blue curtains, surrounded the space. White glossy cabinets reached the ceiling. In the center, an island held a six-burner stove with four barstools tucked neatly beneath its edge. At the far end stood a breakfront cabinet displaying powder-blue china and framed family photos.

A ceiling fan buzzed softly above Beth's head, carrying the scent of bacon and toast through the room.

Beth often wondered what it'd be like to crash one of the slumber parties the girls gossiped about in school. *This must be what it's like,* she thought. *Awful. I hate being somewhere uninvited.*

Outside, a child squealed with delight. Oddly enough, the sound offered Beth a drop of comfort. She turned her head to see Chris standing guard. As long as he had the family in sight, she was safe.

Crayon magnets held a calendar, finger paintings, and photos of a young girl on the stainless steel refrigerator door. Beth reached for the handle, then froze. A sour feeling churned in her stomach. Seeing those genuine smiles and the calendar's notes hit her hard—it meant a real family lived here, with a little girl who went to school and painted pictures.

Just then, a lawnmower rumbled to life outside. Beth snapped to attention and jerked her head towards the window.

It's only a mower. You're not hurting anyone, and it's only food. These people can afford to lose some of it.

Beth nodded at the voice in her head and tugged the handle.

With trembling hands, she grabbed anything small and handy: two unopened packs of hot dogs, several baggies of lunch meat, two one-liter bottles of water, a bag of kiwis, a few apples, and a thick white block of cheese.

You forgot to take the pack off!

Arms full, Beth kicked the fridge door shut and rushed to the counter beneath the open window, stuffing everything into the backpack. "Chris!" she panted over the roar of the motor.

The child's voice drew closer. "Okay, mommy! I want soda!"

The back door opened and shut. Seconds later, the girl from the photo ran into the kitchen, heading straight for the fridge. She wore dirty jeans, a purple jacket, and three pigtails high on her head. She didn't notice Beth standing just a few feet away.

"Missy, don't run in the house," the mother called from the backyard.

Beth froze against the counter, stomach twisting. She felt ridiculous standing there with a backpack full of stolen food.

"Okay, mommy!" The girl pulled out a can and shut the door. Bottles clanked against the inside shelf. "Got it!" She whipped around in a large circle, then stopped suddenly. Her jaw dropped with a muffled gasp.

Beth squeezed her eyes shut and braced for a piercing scream. To her surprise, the child didn't make a sound. After a few seconds, Beth peeked her eyes open. Dazed, the girl stared at her, cocking her head like a curious dog.

Beth gave her a pinched smile. "Hi."

"I dunno you. Are you mommy's friend?"

Stay calm.

"Oops, you f-found me. I guess you w-win."

Footsteps scuttled across the grass outside the open window, breaking the delicate moment between the girls. Beth thought she heard Chris whisper her name. She spun around and tossed the pack out the window. One foot lifted towards the counter—ready to leap—but something made her pause and look back at the girl.

The child stood still, watching. Something about Beth held her attention. She forced a smile. "I'm…uh, the expired food police," she said. "You don't want your family getting sick, do you?"

The child smiled back and held out a tiny arm, swaying the can in her hand. "Wanna soda?"

Beth froze. The kindness hit her like a wave—unexpected, undeserved. Tears welled in her eyes. She didn't know if it was the guilt or the girl's open-hearted offer, but her chest ached. Unable to stop herself, she reached out and took the gift. "Thank you," she whispered. "I must fly off now. Other families need my help."

The child giggled, revealing a row of crooked teeth.

Every second stretched like a wire ready to snap. Beth forced herself to turn away and clambered onto the counter. Beside the sink, piled with pans and soiled dishes, sat a roll of paper towels and a digital radio.

Toilet paper!

She grabbed the items and leapt into Chris' arms. The pack slipped, smacking the ground. A pack of hot dogs tumbled out.

"Jeez, Beth!" He crouched, snatched the pack, fumbled the zipper shut, then lurched up and grabbed her wrist. "C'mon, let's move. Now."

10

THE GIRL

"This cheese is good!" she said, cutting into the white block with her fingernails.

Chris squeezed another piece of turkey into his mouth. "Wait till you try these cold cuts."

After running five hundred feet down Ditchburn Street, Chris insisted they return to the clearing in the woods. A man had been mowing behind the house they'd broken into, the noise drowning their footsteps and easing their escape.

"We gotta go back," he'd said. "The trees won't block the rain, and we need a secret place to eat."

Beth hated the idea of returning to the woods but, with no other options, she relented.

Clouds thickened and darkened as they returned to the forest, turning day into dusk. When they reached the hole in the woods, thunder growled above them like an angry lion, the air heavy and damp.

Hungry and thirsty, they sank onto the remnants of their pile to eat, planning afterward to find shelter somewhere warm and dry.

"You picked some good stuff, Beth." Chris lifted the water bottle to his lips. "But I have no idea what these fuzzy things are supposed to be," he said, eyeing the kiwis.

"Thanks!" Beth took a gulp of water and grinned, dizzy from the burst of flavors in her mouth. Sitting cross-legged, the canned soda rested against her hip. "I think they're fruit. I heard Aunt Phyllis in California eats them."

The sky ignited, the clearing lit by a sudden flash. Seconds later, another rumble of thunder fell from all directions.

Beth flinched, her water bottle slipping in her grip. "We should get going, Chris."

Chris swallowed his last bite, nodded, and stood. Beth followed. They packed the rest of the food and water into the backpack, but she kept hold of the soda can. That was her prize.

For the first time, Chris noticed the hand radio dangling from her wrist. He snatched it and turned it over in his hands. "You took this?" he asked, brows lifting.

A wave of shame crashed over Beth. For a moment, she'd forgotten what she had done. Back in the forest, all she'd cared about was food. Now, the guilt struck hard, like a hairbrush smacking her skull. Half expecting the girl's mother to be standing behind her, she winced and rubbed the crown of her head, then peeked over her shoulder. "Uh...I grabbed it on my way out."

Chris eyed her for a second before turning his focus to the radio's knobs and switches. His eyes glazed over, lost in thought. After a moment, he nodded and slipped the radio into his pack.

It was time to move on.

O   O   O

"This stinks!"

Rain spilled through the foliage like a web of falling streams. Sneakers slapped puddles, soaking their socks and chilling their feet.

The twins tussled along a narrow path, rain slapping their skin like blunt needles. Branches scraped, sprigs clawed as they pressed forward. Chris spotted a limb propped against a tree and grabbed it. At two feet long, it was sturdy, easy to swing. Perfect for clearing the way.

Rain morphed into a deluge in minutes. Beth could barely hear her footsteps. Cold air bit her skin as she tried to walk with arms wrapped around her chest. Her head ached, and her teeth rattled like tiny bones in her mouth. "This is horrible," she grumbled. "Maybe we should have gone into a stupid foster home."

Chris struck a branch. "Keep your eyes open for somewhere to camp. We've both been stuck in the rain before, so don't complain."

Beth narrowed her eyes. Chris had gotten good at dismissing her, especially after joining his new sports crowd. Now his anger turned infectious, spreading like a virus.

Something raw and involuntary awakened inside her, consuming her focus. A torrent of emotions flooded every cell, leaving no room for logic.

Beth stopped in her tracks. Aiming forward, Chris hadn't noticed. "I don't want to be out here, and there's no place to go! We can't do this by ourselves, Chris! I want to go home!" Blind fury erased all concerns about the rainstorm as she ran off, sodden sneakers splashing through the swelling puddles.

Chris spun around, but she had already vanished into the soggy backdrop. "Beth, are you crazy? You can't leave!" he hollered through the rain.

O   O   O

It didn't take long for Beth to grasp the severity of her situation. She'd abandoned her brother in the woods during a rainstorm. Cold and alone, thirst clawing at her throat, she clung to the canned soda in her frozen hand.

Low, thick clouds loomed overhead, condemning her naivety and misdeeds. Rain pelted her arms and face; wind pushed against her skin. Hair clung to her cheeks like a paste, sweat beaded her brow. She couldn't stop shivering.

Beth longed for her warm bed and journal, but reality hit hard: her house was gone. Defiant, she pushed the thought away, telling herself the fire was just a cruel rumor her survival instinct made up. She planned to read her beloved books again, breathe in lavender from warm sheets, sleep late, and disappear beneath the covers. Hope was all Beth had left.

After what felt like hours of hiking, she caught her breath

against a fallen tree. Bones ached. Mouth ran dry again. Without Chris to guide her and the sun hidden behind clouds, she had no idea which way to go. Her last hope was that a forest ranger or lost tourists might cross her path, someone who'd listen and take her to the police. She didn't care what punishment was coming. The woods were worse. At least the police would put her someplace warm and give her something hot to eat.

Examining the soda can, Beth's hand moved to the tab—then her survival voice slammed the breaks.

Don't.

Beth paused, weighing her next move. She nodded and released the tab. Drinking now would be foolish. The soda offered support, a reminder that kindness and warmth still existed in the world.

Desperate for spit, she dragged her tongue across the roof of her mouth. The insufferable dryness sparked memories of sitting in the dentist's chair. Dr. Morris, in his white jacket, handlebar mustache, and slick black hair, pushing cotton into her mouth to soak every drop of saliva.

Beth looked up. Raindrops touched her lips, sprinkling her tongue with sour taste.

Her hand drifted to her back pocket. Like the soda, the diary should have offered comfort, but her stomach dropped when her fingers touched empty fabric. Her eyes snapped open, head darting in every direction. "Oh no! My journal!"

Tears stabbed her eyes, but she shook them off, calling to her inner voice. "We have to go back and find it!"

Where will you go? You're in the middle of the woods.

The voice was right. Beth had no idea where the book landed. Fresh shame plunged into her stomach. She hadn't just deserted her twin; she'd turned her back on her closest friend.

Hours passed. With each step, the urge to find an exit trail or call for help faded. Bricks filled Beth's shoes. Her foot caught on a rock. She stumbled into a branch and clung to it with everything she had.

Focussss. We'll get through thisssssss.

Blood pulsed in her head. Trees spun; the forest became a Tilt-A-Whirl. Her head felt like a gangly plastic doll on a spring. Images of Chris alone in the woods appeared, refusing to fade. "Chris...?"

Beth squeezed her eyes shut. Her head pounded. Was this hypothermia? Flopping from tree to tree, she cursed herself for letting her mind drift during those early morning health classes.

A gust of wind rose, and soft humming—like singing—radiated above her. Through the rain, wind whistled in her ears, brushing her face like sun-dried linen. Her surroundings faded, revealing a path ahead.

She had to go back and find Chris.

Beth turned on her heels and staggered the other way, hoping the path led back to her twin.

11

THE BOY

Hours had passed since Beth took off, leaving him alone.

Clouds parted, revealing soft blue fragments of sky. Sunlight beamed down patchy streaks of light, glinting the greenery. Golden rays slipped between tall tree trunks, casting shadows like steady skeletons. Chris trudged up a small hill, searching for his sister.

He was furious at her stupidity. How could she run off like that? What had he done to make her so angry? Why did girls have to be so freaking emotional?

Chris had to find her. He hated to admit it, but her disappearance rattled him, as if some mysterious force had sucked out a piece of himself. He felt alone, fractured, and hated it. Beth was loyal and trusting, always at his side, shadowing along— something he hadn't realized until now.

His knapsack weighed down his shoulders, twigs whipping his face and scratching his arms. Exhaustion and hunger dragged on his mind and body.

Still, he marched on.

He pictured Beth racing through the trees, frantic and drenched like a lost child from some cryptic nursery rhyme. Would a shrewd stranger spot her, fake concern, and snatch her up? What if she tripped on a root, fell into a creek, and cracked her head open? Both were possible since Beth was gullible and, well, darn clumsy. After all, Dad had once named her "Clumsy Turtle" during those playful wrestling matches on the living room floor.

Chris paused against a tree to catch his breath, taking small sips of water. Awaiting some sign that would lead him in the right direction, he looked skyward. Magpies and robins sang in the trees, oblivious to the drama below.

He capped the bottle, pushed the pack higher on his back, and headed west towards the fading sun.

The obstruction in his back pocket became unbearable, the sharp corners jabbing his rear end. Unable to ignore it, he stopped, pulled out the provocation, and examined it. Tiny white hearts dotted the purple cover, and the word "Diary" appeared in decorative font on the lower right corner.

Chris stared at the book, curiosity growing. The cover, wrapped in a plastic sheath, remained unscathed. "Screw it." He flipped it open. Rain dampened the purple-lined pages; some entries bled purple ink. He peeled apart two pages and glanced at a random paragraph.

Tonight I cried and cried because my mother hates me. I don't like my family sometimes! Even though I write to you, I still talk to 'her.' I tell her about my problems because no one else will listen. I talk to her a lot.

He sucked in a breath, flipping to another page.

As you know, I hate my mom (a little). I can't take it anymore. My mom favours my brother. For instance, she's a lot nicer to him and when he does something wrong, she just (maybe) yells at him, and it's the opposite of me.

Chris snapped the book shut, dropping it into his pack. "Arrrrgghhh!"

The outcry boomed through the trees, the disturbance startling a flock of birds into flight from high branches.

Desperate to track down his comrade, Chris stormed on.

THE GIRL

THE GIRL

Staggering on, her head buzzed like a swarm of hornets.

Tiredness and confusion consumed her. Beth fought to stay awake, aiming towards a shadowy shape. She reeled to it, hoping whatever it was could rescue her from this hell.

Shivering, she lifted her arms to it. "H-Help..."

Like a mirage, gray timber wrapped in soggy vegetation came into focus. But it wasn't a person or an animal—it was a building nestled in the greenery.

Staaaay focuuuused. Staaaay awaaaake.

Beth grew nauseous, her legs weak and rubbery as if the biting chill dissolved her bones, leaving behind strained tissue. Her throat felt hot; she circled her tongue around her mouth for saliva. Her toes tingled. Even her hair hurt, like needles pricking her skull.

Moments later, her muscles betrayed her and she crumpled to the ground, escaping into a sea of black.

THE BOY

THE BOY

The sun hung low, ready to melt into the horizon.

Chris drank his last drop of water nearly thirty minutes ago. The bottle reserved for Beth sat untouched in his pack. He did everything to distract himself from stealing a sip. That was for her. And once he found her—and he would—she'd need it more than him.

Snapping twigs and rustling leaves under his shoes drowned out any chances of detecting a river or stream. Every minute counted. The pursuit had to be constant, relentless. From now on, he planned to stop only to pee.

Keeping an eye on traces of dew and drizzle collected on low-hanging leaves, Chris chewed on the front of his shirt, sucking down any moisture he could. He knew better than to drink rainwater, especially off dirty leaves and branches. But for the first time, he defied his scout leader's rule and pulled off his cap, holding it out.

Fifteen minutes later, he'd collected half a cup. Chris paused to pour the reserve into his empty water bottle, then gulped it down, grimacing. It tasted greasy and metallic, like chewing aspirin.

Desperation grew by the minute. If he didn't find Beth soon, he'd have no choice but to stop and camp before nightfall. Wandering wet through the woods at night was asking for death. A small part of him hoped Beth had found her way out, maybe reached a police station. At least then, she'd be safe and dry.

But Chris knew better. He felt it.

He thought back to the break-in. He still couldn't believe they'd gotten away with it—and that Beth hadn't put up a fight or refuse the idea entirely. The thought made him smile.

A two-foot-long forked branch nestled in the soil caught Chris' attention. Curiosity drove him to pick it up. He set his foot over one end until it snapped. Now it was the right size, about seven inches long and two inches thick. Perfect.

He wasted no time heading off again. He fished the penknife from his front pocket and began stripping away the wet, mossy bark. He tucked it into his back pocket after a few minutes. Finding cloth was unlikely, but he kept looking.

He struck a branch with an open palm. "Damn, Beth! Where the heck are you?"

12

CAPTAIN RAMSEY and DAVID POWELL

CAPTAIN RAMSEY and DAVID POWELL

"You're damn right that I'm angry. I'm furious!"

While Chris carved his makeshift slingshot, Douglas Ramsey and David Powell questioned the single mother at Dominion Gardens. Hearing her little girl ask who "Mommy's friend" was, Mrs. Alperstein assumed Lara was playing one of her usual games. She was always inventing stories. Only later, after noticing the dislodged kitchen window and the missing radio and food, did the truth set in.

She reported the break-in immediately.

Sitting with the officers, Mrs. Alperstein fought to compose herself. She didn't want to alarm Lara, still playing in the backyard. "I'm furious that this girl—this *kid*—stole my peace of mind. What is happening with kids these days, anyway?"

They sat around a circular oak breakfast table at the corner nook in the kitchen. The woman sat facing the backyard windows, her eyes fastened on Lara's every move.

Powell scribbled the woman's answers into a crisp new notepad. With his lean frame, tousled dirty-blond hair, and sharp green eyes, he could have passed for a college student rather than a cop. For most of his five years, he'd been stuck behind a desk, until Detective Sanders arrived from New York and shook things up. After a brief stint with Sanders, the captain teamed him with Barry Warsoff. But Warsoff, newly promoted to lead officer for missing persons, was busy chasing down leads on the twins. The Alperstein case was low priority, so the captain brought Powell along for some hands-on training.

Mrs. Alperstein insisted the officers avoid questioning her daughter. Instead, she shared every detail about the intruder with them. "…and my daughter kept repeating how small the girl was. About this high," she said, raising a flat, shaky hand several feet from the ground.

Shaken by neighbors' reports of break-ins, Mrs. Alperstein installed surveillance cameras hidden behind decorative ornamentations over the front and back doors. Since the twins avoided the entrances, the cameras caught only their profiles as they slipped alongside the house.

Ramsey guessed the intruders were harmless kids, maybe even homeless.

Horrified, the mother gaped at the captain's theory. "But you must take this seriously!"

The soft-spoken captain furrowed his bushy, salt-and-pepper brows. "Yes, ma'am," he assured her. With over twenty-five years on the force, his careworn eyes and weathered face showed every dent of anxiety earned on the job. "Someone broke into your home and threatened your child. We're taking this very seriously."

Powell snapped photos of the kitchen and the package of hot dogs pressed in the dirt outside the window. The storm had erased all footprints.

Ramsey called forensic identification officers to collect fingerprints and hair fibers. He retrieved the security footage for analysis.

Once forensics arrived, Ramsey and Powell thanked the anxious mother and excused themselves. As they walked to the squad car, reporters called out questions. Ramsey told Powell to ignore them. They had nothing concrete to share, and besides, Officer Castaneda handled the media.

The officers headed back to the station, turning south on Ditchburn Street. Ramsey hunched over the wheel, lost in thought. "There are a few things I'm still trying to understand," he mused.

Powell focused on the photos taken at the scene. "Hmm…?"

"It's unusual a suspect of a B&E, especially in this neighborhood, would be so young—and female."

Powell blinked, breaking his gaze from a bird's-eye photo of the hot dogs in the wet grass. "Yeah...?"

Ramsey scratched his stubbly chin. "Such an arbitrary crime," he said. "And she took food, not much else. That house held valuables. Apart from a hand radio, they didn't take anything worth of value."

David nodded slowly.

"This is the first home invasion I know where the stolen goods were hot dogs and cheese."

Powell snickered. "What are you saying, Captain? That you don't trust the lady's story?"

"No." Ramsey shook his head. "It's just...something's not right. Why just food and a radio? Why risk breaking into a house with the residents in the backyard? Are kids now looking for a more intense rush? Maybe the thrill of snatching candy bars and video games lost their luster?"

Powell nodded, his mouth forming a wry grin. "You always said criminals aren't the sharpest tools in the shed, Captain."

The captain didn't blink an eye.

A few minutes passed before Powell spoke again. "You want to try again tomorrow? Maybe convince her to let us speak with the kid?"

"Forget it," said Ramsey quickly. "Once we look at the security footage, we'll get a clearer picture of everything."

David nodded, returning to the photos.

They pulled into the station and shot up the entrance stairs towards the far right corner into the captain's office. Sullen, fluorescent lighting flooded the grubby white walls crammed with maps of New Jersey and corkboards pinned with "Missing" and "Wanted" flyers.

Back in his office, Ramsey grabbed a fifteen-inch monitor. "Sit down," he said. "Okay, watch closely."

Ramsey jumped to the time code when Mrs. Alperstein said the kids first appeared. The officers watched a boy and girl creep towards the side of the house. Ten minutes later, they returned. The little girl's description matched every detail.

"Jeez," said David, squinting at the screen. He had his arms crossed over his chest, shaking his head. "These perps are getting younger, aren't they, Captain?"

Ramsey shot his deputy a stern look. "Dave, I told you again and again to expect the unexpected." He pointed at the screen. "They don't look much older than what—thirteen?"

The boy wore a baseball cap and carried a knapsack. Standing nearly two inches shorter than him was the girl. Both wore soiled clothes and sneakers.

After watching the clip a third time, Ramsey spoke up. "They don't have cameras covering the side of the house. No proof the kids tampered with the window or got inside. But the little girl's story about the soda appears to hold up. See her holding something on her way out? If that's a can of soda, it wasn't there before. If we assume—at least until the forensic results arrive—that these two kids burglarized the house, I must admit they're resourceful."

"Sir…?"

"The kids," Ramsey added. "Where would kids that age learn a skill like that? Dismantling glass from a window frame?"

Powell shrugged. "Good question. Still, they don't look threatening. See how scared they are running away? I doubt they'll come back."

"No reason not to take this seriously, Dave." Ramsey released a long, restless yawn. "Do your due diligence."

Powell took a moment to skim his notes. "So…?"

Ramsey's eyes narrowed at his deputy. "Head back to Dominion. Knock on some doors and see what you can dig up. Then file the report. Once the prints are in, send them off to the lab. And don't forget to report this to Warsoff."

13

THE GIRL

Sitting at the kitchen table across from Dad and Chris, she snatches up the serving tongs. The aroma of spaghetti, glistening with olive oil, fresh garlic, and cracked pepper, swirls around her, flooding her nostrils. Mom is nowhere in sight.

Beth smiles. There's no pressure to eat. Hunger is the driving force tonight; she craves the garlic's spice and the oil's fruitiness on her tongue. She may even ask for seconds.

Then Dad pulls the thongs from her hand. "Stupid," he barks, passing them over to Chris. "You weren't assigned to it!"

Beth's jaw falls open, shock flooding her features. She battles to dam the tears threatening to spill down her burning cheeks. In a sudden burst, she bolts upright, sends her chair skidding back, and storms from the kitchen to her bedroom.

A swarm of wasps circles her bed. Beth lashes out with a pillow, scattering their bodies like ink stains across the white comforter. Exhausted, she collapses to her knees, burying her head in the mattress as tears slip down her cheeks.

Her door bursts open. The sudden breeze blows bug fragments into the air like black dust. "What's going on here?" a voice calls from the doorway.

Beth's head snaps up. She glances over her shoulder and sees Erica, Chris' crush, glaring down at her with long blonde hair and arms crossed beneath her large breasts.

"Who do you think you are, barging into my room? You're not my mother! I don't have a mother!"

Buzzing noises pulled Beth from her dream. Darkness fell, the air cold and still. For a moment, she wondered if she was dead, but her chattering teeth told her she was alive. A lightning bolt shot through the deepest part of her brain where her head smacked the ground, affirming her existence. Death wasn't cruel enough to cause physical pain, was it?

Beth took shallow breaths, dazed. Was she home? In a hospital? Had she slipped from one nightmare into another?

The musty smell reminded her of Chris' bedroom. She wriggled her fingers and toes against the mattress. *My bed,* she thought. *I'm in my bed! The fire and the woods was just a nightmare!*

It took a moment for her eyes to adjust to the darkness. Then light tinged random shapes around her. She turned to the right and spotted a window. Darkened with dirt and more tall than wide, it looked nothing like the one in her room. Her gaze lifted to a hole in the ceiling, revealing an endless sky and sweeping clouds.

Burrowed in a blanket that smelled like a moldy shower curtain, Beth felt warmth between her legs and under her arms. A shiver raced through her, the hairs on her arms rising on pointed goosebumps.

Crackling. Buzzing.

The sudden noise jolted her upright. Pain flared in her head, and she grimaced. Something shifted on the mattress. Holding her breath, her eyes sailed down to see what caused the warmth. But it was too dim to tell.

Oh no, you must have peed yourself.

Confused with fear, Beth shifted against the cushion. Something solid rolled against her. She reached back, fingers closing around the unfamiliar object, and lifted it into the dim light. It was heavy, warm, and unmistakably a water bottle from the girl's house. Her hand wandered to the right, brushing against another. Pulling the blanket aside, Beth stared down in disbelief—her clothes were gone, leaving only a training bra and underwear. A lump rose in her throat as she slipped her hand between her legs and found another water bottle.

What the heck? You part of some experiment or something?
Crackling. Buzzing.

Beth flinched, her eyes darting in all directions. The sound came from outside, but close. Instinct told her to scream for help. She opened her mouth and drew in a breath. Then her survival voice screamed in her head.

Don't!

She snapped her mouth shut, biting her top lip. If she'd been kidnapped, panicking would only make things worse. Whoever was outside could burst in any moment and hurt her. Her mind raced for a plan.

Beth had spent countless nights with Chris watching low-budget horror films from the '80s and '90s, stories not so different from where she found herself now. The characters awakened, usually in some drugged stupor, soon realizing they were in a terrible place, shackled to rusty pieces of furniture. Terrified, they'd curl up sobbing, awaiting their destiny. Beth tried to imagine what she'd do in those situations but always came up short of a quick plan.

If you learned one thing from those movies, it's that panicking makes things worse.

Nodding, Beth searched for anything to use as protection. Her right hand slid off the mattress and touched something hard: a pointed piece of wood two, feet long.

She picked it up. *This can work.*

She edged over to the side of the mattress and wobbled to her feet, wrapping the blanket around herself. She dodged from the window, hiding from whoever was outside. Another sharp pain fired through her brain, nearly knocking her down. Wincing, she waited for the throbbing to ease. Her feet felt like blocks of ice. She looked down.

He took your shoes and socks, too? What kind of freak is this?

A few feet ahead, a sliver of light leaked beneath a door. Beth crept forward, the floorboards creaking under her feet. She pushed the door open; it hung on leather hinges and didn't squeak. It opened south onto a mess of trees and grassy plants, the sinking sun to her right. The last light fought through a sea of greenery, creating a jumble of shadows. A gust of damp air slapped her face, sharp scents of oils rising from the vegetation.

Buzzing. Crackling.

Beth's eyes shot to her right. She tightened her grip around the wood, her heart hammering against her chest. With the other hand gripping the blanket, she crept outside, stepping onto a concrete slab beyond the door. A bitter cold stung her feet. The door crept shut as she craned her neck towards the sound.

A crackling noise echoed in the distance. Beth shrieked and jerked back, nearly dropping the blanket.

Chris spun around, the radio tumbling from his lap to the ground.

Buzzing.

Neither of them spoke for a moment. Then Chris turned back to the radio. Indignant, he slapped it with an open palm. "Shit. Just had it."

"Chris? What's going on?"

THE BOY

He sat on a log in a twelve-foot-wide clearing, the floor thick with packed dirt and dotted with young spruce. Rainwater pooled in shallow patches and tall pines ringed the space, light filtering through the canopy in shifting fragments. A small fire crackled in the pit before him.

"Everything's okay. You're safe, so you can drop that." Chris glimpsed over his shoulder, eyeing one side of his sister. "The wood, I mean. Not the blanket."

Beth glanced down at herself, cheeks flushed. She dropped the wood, clutching the blanket tighter around her.

"I found you on the ground and took you inside."

Beth stared at him, stunned.

"Your clothes aren't dry yet, but you should probably sit by the fire and get warm."

Beth paused, then stepped towards the fire pit. Trees stood black against the indigo sky, their shadows tall across the clearing. A few fallen branches lay scattered, but the ground was mostly clear—no thickets, no roots to twist through. A weeded path ran from the door to the pit.

She sat on a mossy log angled away from him.

Chris fidgeted with the metal antenna, frustrated. He'd never seen a radio like this. It had a small speaker, two knobs, old enough to belong to Mom and Dad as kids. Dry mud stained the knees of his damp jeans. He wore a different T-shirt: "Second Place Means You've Lost" scrawled in bright yellow cursive. His sneakers, once white, were caked in brown mud.

"You okay?" he asked.

"I don't know. Am I?"

His mouth curled into a grin. Why did girls always answer questions with questions? He set the radio aside, feeling emotionally strained, more disappointed than angry. His eyes were bloodshot.

He picked up a branch and began poking the wood in the fire. His gaze lingered on the flames, studying the sparks before they vanished into the air. It was all he could do to avoid standing up and smacking Beth across the face. He couldn't believe how stupid she acted.

"You shouldn't run off like that," he said, swatting a mosquito against his cheek. "I know this isn't easy. It sucks. But you can't just take off like that."

Beth peeked at him and gave a small nod.

Chris gestured at the ground near her foot. "By the way, there's some water. But take it easy. We don't have a lot left."

"Thanks."

He closed his eyes, drawn to the crackling fire. Warmth grazed his skin, loosening tense muscles like a warm bath. A sudden chill snapped him awake, and he looked over at Beth. She shivered. He fished a dry T-shirt from his pack and tossed it to her.

She smiled, nearly dropping the blanket. She glanced at him

with shy eyes. He turned his head as she pulled it on.

They sat in silence.

"Chris?"

"Yeah?"

"How'd you find me?" Beth motioned towards the shack. "I mean, what is this place?"

Built from abandoned construction debris and repurposed waste, the single-room shack measured fourteen by eleven feet. Slate-gray wooden planks, rutted and worn, formed the walls. The roof patched overlapping asphalt shingles and wood shakes, topped with tin sheets to seal holes. A single window, four feet high, was missing two of nine panes; one glass bore a spiderweb crack. The splintered, rotting green frame barely held on. Foliage crept over the east end, nearly swallowing the shack. Pressed to the back stood a shed half the shack's size, nestled among thick brush and trees. The southwest side had been cleared of trees. Behind the shed, Chris had spotted a narrow path running a hundred feet north to a hole in the ground.

Beth scooped up the bottle by her foot, took a drink of the water, and frowned. Chris knew it tasted metallic. "Chris…?"

He braced himself before turning to his sister. "You were unconscious not far from here," he said, pointing over her shoulder. "I didn't know if you were alive or dead. But then I saw you breathing. Good thing I found you."

He dropped the poking stick and grabbed the Y-shaped branch resting by his foot. Using the penknife, Chris carved out one-inch prongs from both ends. "You seem fine now, but I think you had hypothermia. Lucky for you, *someone* paid attention in health class." He shifted his weight. "I figured the hot water bottles would help warm you up." He glanced at her, his voice rigid. "I had no choice. You needed to get out of your wet clothes. You could have frozen to death."

Beth nodded, unveiling a sheepish smile.

"Don't worry," he added, dropping his voice. "I couldn't *see* anything. It was dark."

Beth's cheeks reddened. "What time is it?"

Chris shrugged. He wasn't wearing his Islanders watch, having tucked it in his pocket when the rain started. "Who knows? Probably around seven." After a pause, he added, his tone spry, "Hey, you don't happen to have a hair tie or rubber band, do you?"

Beth shrugged, shaking her head.

He sighed.

"How'd you do that?" she asked, nodding at the fire.

Chris placed the branch aside and picked up the longer stick, nudging the fire again. "One of us was a stupid boy scout, remember?"

"That's not what I meant," she mumbled.

"It wasn't a big deal. I had matches, and this pit was already here. It wasn't easy, though. Everything is wet from the stupid rain."

"How'd you do it then?"

Chris motioned over his shoulder to the shack. "There were pieces of dry wood in there."

"Where'd you get the matches?"

"Damn, Beth. You should study law or something."

"Huh?"

"The bar, okay? When I went inside to piss, I took a pack of matches—oh, and if you need to go, I took some toilet paper from the bathroom." Chris figured girls didn't get their periods until seventh or eighth grade, but he wasn't sure and didn't want to ask.

"I suppose a bathroom is out of the question."

He bit his upper lip, stifling a retort.

"I mean, thanks. That'll help."

Chris stared up at the moon, but the more he tried to lose himself in its glow, the sharper the memory of Beth sprawled face down in the dirt became. Seeing her motionless in the mud had convinced him she was gone. His legs went numb, and he collapsed, gasping for air, his face pressed into the cold ground. Pain blazed through his chest, and acid burned his throat as he fought the urge to vomit. Not even a fastball to the groin or the sting of losing the state championship compared to this. Even the memory of medics wheeling Mom and Dad away under white sheets could not touch the raw agony that pinned him to the earth.

Only after turning her over and seeing her chest rise and fall did he cry out in relief. Too weak to lift her, he dragged her inside the shack by her feet.

The experience had opened his eyes. He realized Beth couldn't handle the outdoors, and accepting that felt like betrayal. "I've decided something," he said.

He saw her brace under the blanket, holding her breath.

"Me too," she said. "You're right. We shouldn't turn ourselves in. I don't want to get separated and sent to some foster care or orphanage."

That was the last thing he expected her to say.

14

THE GIRL

Between seeing Chris by the fire and now, she had resolved to stay. Leaving him felt wrong, cruel.

Moments ago, Beth had never been so scared—expecting a perverted stranger to carve her up or squeeze a rope around her throat.

Then she saw Chris.

The discovery sparked a buzz she hadn't felt since locking eyes with that cute, brainy kid at school. It was recess; while other kids played outside, Beth wandered the library searching for a new book. The boy, absorbed in a thick hardback, looked up with glassy blue eyes behind thin-framed glasses and caught her gaze. Curious, she studied the yellowish ring around his left eye. Distracted and prone to daydreams and staring, Beth often drew mockery. But the boy offered a faint smile. Petrified to hold his gaze, she looked away, never looking back.

Chris shook his head. "This is screwed up. It was stupid bringing you out here. I can handle it, but you…"

"…can't?"

"Once you eat something and get dressed, I'll walk you back to town. Or better yet, we'll get someone to drive you. Yeah, that'll be easier. Safer, too, now that it's getting dark."

Why was he so eager to get rid of her? Did he hate her that much? Knowing any dispute would only bring tears, Beth stayed quiet. Chris, like Dad, was stubborn. And if the last few hours showed anything about her survival skills, convincing him seemed pointless.

So you're just gonna sit here and say nothing?

Minutes passed under heavy silence.

"You hungry?" he asked.

Tears blurred Beth's eyes. Inside, she screamed. To hold back the flood, she curled her toes like fists, anything to dull the sting in her chest. Eyes fixed on the flames, she pressed her lips tight and nodded. The thought of food made her stomach growl; Chris laughed and pulled a package of hot dogs from his pack, skewering one on a pointed stick.

"Here," he said, handing it to her. "This is yours."

"What's this?"

"Duh. You're supposed to hold it over the fire and let it cook. Like toasting marshmallows."

Beth twirled the meat over the flames, inhaling its thick, smoky aroma. If Chris hadn't been watching, she would have swallowed it raw. But since he'd taken the trouble to carve the stick, the least she could do was let the hot dog cook.

An unsettling thought crept in: the faster she ate, the sooner Chris would send her away. It was like the awkward flight home from vacation—wishing time would speed up, only to realize the landing marked the end of something good. Beth had never flown, but after years of reading adult paperbacks, she could imagine well enough. "You're not having one?" she asked at last.

"Nah. I already had a couple earlier. I'm good."

She scrambled for a way to convince her brother to let her stay. Nothing came.

After two hot dogs and a bottle of water, she felt better, energized.

It was time to go.

Inside the shack, Beth struggled to pull on her damp jeans. Afterward, Chris asked her to search the area for a rubber band, anything he could use for the slingshot. Not only was he sending her away, now he wanted her to scavenge for parts for his stupid toy.

She half-heartedly searched while he kicked dirt over the fire.

A soft rustling grabbed Beth's attention. She spun her head towards the sound and spotted a squirrel ten feet away, frozen like a statue. "Hello there, little one. You lost?" As if disturbed by the strange creature's presence, the squirrel's head jerked side to side, its claws twitching. "Looking for a friend?"

Specks of purple beneath wet leaves came into focus. Beth froze—her journal! Her mouth fell open. She glanced over her shoulder, then crouched to scoop it up.

The pages were moist and crusty along the edges. She pressed the book against her chest with both hands and grinned like a child on Christmas morning. She peeked over her shoulder again before slipping it into her back pocket.

"Find anything?"

She spun around, shaking her head.

"We gotta go anyhow. It'll get dark soon."

Beth's smile fell. What was the point of fighting? Chris would win. He always won.

He insisted she wear his Islanders jacket, a peculiar gesture since he was the one staying outdoors. As if he could somehow decode her thoughts, he said, "Don't worry. I'll be okay without it."

"But you'll need it more than me."

Chris tossed it to her without a word.

They hiked downhill to the ruts leading towards the forest's edge. A band of tall beach plum shrubs, wrapped in snowy white blossoms, lined the trees. Strangely, Beth hadn't noticed them last night.

Chris pushed through the patch and crossed the lea towards Ditchburn Street, Beth close behind.

THE BOY

THE BOY

He stuck out his thumb and waited for a car to turn the corner.

"As soon as we flag someone down, have the driver take you to the nearest police station. Tell the police who you are and what happened to our home."

Beth bit her lip. "Okay."

He looked over his right shoulder and caught sight of Beth's faraway expression. She looked ashamed. He felt a pinch of guilt about pressuring her into that house, but what else could he do? They needed to eat, and he couldn't fit through that window. Besides, they were better off with him keeping watch.

Attempting to lighten the mood, Chris forced a laugh. "Those people are so rich, they probably won't even care about the food. Okay, they have to fix the window, but it's no big deal. So don't worry about that, alright?"

Ditchburn Street came around a bend from the left before stretching west miles ahead. Dense trees lined the other side, branches extending overhead like coiled snakes. The tarmac was dark and smooth and looked freshly paved. The city had built a new highway across town a few years back, dissuading commuters from using the lengthy back roads. Except for locals, most used the interstate that bypassed small towns like Wanapatchee and Rookwood.

Wind rushed down the road, sending litter dancing along the rocky shoulders. The road lay hushed and empty.

"Once someone pulls over, I'll talk to him for you." Chris could feel the weight in the air, his sister's breathing over his shoulder. He was not blind to her distress but knew to distance himself. That made things easier. "You hear me?"

Squeezing the jacket to her chest, Beth blinked and turned to him. "What about you? Why won't you come with me?"

A vision of the purple-lined page flashed in his mind. Hours earlier, bored during a pee break, Chris rummaged through his pack and flipped to page fifty-two. The words glowed like a neon sign.

At first glance, he rolled his eyes and snorted. He'd convinced himself it was just one of those things girls write when upset over something silly.

Then it hit him. Thinking something bad was one thing—a passing thought—but taking time to write it down was another.

Words on a page held power.

Wheels spiraling against asphalt snapped Chris back. He blinked, then stepped into the road, waving his arms.

An SUV steered around the curve, beams emerging around the bend. He held his breath. The vehicle zipped down the road as fast as it came.

"Damn." Chris dropped his arms, looked over at Beth, and shrugged. She offered a weak smile.

A minute later, another car approached. He raised his arms again. A dark gray sedan steered towards the side of the road just beyond them. Gravel crunched beneath the slowing tires.

Chris told Beth to stay put, then jogged up to the car and peeked through the open passenger window.

"You lost, kid?" The driver, a round face man with dark gray hair, wore jeans and a long-sleeve shirt. He looked forty, maybe fifty. Apart from a balled-up sweater in the back seat and two empty coffee cups in the center console, the car was neat, free of clutter.

Chris told the driver his sister meant to catch the bus, but they'd lost track of time playing in the woods. He gestured to her and saw her watching him, studying his every move. The driver turned his head, looked at Beth, then nodded. She dropped her gaze, suddenly fixated on cracks in the concrete.

Chris gave the man a thumbs-up and sprinted back to Beth. He told her the driver would turn around and take her to the Wanapatchee police station. "I told him Dad's a cop, so you'll be safe. He thinks you're visiting him at work. You'll be fine."

Beth said nothing. After a moment, she nodded.

He walked her to the car. She drew him into an embrace, her arms holding on just a moment past what Chris could bear.

"I wish Dad gave us those cell phones for Christmas," she said, her voice muffled against his shoulder. "Then we could stay in touch." She wiped her eyes with the back of her hand.

Chris broke the embrace and grinned. "I'll see you soon, okay?"

Seemingly unconvinced, Beth nodded and slipped into the

sedan, gently shutting the door behind her. She caught the driver's eye, worked up a smile, then turned back to Chris, the smile fading.

They held each other's gaze for a moment before Chris looked back at the driver. The man waved, then glanced over his left shoulder before merging onto the blacktop. He said he'd wait for the U-turn a mile down the road—safer that way. Familiar with the stretch, Chris nodded and watched the car shrink, disappearing beyond a rise.

Beth didn't take her eyes off him the whole time.

Watching her fade away, Chris was jolted by a sudden memory. Last summer, he found a stray Doberman crawling across the baseball field. The chocolate-colored puppy dragged an injured leg, its pale pink tongue lolling from the side of its mouth. No collar or tags, so Chris took it home.

Mom and Dad objected, and three days later, Mom called a friend in South Jersey to take the dog. "How can you take care of a dog when you're at school during the day and playing sports at night?" Mom's friend owned a farm with plenty of land. A perfect place for a puppy, she said.

Chris had never imagined a bond with the dog hitting so hard and hated himself for bringing it home.

Heated tears welled in his eyes as the woman led the dog into the back seat. With Mom beside him and Beth watching from the porch, it took everything he had to keep the tears from spilling as he watched his new friend disappear down the road.

Chris never forgave Mom and Dad for that.

He blinked back to the present. Marooned, he turned, dug his hands into his pockets, and headed into the woods.

15

THE BOY

THE BOY

"It may sound like the premise of a Hollywood film but isn't. More like a nightmare for a mother and child who, just this morning, suffered a senseless break-in right here in town. The mother reported that her child saw a young woman inside their home, holding stolen food. The child, unharmed, was not available for questioning.

"Suspects removed a glass pane to enter through the kitchen window. The mother requested to speak tonight, hoping this story prompts other parents to discuss this chilling but important issue with their children."

The story shifted to Officer Castaneda's report.

"The family cooperated fully throughout the investigation, and we're pleased to note no harm came to them. The suspects' identities remain unknown. Thanks to the child's description and collected footage, authorities expect to identify them by tomorrow."

Chris switched off the radio. It was nearly eight o'clock.

He located the local all-talk AM station. The odd-looking device proved to be an all-purpose livewire emergency radio—a long-range AM receiver with a high-sensitivity FM band. It also served as a powerful LED flashlight. A handy tool.

The shack stood nearly two miles from the forest's main entrance on Skyway Drive—twice the distance from the path the twins took from Ditchburn Street. Once a rutted track, the path had grown rough and narrow, weeds and roots sprouting from the dirt. And yet, Chris reached the area faster than expected.

Twilight arrived, draping the room in shadows. Six feet above the ground, Chris gazed down through the fractured window. The trees loomed like tall, black creatures gesturing in the breeze. For some reason, Chris thought of *The Wizard of Oz.*

The loft where he sat pressed against the back wall, nearly two and a half feet deep, stretching from end to end with enough room to stretch out. Chris hated heights—actually, feared them—but the thought of lying on that dusty mattress in the dark, the floor creaking beneath every move, felt worse. He felt less helpless sitting tall at the back of the room, facing the entrance.

Bad things happened at night. If the radio's battery faded, a hand-crank generator provided backup power, making the light safe to use. But using it risked attracting attention, especially after dark. The light cast chilling shadows, like evil spirits in *Ghost,* a movie Mom liked.

In his bedroom, Chris kept nightlights. His favorite was a silver NHL Stanley Cup. But after a sideways glance from a friend, he yanked it from the outlet like he'd forgotten it was there, and tossed it into the closet among forgotten trinkets. Soon he found solace in watching television before drifting off to sleep.

The shack was a crude wooden structure, dust-caked with spiderwebs hanging in the corners. Burnt umber paint made the walls seem angry, cracked and chipped like swarms of insects nesting from floor to ceiling. To Chris' left lay a mattress. A bench ran along the right wall, with a rusty sink and broken tap. The washbowl's pipe stopped above a metal bucket, a ceramic jug resting beneath. Scruffy rags hung on nails beside the sink. Aside from the shelf and mattress, only a small handcrafted table and chair stood in the back corner.

Chris rested his head against the plywood wall, reflecting on the news. The reporter's words and tone painted the twins as criminals bent on terrorizing residents. But little happened in Wanapatchee; a story like this was sure to draw attention and ratings—a prime opportunity for a small-town journalist.

More concerning was what happened inside that house. A kid had seen Beth—and Beth said nothing. For some reason, she kept it a secret. Why? What was she hiding? If only Chris knew what happened in that kitchen. Damn that lawnmower.

Why hadn't he crashed at George's? Instead, he'd gone into the forest. George's mom would've welcomed them both, no question. But that was a fantasy, right? After a day or two, she'd be calling the state.

Chris took stock of the remaining provisions: eight ounces of water, a small block of cheese, some deli meat, half a pack of hot dogs, two apples, and a bag of brown fuzzy things. Not enough for two days.

He needed a plan. Sneaking into another house was risky. He considered starting a fire to cook and keep warm but dismissed it. Too likely to draw attention from hikers, hunters, or rangers.

He eyed the raw hot dog. Hell, he'd eaten worse on a bet. But chomping cold mystery meat alone, without his buddies to cheer him on, killed the appeal.

A swift breeze slipped through the hole in the window, stirring putrid odors in the room. Whether he stayed a day or a week, Chris had to make the best of it. Tomorrow, he'd patch the ceiling and fix the window. He'd picked up a few tricks watching Dad handle repairs and felt up to the task. Tools and extra lumber waited in the shed.

Hugging the bundled shirts to his chest, Chris curled up on the loft. The wood pressed into his shoulder and hip.

He hated being alone. He wasn't used to it. It felt like a sentence. Friends and teammates were always around. Even at night, he'd be with Dad, watching hockey or baseball, laughing whenever Dad ranted about players making dumb decisions.

Now there was no Dad. No friends. No television. Not even a sister flinging things on the other side of the wall.

Nothing but growing darkness.

And crickets.

A horrible word flashed in Chris' mind: orphan. He and Beth were now orphans. He thought of that movie she liked—*Annie*. But there was no bald billionaire welcoming them into a world of polished floors, dancing servants, and delicious food. So what did it mean, living without parents? Would he be forgotten, discarded by society like some sex worker?

Tears clouded his vision. He wiped his eyes with his hand.

There was too much to think about. He needed to shut the world out, forget everything for a minute. Maybe even sleep, if he was lucky.

The boys at school talked about it. With Dad at work and Mom and Beth grocery shopping, Chris did it watching the Super Bowl. He even tried it in a school bathroom stall, risking detention and punishment. But what did it matter? Playing it safe was for cowards.

Chris let his mind drift to Erica, how she'd comb her long, blonde hair with her fingers, flipping it back on his desk like waves of yellow yarn. Normally, he'd have swiped it aside and returned to reading. But not with Erica. He looked forward to the scent of her cherry almond shampoo.

With curious eyes and a headband, she reminded him of Alice in *Alice in Wonderland.* One of the prettiest girls in the class, she wasn't snobby like the other girls. She'd even been kind to Beth.

Erica was also one of the first girls in class to develop breasts— small but firm and round, like Grammy's teacups. Chris would sneak peeks whenever she scribbled answers on the chalkboard, fascinated.

Blood rushed south to his groin as he rolled onto his back. A grin spread across his cheeks, drifting him into a world of blissful indifference, where shunning life's concerns felt effortless.

THE GIRL

THE GIRL

As Chris listened to the news, she hobbled through a brush, face and arms dotted with blood, a revolver clutched in her hand.

Returning to this pitiless place was unthinkable. Insane. But it was the only refuge. No bedroom lined with bears and kitten posters. No white desk with its matching chair. No bed with the cotton comforter.

Worst of all, no books. Just a scorched pile of carbonized hardbacks and ash.

The only reason to return to Schicara Drive would be to see Mrs. Calmin. But going back felt like chasing smoke—faces and memories you longed to touch but couldn't.

Chris was all she had left, and Beth needed his protection. With all the courage and confidence of a storybook hero, he'd save her from the monster.

Yes, he'd pushed her into the car like a chunk of meat into a shark's mouth. But it was well-intended. It had to be. Watching him shrink in the rear window, Beth realized how thrilling it had felt, slipping inside that little girl's house—cells rushing through bones a million miles an hour. She'd never felt so alive.

Run! Run your butt off! It's just Manhunt—a game! Hit the safety zone before he tags you. MOVE!

16

THE BOY

He clung to his dream, unwilling to let it slip away. He and Erica were rolling on the pitcher's mound, touching places his bald, uptight health teacher would call "inappropriate."

Moments before waking, her laughter turned into a shriek.

Chris had always thought dreams were like silent films—black-and-white, flickering pictures. But he remembered her laugh. And her hair, spread across the clay slab like the feathers of a golden peacock.

It took a moment before he realized he wasn't in his bedroom. Fuzzy details from yesterday drifted back.

A sound yanked him from the haze. He lifted his head from the balled-up sweatshirt, listening.

Was it a loon? A coyote?

A minute passed in silence.

Chris scowled and shook his head, forcing his eyes open.

Through the window, pieces of night sky showed above a black, eerie ground. Gray light slipped through the cracks, slicing the darkness into strips. Like a mausoleum, everything was deathly still.

His mouth gritty, Chris dug into his pack and drank the last of the water. It was barely enough to coat his throat. Just as his head touched the sweatshirt again, a shrill pierced the night. Not the high-pitched laughter from his dream, but the bone-chilling shrieks girls made in horror films.

Pulse racing, he shot up and snatched the penknife from his pocket. It felt puny compared to the weapons he'd held proudly in the garage. Dad had taught him to protect Mom and Beth on stormy winter nights that sometimes kept him stuck in the city."

If not for nosy police and neighbors, Chris would have cracked the safe. He knew the combination—it was the only number he'd memorized besides his and Beth's birthdays. Inside the five-foot steel chest lay several semi-automatic handguns, two shotguns, and a larger weapon that fired many bullets fast.

If anyone dares darken our doorstep, Dad had said, *you need to know what to do—and how.*

Chris felt honored by the responsibility and vowed to keep the combination secret from friends, from Beth, even from Mom. Beth had a loose tongue, and Mom was hot-blooded.

Don't tell your mother, warned Dad. *She'll get mad at me, try to kill me in my sleep, and probably shoot off her foot.* One look at Dad told Chris he was serious.

Chris wondered if the police had raided the fireproof safe, the thought of Dad's possessions in other hands sparking outrage.

Another long, unnerving cry echoed in the distance.

"What the hell?!" Chris froze.

A sudden breeze whistled through leaves, sending a sharp chill into the room. Branches rapped against the roof and walls. Chris wiped the chilled sweat from his brow and climbed down the creaking ladder. Tightening his grip on the penknife, he inched the door open.

The door opened to a sea of green and gray, the air thick and chilly. Silence hung over the forest.

No red eyes peered between the trees. No beasts crowded in.

Sighing, Chris pulled the door closed and raced up to the loft, body pressed against the wooden slab, clothes and knife tight to his chest.

Trying to fall back asleep now was futile.

17

THE BOY

He lay on the forest floor, head resting on a paper towel roll, watching his first sunrise.

Amber light twinkled past black tree trunks and feathery patches beside the shack. Birds broke the ghostly night with early morning hymns.

Chris watched the sun's buttery light gleam through the birches, entranced by the giant ball's indifference.

Aside from stumbling outside once to pee, Chris stayed tucked in the shack, hands wrapped around the penknife like a tiny sword. Fear faded with the morning light; eager for fresh air, he rushed outside.

The clean, brisk air revived his tired muscles. Chris managed to stay alert through the longest night of his life, pondering unforgettable sports plays, school moments, even spirituality.

Was God real, or some money-hungry cult's invention to scare people? And if God *was* real, why was he so mean? Maybe God was a girl—vicious and clever, hiding hate beneath a smile.

Mom was an obvious example. No surprise to Chris that she favored him over Beth. He was the smart one, required less work, and was easier to love. He could brighten a room with a joke, impersonation, or silly dance. Loving Beth took effort. No one wanted to be around a girl who soured a room with her troubles. Distant, gloomy people only reminded others of their own pain.

Chris often felt torn between defending his sister and enjoying the favoritism, but it was easier to stay quiet. When Beth broke dishes or muttered snide comments, he sometimes wondered if she welcomed the abuse. She took every punishment without protest. After a hard slap and a biting remark, she'd spin away—eyes wet with hate—and storm into her room.

Maybe it was fear of Dad's reaction that kept her from fighting back. It never mattered who was right. Moms and Dads were always on the same team.

During the night, the dark and its chilling sounds drowned out Chris's guilt. With daylight, regret returned. He hated the thought of handing Beth to the police. They'd toss her in an orphanage or with some foster family, for sure.

Part of him almost hoped she was leading the cops to him now. At least then, they might stay together.

He remembered Michelle, the redhead with freckles from math class, whispering that her stepfather watched her while she pretended to sleep and when she showered. That explained her smelly hair most days.

If a stepfather did that, imagine what a foster father might do.

Sending Beth off with the driver had felt right. The man looked concerned and even smiled.

Never trust a man who doesn't smile, Dad used to say. Strange, coming from someone who rarely smiled himself.

Still, Chris couldn't shake the feeling something had gone terribly wrong. A sick churn sat in his stomach all night. He nearly puked a few times, but fear of rushing outside to do it kept it down.

His stomach rumbled. He pulled out the last deli slices and an apple from his pack and wolfed them down. Barely satisfying, but enough to wake him up. The remaining food was enough to last maybe two days, but the water was nearly gone. Finding a source would take time. He had to move, fast.

First, he needed to double-check his supplies: dry clothes, socks, water bottles, baseball, and a hat—and he needed them all. While fastening the pack, something shifted in the outer pocket. He unzipped it and found the compass he'd taken on his last scout trip.

"Yes!"

Despite Mom's nagging, it wasn't worth unpacking after a trip.

Chris slung the pack over his shoulders and used the compass to head north, the glinting sun over his right shoulder.

There was water in these woods. Tributaries crisscrossed the area; some would lead to a stream, maybe a river. It had been a year since he was a Boy Scout, but he remembered his leader's talk on solar water disinfection. Sunlight could kill bacteria and viruses. He didn't have many bottles, but it was a start.

The jug! Plenty of dry matches remained, and with the container, Chris could boil water over fire.

He smacked a nearby branch and grinned.

The incline felt steeper today, the backpack heavier than before, like carrying a squirming toddler on his back.

Chris paused, wiped his forehead, and rummaged his pack for the heaviest item. Not the weird, fuzzy fruit, but the baseball. Tossing it to himself would stave off boredom.

Thirty minutes in, footpaths appeared, like deer tracks. Chris pulled out his penknife and scanned the area. A soft, constant clamor, like an endless guitar rift, rose from the west. He turned left and listened. The prints forgotten, he shifted towards the sound.

Just off the path, faded ruts stamped the forest floor. Chris traced them nearly five hundred feet until they merged with an unpaved road, steering him back to familiar ground—the same route he'd taken Beth yesterday. Ahead, the greenery split, revealing patches of field beyond the trees.

The sound grew louder.

"Shit!"

He dropped to the forest floor and froze.

Had he walked into a trap?

The police might have spotted him yesterday and set a bait. Raking his fingers through brush, Chris spotted Ditchburn Street, bare as a winter field. It took a minute for his breathing and heartbeat to settle before standing again.

He crept out, expecting a half-circle of police with shotguns balanced on the doors of flashing cars. Shuffling across the field to the northwest, he pictured a mouse creeping towards cheese set on a trap. Five hundred feet later, he crossed over a small hill.

A sedan sat beside the road.

Or was it?

It looked like the same model, definitely the same color. Grimacing at the noise, Chris quickened his stride and braced as he rounded to the driver's side.

Beth sat slumped in the seat, head pressed against the horn, unmoving.

"What the...?" Chris slung off his pack, dropping it on the pavement. He yanked the door open. "Beth!"

No response.

He grabbed her shoulders and pulled her away from the wheel, silencing the horn.

A chilling silence.

She fell against the seat, eyes closed, mouth parted open. Red smears painted her clothes and the dashboard.

Chris sucked in a breath, gooseflesh prickling his skin. Nausea churned in his gut. Hands trembling, he touched Beth's shoulder. "Beth? Come on, wake up." His voice was thin, weak.

He pressed an ear to her chest. After a grueling pause, dull thuds broke through.

Chris blew a sharp breath, patting her body for wounds. She wobbled against his touch, offering no resistance.

The blood wasn't hers.

It had to be the driver's. Where was he, and what the hell happened?

On her lap lay pink sunglasses and a water bottle. A bloody revolver sat beside a wallet on the dashboard.

Chris picked up the snub-nosed revolver, noting the Smith & Wesson .357 Magnum stamped on the barrel. The weapon felt heavy in his hand. Dust coated the muzzle, and when he sniffed it, a faint scent of gunpowder flowed up his nostrils. Pressing the release, he ejected the cylinder, revealing six chambers—five loaded, one empty.

Leaving the weapon was dumb and dangerous. He pushed back the cylinder and slid the revolver into the front of his jeans. Then he dropped the water, sunglasses, and wallet into his pack.

Something twinkled in the passenger footwell. Chris squinted at the object, then crossed to the other side to pick it up.

A bullet casing.

Only now did the sharp scent of gunfire hit him.

Strangely, the car's exterior looked untouched, no cracked windshield, no dents. Nothing to suggest a crash or struggle.

Chris slipped the casing into his pocket, bile stinging his throat.

He needed to think fast. He needed a plan.

He seriously considered standing in the middle of the road, wildly waving his arms. It might work, if he didn't end up a stain on the asphalt or run into another lunatic. Besides, last time reaching out for help blew up in his face. And what if the driver was coming back to hurt Beth again?

Getting his sister to safety was critical. The shack was close and secure enough. Last night had been terrifying, but no wolves, bears, or psychopaths had come crashing through the door. Chris would carry her, wait for her to wake up, then return to steer the vehicle out of sight. How hard could it be? The keys were still in the ignition.

He rushed to Beth, sliding one arm under her knees, the other behind her neck. As he pulled, a gasp fled his lungs. "Damn, Beth. You're not as light as you look!" Determined, he managed to lift her after two more tries.

"Damnit."

The pack lay on the ground, compass in his pocket. No way to grab both without setting Beth down first. And that would mean lifting her again.

Swearing under his breath, Chris set Beth on a patch of grass, seized the compass, and slipped on the pack. He drew in a breath, braced himself, and heaved her up with an angry cry. He pulled too hard, stumbling back against the trunk of the car. Beth's head lolled against his chest, limbs dangling like wilted branches.

Chris didn't realize how absurd the plan was until he'd stomped a hundred feet across the field. Twice, he had to stop, panting, balancing her on his bent knee. Tucking the revolver into his jeans had also been stupid. One wrong move and the thing would blow a hole through his crotch. He slipped it into an empty pocket inside the pack.

By the time he reached the forest's edge, sweat glazed his face, and his underarms were soaked.

"Anytime you wanna open your eyes and start walking, I'm good with that!" he panted, gasping every other word.

He battled into the woods, Beth rocking against his gasping lungs. Birds crooned, welcoming them back into the wild.

The glow of the morning sun softened Beth's face, making her look peaceful, almost doll-like. It was hard not to stare.

Carrying her through the forest, though, was exhausting. Brutal. On flat ground, Chris carefully dragged her by her arms, grunting. "Sorry, Beth, but lunchmeat and apples don't cut it, you know?"

It took over an hour before the endless path gave way to a brook. About a hundred feet beyond, the clearing lay waiting.

Chris turned the knob with his arm and dropped his sister onto the mattress. A cloud of dust puffed out from the tattered cushion. A slant of sunlight leaked through the west window, shining a soft, rosy glow on her face.

He yanked off his pack, feeling ten pounds lighter. His back and shoulders burned, as if he'd pitched five games back-to-back. He fell to his knees, panting against the floor, breath loud in his ears, clothes clinging like plastic wrap, jeans damp around the ankles.

He took a moment to steady his breathing before standing and grabbed the water bottles, setting the one from Beth's lap by the mattress.

A blue jay zipped across the clearing, flickering leaves as Chris trudged to the fire pit and sank to the floor. His throat felt raw, every swallow like sandpaper.

He reached for the radio and switched it on. Static crackled before an announcer chimed in with a traffic update. Then sports— news that would've grabbed his full attention just two days ago. A jingle led into local reports on budget talks and public schools. Then came the report.

"In Wanapatchee, a house fire responsible for killing two adults may no longer be a mystery, says the sheriff's department. Officer Wade Castaneda has the details."

Chris sat up, leaning into the speaker. He pulled the Islanders watch from his pocket.

9:36 AM.

"The sheriff's department has launched an investigation. The coroner's report shows the deceased had blood alcohol levels. Forensic officers found large amounts of alcohol surrounding one victim. The fire, however, has yet to be ruled accidental."

Castaneda cleared his throat. "We have few clues about the children's whereabouts. We're working with Wanapatchee firefighters and Northern Jersey public service teams. Local and regional stations have been notified. Neighbors are cooperating with state and local authorities, providing descriptions and photos. The station has received numerous calls from volunteers offering help. We appreciate everyone's support, and will reach out if assistance is needed. Meanwhile, anyone who has seen the children should contact the station immediately."

After a faint question from a reporter, Castaneda replied, "Yes, there is some suspicion, and we are looking into that. But there is no solid evidence at this time that would indicate either of the children was in any way involved in the fire."

Chris swallowed hard.

He switched off the radio and dragged himself back inside the shack, limbs heavy, body like lead. He stood over Beth, studying her with stony eyes.

She hadn't moved.

It was uncanny—how they'd managed to cross paths again so soon. Was it a fluke he happened to hear the horn?

His eyes flicked to the bare patch on the mattress. It stank of urine and looked like a family of moths had eaten through it. Still, it looked more inviting than the loft or the cold dirt.

Before he could decide, Chris sank to the floor, his bones melting like butter.

O   O   O

When he woke, he was startled to find himself sprawled on the floor. Falling asleep was a blur, though he remembered listening to the broadcast outside.

He dug into his pocket and snapped on the watch.

3:18 PM.

He'd slept nearly six hours.

Sitting up, Chris grimaced at the stiffness in his back, the dryness in his mouth.

Beth hadn't moved. Her chest rose and fell in steady breaths.

He needed to act before dark. Moving the car was critical, but water came first.

After taking a moment to collect himself, Chris stepped outside into the dry, cool air. He wolfed down a raw hot dog, then tucked the revolver into his jeans, no longer concerned by it firing off by chance.

A blue jay nestled on a branch beside the clearing as he headed towards the footprints he'd spotted earlier. He waved at the chirping bird. "See you later, buddy."

He thought of leaving Beth a note but had no pen.

18

THE DEPARTMENT

Forty-eight hours has passed since the Pacelli twins vanished.

Fire crews and forensic techs had gone over the Alperstein house, collecting samples and ruling out chemical or electrical causes. While Ramsey's team spent the last twenty-four hours chasing leads, forensics swept for fingerprints and hair fibers. The team delivered their bags and swabs to the lab, then uploaded the evidence to a shared database used by nearby precincts.

Barry Warsoff ran the prints through the system. The prints were dead on with those collected two years earlier.

The twins weren't among the half-million children abducted in this country. That brought Ramsey a measure of relief; over eighty percent of abducted kids were killed within the first twenty-four hours. Kidnappings were rare in Cassic County—rarer still involving siblings—but Ramsey no longer believed a girl like Beth Pacelli incapable of burglary. Children were capable of monstrous acts, especially in towns like this.

Three years back in Rookwood, a high school honor student smothered his six-month-old brother with a pillow. The boy then strolled into his living room, joined his parents on the couch, and munched on popcorn while watching an episode of *The Sopranos.* Jealousy, as it turned out, was the motive.

The captain's stomach dropped. He leaned back into his leather chair. *What in God's name was happening to this country's youth?*

Nearly two hundred kids vanished in Jersey last year; the Pacelli twins were the first within the captain's jurisdiction. A team spending much of its time breaking up bar fights, domestic disputes, and rowdy high school parties now faced intense pressure. The twins posed a new, unusual challenge.

With the search party underway, Ramsey considered sending a pilot in the air but dismissed the idea. The mayor would frown on upsetting the budget for a helicopter search, especially since the twins could be anywhere by now.

Waving a manila folder overhead, the captain marched out of his office, heading straight for Dave's desk. "You're on patrol this afternoon, Powell."

The deputy flicked his head up from an inch-high stack of paperwork.

Warsoff was out on assignment, so Ramsey instructed Powell to scout the circumference and neighboring zones of Dominion Gardens alone while Sanders coordinated case files and took calls from residents offering leads. He'd spoken to countless people claiming to have seen the twins on a playground or in a hardware store with grim-looking men.

Confused, Dave shot up from his desk, rifling through files and photographs.

The captain instructed Officer Garrett Reid to resume gathering the twins' histories from neighbors, teachers, classmates, and friends. They needed a clear sense of the family dynamics. Was there abuse at home? Had Beth and Chris tried to run away before?

Reid, a stalky officer with thick black hair and a round, oily face, knocked on Detective Sanders' desk, his portly body swaying with each step. "Good time to catch up on that backlog," he called out. "See you when we return from the outside, Shooter."

Powell darted off several paces behind Reid.

Sanders glared at the officers pushing through the glass doors.

But inside, he was laughing.

No one suspected he'd copied Dave's photos and data. The documents lay inside a green file, waiting on his kitchen table.

19

January, 20 years ago...

THE WOMAN

She sank down, legs quivering beneath the weight of her growing belly. It was her third trip to the bathroom that hour. She felt like an infant, relearning how to sit and stand.

A minute passed before the woman settled onto the couch, wrapped in a worn blanket. The dog-eared paperback beside her forgotten, she clicked the remote. The TV ticked on, casting a blue, sickly hue across the room, reflecting the mood inside her. To her right, a sprinkle began tapping the window.

Her eyes wandered the dim space, and she sighed, her hand resting on her belly. Mismatched lamps dipped in the middle of two large cardboard boxes used as makeshift end tables sat on either side of the couch. The couch, faded from its original bright yellow, held depressed cushions, the fabric thinned at the arms. It was a housewarming gift from her parents, picked up at the local thrift store.

The modest two-bedroom house settled on a hill overlooking the city's edge, not thirty miles away. Low ceilings and dated paneled walls enclosed the space. Thin curtains framed the single south-facing window in the living room, filtering watery light even on sunny days. A threadbare carpet covered the hardwood floor beneath.

But none of that mattered. With help from both parents, Linda and her new husband took pride in acquiring this place. It was their first home, and it was perfect.

A crash of thunder punched the sky. Linda flinched and gripped her stomach. Having spent her entire life in this town, you'd think she'd be used to the sound by now, as common as braying sirens along the city streets.

But tonight, fear pricked the woman's insides like hot skewers on pincushions. An unbearable dread twisted inside her, edged with quiet resentment for the man she loved.

"Don't leave," she'd said as he pulled on his coat at the front door. Stiff and distant, he seemed indifferent to the silly little lives around him. But with her, the lines on his face vanished, eyes widened and softened, muscles relaxed. The reason was clear: she disarmed him. And she relished that power, like that night outside a downtown nightclub when he wanted to confront a drunk man grabbing an even drunker woman. Fists trembling at his side, breeze tossing dark hair across a sweaty forehead, all it took to mollify him was cupping his reddened face, locking eyes, murmuring his name. It was like injecting a sedative into his vein, the tanked-up man forgotten.

Only tonight, her pleads didn't penetrate. Her husband pecked her mouth before turning away, leaving her alone in the house.

Something about tonight felt wrong. That feeling just before something horrible happens, like the rising music before a clichéd *BOOM* in a scary movie, or the breathless pause before a brutal scene in a novel. And usually, the woman's instincts were dead-on.

Pushing aside her instincts, Linda forced a laugh. He'd called her silly, and he was right. He was rarely wrong. So sharp, in fact, his smarts sometimes unnerved her.

She leaned over the cardboard box, used the cheese knife with the serrated blade to cut another slice of pepperoni, then stabbed a green olive with the fork tip, popping it into her mouth. Cravings, courtesy of the insatiable lives growing inside her.

She glanced at the clock.

11:42 PM.

Her husband would be home in less than six hours. A long time to wait. His new career paid poorly, so he picked up two nights a week tending bar at the local pub. *We need the money*, he'd said. One last chance to save for that relaxing, well-earned getaway to the Poconos before the twins arrived in less than three months.

Linda had begged him to take the earlier shift, but he refused because nighttime brought better tips. It wasn't long before that understanding part of her gave in. That's what partners do. They compromise. Especially when planning to spend the next sixty, seventy years together.

The woman's eyes glazed over twelve channels: commercials, a Yankees game, insipid infomercials hawking cures for thinning hair and weight gain, and news segments dramatizing the city's latest atrocities. Cable was one of the promised perks of her husband's new career.

But the TV barely held Linda's attention. Her eyes dropped to her stomach, returning to what had come naturally the past few months.

Tony—the book said it meant "priceless one."

Barbara—I like this one. It's classic, charming.

What else...?

Jeffrey. She remembered a coffee mug dangling on a hook in a gift shop in Mystic, Connecticut. It said, "peaceful one."

Another bolt of thunder split the sky.

Alice—means "noble," doesn't it? Beautiful. I like this one.

Richard—an attractive, handsome name. Respectable. Maybe because she was thinking of Richard Gere.

Sarah. Linda remembered the meaning: "princess."

She grinned.

Andrew—I think it means "strong and manly." I like this, too.

Charlotte—a lovely name. Feminine.

All two syllables. Easy to spell, easy to say. No spiteful school kids would mock these. Tomorrow she'd offer them to her husband, eager for his opinion.

Twenty minutes ticked by, and Linda couldn't shake the prickling tension beneath her skin. A sharp finger stabbing her goose-fleshed shoulder, again and again.

A faint, whishing sound seized her focus. She tensed and tilted her head. Thoughts flickered to the Glock in the drawer beside the bed and the stack of hollow-point bullets. She envied how her husband handled the weapon with the ease of a baby with a rattle. His career trained him on handguns, rifles, and shotguns, yet repeated attempts to assure Linda of its safety failed to ease her mind.

An unsettling desire struck her to push herself up, wobble into the bedroom, and seize the handgun.

It's just nerves. Stop driving yourself crazy.

She chewed over more names, but it was no use. Her mind refused to focus, drifting back to the sound she swore came from the kitchen.

A chill crept into the room.

The blanket covered Linda from chest to feet, and heat sieved from the radiator.

But cold pressed against her skin.

No longer convinced it was her overactive imagination or hormones, her spine arched tight, like a startled cat sensing something invisible.

The curtains ballooned with ghostly breath and sailed across the closed window.

20

THE BOY

He hiked northeast up a knotty path. Branches crunched under his sneakers, now looking like they'd spent days in a soggy trash heap. Insects droned around his head, testing his patience.

Overhead, birds chirped, chattering about the peculiar creature wandering through their world below. Flipping the baseball offered some relief, but it slowed his pace and sent him stumbling over one too many roots. For now, it was smarter to focus on the compass. Boring, maybe, but wise.

Searching for water was something Chris never imagined doing in a million years, but he was surprised by how much it stimulated him. Okay, not as much as pitching a no-hitter or locking awkward gazes with Erica in class, but it gave him purpose. He was starting to feel like a leader. A commander.

But even officers had limits, especially after dragging themselves into the woods with little sleep and even less food. Chris' legs ached and his head throbbed. The warm, questionable water from the baseball field fountains sounded delicious now. If he didn't find water soon, he'd be back to stealing, and from someone's hose this time.

Chris sparred with memories of everything that had vanished from his life: Mom and Dad, a warm home, good food, friends, clean underwear.

For the past couple of days, he'd managed to keep faces and conversations buried. But the past was a disease. You could only fend it off so long before it rushed up and poked your brain like a blade.

His resolve thinned as pieces of his life emerged.

How many times had he leapt out of bed after Mom was asleep to catch the end of an Islanders game with Dad? Too many to count. Strange how it never bothered Dad, even on school nights. *What a friggin' jerk!* and *You must be kidding me!*—two of Dad's go-to lines, always paired with flared nostrils and flushed cheeks. Chris used to find Dad's passion hilarious.

And Dad must have enjoyed those nights too, having someone to laugh at his jokes and fetch his beers. A shake of an empty can was all it took for Chris to know his cue. He especially liked using the can crusher, mounted above the garbage can in the garage. It never took more than a week to fill a twenty-gallon bucket.

Then pictures of Mom surfaced as clearly as images on a screen. Like the way she'd scrunch her pale face when Chris repeated dirty jokes he picked up at school. Or how she'd chase him, laughing, after he slipped foul words into the grocery list on the fridge.

Everyone knew Mrs. Pacelli as the woman with the dirty mouth sitting in the bleachers, a thermos tucked between her feet. She'd insulted so many umpires, they knew her by name. Chris lost count of how many times they'd threatened to kick her out of the stands.

Air rushed from his lungs, and he bent over, tears burning at the corners of his eyes. Every muscle tightened. He clenched his teeth to smother a scream.

"C'mon, man," he snarled. "Keep it together."

Self-coaching usually got him through the hard stuff, but not now. So he stood up straight and did the only thing he could think to do: focus on the bark of the nearest tree. He studied the black cuts. They looked like open sores on brown skin.

Still, a drop escaped, trailing down to his jaw. He didn't wipe it away; that would mean admitting it was real. And he was a boy. Boys didn't cry.

The tear clung to his cheek, as if to say, Hey, you can't ignore me forever.

Chris growled, "Screw off."

A minute later, faces and memories dissolved like vapor.

An hour passed. Everywhere the path led looked the same. Nothing but vines and nettles filled the gaps between trees, raring to tear his clothes and slice his skin.

Boredom could drive people crazy. He had to stay occupied.

But how? He wasn't the creative one. Beth was.

Soon, he invented a game. Chris pictured Richard Dawson, the lively *Family Feud* host from the eighties, whose reruns popped up after Mom lost interest in the Home Shopping Channel. Dawson was fearless and hilarious, always hugging contestants and sometimes even sneaking a kiss.

What a wild job, Chris thought. If he pulled a stunt like that at school, he'd probably be sent home for harassment or worse.

Richard appeared behind a podium on a blue and gold soundstage, wearing a dark suit and red tie. His face tan, his grin polished. Chris wore an Islanders jersey with "Bossy" stitched on the back. The show was live, airing across the world. Boys at home watched with jealousy. Girls with desire.

"Ladies and gentlemen, our returning champ—and youngest contestant—Chris Pacelli!"

—jump over that rock—

The crowd stood and roared.

"What a lively audience we have today! Wouldn't you agree, Mr. Pacelli?"

Chris smiled and winked at the crowd, prompting a surge of laughter.

"I see you're wearing your favorite jersey. Lucky you, because today's category is sports trivia."

The crowd quieted as Richard pulled out the blue card.

O   O   O

Immersed in the show, Chris nearly missed the animal tracks. He called a station break and dropped to one knee for a better look.

The prints were small and narrow. Maybe a rabbit or a fox. The steel in his waistband pressed into his belly, and for the second time, he considered shooting something. Hunters had done it for centuries, so why not him? At least he'd be doing it for food, not for sport.

Still, the thought of stopping a beating heart, even to survive, made him queasy. But he knew he'd be good at it. He could fire any ball or puck on target, even toss food into the air and catch it in his mouth every time. He had killer aim. That had to mean something.

Then, behind the wind, came a strange babbling sound. Chris sprang up and kept walking, slowing his steps. But the scrape of his shoes across the forest floor made it hard to tell where the sound was coming from, so he stopped often to listen.

About two hundred feet later, the trees opened to a narrow channel leading to rushing water. The stream was four feet wide and cut through the woods ahead, running out of sight.

"Yes!"

The channel's slope was gentle, not fast enough to keep bacteria and other microbes from growing along the streambed.

At the bank, Chris dropped to his knees at a riffle where the water moved quicker than the still pools on either side. It was hard to resist drinking until his stomach burst, but he didn't want to repeat Beth's mistake and end up pissing out of his butt.

He pulled out the bottles, dunked them into the stream, and flinched. "Damn." The water felt icy, like a pool on the first day of summer.

He pictured the stream feeding into something larger, maybe a river. A perfect place to shed the clothes now clinging to him like plastic wrap. And the water there would run smoother, deep enough to bathe.

After filling the bottles to the rim, Chris capped them and stuffed them into his backpack.

He checked his watch. Only a few hours left before dark.

He crawled to a spot where the current slowed and peeled off his shirt. He drew a few deep breaths, then dunked his head. For five long seconds, he raked his fingers through his hair. He flipped back, and like pieces of shattered glass, water sprayed in every direction.

"Damn, that's cold!" Cold, but invigorating.

Chris splashed his chest and underarms, then dried off with the dirty, sweat-soaked shirt. He shoved it into the stream, brushing away the bugs and grime.

Mom would be proud—her son washing his own clothes.

Chris shook his head.

That shirt is filthy, Chris. Another day and it'll walk to the hamper by itself!

Shut up.

He slipped on a clean shirt, hooked the Yankees cap to the front loop of his jeans, and headed southwest.

○   ○   ○

Somewhere between soaking his head in freezing water and scaling the tree, Chris decided he'd be the hero of this story. And truthfully, it felt damn cool.

Finding the same exit was easy enough. About a mile from the edge of the forest, he spotted a vantage point in a towering maple. The compass helped, but climbing the tree was more fun. Yesterday, he even carved notches in several trunks, using the marks to find his way.

Chris made good time, but he had to move fast to beat the dark. That was going to be tough with the extra weight.

Ditchburn Street stood quiet again, a car passing every minute. To a passing driver, the day looked like any other ordinary weekday.

To avoid being seen, he skirted north along the tree line for about two hundred feet, then slipped out through a break in the shrubs and crossed the field towards the sedan. The whole maneuver made him feel like a soldier preparing to strafe the enemy.

There was the car, just as he left it.

Seeing nothing inside worth taking, Chris pulled the blood-smeared trunk latch. The door popped open.

He set his pack inside and released a breath. A bag and a brown leather flight jacket sat inside the trunk. He pulled the jacket on. It settled heavy on his shoulders, warm against sore arms.

Beneath it were papers clipped to a board, a Men's Health magazine, a few pieces of cardboard, and a stencil kit. Since Beth liked to read and write, Chris folded the papers, tucked them into the magazine, and placed both in his backpack.

At the back of the trunk sat an unmarked black bag. Pockets lined the outside, each one holding something different: a small flashlight, leather gloves, handcuffs, and pens.

Chris unzipped the case. The top flap held three compartments stuffed with aspirin packets, hand sanitizer spray bottles, a stick of deodorant, and anti-diarrhea medicine. The right pocket held two batteries and a pair of binoculars. The left pouch had a red can of pepper spray, a bottle of 100 SPF sunscreen, and some loose change. A half roll of duct tape and a travel mug sat in the back sleeve.

He peeked into the center pocket and froze.

A black handgun.

Chris gasped and staggered back a few steps.

Over the roar of a rusty Trans Am missing its muffler, he could hear his heart pounding. By the time he looked up, the car had passed.

He edged back to the sedan and picked up the pistol. It felt lighter than the revolver. A loaded magazine sat beside it. He pulled the bag closer and packed the items into his knapsack, leaving out the batteries and stencil kit.

A bolt cutter caught his eye just as a car pulled up behind him.

21

DAVID POWELL

"Having some car trouble?"

The officer exited the squad car. He looked over the trees on each side of the road before approaching the sedan.

On the surface, the car looked fine. No flat tire, no smoke rolling from under the hood. Powell's first thought was the driver had pulled over for a piss break. It happened all the time. Then a kid struggling with something in the trunk caught his attention.

Having just cruised the main roads and developments of Wanapatchee, Powell decided to take a quick drive towards Rookwood before reporting back to the station. It had been a quiet afternoon. Most people were still at work, kids in school. No signs of suspicious activity, not even a speeding car. Taking in the scenic beauty and earthy smells of Ditchburn Street, Powell remembered Warsoff's tip about making an effort to establish a good rapport with the community. It builds trust and keeps a tight, loyal union with the people, he said. Something we desperately need nowadays.

The boy spun around, eyes wide. "Huh?"

The officer put his hands up. "It's okay. I'm a police officer, here to help. Are you in need of assistance, son?"

The boy exuded nervous energy. He stood silent, eyes locked on Powell's badge and nametag, widening his stance in a lame attempt to conceal the trunk's contents. These reactions were common enough. Most people, especially kids, got nervous whenever police drew near. But in the last ten seconds, Powell sensed something odd. This kid carried a questionable aura, no doubt about it.

The oversized jacket and baseball hat dangling from his belt loop caught Powell's attention. The boy shifted his weight, giving Powell a glimpse of the sedan's license plate.

Powell caught his breath. He pressed his lips together and flashed a look at the blue and orange backpack in the trunk. "Are you alright, young man?"

No response.

He studied Chris Pacelli, squinting with recognition. He'd examined the twins' photos and the Alperstein footage enough times to know every feature, from the arches of eyebrows to the shapes of ears. Chris' round light-brown eyes and the subtle dip of his cupid's bow looked all too familiar.

That's when Powell caught sight of the slightly open door and the stark red puddle beneath it. Someone had been hurt. Was the boy in danger? Was this his car? He looked back at Chris. Besides a few scrapes on his face, there were no clear signs of abuse or bleeding, though his eyes said otherwise.

They met each other's gaze.

It was clear the boy was scared. He'd just lost both parents in a house fire and was probably still in shock. But when those eyes flickered left and right, Powell wondered what he was hiding. He believed in the goodness of the community and its people. This boy was no different. Aside from detentions at school and a few fights on the bus, Chris Pacelli seemed like a regular, clean-cut kid.

So what was going on? Had someone pushed the twins to burglarize the Alperstein house? Was that someone nearby, watching from the woods?

"Son?" he spoke softly. "I'm going to ask you a question. It's safe to shake your head yes or no. Okay?"

No response.

"Are you in any danger?"

Nothing.

"Are you or anyone else hurt?" he asked after a pause, eyes fixed on the boy.

Silence.

"Are you alone—"

"What do you want?"

The boy's lips parted, hesitated. Powell waited. When nothing came, he said, "I just want to help you."

The boy took a defensive stance. Powell could see his muscles tensing as if preparing for an attack.

He took a half-step back. "Why don't you tell me what's going on, son?"

"Don't call me that." The boy's eyes narrowed, his mouth tightening. "Just leave me alone, please."

Powell shifted his weight and leaned closer to the trunk. The backpack sat to Chris' left, a pair of handcuffs hanging out the side. "I'll call you whatever you like. How does that sound?"

The boy peeked over his left shoulder, hands trembling.

"No need to be afraid. Hang tight. I'll be right back."

THE BOY

He was screwed. Recognized from the news, caught in the middle of another crime.

The officer seemed genuine, but his poker face betrayed him. He knew Chris.

"I'll call you whatever you like. How does that sound?"

Chris' mind raced for words, anything to divert suspicion. Normally, he was slick under pressure, able to spin a lie better than anyone he knew.

My batting average is 500.

Yes, ma'am. That is my mother's signature on my test.

Did you know my granddad invented Big League Chew?

But all the confidence that once came so easily drained through his pores like blood from a gash. Even if he could say something intelligible, then what? "Sorry, officer, for breaking into that house. Oh, and I have no idea how all this blood got here. And I wasn't stealing anything. By the way, please don't search me."

No doubt, the officer would cuff him and toss him in the squad car, locking him up with crazies until gray hair sprouted on his balls.

The officer's eyes settled on the sedan's license plate. He stepped back towards his squad car. "No need to be afraid."

What was he looking at, and why was he so damn nosy? Now he'd probably call for backup and inspect the car. What would happen to Beth? She'd die out here without him. Or worse, be picked up or surrender and taken into an orphanage or a hideous foster home. Not many people were itching to take in a confused, abnormal twelve-year-old girl.

No way Beth remembered, but Chris had once picked up one of her books—or more accurately, stolen it, shoving the five-hundred-page paperback into his backpack. In the story, a mother murdered her cheating boyfriend; that foolish, selfish act triggered her young daughter's treacherous journey through a string of drug-soaked foster homes. The story haunted Chris. The girl's journey felt painfully real, as if pulled from the author's life rather than imagination. Picturing Beth trapped in a world like that was unthinkable.

That was the last time Beth strolled into Chris' room without knocking. She'd caught him reading the book and asked why. Shrugging off the discomfort, Chris said, "Dunno. Just bored." What he wanted to say was, *I wanted to know what got you so upset.*

"Hang tight for a minute. I'll be right back." The cop paced back, studying Chris. The door was already ajar, and he slipped into the driver's seat.

Chris felt sweat drip down his back. The officer must have seen the mess in the car, the blood. And Chris held the weapon that did it. Once the officer picked up that radio or punched the laptop keyboard, it was over. No more blue skies. No baseball. No girls. No hope.

Chris found himself in motion before his mind could catch up.

"Uh, no need to walk over here. Please stay back at your car."

"Please," said Chris, the revolver heavy in his pants. "I'm fine. Everything's fine. No need to…"

DAVID POWELL

DAVID POWELL

As he reached for the CB, the boy took long strides towards the car, panic in his eyes. He lingered by the open door, staring at Powell's hands.

"Please. I'm fine. Everything's fine. No need to…"

Powell's words went terse. "I'm going to ask you one last time to walk back to your car."

The boy's eyes glistened, hands twitching inside long jacket sleeves. He scratched the back of his neck. Powell saw steel as the boy's shirt lifted an inch above his waistband.

"But you don't have to do anything. I mean, everything is cool. I don't need your help."

Powell swallowed hard. "Step back, son. Right now."

Chris did what he was told, raising both hands.

Until now, no circumstance had ever called for a weapon discharge. But like Warsoff said, every cop ends up doing it at some point. Powell never imagined it would happen so soon. And with a child, for God's sake.

Fighting to stay calm, he stepped out of the vehicle, hand resting on the Glock at his waist. His voice stayed firm but soothing. "Put your hands behind your head, son."

The boy's eyes flickered. Powell moved to draw his pistol, but in that instant, the boy yanked out his own and held it steady with both hands.

"I said, don't call me that."

THE BOY

THE BOY

Before taking a step back, Dad's words echoed in his ears: *When dealing with police, move slow, look them in the eye, and most of all—show respect.*

He saw the man swallow down a chunk of fear, his Adam's apple bobbing. His eyes tracked the officer's right hand as it edged towards the black handle.

The air went still.

Chris caught the faint whisper of wind through the trees. Then panic surged, mixed with anger. He wasn't guilty. He wasn't going anywhere. And neither was Beth.

Fear flushed his face, then gave way to aggression. His eyes narrowed to slits.

The officer crept his hand towards the Glock. But Chris was faster. He'd drawn the revolver a hundred times in the woods, testing his speed, picturing an old Western duel. He never imagined putting the drills to use. It slid from his waistband as smooth as porcelain.

"I said, don't call me that."

The officer's eyes bulged, his left hand extending in front of him. "You don't want to do that, Chris. I know you're scared and alone. I'm here to help, not hurt you. Now drop the gun and step back."

He was lying. That's what police do—that's what all adults do. "I'm not going anywhere. We didn't do anything wrong!"

The officer spoke fast. "Drop the weapon and step back. I don't want you doing something you'll regret. Do you understand?"

What the hell was he supposed to do now? He sure as hell couldn't run. Not into the woods. Not anywhere. The police would find him. "Don't talk to me like I'm stupid. I'm not stupid."

The officer nodded, his left hand creeping to his side. "Alright. You're not stupid. Got it. Everything's cool. So go ahead and drop the weapon now."

Tears welled in Chris' eyes. "Stop telling me what to do! You're not my dad!"

"I'm not your dad," assured the cop, brushing the handle of his weapon. "Everything's okay."

A wild idea flashed through his mind. What if he shoved the man into the trunk, then sped off to some deserted lot? He could phone in an anonymous tip, drop the location, and disappear before anyone knew he was there. The police would find the officer, but Chris would be long gone. The plan sounded freaking crazy, borderline insane. He would have to master the CB radio, learn to drive on the fly, and pull it all off in twenty minutes. Still, maybe— just maybe—it could work.

The officer drew his weapon, catching Chris off guard.

The revolver bucked in his hand so hard it nearly jumped into the air. A vulgar boom followed, the bullet tearing through clothes and skin.

The officer fell back onto the concrete, pressing a hand against the hole underneath his collarbone. He looked up at Chris with wet, pleading eyes.

His limbs locked, chilled and stiff, as if sealed in a freezer. The man coughed up blood, but no sound came out. The blast had been deafening; the ringing echoed in Chris' ears louder than after a hockey game at the Nassau Veterans Memorial Coliseum. It felt like watching a silent film, only in color without the shaky clips.

Finally, Chris moved. He stepped forward, revolver loose at his side, gaze distant on the empty road.

Another cough cracked the silence like thread snapping in the dark. He turned to the officer.

I'm sorry, he thought. But before the words could leave his mouth, the man stilled, eyes sliding shut, lips parting, his body sinking against the cold asphalt.

22

THE GIRL
THE GIRL

She shuddered awake, her breathing slow and steady. Tight knots gripped her joints.

An orange sheen bathed the space through a dusty beam of light. Through the hole above, a wispy cloud drifted, soft as a feather. It was soothing, the shock of awakening in the shack fading like a dream.

Beth shifted her weight on the mattress, groaning at the burn shooting up her right thigh. The limp bed and timber walls reminded her of summer camp and how counselors had set her cot in the middle of a cabin with four other girls. In that room, they stared at her like a bug creeping on the ground; they waited for the right moment to crush her and watch everything inside leak out. They picked at her clothes, her haircut, how she walked, spreading rumors she liked girls and had no breasts. One counselor, a tall redhead who called herself Koala, regarded Beth with cold, passive eyes.

The boys at camp were lucky. A couple of punches, some name-calling, and it all blew over. Then they went back to enjoying summer as though nothing happened.

What stopped Beth from unleashing havoc in that cabin was Alexis Johnson.

She rose to her elbows, then pushed herself to a standing position. Her leg gripped under her weight, and she leaned against the wall to steady herself. A half-empty water bottle on the floor caught her attention. She'd read somewhere that the human brain is over eighty percent water and often wondered how long a girl could go thirsty before her mind dried up like a fig.

Beth grabbed the bottle and pushed open the door, stepping outside. An afternoon breeze brushed her skin as she hobbled across the clearing towards a pile of black twigs and white ash. The air was dry, not as cold as yesterday. She settled on a log and scanned the area. Where was Chris? How long had she been asleep?

He's probably taking a pee. And I don't know.

Dusk was still a couple of hours off, soon closing out another day in the woods. Beth couldn't deny the beauty of sunlight burnishing orange and yellow beams through the trees. An Albert Bierstadt painting came to mind. Chris would think she was nuts, but she missed the library, flipping through prints by artists like John William Godward, Lord Frederic Leighton, and John William Waterhouse. Beth knew she lacked the shine and beauty their muses had, and often wondered what it felt like to pose for a secret society of young, revolutionary thinkers.

Her eyes dropped, and so did her mouth. Blood crusted her clothes and fingers. Her hands shook as she searched for wounds.

The blood wasn't hers.

She spoke, barely above a whisper. "Chris?" She thought about calling out his name but stopped.

Wait! You're a criminal. You have blood all over you. Do you really think it's smart to draw attention?

The voice was right. Besides, Chris wouldn't hear her anyway. Beth bit her lip as tears of frustration brimmed.

Chris wouldn't just leave. He'll be back. He would've left food if he didn't plan to return.

Beth nodded. She stared at the bottle, then raised it to her lips.

A bird fluttered above her head for a minute before darting behind the shack, disappearing into the shiny abyss.

Beth stood and walked back inside. She closed the door behind her, then paused and examined the space. The air was stale, musky. She looked down at the sunken spot on the mattress.

This is home now, isn't it?

She crawled onto the mattress, wincing at the pain. She curled into a fetal position, fists closed beneath her chin. The coppery smell on her hands overpowered the stench in the room. Finding the blood had shifted everything, making what came before feel almost trivial. It was as if she'd drifted off a few days ago and woken in someone else's cold, fractured life. She was learning the world didn't care who it offended, or who it hurt.

Beth imagined a storm pulling in sheets of rain through the hole in the ceiling, drowning the building and everything in it, including herself. She would dodge every instinct to survive and let the water fill her mouth, her lungs. She would become one with the storm; with it, she would disappear, drifting into a hazy vortex like the bird in the trees.

Beth closed her eyes. "Mommy…?"

Minutes later, she fell back to sleep.

THE BOY

THE BOY

The fear of being crushed by King Kong on some ghostly city street never stood a chance against this nightmare. A beast, tall as a tower, stomping you like a boot on a beetle—that was scary. But standing in front of a dead cop—a man he had shot—brought a kind of fear Chris couldn't even begin to grasp.

Executing soldiers, scorned hookers, and drug dealers on a twenty-inch screen hadn't prepared him for the weight of this moment. He'd thought years of punching game controllers might give him a sense of what it felt like to shoot someone in battle or on the street.

He was wrong.

The feeling was heavy, like liquid lead dragging through every vein and artery. Chris had stopped a human heart.

Seconds after the officer took his last breath, Chris vomited up chunks of mystery meat and water onto the pavement. It splattered against his muddied sneakers, stopping an inch short of the officer's leg. He wiped his mouth with a dirty forearm, grabbed the man's feet, and, careful to avoid the puke, dragged the body towards the cruiser's trunk. As crazy as it sounded, it felt like the right thing to do to keep the officer with his own car.

The man weighed at least one hundred sixty pounds. Chris was solid for his age, but when you're a kid dragging a body twice your size and weight, it hardly matters.

For a moment, he thought he could squat inside the trunk and pull the body in.

"Yeah," he huffed after a few useless tugs, "this'll work!"

A sound came from behind, a car approaching from the west.

"Oh, shit." Chris released the body and froze, praying the driver wouldn't see him. The offer's hands slapped the rear bumper before hitting the tarmac, and Chris winced. Maybe the driver would see the police car and think it was just a routine stop.

The tires slowed.

Chris stayed still, awaiting his fate. For a moment, he wasn't sure if he wanted the car to pass. Maybe the driver would pull over and end this nightmare once and for all. He wondered what was worse: caged behind metal bars or trapped among wooden trunks.

No longer able to bear the suspense, he inched an eye open. Using peripheral vision, Chris spotted a white SUV heading east towards Wanapatchee. It passed by, picking up speed two hundred feet down the road.

He huffed out a breath, wiping sweat from his forehead. Luckily, the cruiser was parked on a slant, the trunk angled towards the field. The driver must not have seen him or the body.

He hopped out of the trunk and rushed to the passenger side, opening the door. His throat tightened as he unfastened the duty belt from the officer's waist and set it behind the back tire. Once he pulled the body close enough to the open door, Chris crawled into the car, hauling the man in by his armpits.

With the man's legs dangling outside, Chris climbed over the body and folded them into the footwell. His nerves twitched at the crooked angle. He pushed the man's back against the seat, shut the door, and stepped back.

The officer's head rested against the headrest, facing him.

Chris looked away and caught sight of the duty belt. It held a Glock G43, two loaded magazines, pepper spray, a radio, a baton, a taser, a flashlight, gloves, and keys. He thought about taking it all, but the pistol weighed heavy in his gut. Instead, Chris pulled out the handcuffs, flashlight, and gloves. He stuffed them into his pack, tossed the belt with the rest of the gear into the trunk, and slammed it shut.

He wiped his hands on his jeans, sucked in a deep breath, then climbed into the sedan and shut the door behind him. With his head locked forward, Chris frowned at the speckles of blood on the windshield. Beyond the red stains, a mile up the road, a distant golden sparkle rested against the landscape: the town of Rookwood.

He studied the cluster panel. The go-kart he drove at George's birthday party looked nothing like this. But years of watching Dad drive the van gave him the confidence to try. His fingers shook as he struggled to turn the key. After a few tries, the engine growled to life. Cold sweat beaded on his face again. Chris licked his dry lips.

Exhaling hard, he pressed his right foot on the brake. The sedan bucked as he shifted into drive.

"Okay, let's go."

Gripping the wheel, Chris eased up on the pedal and drifted forward. Tires bit into the graveled shoulder as he pulled the sedan out of sight of the road.

He reached the police cruiser. Chris went for the door, then stopped himself. On his list of things to do before he died, stealing a police car wasn't one of them.

After a moment, he talked himself into pulling the handle and tossed his pack into the back seat. He slid into the driver's seat, shutting the door behind him. Attached to the center console sat an open laptop and a GPS device. Chris swallowed hard, wondering if the officer had keyed information about him into the computer. He unhooked the device from its base, setting it on his lap.

He reached for the brake pedal, but it was just out of reach. His sneaker barely grazed it. He fumbled with the seat lever, shifting himself until his stomach pressed a few inches from the steering wheel. His hands clenched tight around the vinyl, muscles trembling.

"Okay, Goose. You got this." His fingers twitched but didn't loosen.

Chris made a hesitant U-turn on Ditchburn Street and headed towards the heart of Wanapatchee, keeping a cautious 35 mph. Cruising down the bare road, he fought the knot tightening in his chest, pretending it was his own car. Soon, worry drained from his body, and he even caught a fleeting, shaky smirk.

Rearwood Avenue was a two-lane road stretching across town. Rush hour had begun, and cars crowded the street. Chris eased through a green light and sighed. Seeing a dead officer at a red light next to a kid driving a police cruiser was sure to raise eyebrows.

The town's strip mall came into view. Shops would be closing in the next few hours. Parking along the lot's perimeter, folks would think police were monitoring traffic.

Chris flicked the turn signal, signaling a left.

An oncoming driver stopped, granting Chris the opening to turn. Their eyes locked for a heartbeat; Chris felt the weight of the man's curious stare. He turned the wheel, unaware of the silent judgment as the front tires thumped over a speed bump, sending a sharp jolt through the car.

About twenty parked cars, mostly lining the storefronts, scattered the lot. It took several tries to park the cruiser between the faded white lines.

Chris shifted into park, pulled the keys from the ignition, and exhaled. "Holy crap," he mumbled.

The elephant in the car called to him. Despite himself, Chris turned his head. The air grew still; the officer lifted his head from the headrest. A wet hole glistened beneath his collarbone, brown hair veiling his eyes. Their gazes met.

Why did you do this to me?

Chris stared into the officer's eyes, slack-jawed.

You don't think you're going to get away with this, do you?

"I'm sorry," Chris whispered. "It was an accident."

Accident? The word oozed through him, thick and slow.

That's not how this works, kid. You really think this ends with you driving off into the sunset?

Silence filled the car, heavy and still. Chris shut his eyes, shook his head hard, yelling for the voice to stop.

You can't shut me out, kid. You invited me in. I live here now.

Chris's eyes flew open.

I know every corner of you.

"No, you don't! I won't let you do this to me! Get out of my head!"

He yanked the handle and leaped outside the cruiser, slamming the door behind him.

O   O   O

After a quick look around, Chris slipped the laptop into a green garbage can. It rattled against the metal cage. Nestled between a market and a drugstore, he spotted the music shop that started it all.

Getting back to Ramapo Forest required strategy. Rearwood Avenue was out. Someone would spot him for sure on a busy street. He wasn't comfortable taking side roads, but the compass would help him stay on course.

He took the first road north, an industrial street lined with four-story office and medical buildings. Across the way sat a near-empty parking lot. A thousand feet in, the road dead-ended.

The pack thudded against his back as Chris weaved between buildings and trees like a soldier cutting through enemy ground. After several twists and turns, he reached a residential street and crossed into a park. He marched past it, keeping his head down. A large woman in gray sweatpants and a yellow blouse pushed a girl on a swing. With each shove, the child squealed with laughter.

Chris kept his head down, sprinting towards the baseball field.

Orange and indigo streaked the sky above the straw-colored grass. Vinyl banners rustled along the chain-link fence around the outfield, faded and familiar. The smell of cut grass carried him back, and Chris grinned.

He stepped onto the infield and made his way to the pitcher's mound, tugging the brim of his hat. He set the pack down and pulled out the baseball, curling his thumb and index finger around the worn leather. He could feel the eyes of the crowd on him.

He closed his eyes, then opened them.

The hardships that brought him here melted away. All that mattered was this moment—and the dusty slab of home plate. He was Chris Pacelli: ballplayer, proud son, and the only twelve-year-old in Wanapatchee Little League history to play every inning without ever striking out.

Five-hundred-watt lights baked his back like the summer sun. From the massive speakers, Volbeat's "Radio Girl" thundered across the field. Thousands of fans from all over the state packed the stands. Chris felt as powerful and precise as Mariano Rivera, the legend with a 95 mph cutter known for snapping bats.

Above his right shoulder, a bird hovered. He thought of the blue jay keeping watch for him by the shack.

He stepped into the windup, eyes narrowing. "Batter takes his position. The Goose considers the pitch. Two outs. One man on second, another on third. One more strike to win the game."

Chris turned towards third base, arms loose at his sides. "Wait. The Goose is taking signs from the catcher."

The crowd fell silent. Chris gave a nod, then settled into the set. "…aaand here's the pitch…" He rose into the balance point, then lunged forward, firing the ball. It cut through the air, bounced in the dirt, and clattered off the metal fence.

"Strike three! The Wanapatchee Warriors Win! UNBELIEVABLE, THE GOOSE DID IT AGAIN!"

Chris jumped up, arms raised like a superhero ready to fly.

The revolver slipped free, thudding into the dirt at his feet.

The fanfare faded, then vanished into silence. The grass lost its green, curling into brittle yellow blades, as if memory itself had dried up. Chris mouth slackened, the corners pulled down by something heavier than sadness.

He dropped to one knee and picked up the weapon. It felt icy against his palm, cold and unforgiving—unlike the baseball that had rested in his hand, trusting him like a baby trusts its mother. Residue clung to the barrel and edges of the cylinder, smelling sharp and bitter.

You don't think you're going to get away with this, do you?

Chris' eyes blurred. A tear fell on the barrel, then several more.

Would he ever play ball again? It seemed impossible now.

You really think this ends with you driving off into the sunset?

Something inside his chest crumpled. Chris dropped his head into his hands.

He cried—the first time since losing by one run to Secaucus in the state championship. The sobs came hard and silent, no sound escaping his mouth. What broke free was not anger unleashed from the gates he'd kept closed, but a slow, crushing shame.

No longer hiding behind the dugout, Chris purged his crimes in full view of the world.

23

THE GIRL

THE GIRL

She woke to the sound of a goldfinch chirping on the fractured windowsill. Its head jerked side to side, as if scanning for threats.

Beth smiled. "Are you watching out for me, Tweety?" Her voice scraped out, frayed and thin.

The bird kept twitching, unmoved. Its melody was gentle, not like Mom bursting through her bedroom door at 7AM.

Beth stepped outside, then paused. The sun cast a steady line of orange and yellow along the horizon. She blinked, unsure of how long she'd been asleep. Spellbound, she sat onto a log and rested her chin in her hands, watching her first sunrise.

Her stomach grumbled. She ran her tongue over her teeth, wondering how long it had been since she'd brushed them.

Part of her wanted to wait for Chris since she lacked the tools to find food and water. But what if he got lost and was trying to find his way back? What if he grew tired of her leeching and abandoned her?

Beth shot up and seized the nearest stick, snapping it in half. The sound empowered her, and she charged out of the clearing.

Waiting around for death was no longer an option.

O   O   O

Oh my God!

It took only a couple of hours to reach the stream Chris had discovered the day before. And what a beautiful vision it was.

Beth dropped on a sandy point bar and placed her arms in the water, bracing against the frigid current. Then she relaxed, enjoying the riffle kneading her fingers like a massage. She slipped her head under, the cold striking her face like a prickly brush. But she stayed down and let herself swallow a few drops, just enough to coat her throat. Curiosity led her to peek open an eye in time to watch a shoal of sunfish sail by.

Food was near. Beth couldn't kill something furry, but something slimy seemed more her speed. And there was no one around to belittle her efforts. But how do you hook a fish without a pole?

You need a net. Look around. There must be something to use.

But Beth's world offered only sticks, leaves, and rocks.

Then, as she picked at the hem of Chris's shirt, an idea struck.

Down several yards, the stream narrowed and squeezed into a tight channel; it picked up speed before merging into an eddy. The downstream, swirling current could work to her advantage.

Beth held her breath and pulled off her shirt, the training bra offering the illusion of protection. Mom hadn't wanted to buy it. *Why waste money on a bra if you don't have anything?* she'd said. But Beth had insisted.

Words or actions—nothing could hurt worse than a mother.

The exposure left Beth sheepish around the unseen birds and creatures of the woods. But hunger had grown fierce. She slipped off her shoes and damp socks, then moved to a spot with a secure place to stand. She rolled up her jeans and eased into the water. Stepping her bare feet onto two rocks, Beth bent down and dropped the makeshift snare into the stream. The current pulled the shirt back between her legs, and she pulled it tighter.

She spotted several blue and orange sunfish whirling by and pushed the shirt out to trap them. Without effort, they dodged the snare and sailed between her legs into a pool of water before slipping into another riffle.

"Rats!"

It wasn't long before several more fish appeared, and this time one drifted into the trap.

"Yay!"

Beth rounded the shirt, wrapping the fish like a baby in a blanket. It squirmed wildly in her grip as she dragged it to the edge. She lifted the shirt from the water, but it was slipping fast. She tossed the fish against the hillside. Strings of water sailed behind it as it landed beside a cluster of rocks.

The fish wriggled in the dirt. Beth's grin vanished as she stared into its unblinking eyes, desperate for water to flood its gills. She looked away, swallowing the bitter weight in her chest. Seeing death again, and so soon, slammed into her harder than she expected.

Feeling exposed and cold again, she hugged her bare skin, then wrung water from the shirt. She looked back at the fish and saw it had stopped squirming. Pressing her lips together, she crouched and pinched two fingers around its tail. This fish was five inches long, big enough to satiate, at least for now. Beth stared at it, thankful it looked nothing like that clownfish, Nemo.

"How am I going to do this? *Can* I do this?"

Longing for Chris' pocketknife, Beth set the fish down on a large rock and looked around for something to slit it open.

A group of limestone rocks the size of a child's fist came into focus. Beth chose the one with the sharpest edges. Squinting, she slit the fish along its belly and let the orange mucus-like fluid ooze out, squeezing her forefinger inside to push out the remaining guts. The fish slipped from her wet hands and flopped onto the dirt. A sharp chill ran up Beth's spine, and she shuddered around in a circle.

"Gross!"

You can dance around all you want, but you still have to do it.

Sighing, she picked up the fish. After a gentle pull, the bone came free, intact. She used the sharp edge of the rock to jab out its eyes. Doing so triggered a memory of an old horror flick. The killer had stomped on his victim's head, juicing the man's eyeball like a vile cherry before it popped out towards the camera.

She held the fish under the water, letting the current wash away the last of the guts and bones. Inch by inch, Beth tilted her head back, opening her mouth before snapping it shut again. An old video flashed in her mind, one with a lifeless head and a bland song chanted with chipmunk voices:

> *Fish heads, fish heads*
> *Roly-poly fish heads*
> *Fish heads, fish heads*
> *Eat them up, yum!*

All the deflecting in the world wasn't going to erase the melody, because memories—especially terrible ones—always found a way in.

> *I took a fish head out to see a movie*
> *Didn't have to pay to get it in*

Again, Beth tilted her head back. The fish hung six inches from her closed mouth, a damp, rotting sea-smell filled her nose.

> *They can't play baseball*
> *They don't wear sweaters*
> *They're not good dancers*
> *They don't play drums*

"For God's sake, shut up!"

Beth closed her eyes, opened her mouth, and chomped down on the top half of the fish, chewing several times before swallowing. Bits of sour meat slid down her throat.

Good Job. Now, the rest.

Grimacing, Beth dropped the rest into her mouth, not bothering to bite off the tail. Doing so would make her gag. She slurped water up from cupped hands, swirling it in her mouth before spitting it out against the dirt. After a burp, her stomach settled.

Giggles poured in. Beth had courageously done the unthinkable.

I'm proud of you.

She beamed, the warmth of the words settling in her chest. Words she'd never heard before; words that felt both foreign and long overdue.

She rinsed her greasy, scale-ridden hands and thought about pulling on the wet shirt, but decided against it. Beth didn't know if it was the meal or the feeling of achievement, but she felt restored.

She wandered south along the stream, a hum slipping from her lips. Unbeknownst to her, Chris lingered close by. He was not missing, nor fleeing, but motionless at the ravine's base, a dead body by his side.

24

THE BOY

THE BOY

While Beth ate the fish, he awakened against a rocky incline.

He'd passed out with his back crooked, one leg twisted under his butt. The steep slope of the ravine left him nearly vertical, pinned against the rocks. His back and head ached.

Chris wiped the dirt and wetness from his eyes with the back of his hand. The moon barely offered any light. With just a flashlight, he'd slipped, trying to examine the blood-crusted hand gripping the orange sleeve of his Islanders jacket.

The body lay face down in a mud-filled rill, its head turned away from Chris. Convinced it was his guilt-ridden imagination, Chris forced out a nervous laugh, then blinked. The body stayed.

A bolt of pain shot up his back, but the urge to move outweighed the hurt. Inch by inch, he stood, brushing dirt from his face, eyes fixed on the body.

"Hello. Sir…?"

No movement.

Chris' Yankees cap sat on a pile of debris next to the man's foot. He snatched it up, knocked it against his thigh to shake off the dirt, then placed it back on his head. The revolver pressed against his belly, and he felt a brief relief that it hadn't gone off during the fall.

"Who the heck are you, and what the hell are you doing with my jacket?"

There was no question the man was dead. His head lay cracked open on top of sharp rocks. Circling the body, Chris studied the man's face and gasped. The eyes and mouth were open, blood pooling underneath his head and legs. Chris recognized him as the driver. His usual knack for judging character must have failed him this time, and he'd put his sister in the hands of a possible madman.

He knelt next to the body and pulled the jacket from the man's loose grip, sliding his arms into the muddy sleeves. He flinched as the wetness pressed against his back.

"Looks like you were one heck of an Islanders fan," said Chris, "but this is mine, not yours."

His head throbbed. The aspirin would've come in handy now. Chris looked around for his backpack, then remembered slipping it off before heading down the hill. He hadn't wanted it throwing him off balance. He scoffed at the irony.

The sun filtered through a thin canopy above the thirty-foot drop. The five-foot-wide ravine sliced the ground, like the aftermath of a movie earthquake. Chris remembered climbing most of the way down before slipping into the dark.

The slope out of the ravine was steep but manageable. He took a few minutes to map the safest path up. Crouching to tie his laces, Chris grimaced at the pain shooting through his body. He knew better than to leave the dead man exposed. He gathered rocks, dirt, and leaves, covering the body and carefully placing a few stones on the man's back. When it was done, a sudden urge to pray stirred inside him, though he had no idea how.

"Uh, hey…God? Bless this man. I don't know what he's doing here, but make sure he rests in peace. Amen."

Chris took a deep breath, stepped onto a boulder the size of a beach ball, and started up. One tread at a time, he balanced against the jagged wall. Each stretch sent pain flashing through his bruised back, but he refused to break. A rock he thought secure slipped under his weight, nearly sending him to the bottom. He caught a root jutting from the side as rocks and dirt tumbled past, slamming into the ground below. The sound echoed through the ravine. He didn't look down. Eyes shut, he searched with his foot until he found solid stone.

Finally, he reached the surface and collapsed onto his back, lungs burning. Pain flared through his shoulders and hands, but he let it wash over him. The climb had stripped skin from his fingers, chipped his nails to the quick. He lay there, blinking at the sky until his breath slowed. With a heavy breath, he turned his head, eyes dragging down the ravine.

What had once been a body was now just a rough pile of soil and stone.

Chris pulled a crumpled packet of aspirin from his backpack. He needed water, but even a sip might break his control. Instead, he worked his tongue, coaxing up just enough saliva to choke the pills down dry.

A sour stench fired up his nose. For a second, he thought it was a dead animal. Then something caught his eye. Brown chunks of meat scattered across a cluster of stones a few feet away. As he crawled towards the smell, his vision blurred, but sharpened again at the sight of small puddles of blood. "...Beth...?"

Chris pulled the compass and pushed through the trees, moving southwest towards the shack.

THE GIRL

THE GIRL

She roamed between the trees with more energy than she'd felt in days. As she slid on Chris' damp shirt, a strange memory came to her. A flash of gym glass.

Beth was a master at feigning distraction to avoid the unease of acting alone. While the girls changed, she fumbled inside her locker until the last left for the gym. Then she'd slip into her gym shirt in the corner. The boys were relentless enough; the last thing Beth needed was girls rubbing their hands on the wall and saying, "Oh, Beth!" their laughter ringing off tiled walls.

But the sting of those insults was fading. Beth caught and ate a raw fish with her bare hands. How many kids can say they've done that?

Dehydration set in, and her head began to ache. Scratching

mosquito bites on her arms, Beth ducked under branches and stepped over a blanket of fallen sticks, roots, and rocks. The romanticism of catching her first meal was already fading.

It felt like hours had passed but midday remained out of reach. Social studies with boring old Mrs. Caligaria was never this tedious. Kids called her Mrs. Caligula, and Beth laughed with them, not knowing why.

The calming rush of the stream called to her. It reminded her to rest her legs and breathe. Dipping her feet in the cool water, Beth sighed, enjoying the current against her bruised skin. Birds chirped behind her, and she wondered what they were saying to each other. Gazing at the clear water made her mouth water. She cupped her hands and scooped some up. As she slurped, her throat opened, welcoming the cool drink. Then she splashed some on her face.

"That's nice," she crooned.

As her gaze drifted across the stream, Beth caught sight of purple violets with spiky heart-shaped leaves swaying in the breeze. A patch of bold beauty among hollow colors. She remembered Mrs. Calmin offering her iced tea with purple blooms frozen in ice cubes. Once melted, she dried the petals and arranged them in Beth's hair, making her feel pretty.

Mrs. Calmin always knew the right words to say. *Frame every so-called disaster with these words, Sunshine: In ten years, will this even matter?*

Beth blinked, holding back fresh tears trembling at the edge of her eyes. She missed the sound of her nickname, missed what it meant.

You're welcome to cry here. Crying with someone heals more than crying alone. Mrs. Calmin said that the day Beth's fat English teacher, looking like Grimace, tossed a pencil at her head.

Her stomach rumbled. Beth glared at her belly. Though grateful for the distraction, she fought the urge to beat it with her fists.

Then she remembered the purple, olive-sized fruit just beyond the mouth of the woods.

You thinking what I'm thinking?

A minute later, she slipped on her shoes and socks and headed south, keeping the stream to her left. She marched through tall pines and shrubs that reached her knees. They pressed against her jeans, piercing her legs with tiny thorns. The thought of the greenery being alive made the hair on her body stiffen. She wondered if it despised her for pressing its branches into the dirt. They reminded her of a scary film about evil plants slinking into people's bodies through their mouths and wounds.

But Beth's zeal for water, food, and freedom outweighed that fear and pain. She fought on.

The stream babbled like a soothing voice you never wished would shut up. It felt friendlier than the voice spitting remarks: *Why did you take that turn? You wanna pick up the pace?*

She had to find the forest's edge. And snatch those beach plums.

THE BOY

THE BOY

"Where the heck did you go now?"

She must have gone to pee or wandered off. He thought about looking for her, but finding her among thousands of trees was impossible. Besides, he'd be useless without food or water.

With everything that had happened in the last twenty-four hours, Chris had forgotten to eat. Hunger festered in his gut like an ulcer, demanding attention and relief. He pulled out the remaining food: six hot dogs, some cheese, one apple, and a bag of brown furry balls.

Setting two hot dogs on the fire grate, he bit into the apple, juice coating his mouth with sweet crunch. He couldn't help but laugh. Mom had begged him a hundred times to snack on fruit. *Chris? Want a nice, red, juicy apple?* she'd ask with a smile, eyes wide like gumballs. Unmoved, he'd always shake his head and aim for the pantry. Mom could always convince Beth, but never him.

Water had never tasted so good, despite the metallic flavor from heating in an old pot. Chris popped a piece of cheese into his mouth and chewed on a warm hot dog. He wanted to save it for Beth, but hunger triumphed.

Once finished, he balanced an empty bottle between his feet and poured in the remaining water, sealing it.

That was for Beth.

He took stock of everything taken from the black bag and smiled, pleased but not surprised at his own resourcefulness. He flipped the deodorant between his hands, then set it aside and turned his eyes to the bolt cutter. It was heavy, like a block of ice with steel jaws and cushioned red rubber grips. He'd seen Dad use one to cut chains in the backyard fence and thick branches in the yard.

A wave of sorrow broke over Chris. Thinking of Dad brought him home, back to his hard-earned trophies and medals now buried in ash and rotting wood. He needed a distraction, something to burn off the ache.

Fix the roof.

Chris stood and grabbed the radio. Music, maybe a ball game, might fill the silence while he worked and waited for Beth.

25

THE DEPARTMENT

THE DEPARTMENT

"So, I was closing the store and thought I'd offer the officer a drink and snack, right?" The man was in his late forties, tall and lean, with silver hair pulled back in a low ponytail that fell to the middle of his back. "At first I thought he was sleeping. Then I noticed the blood."

The captain leaned into the vehicle. He thanked the store owner for the call and sent him on his way. Then he requested a crime scene crew, asking for Detective Warsoff and Officer Castaneda to assist.

They came upon the cruiser, and hours later, the sedan. At the second scene, where a jogger had spotted the retired officer's car along Ditchburn Street, Ramsey called in Deputy Reid and Detective Sanders. He didn't need to run the plate to know it was Bennett's. Folks tend to advertise their profession or how they define themselves on their car.

The town had built I-193 several miles away, and everyone in the department knew Bennett wouldn't trade the florid scent of pine along Ditchburn Street for the convenience of a freeway. Since its construction, his appreciation for the road only grew, especially in his final years on the force. No scowling commuters tailgating one another, no brassy car horns, no accidents. Just a smooth road populated by trees, leading the people out of Wanapatchee.

People were creatures of habit, and Bennett was no different. Though retired a year, he kept the routine of shooting at the range every Wednesday and Friday. Hell, he even kept his old duty bag in the trunk. It was wise to stay prepared, keep emergency supplies close.

Now Bennett had been missing for twenty-four hours, according to his family. The captain took no chances and launched a full investigation.

By midday, news vans, police, medics, and curious citizens crowded the strip mall parking lot.

The captain arranged for forensics to lift fingerprints from both vehicles and ordered a rush to the lab, eager to see if they matched. When the pathologist arrived, he checked the cruiser, signed a warrant for an autopsy, and handed it to Ramsey before joining the officers inspecting the sedan. The on-site coroner saw no point in sending Deputy Powell's body to the hospital. Instead, they transferred him to the town morgue for the medical examiners to perform the autopsy.

But no one needed to wait for the examiner's report to confirm the identification.

"Are you concerned about Bennett, sir?" asked Detective Warsoff once the clamor died.

Ramsey, a sullen look in his eyes, shook his head unconvincingly. "Of course not," he said. "Bennett was a sharp officer. A smart man."

"That's not what I meant."

Ramsey shot him a look. "What *did* you mean, Barry?"

Warsoff shrugged. "I was just wondering. Don't you think it's as good a time as any to call reinforcements?"

"I've already thought of that."

"Maybe we ought to allow state police to get involved—" the captain shot a look at the deputy— "sir."

A murdered officer and a missing retired detective were bound to bring a swarm of cops and agents to their small town.

"The FBI is insisting on taking over the investigation, Barry," said Ramsey crisply. "You just find me a witness. Someone who saw something. Anything. I've got Reid and Sanders doing the same across town."

"Sanders, sir?"

"You heard me. I don't want anyone going out alone. I know

Reid can handle himself, but I'm not taking any chances. Not until we locate Bennett."

The detective nodded.

Ramsey sighed and shook his head. What a mess. The pressure settled on his shoulders like a fifty-pound bulletproof vest. State police were on his back, pressing to take over the investigation, but he'd be damned if he let that happen. For twenty-five years, this had been his town. His jurisdiction. A couple of missing kids and a dead officer didn't change that.

But for a small town in northern New Jersey, murders were rare. And since word had spread, the department received calls from officers in Rookwood and Hollis offering to transfer in and help. The captain continued to assemble large search teams, pulling civilians and police from both towns. He even knew hunters with dogs eager to join the effort and offer their services.

26

THE BOY

"...we received a call from a witness who reported discovering a body inside a police cruiser. Responding officers located the body in the passenger seat. The victim had been shot in the chest, with no signs of movement or breathing. A large amount of blood was present inside the vehicle." Officer Castaneda's voice thinned. "At that point, additional units were requested at the scene."

A reporter interjected. "Is it true the Pacelli kids may have been responsible for at least one of these incidences?"

A pause. "A ballistics expert examined the wound and determined the shot was fired at close range, from below. The Wanapatchee Police Department finds no evidence linking the Pacelli kids to either case. However, we do have reason to believe they may be armed and are currently wanted for questioning."

Chris listened to the report while tidying the shack. He swept along the walls with a broom and caught himself laughing. When had he last held one? Inside the house was Beth's job; Chris handled the lawn in summer and took out the trash now and then.

He dragged the mattress outside, propping it against the shingled wall. Wrapping one hand around the corn whisks and the other around the stick, he hammered the cushion with brute force. Dust burst from the padding in thick clouds. He yanked his shirt over his mouth and nose to avoid coughing.

"The Goose approaches the plate, the bat raised just slightly over his right shoulder. Let's see if he can beat his record, folks. He's ready for the first pitch. Aaaaaand..."

Thump!

Chris blasted the stick against the cushion. Another patch of dust curled out, floating overhead like a storm cloud.

It didn't matter that his lungs burned, arms ached, and palms blistered. An engine roared inside him, pushing him faster through the sting. He uncovered a fresh, fierce layer within himself—packed with new endurance he never knew he had.

"Over the fence it goes! The Goose has done it again! It's no surprise who the—*whack!*—hero of—*smack*—!"

With each blow, his swings hit harder. Then the stick snapped in two. Even that didn't stop him.

"—this game—*punch!*—is!"

He switched to fists. Grunts and groans tore from deep inside, biting through clenched teeth.

Finally, Chris kicked the broom pieces aside and let his butt hit the broken timber by the firepit. Sweat covered his scalp, dripping down his face and back. His eyes were moist with tears. His breathing had intensified to wheezing, taking a few minutes to return to normal. Then he drank the rest of the water.

The man on the radio predicted rain. The next step was patching the roof. Dad loved to fix things, and Chris was no different. Once done, if time allowed, he planned to steal a peek and watch the fuss he created.

He felt amazing. Stronger. Ready to keep going.

The builder must have used the extra lumber to carve spare shake slabs for the roof and siding. Standing on his toes, Chris stacked a load of slabs on top of the shed. He lacked the patience to find something to stabilize them; stacking would keep water, leaves, and bird crap from leaking inside. Good enough for now.

He stepped on the uneven ridges along the shack's edge and lugged himself onto the shed. He raised his right leg over the edge and pulled up, landing face down in a mass of branches and crunching leaves.

"Shit."

Stiff foliage cushioned the landing, keeping Chris' forehead from striking the roof's ridge. He inched to his feet and looked around. Best to leave the branches and bed of leaves alone. They offered insulation and helped camouflage the building.

Chris placed six slabs over the holes, then gathered fallen branches, arranging them for added protection.

It wasn't until he sat down that he realized just how high off the ground he'd been. He smiled to himself, letting his legs dangle over the edge. From this height, movement could be spotted for miles.

A blue jay sailed across the clearing and settled on the roof. Its sapphire feathers, laced with white, offered a sharp splash of color against the green and black. It hopped along the uneven surface towards Chris, then stopped on a wilting branch.

Chris spotted a black spot no bigger than a pinky nail on the bird's chest, a faint smile on his lips. "This is my territory now, Blake."

The bird studied him through the leaves, head angled as if trying to understand him, before launching into the air.

THE GIRL

Scowling at the forest floor, she stopped where the weeded trail feathered off into nothingness. Once again, Beth's instincts failed her.

An image of Mom's pointed face flashed in her mind, index finger and thumb pinching together for emphasis while saying, *Stoopid. Ya stoopid!*

Without water and with an injured leg, she risked another collapse. Maybe worse. She had to find her way out and fast.

It's your call. I leave it up to you.

Beth rolled her eyes at her sense of reason. "Great. *Now* you clam up?"

Something caught her attention, and it wasn't green or black or wood. It stood a hundred yards away at the end of a rocky path. Curiosity drove her forward like a mosquito to an open vein.

It appeared like a dream—tall cement rows buried in a sea of foliage and timber. Fifteen-foot-high walls stood among the trees. The remains of Van Slyke's castle.

Beth shook her head. "I must be seeing things again."

She wandered beneath towering stone canopies topped with rusted iron beams. The fire had left nothing but a stone shell. The roof was gone; the window casements held no glass. Green lichen covered the rows of chunked stone.

Above one was an arched hole. Beth ran her hands over the mortar between the stones, feeling its graveled texture against her thirsty fingers. She frowned at a large red face, the size of a pizza, that looked like a sinister pumpkin, tainting a pillar to her right. A rusted cast-iron bathtub stood between two walls with large sections cut out for windows.

She felt like she'd stepped into a fairy tale. And she was the princess. A broken princess. Her castle blasted to pieces like crumbled Legos by blazing cannons belonging to a she-devil with the same pale face, large eyes, and long nose as Mom. The witch couldn't stand the thought of the girl being happy in her beautiful home, so she ordered the military to destroy it.

But instead of locking the princess in some cold, wet dungeon, the witch enjoyed watching the girl wander among the ruins of a home she could never leave. Now trapped in her own prison, the princess could never forget what the witch had stolen.

Like many fairy tales, this one didn't have a happy ending.

A beer can crunched under Beth's foot, snapping her from her trance. She looked down to see a litter of cigarette butts scattered across what had once been a gorgeous marble floor, now a swath of soil. The air leaked from her lungs, and she curled over.

After a minute, Beth stood upright and, clutching her injured leg when it faltered, drifted through the rest of the magnificent maze. She caught sight of the red brick fireplace and felt a crushing desire to crawl inside and curl up in its dank blackness. There she could be safe, like in her fort back home.

It's tempting. But not a good idea.

Her eyes locked on two plastic water bottles several feet away.

Wait. You're not thinking—

"Shut up. You wanted to be quiet, so be quiet. As long as it's not ammonia or bleach or pee, I'm drinking it."

Beth squatted and picked up both bottles, brushing away the dirt; they felt warm and soft in her hands. She uncapped one and sniffed the mouth. A faint, woody smell rose to her nostrils. She wiped the mouthpiece with her shirt and brought it to her lips, testing a small drop on her tongue. It was warm and salty, but it was water. Beth shrugged and poured all eight ounces down her throat. She would save the second bottle for later.

For an instant, she was home, drinking from the hose beside the garage, the sun warm on her face, rough cement beneath her feet, and the memory of a life she could almost reach, just out of grasp.

THE BOY

THE BOY

It took him about an hour and a half to reach the forest's edge. According to the sedan's odometer and compass, he'd driven two miles northwest before abandoning it. Luckily, he had a compass leading him in the right direction. Once he arrived at the edge, he could see what was happening without being near the scene.

As Chris drew closer, his heartbeat quickened, unsure whether it was fear or excitement. Truthfully, he felt stimulated by the thought of the town making such a fuss over something he did.

He checked his watch.

4:38 PM.

He ducked behind a mass of bushes, peering through the gaps. More police cruisers and news vans packed the northwest end of Ditchburn Street—a far too familiar sight. Chris listened to the faint clamor of people on the street.

In the woods, sounds carried three times louder than anywhere else. Chris took care skittering over fallen leaves and sticks among tall thickets. Around here, they stood close to six feet tall, with finely serrated, egg-shaped leaves and snowy white flowers on stout, hairy branches. Over his shoulder, he spotted bushes heavy with red and purple berries, his mouth watering. But there were more important things. Berries would have to wait.

A rustling sound came from his right shoulder, followed by a snapping branch. Frozen in a crouch, Chris held his breath. Panicking and running would be stupid. He stroked the revolver inside his pants, swallowing the lump in his throat.

Richard Dawson patted his back, assuring Chris he could handle whatever came his way.

The crackling sound drew closer, fifty yards away.

"Holy shit. Beth?"

Only now did it strike him: his sister could be dead. He always believed he would sense it if something happened to her, a gut-deep certainty. He remembered the time Mom struck her and she crashed into the coffee table, her mouth colliding with the sharp corner. Chris had stayed behind while they whisked Beth to the hospital, her front tooth chipped, forehead stitched. That night, he'd gotten sick in the bathroom. He would never say it aloud, but Beth seemed to endure more pain than he could.

And there she was, disoriented but smiling. Chris shot a look towards the road to see if anyone had spotted her. No one had.

He darted through the brush like a base runner and, in one swift motion, swept Beth up. He clamped a hand over her mouth, cutting off her cry as he pulled her into the woods.

27

THE GIRL

"Stop struggling, Beth. It's me!" She wrestled against Chris' grip, punching, striking out until he clamped a hand over her mouth.

"S-See?" he huffed. "It's…just me."

Her eyes narrowed, muscles slack. Chris pulled his hand away.

"Chris?" She looked up to see her brother staring down at her. He looked different somehow. His eyes piercing, primitive. "What are you doing?"

Chris shot a look over his shoulder. "We got to keep moving."

Without delay, he led her south through the green maze, letting the compass guide them, even through thorns. He didn't care about the easy route, just the fastest.

He pushed her into the shack and shut the door. Their breathing shallow, pulses racing. Chris peeked out the window. No one behind them. The only force stirring the foliage was the breeze.

Beth stood motionless, her leg screaming. She looked around the room. Everything seemed cleaner.

Chris dropped his pack and collapsed onto the mattress, tucking his head into the crook of an arm.

Beth opened her mouth. Where to begin? Why was Chris acting like an army was hunting them? So many questions, but all she said was, "I ate a raw fish."

When he pulled his arm away, she stared up at the blanket of black that was now the ceiling. The light no longer pierced the holes.

"Huh?"

If she told Chris about the fish, maybe he'd see her differently.

She'd be brave—he might even say so. But the words stuck like a chalky pill, refusing to slide down her throat. Then she remembered the water bottle, dropped in the brush. "Do you have water? I haven't had a drink in a while."

With a grunt, Chris sat up. "Beth, where the heck were you?"

Her eyes widened. "What? Where was I?"

"You can't do this alone! I told you not to run off like that!"

A blank look cut across Beth's face. Whenever drama hit, she clammed up, scrambling to gather her thoughts. Writing was better. It gave time to think, free of the pressure of speech and the shame of tripping over words.

Chris' gaze seemed to pass through her. It took a moment before Beth realized he was staring at her rust-colored shirt and jeans.

"Okay, give me a minute," he sighed. "I don't wanna start another fire until it's safe. Then I'll heat some up."

After tensions eased, Chris set out to sanitize the water. They took their usual places on the logs. He cooked the remaining hot dogs, waiting for the water to cool to room temperature. Thunder rolled across a darkening sky. Mosquitoes circled the clearing, but with their minds on heavier concerns, neither flinched or bothered to swat them away.

Beth's eyes locked on the pot at Chris' feet as she finished her second hot dog. The meat had a delicious saltiness she hadn't noticed before. When the water no longer huffed steam, she said, "I don't care how warm it is. I'll take it now."

Chris set a 16-ounce bottle between his feet and tipped the heavy pot over its mouth. "Be careful," he said, handing it over. "Don't burn your lips."

The bottle sat warm in her hands, like hot tea. She took a sip and grimaced at the heat, then set it down, waiting for it to cool.

Chris smirked.

The sky growled like a bear, rain scent thick in the air. The twins' hair danced in the whistling wind.

As Chris flicked dirt into the fire, Beth looked skyward. She was thinking about the castle, longing to see it again. Drops of water slipped through the canopy, pulling her from the haze.

"What are we going to do?" she asked, glancing at the shack. "We'll get wet in there."

"Give me some credit. I wasn't just sitting around while you were out, doing whatever you were doing." He stood. "C'mon. We'll be alright in there."

Inside, the scent of wood hung heavy. Branches shifted against the window, shards of light bathing the room in a sullen glow. It felt like a hidden basement, holding untold shadows.

Chris clicked on the flashlight. "Damn," he laughed, squinting against the bright glow.

"Wow. Where'd you get that?"

"You should know." He set the flashlight under the corner of the mattress. A mild orange glow burnished the cabin like a womb. In this light, Chris looked ten years older, rugged.

"Huh?"

He lifted his shirt to examine the damage. Red spots coated his chest like pepperoni on pizza. "Damn. You really did a number on me."

"Sorry."

Rain picked up, drumming against the roof. Both were hungry for answers, but neither knew where or how to begin.

Chris shook his head and sighed. He turned to the window, and Beth watched him study the branches fluttering in the wind.

"Where were you?" she demanded. "What happened?"

"What do you mean?"

The last twenty-four hours felt like a strange dream—poignant, reflective, but mostly forgotten. "I *mean*, look at me!" She glanced down at herself. "The last thing I remember is getting into that car. Then I woke up here and went looking for you."

Chris stared at her, studying her for a long moment, as if doing so might unlock the answers he needed. "You really don't remember?"

Beth bit her lip and shook her head, terrified to hear the truth.

Did she hurt someone? Did she hurt him?

Reluctantly, she flashed back three years. Chris had said something to set her off. She shoved him hard across the kitchen; his body slid across the waxed tile before slamming against the pantry door. Every thread of mercy had drained from her body. With chilling calm, she marched towards her brother with clenched fists, like a panther stalking an injured deer. It was as if she'd kept her rage hidden, letting it thicken over the years.

But now, picturing Chris sprawled on the floor with wide eyes, mouth agape, her heart sank with a remorse she'd never known before.

Chris opened his mouth, then stopped. After a moment, he spoke. "You didn't want that man taking you to the hospital, so he let you out. You came back here. And being the klutz you are, you tripped on a root and hit your head."

Beth touched the bump on her head and winced. Chris was right. She remembered Mom and Dad signing a waiver at the hospital, attesting the 48 stitches on her forehead weren't from abuse but her own mishaps.

Beth glanced down at her clothes, confused.

"Don't worry about that," he said. "You fell on a dead rabbit. It was kinda gross but not bad. I guess you woke up and wandered off." He added curtly, "What you didn't know is I was getting water for us."

Was he lying? Chris was a damn good liar. He honed that skill signing Mom's forged name at school. Beth once caught him testing what adults called a "poker face" in his bedroom mirror. He'd worked on it for hours until the innocence looked real.

It all made sense. Shame washed over her. She'd doubted Chris again, even though he only wanted to protect her. "Oh," she mumbled, staring down at her laced fingers.

Chris scratched his neck. "It's cool. No harm done. And I have another shirt for you. Tomorrow you can wash your jeans in the stream."

Beth nodded.

"So, you alright?"

She looked up and shrugged. "I guess. What about you?"

"What about me?"

"How did you…? I mean—"

"What, you think I can't take care of myself?"

"It's not what I meant."

"What did you mean?"

Beth crept down on the mattress, hoping the motion would ease her embarrassment. "Did you hear the news? Are we okay?"

Chris adjusted himself against the fabric and closed his eyes. "Yeah, I heard the news."

Minutes passed as they listened to the rain beating against the shack's roof and walls. Neither would admit it, but the rhythm felt oddly melodic, almost comforting. Beads of water slipped through gaps in the sprigs against the window, sprinkling the warped shelf below.

"So, when do you think we can go back?"

"Go back to *what*, Beth?"

A painful reality check.

The blow landed in her gut like a steamroller, stealing her breath. Until then, she managed to retain a shred of hope that they would leave the woods, no longer worrying about food, electricity, or warmth. It made sense the police would forgive them for stealing food. After all, they were just kids and had lost their home. Still, the thought of police rushing them into a detention center, foster care, or orphanage sounded terrifying. Beth struggled to imagine a hopeful outcome. Nothing came.

Finally, Chris opened his eyes. Beth felt his gaze on her as she picked at the padding beneath her knee. She sensed he needed her somehow—a reason to stay. Otherwise, she'd take off again and expose their hideout. No way would Chris spend his life behind bars, disgraced and judged. Not for an accident. Beth knew he'd rather die.

Chris rose from the bed and climbed the ladder to the loft. He sat down, legs dangling over the side.

"What are you doing?"

He rubbed his eyes. "I'm tired. I didn't sleep good last night."

"You're sleeping up there?"

"Why not? I've done it before. You can have the bed."

"But you can stay down here and—"

"No way you're sleeping up here. Remember what happened the last time you slept on a bunk bed?"

Leave it to Chris to bring up something humiliating. Last year, their class went on a weeklong field trip to Stokes, a 16,000-acre state park in Sussex County. The trip introduced the kids to the glory of the outdoors and the basics of forestry.

Beth was thrilled because Donald Polsky had asked to escort her to the most anticipated event of the year: the square dance. He'd slipped her his school photo during English class. On the back, written in purple ink: *Will you go with me to the dance at Stokes?* Beth had nodded, her stomach doing cartwheels, a nervous smile on her face.

But she didn't stay long enough to attend the dance.

The teachers had assigned her to a cabin with seven girls and four bunk beds. That first night, she dared to sleep on a top bunk. Somehow, she ended up on the hardwood floor, and it wasn't until Mrs. Deako shook her awake the next morning that Beth realized she'd fractured her left arm.

Mom and Dad took her to the hospital for a cast, cutting the trip short and canceling her dreamy plans with Donald. Beth walked around for six weeks with that dumb thing on her arm, Mom's message scrawled in thick black marker—*To err is human. To fall out of bed is dumb*—standing out among other scribbles and signatures.

A week later, Donald's interest in Beth faded, like cheap ink on a valentine's card.

Chris offered his extra shirts. "You can use them to stay warm." he said, the edge of his voice gone. "And don't forget to turn the light off. We need the batteries to last until we find new ones." He settled back on the bundled leather jacket he used as a pillow, closing his eyes. "We'll figure something out, okay? Don't feel bad. I know a lot of guys from broken homes, and they're no better off than we are now."

Beth unzipped the backpack by her feet and pulled out the T-shirts, unaware of the new supplies inside. After slipping on the Islanders jacket, she arranged the shirts over herself like an unstitched blanket, and clicked off the light tucked beneath the mattress.

Darkness settled. The moon cast a soft glow through the window, beneath the door, and through small gaps in the jamb. Just as Beth began to drift off, a voice whispered from above, pulling her from that first spell of sleep.

"You didn't miss out on much. It was a crappy dance, and Donald was a loser anyway."

The words were so faint she barely heard them. Did she imagine it?

They were real. I know it.

28

THE GIRL

THE GIRL

"Leave me alone!"

She stumbled through the grassland that paralleled the road, the revolver heavy in her hand. Her knuckles, pale and tight, pressed against cracked skin wrapped around the grip. She needed to know if the driver was gaining, but the thought of that twisted, bloody face stopped her from looking back.

Beth threw her head back, screaming at the dimming sky. Each step drove pain up her leg like a lightning bolt from the crash, but she kept moving. Fear of what the man would do if he caught her lit something primal. She had to survive.

Outrunning an adult wasn't impossible. Three years ago, Dad had spent the afternoon setting up their aboveground pool in the backyard. After he laid the base, neighbors came by to help line the walls with the ground rails. Curiosity led Beth to peek over the side. It didn't matter that Dad warned her a hundred times to step back—falling in would bring the whole thing down. She kept peering over the edge, stumbled forward, and landed flat on her face. Aluminum whooshed as the pool walls collapsed, wrecking Dad's entire day's work.

Dad bolted after her like a coyote chasing the road runner, dust ballooning like smoke under his feet. Beth shot up from the ground, racing across the yard and down the street untouched. She realized terror, sharpened and intense, could eclipse rage.

"Stop!" the driver called.

Beth knew he'd gotten closer. Stopping, even for a second,

would be her end.

At first glance, the man seemed harmless, even approachable. Back in the car, he'd seen her hugging a jacket and offered a scarf he said was in the glove box. But why carry a gun? And why claim he recognized her? Was he trying to create a connection to make things easier before harming her?

If books taught Beth anything, it was that trusting people was foolish. Stories of men kidnapping girls and disemboweling them for amusement raced through her mind, pushing her to seize the gun from the compartment before he could react. With the car in motion, he spun towards her in shock. The steel quivered in her tense grip, her forefinger pressing against the trigger guard.

"Hey," he snapped. "Don't go touching that, little lady." Then, slowing his speech, he said, "That's not a toy. Just set it down so nobody gets hurt."

He reached out his hand. Beth pulled back against the door, arm stiffening, finger resting on the trigger, muzzle aimed at his cheek.

"Wh-Whoa! I said that's not a toy! Watch where you're pointing that!"

Beth scrambled to recall Chris' one-time thirty-second handgun lesson. George had been staying over, and with Mom and Dad asleep, she caught him flaunting one of Dad's firearms. Beth promised not to snitch if he let her hold it. Huffing, Chris placed the revolver in her hands. "Only for a second, and that's it," he said. Beth never imagined she'd have to put the lesson to use. It just felt good to be one of the boys, if only for a moment.

Beth thought about tossing the revolver out the window, but the driver must have locked it. Nothing happened when she pressed the button. Her only chance was to fling it through an open door. She yanked the handle, unlatching it. Airflow stopped the door from opening more than a few inches before it slammed shut again. Beth shoved her right foot between the door and rocker panel, but the driver snatched her wrist before she could toss the weapon out.

"What are you doing?" he hollered.

Her hand quaked in his grip, his fingers squeezing her wrist so hard she heard something crack.

"Let me go!" She uncurled his fingers with her left hand, then shoved him away with her left leg. With nothing to hold on to, the force drove her against the open door. She squeezed the trigger by accident, striking the driver in the leg.

"Sonofabitch!"

Blood fired out from the wound, speckling his face, neck, and teeth. His foot balked off the accelerator, slowing the car to 10 mph before Beth toppled out.

The door struck her left leg, leaving a fresh bruise and searing pain. A patch of grass cushioned her fall—dumb luck, since planning the jump might have meant broken bones from using her hands to brace herself.

Seconds before tumbling out, Beth's survival voice roared: *Tuck and roll! Tuck and roll!*

She obeyed, tumbling nearly fifty feet across stony earth before bumping into a flowering dogwood tree.

O   O   O

The driver was close, hobbling several yards behind. His right hand, swollen and purple like a mass of crushed blueberries, clutched a sodden blue-red handkerchief against the hole in his thigh. The wound pulsed. Red smears glazed his face; his lips curled over clenched teeth.

It was Beth's nightmare come true—more terrifying than the man in her dreams wearing torn overalls, a bleached mask, gripping a rusty machete.

Her bones screamed, her lungs burning like raw wounds. She spun her head towards the forest, locking on the aperture Chris had led them through. It stood beyond the tree with delicate white flowers. The same ones she had studied moments before, trying to distract herself from the hole in her chest. The tree stood two hundred feet across the field, maybe more. But with her injured leg, it might as well have been a mile.

The setting sun cast a soft pink glow against a powder-blue sky, clouds stretched like pulled cotton. The scene reminded Beth of a Monet painting she'd once seen in a library book.

"Give me the gun," the driver huffed. "I want the gun!"

Her sweaty grip tightened around the revolver. She considered firing a warning shot. It might slow him down, buy time to find a spot to slip into the woods. But what if he kept running? Would she have the courage to fire again? The odds of hitting him from afar were slim at best.

Come on, keep moving!

Reaching the aperture, Beth nodded to her consciousness and vanished into the woods, swallowed by thick greenery. Branches smacked her face as her shoes sank into the marshy ground. The canopy blotted out the last of the sun, forcing her into pockets of fading light. The Islanders jacket dragged in her hand, snagging on low-hanging twigs. Trying to move fast felt like skateboarding underwater.

Fixed on what lay ahead, Beth hadn't noticed if she was alone. For the first time since entering the forest, she spun around.

Hot damn, I think you lost him. He must've given up.

She had lost him. And managed to avoid doing something stupid, like toss away the gun or face-plant in the mud.

Countless nights, the twins had sprawled on the shag carpet watching horror movies, scoffing at characters making stupid decisions, like scrambling up stairs instead of out the door, or tossing their weapons after knocking the killer down.

"I don't care if she chopped his legs off," Beth would say. "Don't drop that ax until the police show up!"

Every muscle begged for rest. But she couldn't stop. That's what a pitiful ingénue would do. Screaming for help was no better. It was the easiest way to get caught and seal her fate within the woods.

BENNETT

Cursing himself for not bringing a flashlight, he hunched forward, vision blurred, and watched the girl disappear into the woods.

He stopped at the tree line and listened. After two seconds, he picked up her direction. He could follow her footprints, check the vegetation for shifting branches, even watch for flattened scat.

The plan was simple. Catch her off guard, restrain her, and retrieve the revolver. He'd done this before.

Once, he'd followed a girl into these woods. A plump teenager sitting by the road, a lit spliff dangling from pale, cracked lips. She wore a long black dress with flared sleeves and glitter nail polish chipped on chewed fingernails. He'd approached steadily, but there was no hiding his intent. She sprang up, flicked the joint into a bush, and ran. He caught her soon enough. Just like he'd catch this one.

THE GIRL
THE GIRL

It felt like hours before she finally calmed.

Too bad there's no merit badge for dealing with stalkers.

Beth pressed a hand against the nearest tree. "Shut up. You're not helping." The run had tightened her throat. Saliva, thick as mucus, coated her mouth, her tongue rough and dry like a snail sheathed in salt.

A sudden rushing sound came from the northeast.

Water!

She pressed on towards the sound, clutching her leg. After pausing several times to steady her direction, she found a narrow flume, probably from yesterday's rain.

Rustling leaves ahead, but no wind. Beth froze.

Don't panic. It's probably just a bunny or squirrel. There are a ton of animals out here. Just don't say, 'Hello,' or, 'Is anyone there?'

Beth nodded and thought of the squirrel she'd seen earlier. She patted her backside. "Oh, no."

It fell out when we rolled out of the car!

Beth scowled. The run had dried her eyes, but tears still welled. Mom was right. Stupid! So stupid!

The rustling started again.

She couldn't tell where the sound came from. She crept forward just as a shadow emerged—dark shiny eyes inside black greenery.

A piercing scream.

Beth spun and tried to run, but her leg buckled.

The driver sprinted ahead. With glossy hands, he grabbed hold of the jacket.

Let go of the stupid jacket! It's just a jacket!

Grappling with the sleeves, Beth spun and raised the revolver. It shook violently in her hand.

The driver froze, staring straight down the barrel.

"Please, let go!" she rasped. "Leave me alone!"

He pulled back his right hand to smack the weapon from her grip. Struggling with the jacket triggered vertigo, and he lost his footing, managing only to strike her hand against the cylinder. The force pushed Beth back, and she fell to her knees.

The driver fell with her, seizing her foot. His vision blurred; he tried to speak but couldn't.

"No!" Beth shook him off with frantic jolts and scrambled to her feet.

The driver snatched the back of her shirt. "P-P-P...!"

He's insane!

Like two worn-out wind-up toys, they collided, feet blundering on the slippery ground. Beth spun, but it wasn't enough to break his grip. Her foot stubbed a stone, and she staggered back, swinging the gun in stabbing motions. On her second backswing, the sweaty steel struck his face.

The driver roared, clutching his nose. The pain only fueled his fury and he lunged at Beth, forcing her to stagger under his weight; she swung the revolver a second time, the metal connecting with his jaw in a sharp crack. His grip on her shirt loosened.

She slipped aside.

He tumbled forward, then vanished. A scream trailed back, cut short by a pointed slab of rock.

29

THE GIRL

Time stretched as she stood frozen, gaping over the edge.

Beth fell to her knees. The revolver slid from her hand, thumping into the dirt.

Let's get the heck out of here.

She ignored the voice and crawled forward, half-expecting to see the driver clinging to the ledge, bloody fingers and bulging knuckles wrapped around a rock, waiting to grab her foot and yank her down.

This isn't some cheesy movie. Don't do anything stupid!

A heavy wind pushed against her back, flapping her hair. A whistle hissed between the cliffs. As she reached the brink, Beth braced herself. She looked down the ravine into a black abyss. The bottom was hidden in shadow; the drop looked at least fifty feet. Far below, a dark patch of ground resembled a life-sized beetle with crooked legs.

A headache pounded behind Beth's eyes. Her stomach turned, her chest jerking forward as a stinging rush fired up her throat. A chunky blend of hot dog and water sprayed against the rocks, flecking her face. She wrapped her arms around herself, shaking and dry heaving. "Mommmmyyyyy. I want Mommmmyyyy."

She cupped her hands to her mouth. "Hello! Can you hear me?"

What the heck are you doing? Are you crazy?

Her voice hung in the air. She spat out a strand of saliva clinging to her lip.

The voice ordered her to run away, but a crushing weight

stopped her. Her body refused to move. If she stayed, a bear or coyote might wander by and deliver a fitting punishment, like rip off her limbs and pound her meat and flesh before crunching down on the bones. Then she'd disappear, no more pain.

You have to move now. Before it gets darker.

The voice was right. The sky turned, restless in the dying day. Beth knew she had to move. She thought about finding her way back to the car. Every adult had a cell phone these days; she could call the police and face whatever penalty the law handed out for robbery, murder, and criminal possession of a weapon.

She wobbled to her feet, grabbed the revolver, and spun around.

Every angle looked the same, like a giant mirror reflecting the same patch of vegetation at every turn. Beth thought of *Alice in Wonderland* and how anxious the girl must have felt slipping down the rabbit hole into strange, freakish territory.

Her leg and throat stinging, she tracked her footprints. Her foot caught on a tree root, and she reeled forward, crashing into a heavy bush. Every obstacle reminded her nature ruled, not humans. She was just a plaything on indifferent land, an amusing distraction for squirrels and birds.

Just keep moving. No time to stop.

"Shut up."

Hey, don't be mean. I'm all you have now.

She curved around trees, eyes glued to the footprints in the dirt. It wasn't long before they stopped at a stretch of land covered in pine needles and flattened grass. She stared at the ground, eyes wet.

Hey, look!

The voice pulled Beth's attention to a patch of undergrowth, matted and sunken several yards ahead. She edged over broken branches, spotting a wet footprint—most likely the driver's—next to a brook. The channel steered her southwest alongside a tree that stood out among the rest. With its thick, curved trunk topped with maple leaves, it reminded her of *The Giving Tree*.

As she moved, something caught her eye: a deep notch carved into the bark, sharp and deliberate. Perched on one of its roots, Beth embraced the tree, resting her cheek against the coarse bark. "Why can't you have an apple for me?" she cried. "Or at least a nice voice to talk to me and tell me where to go?"

Something skittered across the earth several feet to her right. The sound faded, replaced by silence. Depleted, Beth closed her eyes and offered a grim smile, waiting for a towering shadow and a booming growl.

More silence.

She opened her eyes and sighed, then veered towards the sound.

Minutes later, the moon's soft light bled through a break in the trees. The opening of the woods.

What did I tell you? What did I tell you! We did it!

Beth shrugged. "So what?"

Part of her hoped she wouldn't find the way out. Her legs would collapse and she'd sink into the earth, turning to ash like countless nameless bodies before her.

You can't think like that. I won't let you.

The street lamps gleamed a golden hue along the road to her left, the tree with the pretty white flowers now a fluffy patch over her shoulder.

The vehicle was nowhere in sight. Beth recalled an oldie song playing on the car stereo; it ended just before she'd tumbled out.

How long could a song be—four minutes? Maybe five?

Inanely, she calculated the distance. At the driver's speed, it couldn't be more than maybe two miles.

"Two more long miles."

Then again, what did she know? While other kids studied math and English inside normal classrooms, Beth was downstairs in speech class tackling the letter S and flipping through books for dummies.

Two trucks sped by, oblivious to the girl hobbling several yards away. They swerved around a sedan's opened door parked askew upon the turf.

Holy cow, there it is!

"Oh please, God. Please let there be a phone in there. *Please!*"

On the pavement, a puddle shaped like a ghoulish inkblot caught Beth's eye. Gooseflesh prickled her skin. Red spots stained the windshield and smeared the dashboard; another puddle pooled where the seat dipped. The scene mirrored snapshots from those true crime shows.

Beth slid inside and dropped into the seat, sighing as her body slumped against the soft leather. A wet backside was the least of her worries. She placed the revolver on the dashboard, thankful to be rid of its hefty weight.

A wool scarf, gloves, discarded receipts, and a bottle of men's cologne sat inside the open glove compartment. She flipped open the console between the seats. A wallet and a comb rested atop more papers.

No phone.

Curiosity nudged her to open the wallet, but doing so would give the driver an identity. She'd learn his name, age, even where he lived. Adults always kept photos, eager to show anyone too polite to look away. Seeing this man's family would be sickening. Burdened with enough remorse to last a lifetime, Beth shook her head.

Don't feel too bad. Remember, this man was a predator.

Beth snapped the console door shut and opened a compartment under the stereo. Her mouth dropped open.

Yes!

Inside sat an unopened package of trail mix and a 10-ounce bottle of water. She started to reach for them, then pulled her arm back. Eating the man's food felt wrong, like peeing in someone's eye after knocking them down.

It's not like he needs it anymore. And your throat hurts, and you're starving.

Thirst and hunger won. Beth grabbed the bottle and the package, the wrapper crinkling in her grip.

Good job.

She gulped most of the water in a single swallow, then shook out enough nuts, seeds, and dried fruit to fill her palm, popping them into her mouth. She barely chewed the second handful.

Hey, calm down. Make it last. You don't know when you'll get food again.

The visor caught her eye next; she flipped it down. Pink plastic sunglasses dropped onto her lap, and she flinched.

What a sicko. Probably a souvenir from his last victim.

Beth looked up and sank back into the seat. Sweat and dirt glazed her face, her short hair wet and stringy against her skin, and a crusted slash scored above her right eyebrow she hadn't noticed until now. The girl in the mirror looked five years older.

Horrified, she turned away. Unlike most girls ogling their reflections, patting gloss on their lips, and combing their hair in the hallways, Beth hated mirrors and never kept one in her locker. Times like this reminded her why.

Imagine how those girls would look after rolling around in the dirt at fifty miles an hour.

Flicking the visor closed, Beth fell back into her seat and let out a pained sigh.

C'mon. What else can you do?

Her head buzzed and her hands and feet tingled. The water did nothing to soothe her burning throat. "I dunno. You're the smart one."

She closed her eyes but all she saw was the wallet. She sucked in a breath and snapped open the console. The wallet was thick, wrapped in dark green leather, with the company name stamped in gold letters on the front corner.

Beth peeked at the license, taking in the man's first name: Jack.

Are you happy now?

"Shut up."

A trunk latch took shape bedside the steering column. Her last memory was reaching over to pull it.

30

THE BOY

Through the window, a beam of light cut across his face, dragging him awake from King Kong's roar. Chris hated nightmares. They were crude and stalked you like painful memories.

You can't shut me out, kid. You invited me in.

He checked his watch.

7:13 AM.

Careful not to wake Beth, he crept down the ladder, his shoulders aching where the bag had thumped against his back. He pulled out the paper he took from the clipboard and scribbled her a note.

> *Getting water. Didn't wanna wake you.*
> *Back soon. Don't go anywhere! –C*

Holding the leather jacket, Chris grabbed his pack and shot a look over his shoulder. Beth lay curled in a fetal position, back to the wall, hugging a bundle of shirts to her chest.

He stepped outside and took a drink. Twenty-four ounces left.

Pulling on the oversized leather jacket, Chris found an inside pocket big enough for the revolver and tucked it in.

Yesterday, he almost told Beth about the driver and the dead officer. But when he caught the confusion flickering in her eyes, the words stuck in his throat. Dad's old warning echoed in his mind: girls could be just as sly as boys, maybe even more so. Beth lacked the typical girl qualities like warmth and beauty, yet she remained just as mysterious and hard to trust.

O   O   O

By noon, he headed northwest with three fish and a grin. The fish rushing into his trap marked Chris's maturity; he was growing stronger, empowered by nature, owning his place on the food chain.

The duct tape failed, so he knotted the tails to a stick with his shoelaces, shuffling the rest of the way back.

Using his compass and acute sense of direction, Chris reached the edge in good time, spotting the tree with the snowy white flowers.

He plucked an olive-sized, reddish-purple fruit and winced at its sour bite. After gathering all the fruit, he aimed for the next tree.

With the sunlight knifing through branches and twigs cracking underfoot, Chris couldn't see or hear the cruiser drifting past behind the trees.

SANDERS and REID

SANDERS and REID

"State police must be laughing their asses off right about now."

Garrett Reid studied the field glistening from yesterday's rain. He snickered, not to mock but to show the detective he was listening. "We don't know for sure the kids were involved."

The air thickened among the officers as Reid forced awkward eye contact, nervous laughs, and heavy nods, feigning consideration for everything his former partner said.

Still, he respected Sanders. With nearly fifteen years patrolling New York's toughest streets, he'd outlasted everyone in Wanapatchee except the captain. Whispers claimed his time undercover in the city's busiest corners had broke him. But despite an imperfect record, he was a tireless worker and was one hell of a homicide detective.

Reid distrusted him, or more accurately, feared him. He wondered if Sanders ever forgave him for confessing the sordid details of that meth addict's house six years ago. Until today, Reid convinced himself the detective had let it go. But seeing those dark eyes burning a hole through the windshield made him doubt.

And here they were, patrolling alongside one another again. Not that Reid had much choice. Objecting to the captain's orders would have been foolish. Their workforce was thin, and every available resource was needed. Pulling Sanders off desk duty was inevitable.

Sanders, seemingly blind to his partner's discomfort, scanned the line of leaf-heavy trees along Ditchburn Street. He ran a hand over his smooth scalp, thick veins pulsing beneath his forearms. His wide, unblinking eyes dominated his face, each blink measured with the precision of a seasoned performer. In his world, every fraction of a second mattered. Even a brief flicker of the eyelids could betray weakness. No one liked to admit it, but being feared was a weapon all its own.

Sanders had lost all taste for fieldwork. Yet with Dave gone and a retired officer missing, an old, unwelcome sensation stirred within him. It clawed its way back, a memory he'd buried deep, now scratching at his core like a knife scraping the last stubborn bit from a mayonnaise jar.

The morning air smelled of musk. It tasted bitter, like rotting salad. Sanders hated New Jersey's smells and understood why folks often jeered the state. The stench reminded him of garbage baking on hot summer streets and hobos pissing in subway stations. But at least New York City was genuine. It didn't hide its inhabitants' plebeian nature. In Jersey, people masked themselves behind horizontal siding and Venetian blinds. They feigned civility.

"Bullshit," said Sanders. "That girl's prints were all over that kitchen. You think that was a coincidence?" The question was rhetorical, of course. The lab results were just a formality, sure to show all the unjustifiable prints and hair fibers. Sanders relied on instinct because it never failed him. He knew better than to trust kids. They were mercurial, careless, often dangerous—especially homeless ones with dead parents.

The bloodstained sedan told much of the story. Bennett was a hefty man, five feet eight inches tall. It didn't take a genius to see a smaller person had adjusted the seat before driving away. The same went for Powell's cruiser. No street cameras showed anyone driving the sedan since Bennett left that afternoon. So the crime scene was close.

The question was how a bullet from Bennett's revolver ended up in Powell's chest.

For a moment, Sanders considered that the media and local politicians with irrational grievances against police had influenced another feather-brained asshole. But the odds of that happening in this small town were slim. He'd planted the seed of suspicion in the captain's mind about the twins, soon to be proven right.

Not that it mattered. Sanders no longer sought approval or needed to impress anyone, especially the gullible small-town officers who couldn't spot a dirty needle in a crack house. He'd been in this business long enough to stop caring about kudos and credit. One reason he even fought the discharge in New York was to avoid the boredom of retirement. Internal Affairs hounded him for months, threatening dismissal and insisting he see the departmental shrink or else.

For three long months, Sanders sat in that office, purging every thought to the skinny, long-legged brunette behind the mahogany desk. It wasn't until he stopped being transparent—a word they liked to push these days—and put on a face that the evaluations approved his transfer.

Reid kept his voice low and controlled. "Just because they busted into a house and took food doesn't make them—"

"I'll bet my left nut those little prints are all over Bennett's car." Sanders's eyes landed on a candy bar wrapper nestled in the grass. "Mark my words."

Powell was green, too young for the cynicism and bitterness that wore down most officers after years of backbreaking service. He carried a refreshing hope Sanders couldn't remember having, though he must have once, before life changed him. Powell spent his entire life in Wanapatchee, much of it exploring Ramapo Forest.

Sanders, a city boy, humored him and welcomed his tips on small-town folk. He even learned a few tricks navigating the forest during an assignment at the old hunter's lodge.

In a moment of idiocy, the detective had fantasized about taking the deputy under his wing like a protégé. He scoffed at himself for entertaining the thought. He felt like an orphan on Christmas morning, finally knowing Santa would never deliver mom and dad wrapped in fat red bows.

Sanders spotted something six feet away in the brush—a small purple book. A diary, by the script on the front. He glanced over his shoulder before crouching to pick it up. The pages were stiff, rippled with bleeding purple ink. He flipped open the cover.

This book belongs to
Beth Pacelli

A crooked grin. "Coincidence, my ass."

Deep in thought, Reid kept his gaze locked on the barren road. "What's that?"

Sanders slipped the small book into his inside jacket pocket. "Nothing. Just thinking."

Heading west in the cruiser, Reid stared at the road, unaware of the boy skirting the trees. The kid wore a dark hat, clutching a backpack to his chest.

Glaring out the passenger window behind black sunglasses, Sanders saw him. He kept his mouth shut, eyes fixed on the boy as he pulled what looked like berries from a tree.

Heat bubbled beneath the detective's calm exterior. The fire in him returned, sizzling in his gut like acid on a slug.

31

THE GIRL

A chill pulled her from sleep. Whether it was the morning air or the nightmare sparking her shaking hands, she couldn't tell.

But was it a nightmare? Hadn't she been half-conscious for a while? In that blurry space, on the edge of waking, she knew she was lying in bed but fought to slip back into sleep.

Morning light leaked through the grime-covered window and cracked walls, bathing the shack in dull gray. A fitting backdrop for the fractured images that lingered like an old, grainy film reel flickering haunting scenes that refused to fade.

A man, the driver, reaching for her.

An earsplitting bang.

Blood spraying like a broken faucet.

Tumbling through the brush like a pinball.

Dashing through the trees, straining for breath.

Blood on hands, oozing like syrup.

The ravine. The scream.

All remarkably vivid pictures. Until now, Beth convinced herself it was her imagination playing tricks. She was no murderer. And outrunning a large man in the woods sounded ridiculous.

She touched her injured leg, blinking several times until the images thinned. The mattress poked her back, so she turned to her side and shut her eyes. The man emerged again, barking through the woods, screaming for the gun. Wrestling on slippery ground, so much blood. That horrible scream!

She pressed her palms to her ears. "I must be going crazy."

Chris could help distract her. "Chris?"

The loft was empty. Beth's confusion shifted to relief when she saw a half-filled water bottle next to the mattress.

Were malnourishment and confusion triggering hallucinations again? Beth saw Daffy Duck nosediving into a pool of water, scooping handfuls into his mouth before realizing it was sand.

She blinked a few times, shaking her head.

The bottle remained, tipped inside a long crack in the wood.

If not for the drink, she would have remained cocooned in bed, swaddled in Chris's shirts like sheets of warm blood. She imagined that the jolt of discomfort she felt stepping out of bed or a hot shower in winter was a taste of what newborns experienced when doctors pulled them from the safety of the womb. Then came the slap, a sting of cold and pain that marked the harsh welcome into a strange new world.

Thirst overcame the desire for comfort, and Beth shot up, snatching the bottle. It tasted warm and stale but soothed her sore throat, sharpening her vision.

"Thanks, Chris."

Rising to her feet, she felt the soreness in her leg subsiding. She wrapped her arms around herself, shuffling to the window. In this light, the woods intimidated her. Dark holes in the bark looked like open mouths, like the freakish trees in *The Wizard of Oz*.

Her gaze traced the delicate lines etched across her face and neck, her ghostly reflection haunting the glass, grateful for the absence of a mirror.

Don't be so hard on yourself. I bet most girls at school wouldn't have made it this far. Heck, they'd probably complain about breaking a nail or dirtying their shoes.

"You don't know that."

Despite the brief flicker of pride she felt for lasting this long, Beth knew Chris deserved most of the credit. He came up with the plan to take food from that house, rescued her twice from the cold, and found a way to get clean drinking water. Without him, she would have died—if not out in the cold, then in the fire.

But he wasn't out there now.

A note on the door caught her eye. Beth smirked, tore it off, and read it. A magazine sat at the foot of the bed. Chris must have left it there to kill time while he was gone.

But where'd he get it?

Maybe that creepy bar?

It must have been the bar.

A man with a waxed chest modeled teal swim trunks on the cover. His muscles looked like smooth rocks packed under his skin.

Red text outlined his body: *Blast Belly Fat! Best Sex Ever! 12 Ways to Defy Your Age! Huge Muscles in Just 3 Moves!*

Intrigued, Beth flipped through the pages pushing cologne, body wash, razors, and condoms, wondering what it was like to be a man. Until now, she'd trusted they were all like Dad: intelligent, headstrong, and distant. But now, she wasn't so sure. Did they have dirty thoughts? Were there things about life they didn't understand? Were they troubled? Did they feel shame?

Beth flipped to the back and came across a quiz: *How Do You Know if She's Into You?* She decided to memorize her answers. It would keep her mind busy and ward off images of the man with the red face and the stained clothes.

O   O   O

She was learning to live with the shack and its shadows. The place seeped into her routine, as if she were slipping into a cast or leaning on crutches. The cabin and the woods wove themselves into her life; perhaps she was being woven into theirs.

Several times, Beth had read the articles on exercise, sex, and work. The magazine had served its purpose, distracting her from the scary images, though never for more than a few minutes at a time.

Not being able to log intimate thoughts left her exposed, a bleeding wound without a bandage. She felt sticky inside. Unclean.

Then she felt herself slip into that safe, quiet spot in her mind, walking down a nameless road, reflecting on people and things from her life. Important, unforgettable things.

Mrs. Caligro's pointed glasses beating against her large, swinging breasts as she walks up and down the aisles.

Wet, blurred eyes, daydreaming under leaves in the backyard. Hair fanning out against the earth.

Mouse, her stuffed penguin, brushing against her skin.

The rich smell of Mom's meat gravy simmering on the stove.

The stink of cigarette smoke.

The stale, intoxicating scent of library books.

That cute boy with the glasses in the library. That smile.

With every replay in her mind, Beth grew more certain that their eye contact was nothing but a jittery mistake. He'd only glanced up to check the clock behind her. Still, when their gazes met, did he notice the same short-haired, skinny girl Beth saw in the mirror?

Another memory surfaced: her thumb trailing caulk between blue tiles, eavesdropping on a locker room conversation. Whispers about something called a "G-spot"—whatever the heck that was.

Later that afternoon, Beth, playing it cool, told Chris what she'd overheard. After a long laugh, he led her into Dad's office and typed in a website. A kaleidoscope of pink skin, mauve parts, and blonde hair exploded on the screen. When Chris finally left, Beth, with awkward curiosity, studied the naked figures. That night, she scowled at her reflection in the mirror.

Whether it was the boy or the sex articles, curiosity sparked. Beth heard it was healthy to be curious, to experiment. She was missing out on something but wasn't sure what.

A strange calm settled over her, no longer bracing for someone to barge through her bedroom door. She closed her eyes and, fingers twitching, probed her skin. She felt silly, like a sighted person trying to read braille.

Then the snap of sticks stopped her. Blood rushed to her face as she yanked her hands away and spun to face the wall.

Seconds later, the door opened.

She stiffened, holding her breath. Maybe Chris would think

she'd fallen asleep, turn around, and leave her alone in her shame.

But footsteps crept over the threshold. They stopped with a thud, followed by heavy breaths.

More steps thumped closer, the planks creaking under the weight. It occurred to Beth that Chris was wearing sneakers. These footfalls were heavy, like hiking boots.

A snicker echoed from the foot of the bed, followed by a shush.

Oh, for God's sake, this is crazy! Tell him to get out!

Beth's eyelids inched open. She could make out Chris' outline, dusty shoes at the foot of the bed. Her stomach churning, she turned her head.

Chris wasn't there. Instead, two seedy men stood holding large guns, watching her.

32

THE GIRL

"Peekaboo. We see you."

Beth jolted upright on the mattress, back slamming the wall. Her arms wrapped tight around her knees.

The man in front of her was huge—over six feet, easy. Taller than Dad. His dark eyes didn't blink. Scraggy stubble framed a thin scar on his cheek. His crooked nose was as pink as his lips; thick eyebrows curled like caterpillars. Like his friend standing at the door, he wore saggy green pants, a jacket stuffed with zippers and pockets, and a bright orange hat. A bruised hand gripped the shotgun at his side.

He stepped closer.

Don't panic yet. These guys are hunters, that's it.

Beth glared at the hunter while he scanned the room, the caterpillars inching closer.

He turned to her, spitting a stream of tobacco on the floor. A bead of spit clung to his lower lip. "You the only one here, little lady?"

"Forget her, Tom. She's harmless," said the man by the door. "We're burning daylight. I need to get something home."

The hunter smirked, eyes locked on Beth. He rested the shotgun against the wall and lowered himself onto the bed. "I think I found something to bring home." His voice barely rose above a whisper.

A gust of damp air pushed into the shack, cutting through the musty smell. The walls pressed in, everything darkening, thinning into mist. Beth saw only a tunnel before her, two chilling men at the end.

"You're my best catch yet this year," he grinned. "How old are you, sweetheart?"

A scream bubbled but didn't sound. It clung to Beth's throat, mocking her for every time she'd judged frozen, tight-lipped victims while vile men loomed over them with knives.

"Can you talk?"

The other man leaned against the doorframe, exhaling.

Lips trembling and mouth sealed, Beth nodded. Her heart hammered against her ribs so loud she wondered if they could hear it.

Okay, this is not good. What can you use for protection?

Head still, Beth's eyes scanned the room for glass, a steel rod, anything. But there was nothing. Chris had cleared it all out.

Some of that wood had nails. Thanks a lot, Chris!

The hunter snorted. He scooted closer and leaned in, their faces inches apart. His breath reminded Beth of the Bronx Zoo. Spellbound, like a scavenger uncovering a wondrous artifact, he brushed aside a strand of hair from her face. She couldn't help noticing the crescent of grime under his fingernail.

"What are you doing here?" he asked.

Panic surged through every nerve in her body. She wanted to scream, to run. But her limbs, stiff as ice, wouldn't move. Beth turned her head to the man at the door. His eyes were locked on his hands, picking at the skin with his nails. He exhaled, long and loud.

"I'm heading outside, Tom. If you don't come, I'm taking off without you. You've got three minutes." Without a look back, he disappeared around the shack.

"Three minutes is more than enough." The hunter scraped his tongue across his teeth. "So you already know my name, sweetheart. It's only fair you tell me yours." His hand crept towards the inside of his jacket, slipped in, then yanked out a package of beef jerky.

Beth gasped, her stomach dropping like an anvil.

The hunter grinned, then popped a piece into his mouth. He chewed like people do when watching obscene acts on TV or the internet. Then he pulled out another. "I see you eyeing this," he teased. "Want some?"

Her stomach growling, Beth shook her head. She'd rather chew tree bark than eat anything this man had to offer.

Don't show fear. Don't give him anything.

"You got something against meat?" he pressed, holding out the jerky. "Go ahead."

The caterpillars crawled higher on his sweat-beaded forehead.

Boys get insulted and angry when you reject them. Men are no different.

Beth raised her arm, her hand quivering like gelatin in the wind.

"Wait." The hunter pulled back, clicking his tongue against his teeth. "If I give this to you, what do I get?"

You know what Mom used to say: don't be stupid. He doesn't care about money. He wants something else.

She cleared her throat, her voice thin and shaky. "I have...nothing to give."

The man flung his head back and howled, flashing yellow teeth and red gums. "Here you go, baby," he said, offering the piece. "For making me laugh. My gift to you."

Beth kept her eyes locked on his hand.

Smile, maybe? No. Too fake. Just stay still.

"Go ahead. Take it."

As she reached to pluck the meat from his grimy fingers, the hunter tightened his grip and stroked the back of her hand before letting her pull away.

He stared for a moment. The caterpillars rose again. "What do you say?"

We have less than three minutes. That's all. Then maybe he's gone. Play along.

"Thank you," Beth said, pulling off a piece with her back teeth. The meat was hard and stale. Still, it was the best thing she'd tasted in days. She had to stop herself from grinning like a fool.

The man pulled out another strip, flicking it into his mouth. "See? Good, huh?"

Beth nodded, managing a smile.

"So, you haven't answered my question. What's your name,

and what are you doing here? Waiting for me?"

She swallowed. "Erica. I'm just—I mean, I'm here camping."

"Erica," he said after a long silence.

"Y-Yes."

"That's a real pretty name, Erica."

"Thank you."

"So, camping, huh?"

She nodded.

Careful. Too eager looks guilty.

"You wouldn't be telling me a story, would you?"

The shack wall shook with a brutal thud. Beth's breath caught, a frightened squeal tearing from her throat.

The hunter kept his eyes locked on her face. "Christ's sake, Bill, I'll be out in a minute!" His expression softened. "Well?"

Beth didn't know if it was fear or tears blurring her senses, but his dark, bristly face began swimming before her eyes like water. The hat, an orange halo, hovering above his head.

Saint Tom. Patron saint of total creeps.

The hunter offered another piece of meat. Beth forced a smile before taking it. She popped it in her mouth, chewing slowly, stalling for time before swallowing. Her body heat rose, and she felt feverish. "N-No, it's true. I'm trying to earn a Girl Scout badge."

"Oh, a Girl Scout, huh?" He pulled back a few inches, looking around. "Where are the other girls? Where's your troop leader?"

Something hard pushed against the shack, quaking the walls.

Boots stomped past, kicking up debris. Then came snarls and heavy breathing.

"Damnit, Bill! I said in a minute!" The hunter sighed. "Don't mind him," he said.

Oh sure. Just ignore the other human bear having a meltdown outside. Cool, cool.

Beth offered a crisp nod.

The hunter drew closer, his thigh heavy against hers. Heat radiated through his clothes, the contact sending shocks through her limbs.

"You know," he said, his palm cupping her cheek. "I've seen you before." Callouses scraped her skin, and she tried not to wince. "I know I have," he added, his thumb tracing down to her lips.

Beth clamped her mouth shut, only then realizing she'd been holding her breath. "H-Huh?" she croaked.

Holy God, he's seen you on the news. He must have.

His face lit up, wide and shining. His breath came faster, sour and hot against her skin. Beth fought the urge to squeeze her eyes shut.

"I-I've done nothing. D-Don't hurt me..."

"There's no hurtin' happening here, baby." He leaned in, pushing her against the mattress, the stink of meat and alcohol assaulting her nose. His breath stirred the hair at her forehead, his face hardening. "But you have to be nice. Why don't you show me what you were doing earlier?"

Beth shoved at him with both arms, but it was like a squirrel trying to stop a bear. She didn't fully understand what boys did to girls, but TV and books had taught her one thing—it was never good.

A slice of memory hit her.

Mom and Dad have gone to bed.

She's watching a movie in the dim family room.

A young couple wrapped in white bedsheets.

The boy writhes on top of the girl like a dying fish.

She won't stop gasping. "It hurts," she croaks.

Sitting cross-legged on the floor, Beth turns to Chris on the couch and asks, "What's he doing?"

Exasperated, Chris says, "He's fucking her."

Beth shudders, mystified why a girl would allow such a thing. There didn't seem to be anything good or reverent about a body slamming into you.

The hunter crept on top of Beth, yanking her into the present. His weight crushed her lungs, making it hard to breathe. She knew what it must feel like to be buried alive.

"I watched you outside." He buried his face in her neck, sucking in air. "Smelled you too. You looked so good, baby."

Something hard pressed against her thigh.

Beth's mind disconnected.

Suffocating in a dark cabin with four vicious girls, wanting so much to be angry. But instead—hurt. Hating herself for feeling hurt.

Halfway across the room comes Alexis Johnson.

She pushes through the wooden door with her bushy brown hair and crystal-blue eyes, like a superhero without a cape.

She doesn't even glance at the other girls. Just marches straight to Beth, pulls her up from the cot, and leads her out into the cheery, blinding sunshine.

They run, hand in hand, stomping through ankle-high weeds, laughing like old-time friends. Forget about them, *she says.* They're just stupid. They don't know you.

Alexis Johnson. Angel. Beth's angel.

A chill pricked Beth's skin, snapping her from her reverie, forcing her back to the here and now. She found her hands pinned to the mattress. Something crawled beneath her shirt, hot breath trailing across her neck.

Footsteps thudded by the door.

This just got worse.

The hunter grunted. "For fuck's sake. Wait your—"

A dull thud shook the room, and he rocked against Beth's small frame, her breath catching in a wheeze before a cry broke free.

"What the fuck?!" He sprang off the bed and spun around.

Chris stood locked in a wide stance, teeth clenched, bracing a bloody bolt cutter in white-knuckled hands.

33

THE BOY

With a tight, leaky jaw and stony eyes, he snarled like a rabid dog.

Using the ball of his foot, he kicked the shotgun from the wall. It clattered to the floor and slid several feet towards the open door.

An eternity passed before anyone spoke.

Beth curled against the wall, trembling.

"Who the hell are *you*, you little shit?"

Chris held still. He gripped the bolt cutter like a baseball bat, waiting for his chance. His legs were jelly; his hands shook on the rubber handles. But his face stayed hard.

The hunter sneered. "Oh, I know," he said. "You—"

Chris struck. He drew the bolt cutter back and slammed the steel jaws into the man's face. The crunch sounded like a fist striking a walnut shell. The hunter reeled, crashing into the sink before collapsing to one knee.

"Chris, no!" cried Beth.

The hunter covered his crooked face, muttering through broken breath. "You're gonna pay for that, you little fuck."

"Leave," said Chris, unmoved. "Walk away. Forget about us."

The man staggered upright.

Beth gasped.

His left eye was sealed shut, bulging red and round like a golf ball. The blades had sliced open his cheek, and blood leaked down like red tears. He pressed the back of his hand to it, snarling. He took a step towards Chris. "You're dead, you little prick."

In one swift move, Chris yanked the pepper spray from his back pocket and unleashed a powerful stream into the hunter's face. The man coughed violently, stumbling backward. He dropped to the floor, writhing and heaving, drool and blood leaking from his mouth, tears streaming from his eyes.

He banged his head against the floor before hacking up a river of brown liquid. "You are so dead, you fuck!" He clawed at the air with his arms, thrashing his legs.

Chris couldn't stop himself from grinning. This pathetic excuse for a man reminded him of a helpless child crying out for attention.

"Oh my God!" shrieked Beth.

Chris, freed from the confines of his own body, became an animal locked in battle—pushed to attack, driven by a primal need to protect. He whipped his head to the right, the manic smile vanishing as fast as it appeared. "Beth, get out of here!"

Beth scrambled to her feet, sore leg forgotten, and ran blind until nearly colliding with a tree at the west edge of the clearing. She whipped around, breath caught in her throat.

Then she screamed.

O   O   O

Inside, Chris inhaled and stepped back from the body on the floor. Pepper spray fumes burned his lungs; puke stained the floor, foul and offensive. "You want some more or are we done?" he said, trying not to gag.

The hunter pressed both palms against his eyes, fighting to breathe. "We ain't done, *you fuck!*"

Chris shrugged and aimed the trigger, but Beth's cry pulled him away from the muzzle. He turned to the window and found her frozen against a tree, mouth open.

Then the hunter leapt up, striking him in the chest before crashing onto the hard floor. Chris' teeth rattled hard as pain shot up into his brain like a bullet. He lost his grip on the bolt cutter and pepper spray; both flew from his hands, rolling and sliding across the room.

"I don't need to see you to kill you, you little shit!" The hunter climbed on top, spitting drool and blood into his face like beads of burning acid. Chris fought to slip away, but his arms were pinned to his sides, trapped by the man's trunk-like legs.

The hunter hammered Chris' chest with savage fists. Cutting pain hacked through his ribs, spots exploding before his eyes like fireworks. Every hit slammed his lungs like a fastball. After a beating he thought would never end, the punches stopped. Fingers raked his face before dropping to his neck.

The hunter squeezed.

Chris twitched and thrashed beneath the hunter's weight, legs flailing but hitting only air. He was trapped, crushed, no match for the man. Dizziness hit hard, the world blurring and tipping sideways. Part of him refused to accept the moment was real. One last shake, then he'd wake on the loft, heart racing, Beth safe below.

"I told you not to fuck with me, didn't I?!"

Beth called from outside. "Chris! What's going on?"

"What's wrong?" the man sneered. "Can't breathe?"

As the smoke thinned, time seemed to stretch, sharpening every detail of the chaos before Chris. This was life-or-death combat, the kind he'd only seen on TV or heard men talk about. Nothing like the after-school scuffles in Aldian Park, where he'd stride away, leaving rivals battered and gasping in the dust. This was war: merciless, unbalanced. Here, his strength was useless. That truth stung deeper than the pain.

Through narrowed eyes, Chris saw the hunter's twisted face locked in a smug scowl. One tooth was missing; a jagged scar cut across his cheek.

This had to be retribution, the universe settling scores for every sin he'd racked up. Still, if this was how he would go down, he'd make sure to leave the world with one final act of defiance.

He spat. A heavy glob slapped the hunter's chin.

Footfalls landed by the door. Then a loud crunch.

"It's about time, asshole! Where the hell—?"

An explosion sliced through the crown of the hunter's head. His body flew several feet behind pieces of skull and brain, smacking the loft wall like eggshells and rotten tomatoes. The blast was deafening, vibrating the walls and floor.

Chris flipped onto his stomach, convulsing and gulping for air. A shrill ringing screamed in his ears and he curled up, coughing and dizzy. When his breathing finally slowed and the white flares at the edges of his vision faded, he lay still, mistrusting his pounding heart.

He pushed himself up, catching sight of Beth motionless on the cold slab just past the open door. Her knuckles whitened around the hunter's shotgun, eyes hollow and distant, fixed on something far beyond these walls.

Dumbfounded, Chris stayed on his knees, paralyzed. Red dots spattered the whites of his eyes like paint on a snowy orchid. His fingertips grazed his throat and he flinched. He inhaled small, controlled breaths, careful not to fan the fire in his throat and chest. Only then did he notice the wet warmth seeping down his leg.

The hunter lay crumbled against the wall, owning the look of a horror film victim. The bullet popped his hat across the room, exposing the missing chunk. Pasty bits of skull protruded through the top of what remained of his head; pieces spread across the planks behind him.

Shivering, Chris turned back to Beth. She stood rooted in place, a hollow, broken shell. Something in her vacant, unblinking stare pulled him back to their kitchen.

The afternoon hung heavy after school. Mom and Dad were out of the house, and he'd pushed her buttons one too many times. She'd slammed her pen onto the table, cheeks burning, and stormed at him, her gaze fierce and untamed. It was as if something had slipped into her body, hijacked her soul, warping her into someone un-recognizable. Chris once dreaded that wild look, but now, strangely, it comforted him. At least this time, her fury was not for him.

"Beth?" he croaked, taking an uneasy step forward.

She stood quiet, trembling.

"Beth?" He tried again, louder. In the impossible case the man was still alive, Chris braced himself before looking over his shoulder. The hunter's pants were unzipped, exposing a patch of white briefs. Chris snapped his attention back to Beth. "You can put that down now."

Still, she didn't move. He placed a hand on her shoulder, gently shaking it. "Hey."

Then her lips quivered. She turned to him, eyes softening, mouth relaxed. Recognition flickered in her gaze.

Chris took hold of the shotgun, easing it down until the barrel pointed at the floor. She let go, dropping the weapon into his hands.

"It's okay. We're okay now."

Of course, he didn't believe it. But what else could he say?

34

THE GIRL

THE GIRL

"C'mon, help me with him!"

Her shoulder throbbed. She stood trembling, standing on concrete, confused until realizing the recoil had shoved her out the door.

She focused on a patch of ground where the wood dipped, inches from the hunter's shoe. It was all she could do to keep from collapsing. Still, everything moved as if underwater. The room tilted, and she braced herself against the door. Her ears rang, smoke in the air. Slowly, she understood what had happened.

Since hearing the hunter's cries, everything shifted fast and slow at once. Knowing something was wrong, Beth's feet slid beneath her, as if on a high-speed conveyor belt. Her footfalls were silent; she couldn't feel her feet touching the ground.

A shotgun leaned against the wall, like the ones she and Chris used to play with. Only this one was heavier.

Cold.

All Beth wanted was to scare the man away. But seeing the life drain from her brother's pale face—those terrified eyes bulging like a bug doused in repellent—triggered a rage she hadn't expected.

She found herself aiming the barrel at the hunter's chest. He'd shouted something and looked up, startling her. Their eyes locked for a fraction of a second, and she saw that grimace before panic and instinct took over and pushed her to pull the trigger. She was shocked the shotgun had even fired.

When she snapped out of her trance, Chris insisted they dump the bodies. The humidity would speed up the decay, and inhaling the stench of rotting meat, along with attracting starved animals, were problems neither of them had the resolve to face. It needed to happen. No time for regret or distress.

Chris peeked his head around the shack. "C'mon, we gotta get moving."

Her eyes glazed, distant, Beth closed the door behind her.

She found Chris squatting over a body, slumped against the shack wall. His knapsack lay open at his feet, and he was pulling long strips of gray duct tape, tearing them off with his teeth. A four-inch gash ran across the man's brow above his left eye, sealed shut and blackened like fresh charcoal. Half his face was wet with blood; his thin lips slightly parted, revealing two crushed pink teeth.

Chris stuck strips of tape to the splintered wall, then rifled through the man's pockets. Loose change, a pack of gum, a round tobacco tin. He unbuckled a leather sheath from the man's waist and pulled out an eight-inch steel skinner. The blade formed an isosceles triangle, like a miniature sword, with "Hand Made" etched on the polished silver. Chris smirked, watching it glimmer in the pale sunlight. "Better than my penknife."

He picked up a green canteen and shook it. Something swooshed inside. He unscrewed the cap and took a swig.

Beth watched, fascinated.

Like a shot, he spat it against the wall. Brown liquid sprayed his face and the body on the ground. "Ugh!" He shivered, tongue flicking.

"What is it?"

"It wasn't water."

"Huh?"

"Booze," he said, sniffing the ring. "Smells like whiskey."

Beth nodded, mouthing, Oh.

It surprised Beth to see Chris snickering as he wiped his mouth with his arm, recapping the canteen.

"You're going to keep it?"

"Hell, yes. It holds about the same as one of those plastic

bottles. And it's strong."

Beth opened her mouth but said nothing. She wasn't talking about the canteen. She hated to admit it, but Chris' cavalier attitude sickened her, almost like he'd done this before. "You killed him, and now you're taking his things?"

Chris pulled out a stick of gum, shook his head, and popped the strip into his mouth. "I'm brave, Beth. I do what has to be done," he said. "Now grab his legs. I wanna tie them together."

Beth blinked, her gaze shifting to the body. "Why?"

Chris exhaled, his eyes on the man's face. "It'll make it easier to carry him to the hole. That's why. Now come on."

Beth stared at her brother. "A hole? You serious?"

"What the hell else do you expect me to do?" he snapped. "Drag him inside so you can cuddle him?"

Oh, he didn't just say that!

The remark struck Beth's gut like a cannonball. She nearly collapsed, her eyes stinging with tears. Ashamed, she turned and crouched, pretending a pebble was stuck in her sneaker. She pulled it off, slapped it against her palm, and shook out the dirt. Once her tears dried, she took a breath, whipped around, and gripped the man's ankles, pressing them together.

Chris grabbed the tape, wrapping it around the calves, knees, and thighs. The whole process took less than a minute. "Ready?"

"But what about...?" She looked at the shack.

"We'll come back for him later. After we get rid of this guy." Then he insisted Beth secure the legs while he hoisted the body under his arms.

Behind the shed, a narrow path ran a hundred feet north to the hole. The body slipped from their hands several times. By the time they arrived, they were both soaked in sweat, swallowing mouthfuls of air. They dropped the body like a sack of rocks. All regard for the deceased had vanished along the way.

Several decaying planks lay over the hole, the edges framed by red bricks about a foot high, giving the appearance of a crude well. But no ladder. No bucket.

Exhausted, Beth collapsed to the ground, catching her breath as Chris knelt in front of the bricks and carefully set aside the planks. When he finished, he turned, wiped his sweaty face with the cuff of his shirt, and rested his hands on his thighs. He looked at Beth. "You ready?"

Okay, this is it. If you do this, there's no going for help. No turning back.

Beth swallowed hard and nodded.

"Wait a sec," Chris said, picking up a rock.

He peered over the bricks and dropped the stone. Five long seconds passed before it clacked twice in the darkness. He looked at Beth and shrugged.

They rolled the body over the bricks until its legs hung over the edge. They locked eyes for a long, hard moment before pushing the rest over, quickly shrinking back as it sank into the black void.

Endless seconds later, the body slammed against the ground, the crunch cracking through the silence.

THE BOY

With rubbery limbs, the twins trudged back to the shack, sneakers crunching over dead branches and needles. Neither had looked at the other or cleared a throat since leaving the hole.

The air stood frigid, but sweat soaked Chris' skin. Dusky clouds swelled overhead, thick with the threat of rain.

He knew the hunter hadn't been Beth's first kill. The moment the body hit the bottom of the well, a chilling thought crept in—a giant black scoreboard lit with yellow-shining bulbs, reading:

Chris: 2
Beth: 2

Thinking of the driver in the ravine, blood soaking his thigh, clutching the Islanders jacket, still made Chris' hackles rise.

He replayed the battle in his head, from spotting the strange man kicking up dirt to landing the final blow with the bolt cutter. The man's constant fidgeting with his hands and jacket had told Chris everything—he'd been waiting for someone. Someone inside the shack.

No one could deny his stealth. With no chance of reaching the shack undetected, Chris had no choice but to launch a full-out sprint attack. He'd waited for the breeze to stir the leaves before slipping behind the thick trees at the clearing's edge. The man either wasn't paying attention or mistook the movement for a small animal.

A moment too soon, the man spun around, his shoulders sagging when he saw it was just a kid. That split-second gave Chris the opening he needed to strike. Beth didn't know his goal wasn't to kill the man, but to knock him out cold.

He'd planned to use the revolver to scare the man off, but a rifle would have made that useless. Instead, he'd circled the north side of the clearing, crept up from behind the shed. After three wide steps, he jumped out, whacking the bolt cutter into the back of the man's head. Clumsy, but effective.

The man cried out, stumbling away from the shack. Chris seized the moment and peered through the window. Branches he'd placed to block out the cold and rain jutted outside. Through the mud-smeared glass, he saw a larger man on the mattress, leaning towards his sister. Beth sat frozen, pressed against the wall.

The injured man had shouted for his friend, then slammed the butt of his rifle into Chris' ribs. The hit caught Chris off guard, like when a football rival tackled him to the ground, snapping his collarbone.

Winded, he dropped to one knee, buying a few seconds to recover. Mud-caked boots crept into his peripherals. A surge of survival instinct and the desperate need to protect Beth rushed through his veins as he tightened his grip on the bolt cutter, pushed himself up, and swung the final blow across the man's head. A muffled cry escaped his throat as steel cracked against the man's skull.

Bent over, he released the weapon and hugged his side, teeth clenched. The blow had rattled his guts, and it took everything he had to avoid howling in pain.

He'd considered taking the man's rifle before going inside but decided against it. Too noisy. Instead, he stuck with the bolt cutter. With his back pressed against the siding, he turned the corner and slipped inside.

○   ○   ○

The twins geared up to move the second body. Chris suggested taking the hunter's jacket and socks for warmth.

"Heck no," Beth frowned.

"He tried to kill us. We may as well take something from that asshole."

"Fine," she said. "But I'm not wearing them. You take them."

Chris pulled off the jacket and socks, spotting a red and black deer skull tattoo on the hunter's right forearm. He bunched them up into a ball on the loft. He never planned to wear them, but if Beth refused, the coat could at least serve as a decent pillow. He caught sight of the orange hat across the room and slapped it onto the man's head, covering the bleeding wound.

Because of the body's weight and the twins' waning strength, moving it took twice the effort. Chris half expected a satisfying crack when the bones hit the well floor, but the sound fizzled out. Instead, he smirked as the body bounced and scraped against the stone walls, thudding into place with a hollow, sickening sound.

With Beth hustling inside to dodge the first of the rain, Chris grabbed the fish he'd left on a boulder after finding the stranger and dropped them into the creel under the sink. He planned to cook them once the rain let up.

He went back for his knapsack. Fat drops tapped his head, and as he threw the bag over one shoulder. He sighed and stepped inside, the weight of everything settling on him.

Beth watched as he placed the shotgun and rifle in the corner behind the table and chair. He arranged the canteen, knife, and tobacco on the mattress.

He reached for the sheath, ready to feel its weight settle against his hip, then stopped himself. He figured he'd wait for Beth to offer suggestions on what to do with the items. This way, he could ease the pressure of being the only one making decisions and taking charge.

Neither had spoken since dropping the second body down the hole. The shack now held a cryptic mix of light and shadow, the silence pressing down, heavier than before. He could feel a shift in the air. It was darker, denser, full of fear, tasting like rotting flowers and sawdust, with the stench of gunpowder hanging thick.

Chris shook his head, unwilling to replay the events any longer. He dragged himself to the window, gazing through the branches. A breeze slipped through the cracks, brushing against the leaves and scraping the glass. He tilted his head up to the patchwork, a smile tugging at his lips. Because of him, they'd stay dry tonight.

Yet a storm of conflict churned inside him. He tried to stoke his anger, but after failing to stop the man from nearly killing him, that fury twisted back on itself, gnawing at him. Grief seemed like a reasonable path, but Beth had already claimed that territory. He even attempted to shrug it all off, pretending the two deaths mattered as little as tossing pebbles at birds.

But nothing worked. Oddly enough, Chris felt hollow.

He let his vision blur through the leaves, glass, and rain, wondering where Blake had gone. "Miss ya, buddy," he whispered.

He imagined the rain as nature's way of christening the land and the cabin. It felt like a quiet pardon, their sins washing away like debris carried down a roadside in a hard, cleansing storm.

He hadn't realized he was rubbing his throat with his finger. He looked over his shoulder to find Beth facing the wall, curled up in a ball with her back to him.

He lifted his shirt to check the damage, cringing. A dozen bruises marked his chest—dark purples and yellows with streaks of red, blending together like some unsightly patchwork quilt. The men were gone, but crude reminders of their existence remained.

Then he thought of Dad and knew he'd be proud of his son for protecting his sister. The thought offered relief.

After changing into dry pants, Chris grabbed the cleansing spray and rag from under the sink and wiped the gore off the wall and floor as best he could. He refused to waste paper towels on that asshole's brains.

He washed his hands, then eased down to the floor. His eyes landed on the package of beef jerky, remembering the berries he'd taken from the trees. He leaped up and grabbed his knapsack, breaking the silence. "You hungry?"

No reaction.

"Thirsty?"

He knew Beth well enough to know she was awake. Sleep for her wasn't rest; it was a struggle, like preparing for battle.

"I've got water but need to sanitize it," he said. "I'd use the pot to catch rain, but I don't want you getting sick. Besides, we should stay inside tonight. We don't know who could have heard..."

She shifted on the bed. Then silence.

"Oh! I caught some fish today. I'll cook it later. And I found berries! They should be—"

"I ate a raw fish."

Did she say, I hate raw fish?

"I'll *cook* it." A long pause as Chris leaned in. "You okay?"

"I never..."

"There's also some jerky—"

"—I never thought I'd be a criminal."

A paralyzing sadness filled her voice, and Chris' chest felt heavier than when it had been pounded with fists. Ordinarily, he would've insisted Beth toughen up, told her the men got what they deserved, then shifted the focus to their next meal.

But these weren't ordinary times. Things were different now.

He grabbed another stick of gum and unwrapped it. Sighing, he said, "Me neither."

He felt an urge to crawl onto the bed and lie beside her.

Back in New York, when Mom and Dad went out and Dena,

the fun babysitter, stayed with them, Beth would pad down the hall to his room and slip under his covers. She said it felt like entering another world. A darker one, with wood walls and royal blue carpet, action figures and baseball cards scattered like crumbs.

And Chris' room had the family fish tank. Everyone had picked a fish as their own. But Beth liked watching them all float among the pink stones and bright rocks, listening to the soothing sound of the bubbling filter.

Lying side by side, they'd amuse themselves by reenacting movie scenes and games with their hands against the shadowed walls. Chris never minded when Beth drifted off beside him. Dad always carried her back to her room anyway.

Now, the thought of lying that close felt wrong. They were no longer children. Besides, Chris lacked the capacity to comfort her.

Beth curled tighter, arms wrapped around herself.

He took the hint.

Sometimes girls needed to be left alone.

35

THE BOY

THE BOY

He didn't touch the berries or the jerky. Eating felt wrong. For the first time, it felt like a betrayal after what almost happened to Beth. Even if she told him to eat, he'd refuse.

The sun had risen, but gray light filled the room. He pressed his forehead against the rain-specked window. The rain picked up, steady and relentless. Droplets streaked down the glass, drawing patterns across his face.

He was exhausted but couldn't sleep. Two bodies lay a hundred yards away, and that fact alone made shutting down impossible. Every rustle in the brush, every owl's call just outside the cabin, made his grip tighten on the revolver.

Despite his heavy eyelids, a strange alertness kept him awake through the night. He sat on the unforgiving floor, reliving legendary sports moments in his mind, picturing what Erica might have worn that day, quietly humming the tunes he missed from his old stereo. He clung to these distractions, desperate to keep his thoughts from spiraling. The urge to switch on the radio and let music drown out the darkness tugged at him, but he resisted. Beth needed her rest.

A voice whispered behind him. "I'm hungry. Really hungry."

THE GIRL

THE GIRL

She had never known deprivation like this. She couldn't tell which aches came from dragging the bodies and which from hunger.

She was exhausted but barely slept. That bloody grimace refused to fade from beneath her eyelids. Even in dreams, the hunter lay on top of her, snarling: *You will never forget this. I was someone's son. I was someone's brother. I was someone's father.*

Then her survival voice cut in. *To hell with those men. They got what they deserved. You know Chris agrees.*

"I don't know," mused Beth. "I don't know anything anymore."

Chris turned. "What?"

With her eyes still shut, Beth sighed. Opening them meant she was alive and forced to face another miserable day in the woods. All she wanted was to disappear. But sometime during the longest night of her life, she'd resigned to stay alive. Like anyone else, she let instinct take over and dictate survival. It didn't matter that she didn't deserve to live. It didn't matter what her heart wanted. Her body ignored her pleas and refused to give in or starve.

What you're facing beats a detention center or orphanage. If you deserve punishment, staying alive is the perfect penalty. Death solves nothing. It's cheating, the easy way out, a dream.

Beth had to agree. If she couldn't face a new day for herself or Chris, she'd do it as penance. "Still have the fish?"

"Uh, yeah. Why?"

"Get one."

"Beth...I can't cook them yet. I need—"

"Just get one."

Chris sealed his lips, swallowing a retort. He grabbed a fish from the creel and held it out. It smelled like the sea, slimy against his fingers. "Okay, here it is."

Beth still hadn't moved. "Do you have your knife?"

"Why?"

"Please just get it, Chris," she said.

After stalling for a minute, he pulled out his penknife and snapped it open. The clicking sound drove her to open her eyes. She sat up and shifted to the edge of the mattress, groaning. Dark purple crescents spread beneath her eyes, her small lips colorless. "You'll probably want a paper towel," she said.

Chris handed over the roll. After several private trips behind trees and bushes, only an inch remained.

Beth tore off a couple of pieces and set them on the floor. Without looking up, she waved for the fish. Chris handed it over, and she plopped it on the paper towels, slicing it open as she did by the river. After scooping out the slippery guts, she yanked out the bone and cut the fish into three pieces, separating the head, body, and tail.

She picked up the head—eyes and all—sighed, closed her eyes, and dropped it into her mouth. The chunk hit her tongue like a weight. She avoided chewing more than necessary for fear of puking. This one was greasier than the first and slipped down her throat in stubborn lumps. Chunks of clay doused in oil.

Stunned, Chris watched her. "Where'd you learn that?"

She kept her eyes locked on the pink fish guts on the wet paper towel and shrugged.

Chris pulled out a piece of gum. "Here. To kill the taste."

Beth shook her head. She needed to taste it. Only a deserved punishment would do. But she needed a drink, something to chase down breakfast. Otherwise, a pair of eyes were sure to crawl up her throat. "Where's that canteen?"

Chris raised an eyebrow. "Canteen? But, it has—"

Beth raised her head, meeting her brother's gaze. Her eyes hardened.

Nodding, he pointed behind her.

Without bothering to smell it, Beth swigged a mouthful and swallowed. Fiery and robust, it poured down her throat like fuel. Her face pinched, followed by a shiver and a coughing fit. Wet and dark, her stomach was a swamp, but no longer empty.

Chris puffed out a long breath and winced. "You okay?"

She handed him the canteen and crawled over to her spot on the mattress. She leaned against the wall, frowning. Her mind swam, and the cramps began to fade. "What about you?" she asked.

Chris had tried alcohol once. Beth saw Dad offer him a few sips of beer last New Year's Eve, and judging by how his face puckered, Chris hated it.

Shrugging, he took a swig. The pointed look on his face failed to hide the effort it took to avoid coughing. He took another drink; this one made his eyes water. Pressing his hand to his mouth, he fought to keep a straight face.

Beth sensed the nausea burning his throat. Smirking, she signaled for him to hand back the bourbon.

○   ○   ○

They passed the canteen through the morning into the afternoon, the burn and crude flavor of the bourbon growing oddly bearable with each sip.

Soon their stomachs spoke up, and they tore into jerky and berries. The meat snapped with salt and smoke, lighting up their tongues like struck matches. Hunger honed their mouths into instruments, catching every edge of flavor. Beth, teeth and fingertips stained purple, thought she'd finally outpaced her brother before realizing the berries had been his plan all along.

The alcohol left her dizzy. She took pleasure in how it liberated her mind and body, and it eased the tension in the room.

Over time, Chris grew oddly focused. Surges of raw emotion weighed on him, and he wore the look of someone being suffocated. Then he excused himself and stepped outside. The rain fell in sheets.

A minute later, just as she stole another sip, Chris returned, hair stuck to his forehead like furry stalactites and shirt glued to his chest. He snatched the canteen from her hands, capping it.

"Hey! What was that for?"

He set the half-empty canteen in the corner. Shivering, he slipped to the floor across from the mattress.

"Well?"

He shot Beth a look. "You've had enough."

"Oh? And how 'bout you!"

"You see me having any more?" he said. "Now take it easy."

She gave up and shrugged it off.

Her beaten expression drove Chris to offer another piece of

gum. She crawled to the edge of the mattress, plucked it from his fingers, and popped it into her mouth. Then she sprawled onto her back, staring at the ceiling. The peppermint soothed her throat, even scraped some of the sandy grit from her teeth.

Time passed in silence.

She rolled onto her side and propped her head up with one hand, her neck limp as a jellyfish. Her mind, murky and leaden like the sky outside, spun back to the last few days—and she laughed.

Chris echoed her amusement. "What's so funny?"

Her laughter sharpened into a cackle. Overwhelmed with emotion, she slapped a hand over her mouth, but it was useless. She laughed about Mom and Dad's death. The burglary. The hunter's broken head. Chris' confusion. The whole thing.

Chris snickered, resting his forearms on his knees. He dropped his head, staring at the floor.

"I just…I…I can't—"

The corners of his mouth pulled tight. "Just say it."

Beth popped up, grinning. "I can't believe I blew that sucker's head off!"

Chris shook his head, and like an old-school Etch A Sketch, the smile erased. "That's not funny, Beth."

She blew a raspberry and threw her arms up. "Whatever! I just did what I had to do."

"Yeah. And you scared the shit out of me."

"Yeah?" Beth held her breath, eyes wide like a tarsier's. "Scared the shit outta me, too," she added.

The wind whistled through cracks in the ceiling and walls as the door gave a long, low groan. The shadows and rain swallowed any chance of detecting visitors, and neither of them dared to check.

A sharp breath cut the silence as Beth spotted Chris's hand drifting towards something near the sink—a revolver.

Images rose in her mind: two dead men swaying in the downpour, black sludge clinging to limbs, gore leaking from open mouths.

"Chris! Is that real? It can't be real! Where did you get that?"

THE BOY
THE BOY

After a minute, he sensed the emptiness outside. He turned to Beth, tracing the line of her stare. The weapon in his hands felt foreign and familiar all at once, its chill biting into his skin. It was no toy, but something that had fused with him, like the old Wilson glove he once broke in under summer skies.

He thumbed the cylinder, voice low. "Beth, why did you throw that man's body down the cliff?"

Beth's eyes found her way back to his face. Her mouth dropped open like a spring snapping in a machine. "Huh?"

"You don't remember?"

"Remember what?"

After stalling for what felt like hours, he told her everything. Finding her in the sedan, the dead officer at the bottom of the ravine. Then he upended his backpack of everything he'd taken from the man's duty bag.

But he didn't mention shooting the young officer by the road. That was his secret.

A long pause settled between them as Chris studied his sister.

She shook her head as if denial could undo the story.

He looked at the revolver. "And I found this with you."

THE GIRL
THE GIRL

"Oh my God." She froze, staring at the weapon.

"After what happened, I wanted to tell you what I knew."

The story sounded unreal. But the longer Chris spoke, the more fragments of her broken memory surfaced. She wasn't going mad; she was remembering what she'd lost.

Beth retraced her recent memories, each one flickering past like a scratchy film, out of sequence and full of static, just like the movies Mom watched from her favorite spot on the couch. The man was not a predator after all, but a police officer. Still, questions hovered in the air.

"It's been on the news," said Chris. "And not just when we broke into the house. Everything. But they haven't found the officer yet. I tried to cover him up."

The world melted into a watery haze, Beth's vision clouded by tears that clung stubbornly to her lashes. Guilt gnawed at her for the two deaths, and resentment simmered towards her brother for burying the truth. She seethed at her parents for leaving, cursed the hunters, and raged silently at God.

She hung her head, eyes tracing the fissures in the floor, half-hoping one would open up and swallow her whole, just as she had with the fish.

Warmth draped over her shoulders, and she melted into it. Boneless and spent, she folded into her brother, burying her face into his chest, grieving the two lives she'd taken.

Chris looked away and shut his eyes. "You're gonna have to tell me what happened."

"What have I done?"

"We're in this together. But we need to get our story straight."

She pulled back. Through glassy eyes she saw a crystallized image of Chris' reddened, wet face. "Chris," she said softly. "Why did Mom and Dad like you more?"

Chris blinked hard, eyes lifting to the ceiling. Then he pulled her gently back against his chest.

A sniff. "I mean…why did Mom and Dad have to die? Did they hate me that much?"

36

THE DEPARTMENT
THE DEPARTMENT

Once the lab results returned, there was no question which suspects were tied to Deputy Powell's death and Detective Bennett's disappearance. The department had the twins' fingerprints from a "Get to Know Your Local Police" event at Wanapatchee Elementary. They matched the prints found at the Alperstein house, the squad car, and Bennett's sedan.

After the mayor's solemn opening speech, a disconcerted Captain Ramsey took the podium before a crowd of eager reporters to provide an update on the case.

"Good evening and welcome to Wanapatchee police headquarters. I'm Captain Ramsey, chief inspector and captain for the city of Wanapatchee. The police service has received an enormous number of media requests. Before I begin, I want to highlight a few things. Media reports have speculated on why we've been keeping details quiet in this case. Please understand that whenever an officer or department faces a traumatic event, Wanapatchee Police Service must first launch a debriefing and after-care program.

"I want to thank those cooperating with the investigation and commend everyone involved for their attention to detail. They have worked and will continue to work on this case for the foreseeable future. Detective Warsoff, Detective Sanders, Officer Castaneda, Deputy Reid, and I have all been working tirelessly on what, for some of us, is the most perplexing and disturbing case we've seen in our careers."

The captain paused, then sighed.

"It has been a trying case, and I want to thank all emergency personnel for their courage and determination in keeping our city safe. I also want to thank the county, Judge Ramirez, the FBI, and the governor. Your support and prayers mean a great deal to us. Thank you.

"Much has occurred these last several days. I will now offer a synopsis of our report."

Looking down at the papers, the captain pinched the bridge of his nose, signaling a firm headache.

"Police received a call from a community member after a body was found in an abandoned cruiser at Wanapatchee Plaza on Melbourne Road. We responded immediately. Upon arrival, Detective Warsoff and I identified the officer as Deputy David Powell. He was pronounced dead at the scene from a fatal gunshot wound to the chest.

"The suspects, known for a break-in at a local residence, are Chris and Beth Pacelli, twelve-year-old siblings. They were recent victims of a house fire on Schicara Drive four days ago, which resulted in the deaths of Alessandro and Rosa Pacelli. These children clearly have emotional trauma, and we will do what we can to detain them and get them help.

"Deputy Powell, who had been on the force a short time, had an encounter with the children that ended in the fatal gunshot. After hours of interviews, investigation, and evidence gathering, we have probable cause to pursue the children and have obtained the applicable warrants. Please keep in mind they are wanted only for questioning.

"The second vehicle involved was found on Ditchburn Street and identified as belonging to former officer and member of this city's district, Jack Bennett. We have been unable to locate Mr. Bennett and are working around the clock. We are also piecing together how these two incidents relate. We urge you to keep Mr. Bennett in your prayers. We certainly will."

The captain looked up, shifting his weight. A tear, caught in the light, glistened in his eye.

"Most officers here are parents and struggle to comprehend what has happened. We are hurting. Our profession is hurting. We are heartbroken. Our concern is the safety of Wanapatchee and its officers. We will carry on with this case with precision and care.

"I will remind you all that this investigation is ongoing and will be for some time. Many questions remain unanswered. I ask for your understanding and patience. We need the full facts, not just pieces.

"Our thoughts and prayers are with the officers and their families. To the victims' families: this is a tragic incident, and the police department is here for you. I will now open the floor to a few questions."

THE BOY

He sprawled across the loft floor, the dynamo-powered radio teetering on his queasy stomach. The buzz faded, replaced by a desert-dry mouth and pulsing headache. The aspirin still hadn't kicked in. Chris had made sure Beth swallowed a couple before she collapsed, face-first, onto the mattress.

He switched off the radio and sat in silence, thinking.

These children have emotional trauma, and we will do what we can to detain them and get them help.

He scoffed.

What did they know about emotional trauma? How could they presume who he was, what he was going through, or how he felt? He was fine. He knew where he was and what was happening. He understood the consequences.

Chris had left the rest of Beth's fish wrapped in paper towels inside the creel. The fish reeked, thick and sour, permeating the space with the smell of a dying sea. It would be hours before the meat turned, but he couldn't stand the stench and saw no world where he'd chomp down on raw flesh and skin.

Heart sinking, he eased down the ladder, stepped outside, and pitched the fish into the brush. He pulled the metal bucket from under the sink. Rainwater may not have been safe, but they had no choice.

SANDERS

Crammed between Warsoff and the captain, mindful of preserving a fixed expression, the detective resisted the urge to fidget. He knew better than to reveal his thoughts. Sanders had a hell of a poker face.

Funny how the captain left out the part about Bennett's blood smeared all over the sedan. Probably to spare the town from further alarm. The calls and letters flooding the station said enough. People were rattled.

But they had a macabre fascination with gore. They embraced fear. That was why they paid good money to get scared in movie theaters and haunted houses, and never failed to brake before car wrecks. The bloodier the accident, the greater the interest.

For a moment, Sanders' mind drifted to Bennett. After his retirement, and with both sons having moved out and raising families of their own, the former detective and his wife decided it was time to downsize and embrace a change of scenery. They both loved New Jersey, and Rookwood offered something different.

Bennett often vented about his marriage to fellow officers, like how his wife hounded him about losing weight. *No man could swallow bitter smoothies and leafy greens every single day*, he'd say. It wasn't long before she eased up on pushing the plant foods altogether.

Sanders imagined Bennett returning to his new place in Rookwood after firing rounds at the range, eager to slap ribeyes on his backyard grill. It was no surprise that when Bennett spotted the kids by the roadside, he didn't hesitate to stop and offer help.

Before bothering with the captain's speech, Sanders ticked through a mental list of what he needed to clean up the mess. He shifted focus when the captain spoke about the department hurting and supporting the victims' families. Sanders could hardly argue with that. He'd seen too many officers hurt or killed in the line of duty, enough blood and funerals to know better.

Once, it worried him. Now, it just made him sick of the whole damn thing. And venomous, stripped down to spite.

The detective stiffened at the mention of the Pacelli twins.

What a load of bullshit.

They didn't need help; they needed punishment. Kids were stupid, but some were sly—colder and more calculating than adults wanted to believe. At twelve, they'd already burglarized a home and killed a cop in cold blood. Now another retired officer was missing. And that was just what the department uncovered.

The girl's prints and hair were all over Bennett's sedan. Same with the boy and Powell's squad car. No question the twins were guilty. Sanders wondered if they even played a part in the house fire. It wouldn't surprise him if they were listening to the broadcast, giggling their asses off.

Frustrated, he needed time and space to strafe the attack. Just as he weighed his grocery list while that shrink jawed on about nothing important, he raced through excuses to dodge the junk assignments piling on his desk. Patience wasn't one of Sanders' strong suits.

But for now, the detective had to bite his tongue and play the compliant cop.

37

THE GIRL

Thin rays of light poured in through the window. Speckles of dust danced in the sunbeams distorted by branches scraping against the glass. Birds chirped from the trees.

Their delight rankled Beth, serving as a cruel soundtrack to her confinement just yards away.

Despite a long night of sleep and promise of a new day, she felt horrible—nauseous, exhausted, a fowl taste coating her mouth. The slightest movement triggered a spike of pain. Her head hung on her shoulders like a cannonball. She imagined the hunter shrunken to the size of a pinky finger, blasting the walls of her skull with his shotgun.

Her tongue felt like a slug baking under the desert sun. Staring at the ceiling, she winced, recalling a tall man with sharp blue eyes and a bizarre mustache stuffing braided cotton slabs into her cheeks. In her old life, Beth feared the dentist. Now, she'd gladly trade a few teeth for a cleaning.

From the corner of her eye, she spotted a travel mug, two aspirin, and some berries beside the mattress. She picked up the pills and set them on her tongue. After sniffing the liquid, she took one eager swig of water.

Beth peered down at a dozen reddish-blue beach plums and smiled. For a moment, she forgot about her swollen head and turned towards the loft, cringing in pain. Chris slept, a soft, careless expression marking his face. He squeezed the Yankees cap in the crook of his arm, his left leg dangling over the side from the knee.

"Thank you, Chris." She popped the plum in her mouth. Her

teeth attacked the fruit, bursting it open and squirting a string of juice across her lips. Once all the pits were sucked dry, she eased back on the mattress and listened to the birds singing outside.

Her mind drifted back to yesterday, forming a pit in her stomach stiffer and a million times larger than the ones in the fruit. Then she remembered the fish and fought to contain her excitement about eating a fresh, beautifully cooked meal.

A thought crossed her mind: if any other boy in school had been her brother, she'd be dead by now.

Beth made a silent, steadfast promise: stand by Chris. No matter what.

THE BOY

THE BOY

By the time he woke, it was already late afternoon.

His stomach churned, and his head felt twice as large as it had the night before.

He crawled down the ladder and stretched, cursing the decision to start the fire at first light. Ordinarily, he wouldn't have been so careless, but the alcohol had driven him to it. It was a miracle he'd even managed to find dry wood.

"Wait!" called Beth as he slid his arms through the straps of his pack.

Tired and hungry, Chris turned to find her standing in the open doorway, watching him.

He stood in a patch of light, hat crooked over one eye, casting a shadow that stretched across the floor.

He widened his eyes and shrugged, his face blank and dark. "Listen," he said. "I've got to head out before we lose more daylight. I won't be long, okay?"

Beth nodded.

He marched to the open door, narrowing his eyes. "If you hear or see anything funny, you have the shotgun, okay?"

His words hung in the air for a moment.

"Okay, Chris."

He exhaled hard. He knew she wouldn't touch the shotgun again. He grabbed the blade at his hip. "Hold on to this instead. And be careful. Don't do anything stupid."

She might have mumbled something else, but he had already spun around and vanished into the forest, haunted by the cold imprint of her written words lingering in his mind.

Why did girls have to be so cruel?

THE GIRL

"Thank you, Chris. Please be careful." As he walked off, loneliness returned, triggering a rolling stomach and racing pulse.

But when her fingers grazed the warm leather, she calmed. The touch assured her that, even with Chris gone, she could hold herself together. Everything would be okay.

Seeing how he carried himself—head hanging low, feet weighted—unsettled Beth. When Chris plodded up to her, she spotted the marks across his neck and sighed. He had done enough; today it was her turn to pick up the supplies. And it would offer a chance to be outside that dark, horrible hut.

But before she could insist, Chris stopped her, proffering the knife.

"…and be careful. Don't do anything stupid."

After he vanished into the brush, Beth slogged over to the mattress, wrapped herself in the tattered blanket, and tried to write. She needed to get everything down on paper. It was either that or scrawl along the walls in a manic frenzy—anything to keep from going mad.

People are dead, and it was all my fault.

She filled line after line in a frantic rush until her hand seized up, muscles slackening as the pen slipped from her fingers.

A hiccup. "Mom…?"

Tears poured in waves, her sobs raw and ragged, like a mother cradling her dead child. Consumed by grief, Beth sat unaware as silent figures gathered at the threshold, watching her.

Part 2

Part 2

Children begin by loving their parents.
After a time, they judge them.
Rarely, if ever, do they forgive them.

-Oscar Wilde, (1854-1900)

A kid came up to me now just the other day
and asked me if I'd thought about what I would say.
If everything came crashing down on top of me,
how would I stay pure?

-"Represent," The Red Jumpsuit Apparatus

38

August, 6 years ago...

SANDERS
SANDERS

He peered through the crack of the open door, straining to hear the child's cries over a booming television. When the owner finally released the chain, Sanders—brushing off Reid's objections—pushed his way inside.

It was a late night, and the Wanapatchee officers did the city of Hollis a favor by responding to a domestic disturbance call.

The single-floor house was small and dim, choked with months of grime. Clear plastic cups, overflowing with cigarette butts and stale beer, cluttered every surface. The stench clung to the air like puke in a sealed car. Sour, thick, and inescapable.

A woman lay unconscious on a tattered couch, a needle drooping from her arm like a sloping flag. The man, lanky, over six feet, wore frayed jeans but no shirt or shoes. Blacks tufts of hair fell into his eyes as he darted around the room, bruises and red welts bright across his chest.

As Sanders stormed inside, Reid inching in behind him, the man grabbed his six-year-old son and yanked him close, using the boy like a shield. His movements were jerky, eyes wide and glassy. Clearly under methamphetamines, he was frantic, fearless, and didn't blink at Sanders' size.

Reid cut in, making several futile pleas for the man to release the child.

"Fuck you! No one's called you! You have no right to be here!" the man snarled.

Furious, drained of what tolerance remained that week, Sanders ripped the screaming boy from the man's sweaty grip, shoving him into Reid's arms. Using the grip of his Glock, he slammed the man across the nose, breaking it in two places.

Courtesy of Reid's loose tongue, that swing earned Sanders another six months behind a desk.

But Sanders offered zero pushback. He'd planned to coast through the next eight years—handle the cut-and-dry cases and paperwork by day, drink with Roger at Lion's Lair by night, then collect his pension when it was all over.

O   O   O

He slapped the green folder on his kitchen table and pulled a whiskey and beer from the fridge.

He dropped down on the beige, threadbare couch with a sigh. A whiff of stale beer and corn chips sprang from the cushions, offering Sanders a faint reminder of last night.

The captain had pulled in the search parties once it grew too dark and cold to continue. As Sanders left the station, Ramsey stood over a map of the town, reviewing the areas already covered and weighing where to send teams next. Sanders had to stifle a laugh. A flicker of guilt tried to push in, but he shut it out.

He didn't care much for the captain, but he didn't dislike him either. The man was old, tired, and soft. Still, he'd welcomed Sanders when other precincts had made their feelings clear. Ramsey believed in second chances, and Sanders admired that, to a point. And he respected the captain's efforts to keep the Pacelli case under local control.

So when the call about Powell came in, Sanders stormed into the captain's office. "What's the use of doing what we're doing if we end up handing the real cases over to state police or a task force?" he said.

Even now when districts from fifty miles out volunteering to assist with the Pacelli investigation, Sanders held his tongue.

Every time he felt the urge to speak up, he thought about the twins. Those smug grins frozen in their photos. He thought about his plan and the satisfaction achieving it would bring. Not just for him, but for the community.

Being marked a hero no longer mattered. After twenty years on the force, Sanders had already proven everything he needed to prove, both to others and to himself.

He looked around his one-bedroom apartment and nodded. Keeping things simple was the clearest sign of a better life. No whining kids. No wife telling him what to do.

The number one wasn't the loneliest. It was the smartest.

He grinned. Not because he was happy, but because he knew he was right, certain he understood something the rest of the world never would.

The apartment had a single window facing north. Sanders never opened the blinds, so the room stayed dim all day, like a forgotten basement. In the afternoons, slices of light bled through tiny holes in the blinds, struggling in a fruitless fight to break through the gloom.

The narrow living room held a couch once tossed beside an overfilled dumpster, a chipped coffee table, and a thirty-inch television. Having few pieces of furniture made it easier whenever Sanders came home late and stumbled around for light switches and keys. The walls were bare, except for a large whiteboard concealing several fist-sized holes. Taped to it was a string of photos and notes from the Pacelli case.

The detective's eyes roamed over the board, searching once more for something he might have missed.

Again, nothing.

He blew out a breath and took two swigs of beer. The can felt light in his hand.

In the beginning, drinking worked like magic, sweeping his mind clean, enabling him to forget at will. Soon, faces and laughter from his New York days faded into a blur. Yet, stubborn memories still pressed against the walls of his mind, squeezing his heart with their grip. He reached for more bottles, but even three a day could not drown out the sound.

It was time for a concrete solution. If his plan didn't kill the demons for good, there was another way. But he'd be ready. And free.

A tear traced down the detective's cheek as he drained the last drop of beer, eyeing the empty bottles and cans scattered across the table. He made a mental note to toss them out later. Then he reached for the remote but stopped himself. Instead, he dug out a small flashlight from between the seat cushions, snapping it on.

Sanders never believed the ends justified the means. That was a lie crooks told themselves to get a restful sleep. Yet he stopped himself from presenting the evidence to the captain and the others. There was something in those pages that could help catch those brats the way they deserved.

The thought poked at the front of his brain until he flipped through the written thoughts of a young girl, hoping chance would deliver a notable entry.

July 10

Today I woke up at 10:30 am. As usual, I was the last person to wake up. My brother (the jerk) went to baseball practice very early in the morning. Today I had to clean my room and vacuum it too. As you know, I hate my family. Especially my mom. I can't take it anymore. My mom favors my brother. For instance, she's nicer to him and when he breaks something or does something wrong, she just (maybe) yells at him. And it's the opposite of me.

Bored, Sanders took a drink and flipped to a fresh, unspoiled page.

September 20

Right now I'm writing to you in the morning because I didn't have a chance to write last night. I just went outside and people made fun of my haircut. I'm so mad! It looks like a boy!!!!!!!!!!

Mild curiosity pushed him to try another entry. Was there a clue hidden somewhere that could lead him to an untold truth?

October 12

Today is the first day I wore a bra. A girl at school saw it when my shirt was a little down. My mom said I don't have anything, but I have some.

The detective blew out a breath, pulling apart two stiff pages.

December 18

st every time I go to the dinner table, everyone makes fun of me! They make fun of my hair and call me Bucky Beaver. Someday I want to run away from home. I know nobody loves me. I'm lucky to have Alexis to talk to when I have problems.

Scratching his neck, Sanders reached for the whiskey.

October 24

Today's a Friday, thank god! I started to write a book a couple of weeks ago. I have all different stories. It's coming out pretty good! Lately, I've been wanting to get my energy back for boys. I want to like them (like other girls do) but my body doesn't (I guess). People think I'm a prude!

The entries were tedious, filled with silly things only a twelve-year-old would care about. But Sanders was starting to get a sense of her personality from the way she wrote, the words she chose. The more he read, the more he found himself drawn into the girl's small world.

December 20

Today my parents got an email warning that my Science average is a 70: C-! My father said I have to study science the whole Xmas VACATION! That SUCKS!

Sanders flicked his eyes to the next page.

December 21

Today I found out that I lost my whole book I've been writing!!!!! Then I did some of it over. I told my mother that I need a stamp to mail a handwritten letter to Alexis. (I had to because she asked me). She said my brother had read it before I mailed it! Before dinner, I wanted to run away just like that. My parents were so mean to me. I can't stand it.

Someone's car door slammed shut in the parking lot just outside the detective's window, breaking his focus.

He needed something substantial. A wild card. Something that would give him an advantage. Without it, no matter how prepared he was, hunting the twins would be like swimming alone in the deep ocean without a life raft.

Every cell in his body told him to approach the boy near the woods. But Sanders knew exactly where that would lead: free meals, cable television, and appeased treatment in a state youth facility, all paid for by law-abiding citizens. He'd watched too many perps walk free after disgusting crimes, courtesy of snaky lawyers and indifferent judges. The system was masterful at manipulating the public, turning criminals into victims. Sanders no longer possessed the resolve to stomach it.

The twins were hiding in the woods, armed. That much was obvious. But for how long? They could move at any time. Because of that, Sanders hesitated to grant them another day of freedom.

Then a brilliant idea surfaced—he wouldn't have to.

He would feign interest in a new hobby. Hell, he could fake just about anything. And there was no need to head to the store, squeezing through crowds of annoying customers and pushy merchants. He would ask his introverted neighbor for fishing supplies. The man was old and kind, with no reason to deny Sanders his toys for an afternoon. If all went as planned, and there was no reason it wouldn't, Sanders would head out before the end of the week.

He turned to a new page; two irregular blocks of text caught his eye. The first was smaller than the second. It listed several names under the heading *Friends*.

The second block held seven lines of people.

Sanders creased his brow and leaned in, the flashlight dangling from his fingers. He skimmed the first line, then read it again.

People I want dead:
Rosa Pacelli (mom), Chris (sometimes)

39

THE BOY

He flipped his head out of the stream, water flying from his hair like a thousand sparkling crystals. The cold stung his skin, but it felt good. Clean.

Earlier, Chris had managed to snag two six-inch sunfish using a V-shaped snare he made from three sticks, his hat, and a couple of T-shirts. Instead of shoelaces, he tied the fish together with thin bark stripped from nearby branches.

At last, he and Beth would have a real meal, warm and proper.

He unzipped the knapsack and dug around for the deodorant. He yanked off the stubborn cap and tucked the stick under his shirt, smearing it beneath both arms.

His eyes hardened, drifting over the glassy water.

All morning, Chris had imagined a crisp, cool drink soothing his throat. But the flow here was slow, bits of dirt and bugs floating along the surface. Unlike Beth, he knew better than to stick his face in and slurp.

A year ago, she'd gone on a Girl Scout trip and, afraid of looking stupid after dropping her water bottle down a hill, drank straight from a creek. It took a full day for her to recover from dysentery.

Chris shook his head, smirking. Sometimes, he was amazed Beth was his twin. It didn't take a genius to see their differences outweighed their similarities. And the gap seemed to stretch with each passing year.

Of course, Beth would argue that Chris was *her* twin, since she was older by a whopping seven minutes.

When fishing the bottles out of the knapsack, Chris scoffed at the fools who left the comforts of home to hunt for overpriced bottled water, all while having unlimited access to their kitchens and taps.

He studied the space, noting the best escape routes in case someone spotted him.

Keep your eyes open. Be ready for anything that tries to attack you. Otherwise, when something happens, you'll have no one to blame but yourself.

But by the stream, that desire to survive and protect seemed to fade. Listening to the birds' consoling chatter and the ripple of the water, he almost believed he was back at the neighborhood lake. By now, he'd be anticipating the next ice hockey match with the other boys.

He wondered how they were getting by without him.

A yearning to recapture the joys and comforts of home flooded the hollow ache in his chest. It overpowered him like a thousand biting emotions, pressing down on him like the bruises on his chest. Would he ever again feel warm blankets on a soft bed, or savor the aroma of pork chops and sausages baking in the oven? He never would have believed that simple pleasures, like blasting crunchy rock tunes in his warm bedroom, could become such a faraway concept. For a moment, the unforgettable scent of onions and Au Jus flooded his nostrils, grating his stomach like nails on skin.

But even after collecting food and water, he felt the same.

Before yesterday, he'd never lost a fight; he hadn't pissed his pants in years. But he had failed to protect Beth—and himself—from that hunter. If she hadn't come back with the shotgun, Chris would've been worm food.

Against his better judgment, he let his thoughts drift, then linger on the young officer.

I live here now.

He remembered those glassy, terrified eyes, frozen in place just before the blast.

Next came the driver, buried in wet leaves, limbs twisted around his torso.

Then the hunters.

And Mom and Dad.

I know every corner of you.

Chris closed his eyes, trying to ignore the burning in his chest and joints. But like a restless child, wounds demanded attention. Every breath pinched his chest like a bloody fist twisting around his heart and lungs.

For a heartbeat, he could almost feel Blake's tiny claws pinching his shoulder, a small comfort he missed more than he expected. Richard, all polished smiles and glittering suits, failed to fill the gap today. And without Blake's playful chants echoing around him, Chris was left with Mom and Dad.

He ached to see them again. Their faces. To hear Mom's smoky cackle and see the way Dad's cheeks flushed when he got mad, drunk, or laughed hard. Chris liked Dad best when he laughed.

Squeezing his eyes shut, he tried to recall the little things—creases, dimples, birthmarks. But only vague shapes came.

Tears swamped his eyes as he stared down the bore of the revolver. One slipped free, trailing down his bruised cheek, stinging a cut. He swiped it away with a closed fist.

You don't think you're going to get away with this, do you?

Chris flinched and lifted his head.

Was that Beth crying?

She had let go last night, but not like at home. Sometimes, he'd slip into her room unannounced and find her sitting on her bed, red-cheeked and glazed-eyed, anger and sadness swirling together.

It was always the same story: Mom, with her sharp rings, had backhanded Beth for something stupid—like talking back while she had a glass in her hand. Beth never stayed quiet when things felt wrong. She'd speak up, especially over dinner, challenging the unspoken rules. It was understood that Chris would eat, leave, and Beth would stay behind to clean up. Each night she fought it, and each night no one listened. But still, she never gave in.

Chris admired her determination. She was shy, but she had fire. Never afraid to take a hit. But lately, something has shifted. Now, she flinched whenever someone got close, like she expected to be hurt. And that broke his heart more than he'd ever admit.

The first hint of sunset gleamed on the horizon. One more hour, maybe, before the sky turned amber and polished the world in gold.

Chris was in no rush to face his sister. Or anyone. Beth had never seen him cry, and he wasn't going to let her today.

But she was hungry. Waiting for him.

Across the stream emerged a fox. Its head poked through the brush in a welcoming game of peek-a-boo. Chris held his breath, watching the animal drink from the stream. When finished, it raised its head, questioning his presence. Its golden coat looked clean and warm, reminding Chris of his dog Tyler.

He locked eyes with it. The animal, in its stillness, seemed to understand his loneliness and pain, regarding him with dark, curious eyes. Chris offered a shy grin. As quickly as it had come, the fox vanished into the thick pine and underbrush.

A strong urge to follow hit Chris hard. The fox could lead him deeper into the woods, so deep no one would ever find him again. He imagined living off the land, lying in the sun, bathing in the stream, fishing. The fox would be his best friend. It would teach him survival, and he'd teach it to catch a fastball with its mouth. He'd name the animal Bossy.

Chris shook his head.

He set down the pistol and dropped his head into his hands. As the tears dried, something new stirred beneath the grief. It wasn't anger, shame, or loss. Something harder. Heat rushed through his veins, slow and thick, tightening his muscles. He felt oddly restored.

It was time to go.

Slapping on his hat, Chris tucked the revolver into the front of his jeans, grabbed the bolt cutter, and stepped into the mirrored maze.

The audience roared at his return, wild and thunderous, like a fiery sea in a hurricane.

40

THE GIRL

She heard a floorboard creak and spun towards the open door.

Springing from the mattress, she lunged at the figure before her. Her feet soared through the air, and for a moment, she was no longer a girl but a wolverine defying gravity.

The boy didn't have a second to react. He stiffened as Beth crashed into him, both of them rocketing through the threshold. She landed on top, pinning him with her knees, blade poised at his ear.

Flashback to two years ago. Winter.

Chris, powerless with a broken collarbone—courtesy of a neighborhood kid tackling him hard during an after-school football game. He's locked in a clumsy, embarrassing brace.

That arrogant kid down the street with the crew cut and dark eyes. Bobby Morrow. Loitering on their property after school, glaring up the brick porch steps at them. He sees his chance to beat Chris at something, then challenges him with four-letter words, dares, the middle finger.

Then Beth is straddling Bobby's chest.

He lay in the snow, breathless, one eye blackening. She's burying his face in the icy, white powder until someone—maybe Chris?—is shouting for her to stop.

Later, he tells her how she leapt off the porch, catapulted towards the boy in a rage, and started swinging.

Snap back to the present.

"Jesus! Get her off of me, Dylan!"

A drop landed on the lens of the boy's wire-rimmed glasses,

crooked on his face. Beth assumed it was rain, until a moment of clarity struck. A stubborn tear had slipped down her cheek. It fueled the all-consuming blaze burning beneath her chilled skin.

A shoe kicked the knife from her grip. It skidded a few yards west of the clearing, a trail of curling dirt charting its course. Icy hands hooked beneath her arms, yanking her away from the boy's cries. Her legs hung in the air, and the world bled into red—even the leaves.

Beth thrashed against the boy restraining her. Spit flew from her mouth like a broken hose. "Leave me alone! Get off of me! CHRIS!!!"

She yanked an arm free, striking him. It was hard to gauge where his face was, but her elbow collided with something hard. His nose?

"Fuck!"

He released her, gripping his face. Her tailbone hit the dirt hard, sending a sharp jolt up her spine.

Spurning the pain, Beth sprang to her feet, eyes darting between the two boys. Silver gleamed in her peripherals, and she raced for the knife. But the smaller boy moved faster. He rolled over, scooping it up.

Everyone froze. Tension hung in the air like smoke. Even the wind seemed to take heed, and silenced.

Don't run. He's not much bigger than you. You can handle him!

Masking her surging pulse, Beth looked at the small boy holding the knife. It quivered in his hands. He hadn't bothered to straighten his glasses. He looked terrified.

See? He's scared. Not us!

Beth flashed a look at the tall boy. He held his nose, lips twisted in a grimace. He stood over five feet tall, with shoulder-length brown hair, frayed jeans, and a black t-shirt. A skull with wings sprawled across his chest, the word Volbeat scribed in gold letters.

She wiped the spit from her chin with her fists.

Tall boy puffed out a breath. "Chill out, man! What the hell's wrong with you?"

Small boy slipped the knife into his back pocket, then raised both hands, palms out. His face softened. "Listen, we're not here to hurt you. We didn't even know you were here."

Beth kept her eyes locked on tall boy, small boy a harmless blur, edging her left eye.

Tall boy coughed. Beth flinched.

A crow squawked in the distance.

"What do you want?" she demanded.

Tall boy rubbed his nose. "Nothing! We're only—we're here checking the place out. That's it."

Beth's eyes darted left to small boy. "Then give me back my knife."

"Genie, if you give this crazy chick that blade, I'll drop her like a wrinkled tit!"

Small boy kept his eyes on Beth. He carried a gentle calm, speaking barely above a whisper. "Dylan, shut up." He drew a long breath and reached for the knife in his back pocket.

"I'm serious, Genie. She'll try to stab you again!"

Paying no attention to his friend, small boy flipped the blade in his palm, turning the handle to Beth. He crept closer, inch by inch, presenting the knife as if it were a secret gift for the most admired girl in school. Every movement measured, his gaze steady and deliberate, eyes fixed on her. He stood a hair taller than Beth, with fair skin, dark blond hair, and eyes that gleamed an electric blue. His green t-shirt and dark jeans were free of logos or rips, a sharp contrast to his companion. "It's okay, Dylan."

As he drew closer, Beth stepped back, impregnable in her unrelenting stance.

Then small boy did something shocking. He crouched down, smiled, and set the knife in the dirt. A thin red scratch stretched across his left cheek. Beth could see the beginnings of a bruise forming on his chin. He stepped back.

"Genieeee..." tall boy warned through clenched teeth.

Small boy tempered, shooting his friend a look.

Beth peeked down at the blade. It rested in a patch of dirt, patiently waiting for someone to claim it. She studied small boy before turning her attention to tall boy, who stood holding his nose, scowling. Slow as mud, she bent over, picking it up.

Just beyond the trees, something fired through the thickets; a sea of brush stirred closer.

Everyone froze before all eyes shifted to the noise.

THE BOY

THE BOY

His name boomed through the air, shaking the leaves around him. His heart hammered, drumming against his ribcage. He could even feel his pulse throb beneath the delicate flesh under his jaw.

The voice was unmistakable. Wild and echoing from every direction. But he knew where to go. He always knew. All he had to do was listen with his blood.

Chris veered off the dirt track, plunging into the tall undergrowth, slicing through it like a bullet tearing down a barrel. Plants slapped at his knees. Hunger spun his head, and every tree shimmered and split before his eyes. Branches whipped his cheeks, bark grazed his skin. But he ran faster. The forest was no longer an enemy. He moved with it, breathed in its rhythm, no longer struggling against its wild embrace.

He crashed through the trees and exploded into the clearing, skidding to a stop between two boys. Beth stood frozen, white-knuckled around the knife. Chris, adrenaline surging, tightened his grip around the bolt cutter.

"Jesus Christ!" someone shouted.

The forest glowed in hazy, buttery twilight. Soon, black skeletons of trees would stretch towards the deepening sapphire sky.

Four kids sucked in sharp breaths, eyes blazing, waiting for the next move.

41

THE BOY

The taller boy, Dylan, spoke first. "What the hell is this? Some screwed-up reenactment of *True Romance* or something?"

All eyes rushed to the boy with the long hair and tattered jeans. He held onto nose, eyes wide as saucers. "Christ, is the mob gonna show up next with machine guns?!"

The kid wearing glasses cocked his head, squinting.

Chris couldn't tell if it was their puzzled expressions or the squeaky sound the tall one made holding his nose, but something drove Beth to loosen her fists at her sides. She bent over, laughing harder than Chris had ever seen.

Birds sensed the shift in the air and took flight above the trees.

Wide-eyed, the kid with glasses forced a tight-lipped grin at Beth. He looked goofy, the frames crooked on his head.

Chris slackened his grip on the bolt cutter, the blood returning, warming his fingers. He caught his breath. "What the hell's going on, Beth?"

She looked up, grinning wide, and studied the boys for a minute. "It's okay." She knew better than to use his name. "They just stopped by..."

Chris glared at the knife in her hand, then back at the boys. "What are you doing here?" he said.

The tall kid shifted his focus from Beth to Chris, intrigued.

His friend finally spoke. "Just stopping by, like she said. We're okay. Everything's cool." He turned to his friend. "Right, Dylan?"

Dylan blinked, then huffed, brow furrowing. "Yeah. We're

cool. As long as she doesn't try to kill us again."

Chris blinked, looked at Beth.

She shrugged and nodded.

○   ○   ○

"Damn, what are you doing with *those*?" asked Dylan, ogling the shotgun and rifle propped in the corner behind the table and chair. "They can't be real." He turned to Chris. "Are they yours?"

Chris slipped past everyone, crossing to the other side of the room. He gathered the weapons and set them beside the bomber jacket on the loft, a silent warning for others to keep their distance. Even though Dylan could grab them with a simple stretch, it was Chris who radiated confidence and courage, leaving no doubt about who commanded the room.

His eyes locked on Beth, and she nodded. His expression said it all: *Not a word.*

The two boys exchanged a worried glance. Dylan frowned, leaning into the corner with arms crossed over his chest.

It took some convincing, but with Beth's assurance, the boys convinced Chris they came as friends—or so they thought. Sensed no immediate threat, Chris let them inside the shack, Beth by his side, maintaining a cautious distance. It was always better to keep your enemies in sight, never at your back.

Chris hitched himself up onto the loft, hooking his legs over the edge, banging the heels of his shoes against the wall. The echo sounded like creepy footsteps. From this angle, he had the best vantage point. Despite his fear of heights, which seemed to fade day by day, he wouldn't hesitate to leap off at a moment's notice if needed. Hell, if Beth could do it, so could he.

"Sorry again for scaring you." The kid removed his glasses, wiped them with his shirt, and slid them back over his ears. His eyes flicked around the room. "But what are you two doing in my hut?" He brushed dirt from his clothes before lowering himself onto the far end of the mattress by the door.

Beth sat at the other end of the bed; Chris noticed her fighting a smile. "Sorry for scaring *you!*"

Chris scoffed. "Wait, hold on here. This place isn't yours."

The boy grinned and nodded. "Yes, it is."

"Oh my God!" Beth looked at Chris, aghast. "We should leave. We gotta leave!" She leapt up, anxiously searching the room for her things, only to be hit by the sad truth: nothing belonged to her.

Eager to quell her panic, Chris opened his mouth. But the same kid cut him off.

"I didn't say you had to leave. I mean, I appreciate you cleaning up, and—" he pointed upward—"don't think I didn't notice the patch in the roof."

A smile began to form on Chris' face, but he let it drop. Earlier, he'd set the fish down on a rock before entering the clearing. He needed to get back before animals found them. And with the light fading, starting a fire was critical. But there was no way he'd leave Beth alone with these two. He had to get rid of them, fast, without raising suspicion. And he had to make sure they wouldn't squeal.

These kids weren't strangers. Chris had seen them at school many times, especially the taller, older one. According to hallway gossip and locker room whispers, failing grades had foiled any shot Dylan had at eighth grade.

Chris wondered if the boy recognized him. Dylan always sat in the back row, jiggling a pen, staring into nothing. Now and then, Chris caught glimpses of his drawings: green stick figures marching over hills, gripping grenade launchers, RPGs, and oversized rifles in three-fingered hands. Stealth bombers drifted across the top of the page, dropping missiles, long, dotted arcs tracking their trajectories.

It was clear Dylan couldn't care less about sports. But the kid had excellent taste in music.

"Ya' know, you didn't have to bust my nose." Dylan tilted his head back, pinching his nose.

"For God's sake, you've taken bigger hits to the face from your mom," said his friend. "It's a little blood. Don't make it a whole thing."

Beth giggled. Chris smiled.

Dylan waved a hand in the air. Chris spotted a red welt across his nose, blood crusting under both nostrils. "Laugh it up, man. I'm glad you're all having fun at my expense. Enjoy your night." His voice came out pinched, nasal.

Chris stared at Beth until she met his gaze. "You alright?" he asked, voice low but steady.

She nodded, stifling her grin. "Yeah. I'm okay."

His pulse started to settle.

A pause.

"No one asked if I was okay."

"Dylan, just stop," said his friend. He turned to Beth. "Don't let him bother you. He's harmless."

Tight-lipped, Beth nodded.

"Wait! Now it makes sense!" Dylan jabbed a finger at Beth.

Chris pulled his attention from the kid on the mattress—the one sitting by his sister as casually as a best friend. A friend he didn't trust.

The twins locked eyes, exchanging looks.

"Genie, tell me you know who they are!"

His friend nodded. "Of course. They go to the same school."

"Think you're missing my point."

The kid sighed, glancing at the twins. "Okay. We saw them on TV, alright?" He smiled at Beth. "At least I think it's them."

Beth kept her eyes fixed on her fingers in her lap.

"I told you, man," sneered Dylan. "They're on the run. They gotta be in hiding or somethin'." He sounded more impressed than reproachful.

"Is that true? It was your home, wasn't it?"

Beth peered up at Chris, awaiting silent instruction. Unblinking, he returned her gaze.

"Don't forget they're also suspects in a police shooting *and* a disappearance!" Dylan called out.

Chris tightened his jaw, glowering at Dylan. Was this kid planning to rat them out? A shaky hand drifted along the cold steel against his belly.

"Hey, relax!" said Dylan, his open hands raised in front of himself. "We won't turn you in. Even though you tried to kill us—"

"Come on, Dylan. Give them a break. Let them talk."

"I'm telling you, man, it's them! We got real-life celebrities in our midst! Outlaws!"

The boy on the mattress held his gaze on Beth, a tiny grin forming.

It didn't matter how sincere he looked, or that Beth had managed to ease up for the first time since entering the woods. The kids looked harmless, but Chris knew better than to trust anyone. Especially outsiders arriving with smiles and warm eyes. "What are you two doing here?" he spat.

"Chris, it's okay—"

The boy on the mattress stood up. "It's alright, Beth."

The sound of this four-eyed kid speaking his sister's name sent shivers through Chris' body, stirring his bones.

"I'm Jason, and this is Dylan."

Chris scowled. "I know who you are." He looked at Dylan.

"Howdy." Dylan flicked a closed peace sign from his temple. "And by the way, I'll live. Thanks."

Chris turned to Jason. "Okay, so you know who we are. And we know you. Mystery solved. *What do you want?*"

"See, I knew it!" said Dylan, one hand on his nose, the other pointing at Chris. "That's Chris, the chick's brother! See, I *told* you!"

Jason waved his friend off. "Don't listen to him. We're not here to turn you in or anything. We didn't expect—"

"What are you doing here?" snarled Chris. These kids knew him, and he hated that. What did they know? What did Beth tell them, and why the heck was she grinning like a fool?

Strangely, Jason showed no signs of concern about them invading his place. He might as well have been hanging out with friends in his living room. "I was saying, I helped my dad build this place a while ago. It's ours."

The kid appeared sincere, but Chris knew better than to buy

into a story that sounded as suspicious as the one telling it. "You built this place?"

Jason nodded. "And my father. Well, my father, mostly. Yeah."

Chris turned to Dylan. "And you. What's your deal?"

"I don't have a deal." Tearing at a hangnail with his teeth, Dylan suddenly looked nervous.

"Dylan, come on—"

"No, I won't *come on*, Jason. Do I have to address the elephant in the room here?"

Everyone stared, puzzled.

"Hello!" he pointed aloft. "The guy's guarding two guns up there. They're probably loaded!"

Chris gave him a long hard look. Then he smiled. "We were hunting. You know, for food?"

Dylan pursed his lips. "Uh, huh."

Keeping an eye on Chris, Dylan pulled a soda bottle from his back pocket. He twisted the cap, and it burst open with a sharp hiss, fizz ricocheting around the room, drenching him in a sugary spray.

42

THE GIRL

Sunset pressed in fast, the sky ready to bloom in blistered orange. The air had grown cold in the cabin, and Beth gladly accepted Chris' offer to wear his Islanders jacket. With it on, she didn't feel as helpless as she had wrapped in the dirty blanket.

Earlier, she'd watched him carry his pack inside and stash it on the loft beside the shotgun and rifle. He'd never let anyone get their hands on what he'd worked so hard to collect.

To her disappointment, he'd snubbed Jason's offer to bring food and blankets from home. But after a prickly silence, he reluctantly agreed to let Jason grill the fish. Starting a fire this close to dusk was risky, but if anyone happened to cross paths with Jason or Dylan, there'd be no alarm. No panic. No violence.

Beth watched as Jason dug through the shed, pulling out steel pots, cups, flatware, extra lumber, two more hard-back chairs, rusty tools, and roof shanks. The hole where the twins had dropped the hunters had dried up years ago, so Jason showed them the hydrant pump his dad had set up on the northeast side of the shack. The pipe stood two feet from the ground, hidden in a sea of scrub and tall undergrowth.

Watching Jason rip away vegetation from the pump, Chris— shoulders raised, hands buried in his pockets—tried to mask his shame while Beth gaped at the newfound treasure.

The twins filled their grumbling bellies with cool water from plastic bottles while Jason and Dylan sat outside cooking. The water was clean and clear, cool as rain on stone. It awakened dormant senses, feeding power and vitality into their muscles. Beth sensed Chris' mood and energy rising.

Staring at the back of his head, she took a mouthful of water from her bottle. Chris stood by the window, watching the boys through gaps in the branches. A loose fist hung at his left side. Now and then, his right hand rose to graze his throat.

From outside, a faint, intoxicating aroma filled the room.

"Will you tell them—?"

Chris spun around. "Sshhh, keep it down. They'll hear you."

Beth shrugged. "There's really nothing to hide. They mean well, Chris. They've already done so much for us."

"You need your head examined or something? Forget what Mom said. Being a girl's no excuse."

Beth winced. "They go to school with us, Chris. You said you knew them. Why can't—?"

"—Used to."

Beth stared at her brother.

Wanapatchee had two elementary schools. One was Catholic, where students wore black and white checked uniforms with ties and skirts. They looked no different from their folks, commuting each morning in starched suits and dark dresses. Beth found it odd they didn't seem to mind living like clones up and down every hallway and classroom.

The four kids all attended the public school; the twins had moved to Wanapatchee from New York in their third year. So Chris knew most of the students.

"C'mon, Beth, don't be stupid. Just because I know them doesn't mean they won't turn us in." He tossed his cap on the loft and ran his fingers through tufts of sweaty hair. "We shouldn't be letting anyone in here. Remember what happened last time people came through that door?"

"But...they're not like that."

"You have a degree in psychology? You've known them for what, ten minutes? Unless there's something you're not telling me."

Nothing Beth did was right. Like Mom and her drinking, Chris had the memory of a fly. Had he forgotten how she saved his life? Did he forget she'd been struggling beside him all this time?

Beth dropped her head and stared at her sneakers, caked in dirt and grime. Arguing with Chris would only make her eyes glaze and fuel his anger.

Ignore him. You know he can be a butthead sometimes.

JASON and DYLAN

Jason sat with his back to the shack, flipping fish with a rusty spatula. Dylan parked himself on Beth's log, a watchful eye on the shack door. Unlike Jason, he didn't trust the twins. He wondered how far they'd go to stay hidden from the public. After all, if they were innocent, why choose to hide out in the woods?

The news reports rattled the town, and that was an understatement. Grown-ups eyed the parks with dread, haunted by fears their children might vanish or fall victim to violence. Such horrors were rare, but youth crime and tense run-ins with police were on the rise.

Rumors rocketed around school hallways and classrooms. Gossip about the missing, murderous twins living on Schicara Drive spread like lava on sizzling streets. Most students knew Chris—or at least knew of him. It wasn't every day their unremarkable town made the news, and the kids found it fascinating. *"Did you hear about Chris and his sister?" "No way they did that!" "Do you think they killed their parents?" "His sister always seemed weird. I wondered about her."*

The girl looked harmless enough on TV, until she tried to dig a blade into his best friend's ear. Chris, though, was a mystery. Dylan wondered if the news had told the whole story. Maybe the missing pieces didn't fit the networks' ratings-driven narrative. Whatever the case, Dylan was intrigued.

Jason, too, sensed there was more to the twins than the reports had let on. He figured there was always more to a story than what the writers, editors, and publishers knew—or chose to push onto the public. Blood and thunder bred attention. And profit.

Dylan spotted Chris watching them through the window and stiffened. They'd discovered the twins' hideout, and the thought of them crashing through the door with guns drawn kept him on edge.

Jason kept his focus on the fish, sliding the spatula under the meat to keep it from sticking to the grill grate. Thankfully, he knew how to cook simple dishes; he'd done it plenty of times at home.

Dylan shifted closer to the fire. It soothed his bruised nose and nerves. "Isn't that the grate thingy we jacked from the Gopple's about a year ago? That shit was hilarious. Last thing I thought you'd agree to."

Jason smirked. "Yeah, my dad would have killed me if he knew we stole it."

Dylan's eyes glazed over in nostalgia. "Yeah, those s'mores rocked. Where'd you tell him you picked it up, anyway?"

"I told him I found it out here, in the woods."

"Ha!" Dylan slapped his knee. "And he bought it! Sorry, pal, but it serves your old man right."

Jason's smile dropped. "I didn't say he *bought* it."

Dylan's face fell. Jason's father was an irascible man with loose hands and a taste for dangerous vices like speeding and drugs. Jason had come to school more than once with bruises on his back, and once with a black eye. At first, he passed it off as a clumsy bike jump gone wrong. But after Dylan caught sight of him shirtless in the locker room, the lies stopped, replaced by long, awkward silences.

Glancing over his shoulder, Dylan changed the subject. "They made themselves at home. Even dug into some of your dad's shit."

"It's just firewood and things. No big deal."

"Why do you give a damn about them anyway?"

The question hung in the air. The fire popped; crickets chirped in the stillness.

Seeing Beth like this had been a shock. She looked tired and desperate, thinner than the last time Jason had seen her. And she was filthy, exuding an odor of someone who hadn't seen soap or clean water in days. She was an orphan now—cold, hungry, and trying to survive in the woods.

While gathering firewood, Jason wondered if he should notify the authorities and lead the twins to food, safety, and proper shelter. Then a cozy feeling, like warm water, washed over him, sweeping away the idea. Helping troubled kids was something his mother would have wanted. And what better way to help than by supporting the twins in their autonomy?

"Wait a minute!" said Dylan, breaking the silence. He leaned into his friend. "You like her, don't you?"

Jason scoffed. "Whatever. What's wrong with helping them?"

"Well, considering they're fugitives, for one," Dylan said coolly.

"Be careful what you say. You don't know what he'll do."

Dylan blew out a breath and shook his head. "I could throw that little guy down in a second if I wanted to. If it weren't for you, I probably would have by now. Just to get those guns away from him."

"Well, it didn't take much to knock you down earlier."

A rich, fragrant aroma filled the clearing, and Jason grinned.

Dylan touched his nose, wincing. "Caught me off guard, that's all. You woulda' been too if a chick elbowed you in the freaking nose."

Jason asked Dylan to wash the plates and cutlery with the hydrant pump. With rolling eyes, Dylan did what he was told.

As he neared the shack, Jason heard voices rising. He shuffled his feet along the sandy ground, careful not to startle the twins.

He eased the door open. "You two ready for some food?"

43

THE BOY

THE BOY

He put his enmity on hold, keeping close to the weapons as he plowed through his first hot meal in a week.

Twilight filtered through cracks in the window, casting strips of light across the shack. The room stayed quiet as the twins ate, broken only by the brassy scrape of forks on metal plates. It took two minutes to wolf down the sunfish Jason had cooked. The food left a mild but flavorful taste in Chris's mouth, his stomach demanding more.

An empty steel plate sat on his lap, his legs dangling over the loft. The meal calmed his nerves, but not his distrust. Beth had already spoken to the boys before he showed up. And now she sat there, far too casual about the outsiders invading their space.

No one knew Beth like Chris did. She was hungry for attention, eager for people to show interest in her—especially boys. Even when kids at school treated her bad, she'd still like them if they left her alone. So what would stop her from giving in now? From trusting the wrong people again? Chris hadn't heard anything about a reward on the news, but that didn't mean the police weren't offering one.

He crafted a mental note: watch the boys closely. Just like he had with a catcher's signals on the infield.

Jason crouched beside the mattress where Beth sat cross-legged, eating. Strings of last light caught her face, turning the grime into something like a mud mask. Dylan stood silent, half-buried in shadow, leaning against the wall near the window, hands in his pockets.

After her last bite, Beth set down the fork and belched. She covered her mouth with her hand.

Everyone froze. Jason blinked at her.

"You don't want seconds, do you?" said Dylan, wrinkling his nose.

"Sorry. I'm just..."

Jason raised a brow. "...Starving?"

"Yes, that too," she exclaimed, meeting his eyes. "I mean, this is *so good*. Thank you—both of you. For helping us."

"I didn't have a choice."

"Dylan—"

"—*But*...you're welcome," he added with a smirk.

Chris could tell Beth was waiting for him to say something, but he pretended to focus on licking juice from his fingers. The air still smelled like gunpowder, and he wondered if Beth or the boys noticed it too. His eyes flicked to the wall. Had they seen the faint stains in the wood? From the corner of his eye, he caught Dylan watching him.

"Yeah, you're welcome," echoed Jason. "I'm glad your brother knew how—"

"Chris," he snapped, whipping his head towards the nerd on the mattress. That fake innocence and proud grin were yanking his nerves.

Jason glimpsed up at the loft and nodded. "—that Chris had the fish. By the way, nice job on the catch."

"How'd you do it?" asked Dylan, mildly curious. "I don't see any tackle."

"Just something I learned in the scouts. And from my dad."

"Hey, buddy," said Dylan, "what happened to your face and neck? Looks like a bear attacked you or somethin'."

Chris froze mid-lick, his expression stiffening.

"Come on, Dylan. They've been out here for a while," said Jason. "Let's see how you look after living like this."

"Don't forget how they smell," Dylan muttered.

Chris kept track of every word and move the boys made. He

caught Jason's discomfort and his attempt to shift the conversation.

"How have you two been holding up?"

God, these guys were nosy. Chris hated it when people knew things he hadn't shared. It felt like a break-in, like they'd sifted through the wreckage of his life back on Schicara Drive. He imagined tearing the glasses off Jason's face and crushing them with the bolt cutter.

"I'm just curious how you've managed this long," Jason added. "You serious campers or something?"

Chris held his eyes on his fingers.

"Hey, is it true you guys tied up a mother and her kid, then jacked a bunch of shit from their house?"

The room stood still. No one spoke for a minute. "We took some food," said Beth finally. "We didn't tie anyone up."

Jason turned to Chris. "Really?"

Chris shot Beth a hard look. *Stop talking!* "Yeah," he said.

More silence.

"Cool!" said Dylan, cutting the quiet. "Pretty badass!"

Tension eased, and everyone laughed. Except Chris. "Who told you we tied them up?"

Jason watched his friend, waiting.

Dylan shrugged, brushing off the question.

"Oh, sorry about your home," offered Jason. "And your folks. That's hard, I know."

"Oh?" said Chris. "How would you know?"

"Chris," Beth warned.

"It's okay," said Jason. "My mom died. Car accident."

"Yup," Dylan added, still picking at the dirt under a nail.

"Oh?"

Jason nodded.

"How sad," said Beth.

"Yeah." A half-smile shaped Jason's mouth. He leaned in.

Beth's breath must've been awful because Chris could see Jason fight a grimace.

"You know," said Jason, "I've seen you at school."

Beth's eyes widened. A smile crept across on her pale lips. "Really? You've seen me?"

"Yeah. You sat in on my English class once. In the back. Mr. Jamison, right?"

"Beth," Chris cut in, "you know him?"

Beth shrugged.

"I've seen you in school," Chris pointed out.

"Yeah, well...I'm in the new annex most of the day."

"He's a genius," said Dylan.

Jason shook his head. Chris could see the dork's cheeks flushing like two red apples. He wanted to bite off pieces of flesh just to watch them rot.

"I'm no genius," said Jason. "It's only creative-type classes the administration came up with. You know, so teachers can create lessons—"

"—for kids who are smarter than the rest," Dylan cut in. "They get smaller classes with other smart kids. Sounds great for them, but the rest of us..." His voice thinned.

"...feel slow-witted...?" said Beth, barely above a whisper.

"Wow," said Jason. "Nice word."

Chris pointed at his sister. "She studies the dictionary." He wondered if she could detect the flicker of pride in his voice.

Incredulous, Dylan snorted. "Uh, huh."

"I'm not surprised," said Jason. "You were—are—one of the star students in English."

Beth giggled and cupped her hands over her mouth, eyes peeking through her excitement. Did she have any idea how silly she looked?

"No, I am not. Not even close."

"Yep. And I know why everyone gave you a hard time that day. You threaten them. Because you're smart."

Chris rolled his eyes. This kid was laying it on thick. The longer he spoke, the less Chris trusted him. No boy was as good and generous as this one pretended to be.

Dylan? He was no mystery. Unlike his meek counterpart, who

knew how to hide things, Dylan was scraggly, blunt. Nothing but elbows and noise.

Eager to change the subject, Chris pointed at him. "I've seen you around."

Dylan tapped his chest. "Junior high, bro."

Chris nearly laughed. Their school ran from kindergarten through eighth grade. Junior high or not, Dylan still walked the same halls as them.

"We've missed your stories," said Jason to Beth. "I mean, I have."

Beth placed a palm on her chest, face rosy with muted giggles. "Me? Really?"

He nodded.

"Okay," snapped Chris. "How about *I* cook for *you* if you can name one story she wrote?"

Amused, Dylan crossed his arms over his chest, waiting.

Jason's eyes stayed on Beth. Wisps of hair fell over his left eye, but he didn't seem to notice. "One was about a popular girl dating her crush. She fell and broke a bone, right? I think you called it *Bad Accident*. Anyhow, the boy dumped her, and then her friends turned on her. It was funny, but kind of sad too. It was darn good. I liked it."

Chris swallowed hard, pursing his lips.

Dylan burst out laughing. He slammed a hand against the plywood wall, making it shudder. "Well, guess who's making who dinner tomorrow! Make sure you use that shotgun to shoot us up some prime meat. I like mine medium-rare."

Chris scowled.

Then Dylan let out a long breath. "Well, kids, as thrilling as this has been, it's late. We gotta head out." He nodded at the door. "Jason, you comin'? I'm sure your dad's going crazy."

A wave of disappointment flashed across Jason's face. "Yeah, we better go." As he stood, Dylan headed for the door.

"How will you find your way out?" asked Beth in sudden panic.

"We'll be alright, thanks. I always—" Jason tapped his back pocket—"bring a flashlight." He turned to Chris. "You okay?"

"Don't worry about us. We'll be fine," said Chris.

Dylan pushed open the door, and light spilled into the room. Beyond the entrance, an army of rust-colored trees stood like sentries. Tall, still, and silent as a photograph.

The boys stepped out.

Then Chris' voice cut through the air, sharp and anxious. "Hey, buddy! You're not gonna tell anyone we're here, right?" He wondered if his words sounded more like a threat or a plea.

Jason turned back. After a beat, he shook his head. "No. You two have enough to deal with." He peeked down at Beth, her head so low her chin nearly touched her chest. "And stay as long as you need."

With that, he stepped out, the door whispering shut behind him, trapping the silence inside as if sealing away a secret the world no longer remembered.

44

THE BOY

THE BOY

Another unrelenting King Kong nightmare claws into his sleep. But this time, the beast doesn't roar from mountaintops or tear through buildings.

It glides beneath the ocean, silent and waiting.

At first, racing through the ocean feels like riding a dirt bike in wet cement. But he's ready now—ready to turn around and beat the beast into submission with his bare hands.

As if suddenly master of the sea, he rockets forward like a torpedo, slicing through water with the smoothness of warm butter. He glances back for a second, crashing into a mess of glowing white jellyfish and curling purple tentacles.

Like a fly bound in a spider's thread, he's tangled, trapped in endless circling fibers and stinging antennae.

Then it appears.

A horrible, dazzling Portuguese man o'war glides towards him. Massive, iridescent, imperious. Other creatures scatter like ash in the wind.

Beneath its massive body hangs hundreds of thick black tentacles, swaying like Mom's fusilli, soaked in her blood-colored meat gravy. They wrap around his arms, legs, ribs, thoughts.

He tries to look away but can't find where to look.

It has no face. No eyes. And yet, it stares.

How can something without eyes stare with such contempt?

He stops fighting. "What do you want?" Bubbles shoot from his mouth, fizzing the water.

The creature doesn't move. Its tentacles tighten. Its soundless, stony stare pierces him like a pitchfork.

"You're not scary. You're just...gross. Uglier than the ape."

It doesn't speak. But now he can hear its silence.

The creature pulls him closer. A tentacle flicks his cheek. Soft, wet, like a noodle. The touch is familiar.

Its features fuse. No longer possessing a gelatinous body, the creature becomes Beth. But her eyes are not hers. They're the sunfish eyes from dinner, glassy and dead.

She opens her mouth. "I don't wanna eat that." The voice is calm, controlled.

Dad's voice.

All the heroism melts away like sweat in water. Thirsty tentacles slurp it up, greedy as mosquitos. He wants to scream again, but the water feels like glass. Dense and sealed.

She—he—it—speaks again. "You're not ready."

Chris' eyes shot open, his limbs flailing like a dying roach on its back. He braced himself, sweat beading across his face. It took a minute before his heart settled to its usual rhythm.

"No, I would never eat that!"

Nonplussed, he rubbed his eyes with the heel of his hands, then looked down at the empty mattress.

"C'mon, tell me. Please."

The morning air felt cool and still inside the shack. Chris stretched his arms overhead, drawn to the voices outside. All he heard now were jumbled words, broken up by girlish laughter.

With a sharp exhale, he hopped off the loft. His socks offered little cushion against the floorboards, the impact quaking the room. He peered through gaps in the branches casing the window. Anxious fingers rubbed his neck.

Jason straddled a log, Beth seated beside him, her back to the shack. He grinned, tucking something into his jacket as she tried to grab it, laughing.

Chris sucked in a lungful of air. What was this creep doing back, and what did he want with Beth?

The dugout buzzed with boyish chatter, secrets traded on the benches. Chris saw the way they eyed girls, their glances sharp and curious, their motives rarely clean. Dad had drilled respect into him, but not every father cared to do the same. For all Chris knew, Jason's dad might despise women. Maybe he'd ran his wife off the road in a drunken rage, or tampered with her brakes while she slept.

Chris bent down, scrambling to pull on his sneakers. He stumbled as he hopped, catching himself with a hand on the wall. Once his shoes were on, his fingers moved instinctively to his waistband. What once felt like cold steel now gave off a strange warmth. No longer just a weapon, the wheel gun had become a companion. Loyal. Protective. He kept it safe, and it returned the favor.

He dashed out of the shack, storming towards them.

Jason looked up, his grin slipping away.

Beth spun around. "Hi, Chris!"

"What the hell are you doing?"

Openmouthed, Beth sat speechless.

"Sorry if we woke you," said Jason. "I was—"

"What are you, freaking stupid, Beth? You want to get caught out here? Why don't you yell louder so the whole town hears you?"

"Okay, pal," said Jason. "We'll just—"

Chris snapped his head to Jason, eyes blazing hot enough to melt plastic. "Don't call me that. I'm not your pal."

Beth shut her mouth, staring into the trees.

Jason shrugged.

"What are you even doing here?" he said after a prickly silence.

"No big deal," said Jason. "I just skipped class today, that's all." He looked at Beth with a sheepish smile. "Not something I usually do, but hey—it's Thursday. Almost the weekend."

Chris blinked. Until now, he hadn't given the days of the week a second thought. In his old life, Monday always loomed like a blue-faced bully sneering over Sunday's fading yellow smile. But out here, each day blurred together. An endless loop of frigid Mondays.

Beth pulled her eyes from the trees. "Jason, what if your dad finds out? Won't he be mad?"

"Oh, yeah. Definitely." He grinned. "But I came back because it's your turn to cook, right? That was the deal."

Beth smiled, stifling a giggle.

Jason had come prepared. From his Spider-Man backpack, he unloaded two fresh toothbrushes, a half-squeezed tube of toothpaste, a pair of worn wool blankets his mother called throws, and a bar of green soap.

Chris eyed the supplies. It had been a full week since a toothbrush scraped his teeth, and the thought alone almost stopped him from kicking the kid in the face. And who wouldn't want extra blankets out here?

He agreed to let Beth and Jason stay outside in short stretches, provided they kept their voices low and avoided disturbing the vegetation. If anyone noticed movement in the woods, Chris had a plan: he and Beth would bolt into the shack and leave Jason alone by the fire.

O   O   O

Starting the fire was easy, thanks to one of the tumbleweed fire starters Jason's dad had stashed in a dusty wool sack inside the shed. Jason insisted on helping, arranging dry firewood into a pyramid while Chris nestled the tumbleweed in the center so the flame could catch.

"Hold on!" Jason reached into his jacket pocket and pulled out a long-stemmed lighter. "Almost forgot this. It's my dad's, but I'm sure he won't know it's gone."

Tired of burning his fingers with matches, Chris snatched the lighter from Jason's hand, showing more enthusiasm than intended. He flicked it on. A tall flame flared, thinning to smoke overhead.

To the twins' amazement, Jason unzipped a soft, four-can cooler slung across his shoulder and revealed three four-ounce cuts of fresh steak. They were thick, ruddy, and glistening.

"I meant to fry them up last night," Jason explained, "but my dad didn't make it home before dark. It was either bring them today or let them turn brown in the fridge."

"Wow!" said Beth. "Those look good!"

Chris's mouth tugged down for a second before tightening into a line. "Yeah. Looks good. Thanks."

"It's venison," Jason added, proud. "Hope you don't mind deer." His eyes were on Beth.

She shook her head and grinned. "I don't mind at all."

Jason launched into tips for preparing the meat. "It's really versatile," he said. "Lots of ways to cook it." He pulled out a few small glass canisters of oil, salt, and pepper—clearly lifted from a restaurant.

Chris scored the meat, then rubbed it down the way Dad used to back home. With his hands, he slapped the steaks onto the grill grate over the sputtering fire.

The clearing filled with the hiss of sizzling meat. Smoke swelled upward in mouthwatering clouds.

"So," said Chris half-heartedly after a few silent minutes, "how do you like your meat?"

O   O   O

It took the twins about seven minutes to inhale their steaks and guzzle all the water their stomachs could manage.

With a shrinking roll of paper towels tucked under his arm and a spring in his step, Chris excused himself to take care of business. He knew better than to go near what had become their underground storage for bodies, so he headed east.

Before stepping out of the clearing, he pulled Beth aside and pressed the pepper spray into her palm. Then he reminded her the shotgun was still on the loft, loaded. "Don't let him inside the shack until I come back," he warned.

Chris waded through fallen branches, kicking aside dead leaves. He couldn't remember tasting a better piece of meat. Sure, Dad would toss a London broil on the grill now and then. But nothing melted in his mouth like that venison.

That jolt of beef in his stomach lit a fire inside him. A new obsession stirred: hunting. It may not have demanded fast legs or a strong throwing arm, but there was power in the weapons, the chase, the game itself. Maybe he'd even ask Jason for tips.

About a hundred yards out, Chris found a spot and dug a shallow hole with the heel of his shoe. He squatted beside a maple tree heavy with leaves. A breeze slipped through the branches, carrying the scent of spearmint.

Then Blake appeared, darting through the green like a flicker of thought. The bluebird zipped from branch to branch, wings flashing in the sun. It circled once overhead—silent and sure— before coming to rest of Chris' shoulder. Uninvited, yet somehow expected.

It perched there, still as prayer, as if it had come not just to watch, but to help Chris remember something he'd forgotten.

"You kidding me, buddy?" Chris turned his head to the bird, keeping the rest of his body still. "You wanna hang out now? This is my alone time, pal."

The bird twitched its neck, a cascade of delicate chirps springing from its charcoal beak, as if carrying a message only the wind could understand.

45

THE GIRL

THE GIRL

"What's it like being a twin?"

It seemed absurd to dismiss the chaos and deaths of the last few days. Doing so required little effort around Jason. Like the chilling winds and winding forest trails commanding her movements, Jason's gaze held Beth in the present. Rather than triggering a cry or angry tears, this anchor left her stomach tumbling like a blouse in a dryer.

Jason had sincere blue eyes that were hard to ignore; they brightened whenever he watched her reactions to his compliments. But eye contact with him sent tiny heart attacks exploding beneath her skin. So she focused on his other features—those furry eyebrows, full pale-pink lips, and the way the right side curled up during pleasant conversation. Beth felt strangely at ease in his company. He was comforting, patient.

As many times as she tried, she couldn't remember a single sentence Jason wrote in class that day. She sat in the back of the room, entertaining her restless mind by drawing crude images of conflict and war on blue-lined paper, as Mr. Jamison astutely called it. And when students stood in front of the class to share their tales, her mind drifted.

Entertaining as he was cute, Mr. Jamison was the youngest teacher in school. Beth loved his outlandish ties and neatly combed blond hair the color of cornhusks. The day she was invited to sit in on his class, they read stories from the Renaissance. He made a theatrical entrance in a toga, a nest hat, and white sneakers. Beth laughed so hard the other kids started teasing her. To them, her voice was grating, like nails scoring a chalkboard. She never went back.

Beth toyed with her hands in her lap. Playing it off like a cramp and not nervous energy, she massaged each finger for effect. "I don't know. It's okay, I guess."

Trying to explain what it was like being a twin felt impossible. Jason had never known the chaos or comfort of siblings. Since his mom passed, his world shrank to just him and his dad. How could anyone put into words what it meant to share a womb, to be so close to another soul before you even took your first breath? How could she make him understand the closeness that existed before a mother's arms ever wrapped around you?

Jason scratched the side of his head. "Yeah?"

Beth looked up and caught him sneaking a glance at the bluish-yellow bruises on her arms.

"I don't know," he said, looking away. "What's with the way he talks to you? It doesn't seem right."

"He looks out for me. For us. It's hard for him, though. It's not easy for me either."

She regretted her words right away. She'd tried to hold them in, but they came out anyway, like something slipping past a broken lock. How could she open up to someone she barely knew? Sharing a classroom wasn't the same as sharing private thoughts.

As if on cue, birds began to chirp gentle hymns in the trees. Beth exhaled what she hoped was a small sigh of relief. Music always made things easier. Jason seemed to like the sounds too. For a while, they sat in silence, light twinkling off his glasses as he held that half-smile, as if listening to something only he could hear.

But behind his eyes was something else. A trace of sadness.

"Can I ask you something?" he said. "Is it true? What they're saying in the news? Do you know what happened to those policemen?"

Beth's head jerked up. She turned to him. "Is that what they're saying? That we know?"

"Well, they have your fingerprints and stuff."

Maybe it was the sound of Jason's voice, or maybe it was just the weight of everything she'd held in for too long. Either way, the words came. She told him everything she remembered since the fire: the break-in, stumbling across the shack in a haze, the men, their accidental deaths. She left out the hunters. Those deaths hadn't been accidents.

Jason didn't interrupt. His eyes stayed on her face the whole time. He looked like a young school counselor, head tilted, elbows on his knees, hands clasped, leaning forward. He kept adjusting his glasses, maybe because he was nervous.

Beth avoided his look. Her hands trembled as she studied them, tracing each line like they might disappear. When the silence dragged on, she imagined Jason's face drawn tight with disgust.

Eyes wide, he let out a long, slow breath. "Wow."

Beth nodded, closing her eyes. "I know. You must hate me."

"Is that what you think, Beth?"

Hearing her name spoken by a boy other than Chris sent her insides churning, like being trapped in a plummeting elevator that hard-stops just before hitting the floor.

"I was thinking, how cool is it that my dad built this place? In a way, it helped save you and your brother's life," he said.

Until then, Beth hadn't realized how important the shack had been to their survival.

"And how tough you are, having to go through all that."

She shook her head. "I'm not tough. I'm just—" She raised her shoulders and dropped them quickly. "—surviving."

"I don't know. You and your brother made it this far without help. If your parents saw you now, I think they'd be proud."

A fresh weight fell on her shoulders. If she'd been standing, her knees would have buckled.

Then came Mom poking her head into Beth's hospital room.

Mom is carrying a single Get Well Soon foil balloon. Peonies, lilacs, pink roses, and delicate periwinkles are arranged in a small glass vase. Tucked between the flowers stands a troll doll in hospital scrubs, its fluffy hair dyed Beth's favorite color: sky blue.

254 | NANCY P. CORBO

The room is dark. Curtains drawn. Night pressing at the windows. She hears nothing but her own voice and the echo of footsteps in the corridor. She lies in bed, wrapped in warm blankets, petting the troll's soft hair for comfort.

At eighteen, Mom enrolled in nursing school. Beth would later learn it wasn't fear of failure that made her quit. It was the helplessness of watching sick, handicapped children collapse onto cold tile floors, knowing she wasn't allowed to help.

"They need to learn how to get up on their own," a seasoned nurse had said, unmoved.

Two days later, Mom dropped out and went to work as a vice president's secretary at a bank.

Tucked in those mechanical beds, surrounded by beeping machines and white walls, it hadn't occurred to Beth how caring Mom had been during the moments she felt most helpless. And one thing you could always count on Mom for was exerting her rights at the nurse's station. *Do your job! My daughter's been beeping for half an hour and no one's helped her! Are you deaf?* More often than not, nurses responded immediately, rushing towards Beth's room in quiet panic.

Another tear slipped out. It lingered on Beth's eyelash before sliding down her cheek; she didn't bother wiping away the shiny trail left behind.

She remembered how distant she'd been from Mom and Dad this last year. By now, they must have forgotten about her, off having adventures with deceased family and friends, like Aunt Maria with her fluffy white hair and gentle nature, or Uncle Fred with his dirty mind and boisterous personality. Beth was the last of their concerns.

Jason must have noticed the change in her expression because his face fell. "Sorry."

More tears dripped down her cheeks as she sat, gazing into what remained of the fire. For a moment, Beth let herself escape into that distant world among the dancing flames.

Jason shifted in his seat, pulling her from her daze.

Wiping the remaining tears with her hands, Beth whispered,

"I'm sorry." It was all she could think to say.

But she didn't know who her sorry belonged to—Jason, Mom and Dad, the town, the dead men, Chris, or the hollow she carried inside.

THE BOY
THE BOY

By the time he returned, the sun had reached its peak. It hung so low in the sky, he felt like he could stretch high enough to sear his fingers on it. The days were getting warmer, or maybe he was building a tolerance to his surroundings.

Only a small heap of charred wood and gray ash remained from the fire. Beth and Jason were nowhere outside.

Fists clenched, Chris headed for the shack. A few steps in, he stopped short, dust sailing around his ankles. A thought struck him: Jason could be useful. Chris could feed him a story, get him to watch the evening news, and report back tomorrow. The TV had more to offer than the radio. More details meant staying ahead. And staying ahead meant making smarter moves.

He smoothed out his expression before opening the door.

Inside, Beth and Jason were sitting on the mattress, talking in hushed voices. Their heads spun around, and Jason waved. "Hey."

Time passed in uncomfortable silence. Chris saw Jason sidestep anything that might set him off—no talk of school, family, anything real. He scrambled for safe topics and eventually, landed on sports, asking about Chris' favorite all-star events.

So Chris bragged about his record-breaking Little League stats, proud that he was the only kid in Wanapatchee to play every game without a strikeout. His earned run average was 2.0, giving up only two runs per game.

Jason listened closely, pulling off his glasses now and then to clean the lenses with the front of his shirt. He held them to the light, checking for smudges, nodding in the right moments. Subtle cues like half smiles and quiet shifts showed he was amused and paying attention.

Chris spoke about the time he and Dad flew to Toronto for his last hockey tournament. As he talked, he remembered a photograph hanging in Dad's office. The Les Four Glaces rink, leaning proudly against the Stanley Cup, grins on their faces. That was where they met Martin Brodeur, the renowned goalie for the New Jersey Devils.

"He was one of the best goalies of all time," said Chris. "And he could barely speak English when we met him."

He had to admit it felt cool talking to another boy, even if Jason had never picked up a hockey stick or knew what a hat trick was.

Then Chris thought about all his hard-earned trophies, now reduced to chunks and pieces of gold-painted metal, plastic, and ash. He yearned to slip back home and salvage his memories. When the story ended, he felt hollow and upset with Jason for making him stir up those flashbacks.

Jason said he'd always wanted to try hockey, but his dad insisted he keep his teeth. Beth laughed at this. She must have remembered her foul breath because she excused herself to the hydrant pump with her new toothbrush, toothpaste, and soap.

Chris seized the opportunity and, acting in an off-the-cuff fashion, suggested watching the news with Jason. After a moment of thought, Jason accepted.

"Can I ask you something?" Jason sat on the mattress, his back against the same wall as the door. From that angle, Chris met Jason's steady gaze.

"Sure, whatever."

"How come you don't turn yourselves in?

Chris wrinkled his forehead. "Turn ourselves in for what?"

Jason explained how he knew about the break-in at Dominion Gardens and what had happened to the officers. It was a story that would make anyone sane want to run screaming or at least cringe in judgment. But Jason played it cool.

Beth had run her mouth. Chris clenched his jaw. "There's more to the story than you know," he said. "And I know what would happen if we went to the police. They'd separate us and throw us somewhere worse than this. No offense."

Jason shut his eyes, nodding.

His silence invited more talk. "And imagine what would happen to Beth if they threw her in a home somewhere. I mean, I could handle it, but not her."

Only Dad could understand Chris' position. Dad would be scared to death to think of Beth in the hands of strangers. Given the circumstances, Chris had no choice but to take on the responsibilities of provider and watchdog for his sister. That was the patriarch's role. He knew Dad would agree.

Jason opened his mouth but said nothing.

An uneasy silence settled in. Neither knew what to say.

"So, let me ask you something," Chris pressed.

Jason grinned.

"Why'd your dad build this place anyway?"

Jason snickered. "I guess he likes his privacy. He says once I'm old enough to go to college, he plans to live out here for good. But," he adjusted his glasses, "I think the real reason was to keep busy after my mom died. He was always outdoorsy, fixing and building things. He's good at it. I'm not, but I like helping him, and he doesn't mind much when I do. He's planning to generate power and maybe even grow his own food. You know, hydroponics and stuff."

Jason went on to say that the area was government-owned, but since his father had once been close with a few councilmen in town, they permitted him space to build here. Other residents built log cabins decades before but eventually left the forest to be closer to society.

"Anyhow, he's not close to done," said Jason. "And he stopped before finishing the insulating felt in the walls. That's partly why you two must be freezing. He just took a break from it for a while. Luckily, he installed that pump. The borehole was pretty much worthless."

"Borehole?"

"Yeah."

"What the heck is a borehole?"

"Oh, there's an old well near here. About the length of a football field away."

Chris stared, his face unreadable.

"You know, for water. By the way, your sister told me how you cleaned the stream water and made it safe to drink. Most people wouldn't think to do that."

O   O   O

When three o'clock came, a roll of clouds veiled the sun, dimming the light inside the shack.

"I'm hungry again," Chris said to himself. He lay on his back, studying the wood patterns in the ceiling. His hand drifted over the revolver at the front of his pants. Beth and Jason sat cross-legged on the new blankets spread over the mattress.

"Me too," Jason agreed.

Beth nodded, running her tongue over her newly polished teeth. Chris did the same. The minty taste reminded him of Dad's favorite treat, Peppermint Patty, and how much he enjoyed nibbling on them after dinner.

"Then how about cookin' us up some grub, jock?" The explosive voice called from outside the window.

Everyone jumped as a breeze blew through the cracks, waving the blankets on the mattress.

Beth shrieked.

Chris leaped up, dodging the ceiling at the last second.

Dylan threw his head back, hooting his unruly laugh. "C'mon, you gotta honor your bets, bro!"

46

JASON and DYLAN

JASON and DYLAN

"That's a cool knife, man."

Dylan watched Chris slide the skinner knife from its leather sheath. The blade flashed, glinting in the light while he turned it over in his bruised hands, his gaze lost somewhere far away. Dylan stayed alert. If Chris snapped, if he reached for the shotgun or let the knife fly, he'd be ready to act in an instant.

Jason's locker sat untouched that morning. At lunch, he wasn't in the library either. Unease prickled at Dylan as he borrowed a kid's cell phone and dialed Jason's house. No answer. Something was off. Heart pounding, he hopped on his bike the moment the final bell rang and tore through the streets towards the woods. He reached the shack window in record time.

Ignoring puzzled stares, he pushed through the shack door and plopped into the farthest corner behind the round table. He leaned forward to get a better look at the knife. The polished blade caught the soft afternoon light. "Where'd you get it?"

Chris raised his head but avoided Dylan's watchful eyes. Despite his obvious tension, his legs swung over the loft like ribbons caught in a breeze. "Thanks."

"Your dad get you that?"

Chris' eyes dropped, landing on the blade in his lap.

Beth caught her breath.

"C'mon, Dylan," Jason said. "Remember, their dad just died."

Chris glanced up and shared a look with Beth. He forced a small smile, mirroring hers.

"Oh, yeah. Sorry, dude."

To everyone's surprise, including the teachers, Dylan and Jason became friends. A year earlier, eighth-graders had started harassing Jason for being a "dirty foreigner" in the advanced classes. Jason wasn't from Wanapatchee but from Hollis, a quiet, shabby community with modest homes on the outskirts. The town had fewer than four thousand working-class residents and was considered low-class by neighboring towns. Most kids lived in the same district as Wanapatchee Elementary, but a small percentage were marked as remarkable by the school board and commuted to attend a special program outside the standard curriculum. Its syllabus was designed to prepare them for high school. Chris was among these students.

Jason was smaller than most kids, making him an easy target who seldom fought back, mostly out of fear of worse punishment. Dylan knew from experience that sneers and ribbing were only the start; soon they'd turn into shoves against lockers, in gym class, maybe worse.

One afternoon, Dylan's parents made him stay late for extra tutoring. The hallways emptied as most kids hurried home, while a few small groups lingered, their voices echoing from club-filled classrooms.

After his session, Dylan walked down an empty, dimming hallway when he heard a lanky eighth-grade jock with a puppet smile and crazed eyes heckling Jason by his locker. A red baseball hat sat high on his head. The boy was pissed because Jason had refused to do his math homework.

"Why not?" he sneered. "You're supposed to be smart. How about sharing some of that knowledge, huh?"

Jason caught Dylan's eyes and looked at him in panic. His face was exposed, less protected with the bully's fist around his glasses.

Dylan dropped his books and rushed in, knocking the kid's head against the locker. The boy hit his knees before Dylan gave him one last kick in the chest.

"How do you like that, you faggot!" he hollered at the kid sprawled out on the floor. "Not so tough without your friends, huh?"

Dylan sat in silence for a week in detention, a crooked grin on his face. Since then, he earned a reputation for being a little crazy, which suited him fine because the kids left him alone. Everyone but Jason.

He slipped into detention to find Dylan, timing his entrance for the moment when Mr. Woodman, nicknamed "Howdy Doody" for his patchy red hair and odd freckles, ducked out for a bathroom break. Hoping for a little safety and maybe even a friend, Jason struck a deal: he'd tutor Dylan twice a week in his failing subjects. Dylan, who'd already endured a second round of sixth grade thanks to math and history, grudgingly accepted.

Glares kept coming, but the bullies kept their distance, afraid of the crazy kid with long hair and loud shirts. To his surprise, Dylan's grades improved and he graduated sixth grade.

"Dylan," said Jason, "someone could have followed you here."

Beth gasped. "Oh my God, Chris."

"Relax,' said Dylan. "Why would anyone follow me? No one has a clue I even know who you two are. And I buried my bike in the weeds." He tapped his chest. "Junior high, remember?"

Everyone let out a breath except Chris. "Yeah, but someone could be keeping a watch on you."

"He's right, Dylan," Jason added. "You should be careful."

"Hey, what about you, Genie? You came here. Ditching class wasn't smart. It made you, like more concupiscent!"

All eyes turned to Jason.

Beth giggled. "I guess you didn't tutor him in English."

Dylan glared at her. "How would you know?"

"Well," she said, cheeks flushing, "Jason may have...urges and things. But I think you meant *conspicuous*."

There was a brief pause before Chris spoke. "Ask her to define it. Dictionary, remember?"

Dylan squinted, mouthing the word conspicuous.

"Flipping through your dad's magazines again, Dylan?" Jason burst out laughing. The twins joined in.

The mood inside the shack lightened, and for a moment they

were regular kids hanging out, sharing a joke at Dylan's expense.

Dylan's eyes narrowed. "Oh, screw all ya'!"

The laughter swelled and despite himself, Dylan let loose, breaking out into a rumbling howl.

○   ○   ○

The smell of sweat and wood smoke clung to Beth like a second skin.

Jason's expression said it all. She carried the scent of the earth and river, her skin rough, coated in sweat and speckled with grime. The soap, a stained rag, and the water pump eased the worst of it, but it was nothing like a real bath.

She insisted on washing up at the stream. Chris said he'd escort her but promised to give her privacy. Jason and Dylan tagged along.

To Dylan's surprise, he found himself relaxing around Chris. He remembered reading in his dad's paper last year about Chris Pacelli, the classmate who led his team to the Little League state championship. Chris had been painted as brave, admired by everyone, and unflappable when things got tough. A kid destined for big things, a young athlete with a bright future.

Now, here was that same Chris, toughing it out in the woods in shitty conditions with no adult in sight. And he watched over his sister, just as Dylan did with Jason. And that earned Dylan's respect.

Unlike Dylan, Jason had grown wary of Chris. Beth kept quiet about her brother, but Jason sensed something was wrong. Chris always kept a gun or knife close, and he had Beth under his control. Jason had come up with a dozen explanations for the purple-yellow bruise along her jaw.

"If my dad didn't mind, I'd let you shower at my house," Jason said. "At least you'd have warm water and towels."

The three boys sat on rocks the size of medicine balls, about fifty yards from Beth. Birds chirped, toads croaked, and the breeze rustled the trees. The sun was a few hours from setting.

"It's cool. Thanks though. Would be dumb to walk around out

there anyway."

Chris scratched a baseball diamond into a patch of pine needles with a stick. The bolt cutter rested beside his left foot, beyond reach from Jason and Dylan. His backpack sagged low on his back.

Dylan sighed, gazing at the crude sketch. "Damn, that sucks." He switched his attention to Jason. "What time did he finally get home this time?"

Jason shot his friend a helpless look.

Chris stopped sketching.

Jason said his dad hadn't come home yet.

"Christ, Genie. That was like, two days ago. You should report that to the police or something—" He stopped himself and looked away.

Chris studied Jason. "Your dad in construction, or what?"

"He's a badass," Dylan jumped in. "He's got an arsenal locked up in his garage. I've never seen shit like that before."

"Whatever. You see that stuff all the time in video games."

Dylan scoffed. "It's way different, Jay."

"Don't forget," Jason added, "after my dad knew I'd cracked the combination and snuck into his safe, he ripped me a new one."

Dylan blew a cloud of hot air. "Yeah, I remember. I still feel bad about that, man."

"What's your dad need all that stuff for, anyway?" asked Chris. "To hunt deer and squirrels?"

Dylan snorted. "No way. He doesn't trust the government, man. Says he's waiting for them to attack in waves or somethin'."

Chris nodded, clearing out a two-inch space for third base. "I hear you. My dad says a handgun can't beat a tank."

Dylan and Jason exchanged a look.

"A handgun might protect your family. But my dad says we have powerful weapons to protect us from enemies, even domestic ones. Like—don't know if this is the right word—a tyrannical government. Ask Beth. She'll tell you."

"Oh, shit!" Dylan slapped his knee. "We were talking about that in class the other day. Something about England's Magnum thing."

Jason cracked a grin. "I think you mean the Magna Carta."

Dylan met his friends gaze, unblinking.

"Remember, it was founded in the thirteenth century to help King John make peace with the rebels. It limited payments to the crown and stopped those in power from taking too much liberty. Just like our Constitution. They say the Magna Carta influenced it."

"Yeah, but my dad says governments take more liberty than they ought to," Dylan said, rolling his eyes.

Chris studied the ground as if searching for answers hidden in the dust.

He shared stories from his granddad's Navy days. How he'd worked in signal intelligence, tracking Russian nuclear threats after the first artificial satellite circled the planet. He mentioned a tense episode called the Pueblo Crisis in 1969, when North Korea seized a U.S. ship, its crew, and their secrets, claiming the vessel had strayed into forbidden waters.

Tracking Russians. Satellites. Spy games. The kind of heavy secrets adults kept locked away from kids. Dylan never cared for history, and most of Chris' words slipped past him, but the steady, confident way the kid spoke made Dylan lean in, hungry for more.

"You know," said Jason, "some people think we won the Second World War because we were armed. If not, the Japanese might've invaded the homeland."

"Christ, Jay, is there anything you *don't* know?"

"I read a lot, Dylan. You know that."

Chris kept his eyes on the diamond in the dirt, raking a few more lines. "My great-granddad served under George S. Patton. He fought in that war. Earned medals. He was a hero."

"No shit?" Dylan raised a brow. "That was a cool flick."

Jason sighed and shook his head.

"'When the people fear the government, there is tyranny. When the government fears the people, there is liberty.' Thomas Jefferson," Chris mumbled.

Everyone fell quiet. A small animal rustled in the brush. The soft roar of the stream carried through the trees.

"My dad was a hero too. He served in the Navy," Chris added. "And his uncles got drafted during the Vietnam War." He seemed to be staring through the dirt into another world.

"Dude, I don't wanna be the asshole or anything, but you talk about your dad like he's still here."

Chris's shoulders tensed.

Dylan met Jason's glare, shrugging. "Sorry, man. Just sayin'."

A hush settled over them. Jason and Dylan watched the dirt, their eyes tracing Chris' hands as he scratched out the crowd around the diamond, dozens of tiny holes dotting the field.

47

THE GIRL

She scrubbed in quick, brisk strokes, the joy of feeling clean overshadowed by the sting of icy water. Her underwear sat on a flat rock, baking in a sunlit patch. Jason's blanket, a pair of Chris's socks, and a fresh t-shirt rested on another rock nearby, ready to grab.

Bathing in a cold stream full of bugs and slimy things stunk. Beth missed her old shower with the blue and white tiles, the high-pressure water pounding her back while silly concerns of the day flooded her mind. But those days were long gone.

She positioned herself behind a beam of light, letting the shadows hide her body. Being naked in the woods made her more anxious than usual, like that time in fourth grade when she chased down the bully who'd punched her in the face.

The rocks sticking out of the pool were slippery. Beth took her time stepping onto one before hopping onto a small patch of earth. Goosebumps prickling her skin, she seized the blanket, wrapping it around herself.

Trees screened the space, offering some privacy. The warmth in the air faded, her underwear still damp. Holding the blanket around her shoulders, Beth pulled on her jeans and then the t-shirt, the Islanders logo bright against the fabric. The thought of the boys seeing her wet underwear clutched in her hands terrified her.

She tucked them into her front pocket.

When the boys appeared, Chris was in front, the bolt cutter resting on his left shoulder and a crude snare gripped in his right hand. He'd hidden the trap inside a shallow hole by the stream, disguised with sprigs and leaves.

Chris planned to take her back to the shack, then return to the water to catch dinner before darkness fell in less than three hours.

"Why can't I just stay out here with you guys?" Beth pushed.

"Because the less of us out here, the better."

Chris had a point, in his own way. Yet returning to that room, where her thoughts mingled with the heavy, musty air, promised a loneliness Beth wasn't ready to face. She opened her mouth to protest, but Jason intervened. "It's okay, guys." He looked at Chris. "I'll walk her back. I know this part of the woods well."

THE BOY

THE BOY

"I wouldn't go in all the way, buddy. Your dick'll shrivel up to the size of a thimble." Dylan stooped along the bank, watching him work the snare.

Chris had agreed to let Jason walk Beth back, but not before pulling her aside. He reminded her about the weapons in the loft, and the pepper spray in her back pocket. Then he squeezed his compass into her hand and insisted they walk as far southeast as possible.

Dylan offered to stay behind. "It's cool," he said. "Jason, take her. I'll hang back with—uh, the jock here."

A clumsy but amusing attempt at praise. Chris smiled, appreciating the nickname.

The plan was simple: if they heard rustling or crunching, he'd duck behind a tree or thick brush, leaving Dylan by the stream. No panic. No problem.

With his jeans rolled past his knees, Chris stepped into the stream and set the snare. The water was freezing. He thought of Beth and how she'd bathed in it just a few minutes ago. "A thimble, huh?" he said, bending over the current with the trap in his hands. "Know from experience?"

Dylan pulled a red lighter and what looked like a hand-rolled cigarette from his jacket. Once lit, he took a few deep hits and let the smoke drift. Gray clouds crept overhead, slow and heavy, sailing along the opposite bank.

After a moment, his eyes glazed over. He held the joint out to Chris, who watched the water rush past his legs. "Wanna hit, bro?"

Chris turned, wincing at the sharp and skunky stink in the air. "No thanks."

Dylan didn't get it. Chris wasn't fishing for fun. This was food—for him and for Beth. He nodded at the snare. "Got work to do."

"Suit yourself." Dylan shrugged and took another drag.

Chris had never known anyone who smoked pot. He'd heard hippies liked it and some older folks used it for pain. But a thirteen-year-old? For fun? "Your folks know you smoke that stuff?"

Dylan laughed, smoke curling from his mouth. "You kiddin'? They'd flip out if I smoked cigarettes, let alone this. Which reminds me..." With the joint pinched between his lips, he pulled a bottle of Visine and a can of body spray from his jacket pocket. "Lifesavers, my friend."

Chris kept his eyes on the snare. He didn't want to miss a single shot at a catch.

"What's the deal with your sister, anyway?" Dylan leaned his head back, squeezing a few drops into his eyes.

Chris shot him a look. "What do you mean?"

"I dunno. I saw her in school a few times. Is she slow or somethin'?"

"You saw her?"

"Yeah. Some asshole kids were pickin' on her."

"She's not slow," muttered Chris, wiping his brow with his forearm. "She's smart. A lot of people don't see it. She's just...misunderstood."

"Holy shit, dude," exclaimed Dylan. "I feel the same way. People don't get me."

Chris grinned and shook his head. He couldn't imagine Beth having anything in common with this sloppy, pot-smoking kid.

A stiff breeze passed through the trees. Leaves swayed in the gust while a few freed from their branches, flecking the stream below. Dylan looked up, watching them fall.

Chris turned his head just as Dylan met his eyes. Dylan dropped his gaze, shoulders tight, staring at his scuffed shoes like they had something to say.

If Dylan and Jason planned to stick around, Chris needed to be clever. With Dylan's mind anesthetized, Chris figured it would be easy to pull information from him. "What's the deal with Jason? Is he cool?"

Dylan blinked, then nodded. "Yeah, he's cool. A good friend. But he became a bit of a dick after the last time I got him in trouble."

"What'd he do?"

Dylan gave a quick, nervous laugh. "I dunno. Just stopped taking my shit, I guess." He cocked his head, grinning. "Why do you care? 'Cause he likes your sister? Don't worry about him."

"I'm not worried," said Chris, brushing it off. "Just curious."

"His dad's the real dick. If Jason tells him you and your sister are out here, the guy'll lose it. Might even call the cops. Try to cash in or somethin'."

Chris caught his breath, standing firm in his gut feeling. Something about Jason didn't sit right. It pressed at him like a finger poking his shoulder, refusing to relent. "Jason said he hasn't been out here in a long time. I'm sure we're fine."

"Well, I wasn't kidding before. The man owns some serious shit. Just be careful. He drinks."

Chris nodded slowly. "What serious shit?"

"Dunno know exactly. Just bigger than the guns you've got back there."

"Uh-huh. I know Jason said he likes to hunt deer."

Dylan narrowed his eyes. Maybe it was suspicion, maybe the drugs. "Yeah, he loves hunting. Even got a tattoo for it."

A fierce heat flared inside Chris' chest. It pulsed before sinking into his gut. Still, he stayed calm, eyes fixed on the water several feet beyond the snare. "Does he take Jason with him?"

"What's with all the questions? Why're you so interested?"

Chris shrugged. "Not really. Just talking."

Dylan laughed, then took another drag. "If you want to talk, let's talk about you giving me that sweet knife of yours. Or better yet, the rifle."

Sunfish swirled around the snare, reeling between Chris's legs. "Shit."

"Missed one, huh?"

He barely had time to brace himself before Dad's temper flared, turning his cheeks crimson. Missing out chewed at him, and losing stung even more when there was an audience. Chris lost count of how many game controllers he'd shattered in his fury. Against people, he always won; against the computer, it was a different story. "This isn't freaking easy, you know. If you want to try, go ahead."

To his surprise, Dylan stood, dusted his jeans with his hands, and kicked off his shoes and socks. He stepped twice into the water before leaping out. "Holy shit! That's cold, man!"

Chris laughed, shaking off his temper. The tension eased, and he steered the conversation back. "Well, his dad seems alright. I mean, it's cool he takes Jason shooting."

"Not really," corrected Dylan. "His dad's a hard ass. Jason doesn't go huntin' with him much anymore. He'd rather hang in the library or humor me by watching me play video games at my house. His dad has a huntin' buddy now, I think."

A pit grew in Chris' stomach, twisting like he'd just corkscrewed around the bend of a rickety roller coaster—the scary ones Beth liked.

As anxious as he was to ask, he decided to wait until the walk back to the shack. For now, impossible as it seemed, he focused on catching dinner.

Minutes later, a swarm of sunfish and a catfish jetted downstream into his snare. Several slipped away, while others struggled against the cotton trap. Straddling on slick rocks, Chris adjusted his stance and tightened his grip on the snare. "C'mon," he muttered.

48

THE GIRL

THE GIRL

Being alone with Jason again churned her gut like an ice cream mixer. She feared what might spill from her mouth once those soft blue eyes locked on her tired brown ones. Mrs. Calmin had the same knack for nudging her to open up. So did Alexis Johnson.

Beth and Jason paced south through blooming brush. She gripped the compass in her hand, but Jason led, confident in his course. She stole glances every few minutes to check their path.

The sun slipped through the trees, and the air cooled to the low fifties, damp and sharp. Beth braced for a cold night in the shack. She rubbed her arms, trying to warm herself, wishing she'd brought the bomber jacket.

Jason offered his jacket; she accepted only after he wrapped it around her shoulders. Warmth blanketed her. "Thank you."

He smiled, then led them down a new path from the one Chris had taken. The trees thinned along this trail, opening space to move without branches scraping skin and faces. White flowers and oblong leaves replaced the spiky underbrush from before. Beth wanted to stop, breathe in the scents, admire the view, but reminded herself this was no ordinary hike in the woods.

Jason warned hikers, tourists, and hunters would soon flood the park. It hadn't struck Beth she might be out here through summer, maybe longer. The thought of struggling through winter in that horrible shack sent a shiver through her. She recalled the film *The Shining* and Jack Torrance frozen in a snowbank, eyes rolled back as if trying to peek at his brain before death.

Their footsteps crunched sprigs and small white and purple shrubs as untold thoughts stirred in their heads. Beth's mind raced at warp speed, but she kept silent.

It occurred to her that Jason's pathway might lead them towards the unfinished well. The hole was deep and dark, but what if he got close enough to look down? Would it stink of rotten meat and garbage? Her stomach flipped at the thought.

Then don't think about it. Distract yourself. Anything else. Hey, check out that butt!

Drawn in by the voice, Beth snuck a glance at Jason's rear end and, burst of graceless timing, snorted a laugh. Jason turned back just as her eyes shifted to a clover patch between her feet, veiling her grin behind the back of her hand. "Sorry. I saw a funny-looking squirrel."

Jason smiled, nodded, and walked on.

Beth wondered if animals caught the scent of rotten meat and climbed down the hole to feed. In a generous world, they already had, clearing the well of everything except the skeletons. Bones didn't smell.

She inhaled, testing the air. Minty evergreen and rich soil sailed up her nose.

They reached the shack in thirty minutes. The route took longer than Chris' but was smoother. Jason avoided the hole but pointed it out after crossing several yards west. "Over there is the well I told your brother about."

Nightfall was still a couple of hours away. Thick clouds dimmed the sun, casting shadows inside the shack. Beth stood by the window, her gaze fixed. The thought of sitting alone in the dark with a boy sparked butterflies fluttering in her belly again.

"I'm sure they're fine," said Jason. "Your brother seems like a resourceful guy. And Dylan—well, I never worry about him."

Beth shrunk back from the window and spun around. Jason stood close enough that his breath stirred the hair on the back of her head. She raced for something to say, fidgeting with her hands, then her hair. It felt awkward not knowing how to feel.

"It must be nice, having a brother," Jason said. He dropped onto the mattress with a thump, then the soft scratching of fabric as he shifted into position.

Beth's nerves cooled. Distance felt safer, comforting. "Huh?"

"I never had a brother or sister. Not even a pet. I was curious what having a brother is like."

She clung to Jason's question, a brief reprieve from the bodies rotting a hundred yards away and the boy stretched out on the bed before her.

The twins had been inseparable as long as Beth could remember. If Chris begged Mom to pin a beach towel around his neck so he could climb the stair posts as Batman, Beth followed as his loyal sidekick, Robin. If one wandered to the corner candy shop, the other trailed behind, clutching a handful of change inside a plastic bank from a McDonald's Happy Meal. If one fired up the Nintendo, the other grabbed a controller and joined in.

That was how it went until fourth grade, when Chris grew into sports and the neighborhood boys. Beth followed along as best she could but soon felt like an imposter, discovering the charm and magic of reading alone.

"We had a pet," she said, her expression falling. "A puppy. We named her Sandy."

"Yeah?"

Beth nodded. "She had problems."

"What kind of problems?"

"She was sick. Real sick."

Shortly after they brought the small dachshund home, Sandy bumped into walls and even tried climbing them. One day, she and Chris heard Mom shriek in the kitchen. A puddle of reddish-yellow liquid, thick as maple syrup, pooled at her feet. Sandy had epilepsy. The vet put her to sleep—as they say. After that, Mom and Dad never bought them another pet, except for Chris' rescue, but that lasted only a few weeks.

"I'm sorry, Beth. That stinks."

Silence returned, cold and deep.

"Hey!" Jason clapped his hands. "Almost forgot. I have something for you."

Fear flooded Beth's veins, her insides clenching.

Please don't be something awful. Get ready.

Her left hand grazed the pepper spray as she glanced left, catching the rifle and shotgun shapes in the dark.

"Check your pocket."

"Huh?"

"It's inside your pocket. You're still wearing my jacket."

Beth's jaw tensed. Her fingers clenched into fists.

"Go ahead," he pressed.

Beth slipped her right hand into the jacket and touched something small. She pulled out a tiny blue book, no larger than two inches long and an inch and a half thick. It sat in the palm of her hand. She looked at Jason.

"It's a dictionary!" he beamed.

A flood of relief washed over her.

Dictionary?

Jason nodded and laughed. "Your brother said you like to study the dictionary. I thought this would help pass the time."

Before she could grasp what was happening, Beth felt her chest tighten. Her eyes grew moist, blurring her vision.

Wow, he was listening.

"Beth?" he said, barely a whisper. "You okay? I thought you might like it. Is it stupid?"

She lifted her head, shaking it. With blinking eyes, she tried to hold a clear image of the boy sitting on the edge of the mattress. He was as still as a chameleon watching its prey, ready to strike with its far-reaching tongue.

Beth longed for her hefty, two-thousand-page unabridged dictionary, its torn red sleeve and bent corners a testament to years of devotion. She hunted for new words from TV shows and books, jotting their definitions into a secret, homemade notebook; she memorized them like spells, eager to slip them into conversation. Doing so drew more confusion and scowls—more than when she brought Mom's homemade brownies to school on her birthday, only to have a classmate crack a tooth on one. The lesson was clear: never show people the limits of their vocabulary. They find it rude, and they hate it.

Beth's mind wandered, then flashed to a memory.

Everyone is sitting at the dinner table.

She stares, stunned, as Mom thumbs through her homemade dictionary.

"I won't snoop in your room again if you can define one word of my choice," she says.

Through clamped teeth, Beth nods. The word is vivacious, tucked under melancholy and above lugubrious.

"Spirited," Beth says instantly. "Lively." Exactly what she wrote in her notebook.

Surprised, and with a hint of resentment, Mom closes the book and hands it over.

"I know this is more my place than yours, but you can sit down. I don't bite. Okay, maybe I did once."

Beth blinked, shaking the memory off.

"Jonathan Elroy. Third grade. He pushed me off the swings to show his idiot friends what a hotshot he was." Jason shrugged. "So I jumped on him, and before I knew it, I bit him on the arm."

"Jason!"

He laughed, raising his arms high. "What can I say? I snapped."

Beth circled the mattress. Her ankle hit the corner, nearly landing face-first on Jason. Mortified, she reached her spot against the wall, avoiding the discomfort of proximity and intimacy. She drew her legs in and rested her chin on her knees, lacing her fingers around her ankles.

Jason twisted around, keeping his spot on the bed. "I'm sure your brother will be back soon. He'll have some food for you. Then Dylan and I can leave, and you two can eat."

Thinking of Jason leaving again left Beth wounded, like being socked in the stomach by the Hulk's rocklike fist. Nothing cut deeper than a goodbye. "When are you leaving?" she asked.

"When they return, I guess. My dad must be home by now."

Beth wanted to scream for Jason to take her with him. She wanted everything he had: a house, a father, a chance to go to school. She'd lost Mom and Dad, but what about a new home? Would society welcome her back or shove her into juvenile detention? Or prison? Why not the electric chair or lethal injection, however they did it in Jersey? She was a murderer, after all.

The truth hadn't touched her until now. Her life wasn't hers anymore—it was already gone. She just hadn't noticed.

"Jason...?"

"Yeah?"

"What is your dad like?"

"My father?"

"Yes."

"Why?"

"I don't know. Maybe because your dad sounds a little like mine. Like how my dad was. Used to be."

She remembered a rare night when her Girl Scouts troop hosted a square dance at the elementary school. All Scouts were encouraged to bring their fathers. Dad worked late, as he often did, and came home after the event was over. Beth was crestfallen.

Later that night, he challenged her to a game on Chris's old-school tabletop NHL set. One match turned into three, and she won them all. Maybe she had improved since playing against Chris, but part of her still wondered.

"I kind of doubt that, Beth," Jason laughed. "Let's just say what my dad lacks in brains, he makes up for in being cool—sometimes. But he can also be an asshole."

Beth slapped a hand over her mouth, giggling.

Jason's cheeks flushed. "Sorry."

"It's okay." She'd grown up hearing worse from Mom than most soldiers did in basic training.

Jason broke into laughter. "I r-r-remember back when my mom was alive, my dad and I had this father-son weekend. We spent the day hunting quail, and later he took me to this tattoo shop. Said I was old enough to get one, but I chickened out. I felt bad, so he got one instead. Probably to prove it wasn't a big deal." He laughed harder. "To this day, I remember how loud he screamed when the guy stuck that needle in his arm. He even made me feed him something to help with the pain."

"What was it?"

"Bourbon. Yuk, right?"

49

THE BOY

Morning came quick. Birds cheeped from the trees, welcoming the new day. Chris wondered if the animals had grown to expect him, maybe even anticipated his presence. He thought about Blake and how strange and sad it was that a bird had become his closest friend. Over time, he'd learned to recognize Blake's tweets. They lasted about forty-four seconds, seven chirps in a row.

Jason and Dylan had stayed longer than planned. Chris caught three fish; Beth offered to let them share the third while she and Chris enjoyed theirs. He could have swallowed all three in two minutes, but for Beth's sake and to keep the peace, he said nothing.

After they ate, Jason said he'd bring back a surprise, whatever that meant. The thought of him returning set his nerves on edge.

He'd spent the last hour deep in thought. Dylan hadn't given him the answers he wanted. Smoking by the river had dulled his mind and twisted his words, making him nearly impossible to understand.

"You awake?"

THE GIRL

Chris's voice, sharp as static, made her flinch. He looked like a corpse in a casket, body straight, hands laced over his stomach. If not for his open eyes, Beth would have called out to make sure he was breathing. "I am now," she mumbled.

She still wore Jason's jacket, wrapped in one of the new blankets. Smooth fleece brushed her dry skin like a thousand butterflies, covering everything but her half-open eyes. She took in her first breaths of the day; the sharp scent of mildew and rotting wood gave way to the blanket's gentle aroma of jasmine and lavender.

For a minute, she let her mind drift and imagined Jason's house. The blanket spread over the back of a fluffy sofa in their family room. Fresh flowers displayed high on the coffee table where the family played fun games like Uno and Life. Maybe some art on the walls and purple air fresheners plugged into the outlets.

As Beth lay awake, watching the morning sun brighten the dull walls, her thoughts drifted to Jason and the pain of letting him go. For the first time, she felt indifferent to Chris's feelings. She had found a new friend, so why would he want to take that away? Why couldn't he understand?

Beth lumbered across the mattress and stood up, rubbing the gooseflesh from her arms. A brisk breeze slipped through the cracks in the window and under the door. It seeped inside the cabin like a ghost, snickering at her discomfort.

"Where are you going?"

Stiff from the cold, Beth heard her neck crack as she turned her head to look at the door. Her bladder felt like a loaded balloon about to burst. "I gotta pee."

Chris rolled over, facing the wall away from her, burrowing his face into the bomber jacket he used as a pillow. "Don't go too far," he warned. "Stay close."

"Uh huh."

The thinning paper towel roll sat on the shelf beside the sink. Beth grabbed it and shuffled to the door, squinting at the brilliant light beyond the threshold. She hadn't felt the sun on her skin much lately, her time outside reduced to nestling in the shade and under storm clouds in small bursts.

Today, the sun was bright and warm. It felt like a veil of soft kisses brushing her skin, and she wanted nothing more than to lie outside and soak it up, just like she did on her heated driveway after an afternoon swim.

A strange, fierce urge to return to the ravine stirred in her, but she didn't trust her sense of direction enough to risk the hike.

So it was the hole.

Chris wasn't watching from the window, so she tiptoed around a bed of roots and stones, then followed the weedy trail to the well.

Beth half expected a pair of scabbed, bloody-taloned hands to be clawing their way up the side of the rocks. Maybe by the time she got there, they'd have pulled themselves high enough for their pallid, broken faces to peek through the sticks and leaves she and Chris had laid down. The thought made her mouth taste like sour milk. But ignoring the dead was far worse than facing them.

If it bothers you that much, then think of going back as penance for what you did.

Beth pulled herself forward, every movement heavy with exhaustion and hope, drawn to the bore in the ground. Deep inside, a quiet voice told her that part of Chris wanted to be found too. Maybe then the nightmare could finally end and the crushing weight of caring for himself and his sister might ease. But Chris was stubborn, just like Dad. He would never give in to anyone, not after coming this far.

She reached the hole.

Since the shooting, the hunter's face refused to disappear. It reminded her of an old horror film she and Chris had stayed up late watching. A madman built a woman out of pieces of other women he'd killed. The gray creature came alive and clawed its dead hand between the man's legs, ripping off his privates. The horrified look on his face mirrored the hunter's when Beth clipped off a piece of his skull.

I know it stinks. But you did what you had to do.

A nod. "Uh, huh."

The voice cut through her doubts, hitting her with the hard truth. Seeing Chris limp and powerless on the floor, his purple face knotted in pain and that man's hands hooked around his throat, lit a fire inside her. His suffering mirrored in her, sharp and unyielding.

Her survival voice hissed low and cold, and Beth shivered. "I can't do that."

Think of it as a baptism for the next chapter in your life. A middle finger to everything that's broken you. It could even make you stronger. Besides, no one's watching.

The hunters, those cruel faces and voices, flashed through her mind like electric shocks.

It's a game. Like the one you played back home.

"Manhunt."

Yes. But instead of guarding the porch, you put the prisoners to sleep with a serum. So they can't escape.

The idea was insane, but it made brutal sense.

Beth let the thought sear through her. A grin split her face, feral and electric. Something alive clawed its way up through the numb that she hadn't felt since Jason's first return to the shack.

She dropped to her knees.

Inch by inch, as if daring the world to stop her, Beth pulled down her jeans. She squatted forward so her weight balanced on the balls of her feet, placed her cold hands over her face, and went.

50

THE BOY

He pulled the radio from his pack and switched it on. The news came first, then the games.

But Chris caught himself.

Reminders of those pleasures would only swell the hole in his heart, fueling his hatred for his situation and those responsible. He needed to be outside. Running, throwing, roughhousing with the guys. He needed to be young again.

After a man chimed in to introduce the next segment of a radio drama, Chris realized there'd be no news today. This week's show was *Zorihon 4*, a sassy P.I. who could slow time. She lived on a planet called Sunanu. With her band of misfits—a zealous techie, a lewd archaeologist, and a sniveling rat monster—she uncovered multidimensional conspiracies, the mob, super villains, and sometimes even gods.

For the first time in his life, Chris cursed Friday.

He switched off the dynamo radio with a grunt. The sci-fi crap wasn't his scene, but Beth would get a kick out of it. He made a mental note to tell her once she returned.

The not knowing was eating him alive. What did the cops know? Where were they looking?

If he'd learned anything during his time in hell, it was that nothing was ever as it seemed, and the impossible could become real in a second.

He tapped the revolver tucked in his waistband, pushed aside his new blanket, and climbed down from the loft. The shack was cold, the kind of cold that crept into your bones. He peered through the window, searching for Beth, but the clearing was empty.

Girls needed privacy.

She needed more than pepper spray. It was a thin shield, fragile and barely enough against the dangers lurking beyond the clearing. She needed the power to stop a heart when it counted.

Chris pulled the Skinner knife from its sheath, turning it over in his hand. No, that would never do. She would never use it.

He glanced at the shotgun and rifle propped in the corner and shook his head. Then he pressed a hand to the cold steel at his waist.

Maybe the revolver.

He already had the bolt cutter, shotgun, rifle, and Glock he'd taken from the man's trunk bag. The wheel gun was simpler than the Glock, easier for Beth to handle. He would part with it, but only after teaching her how to use it.

Minutes later, she returned with a look Chris had never seen before. Her posture sagged from fatigue, but there was something strange in her expression. Her forehead smoothed out, free of its usual creases, and she was grinning.

"What's with you? You look like you ate a canary or something."

Her grin expanded. She slipped past Chris by the door and plopped onto her sunken spot on the mattress. "You mean I look like *the cat* that ate the canary," she corrected.

He rolled his eyes. "Whatever."

Beth shrugged, snatching the tiny dictionary sitting on the bed. "Seriously, what happened?"

She flipped through the pages, her fingers moved fast like she already knew where the word would be.

He leaned in just enough to see the word she'd landed on.

Brave: *[breyv] adjective, brav-er, brav-est.*
1. possessing or exhibiting courage or courageous endurance. 2. making a fine appearance. 3. Archaic. Excellent; admirable. 4. A brave person, warrior.

Chris cleared his throat. "Where'd you get that? Your boyfriend?"

Beth slapped the book shut, holding it in a closed fist. "He's not my boyfriend. I hardly know him."

"Uh, huh. What's the deal then?"

"What deal?"

"You know what I mean."

Beth shook her head, peeking at the small book in her hand. "Nope. Can't say that I do."

"Hey!" Chris slapped the book out of her hand. It whipped through the air, smacked the loft wall, and landed by the mattress.

"What's your problem?"

"*My* problem? You're the one acting funny. What's going on?"

A pause, and then, "Oh, shut up."

"What?"

Beth shook her head. "No, I didn't mean you. I—Chris, nothing is—"

He stomped his right foot on the uneven floor, sending vibrations through the walls. He took a breath and paced to the other side of the cabin, raking his fingers through his sticky hair. When he pulled his hands away, a clump stuck straight up. He looked like an angry parrot.

Beth pressed her lips together, trying not to laugh.

"Those two can't come back here again."

A cloud drifted across the eastern sky, blocking the sun for a moment. Darkness filled the space before the light returned.

Like a child confronting a parent, Beth stood up, huffing. "What? Why not? You can't do that!"

Jason and Dylan had told them what the kids were saying at school. Whispers spread through hallways and classrooms about the fire and the dead police officer.

Did they kill those people?

Oh my God, are they dead?

I never thought Beth could do something like that, but I always knew she was weird.

If word got out that Jason and Dylan were close to the twins, parents and teachers would get involved. The boys would be cornered. Sooner or later, they would give up the hideout. They'd become rats.

But how was Chris supposed to convince her to keep the boys away when she wouldn't listen to reason?

He couldn't tell her about Jason. Chris would rather her hate him than hear what he knew. The truth would crush her. Maybe push her to do something crazy.

Dylan was harmless and fickle, but Chris watched him with suspicion. He was the kind who might betray them if the price was right. Chris pictured him at school, grinning like a fool, hiding his secret.

"You're freaking ridiculous!" His hands trembled as he struggled to pull the revolver from his waistband. He tossed it on the bed. "That's yours now. You need it more than I do. Good luck figuring it out." He marched to the door, slamming his hand against it. "They're not coming back, Beth."

He yanked the door open; its silent hinges whizzed with a jolt, sending it thumping against the shack wall. He snatched his cap, yanked it on, grabbed his knapsack and the canteen, and stormed out without closing the door behind him.

THE GIRL

THE GIRL

She stood alone, dismayed. Was he coming back?

Of course, he is.

Why was he so angry?

Tears came; Beth cursed, fighting them back. Like bitter foes ready to be unleashed, they stayed in the corners of her eyes, waiting. She didn't know whether to bawl into a blanket or cry out into the sky.

What Chris said made sense, but she refused to give in. Not this time. For the first time, her future held a spark of hope because of Jason. He made her feel like she could be herself, like she belonged.

Whether Chris knew it or not, his anger only pushed her closer to her friend.

Beth's eyes glazed, an unexpected memory rushing to her mind.

Long Island. She watches from a distance as Chris shuffles alone across the fresh grass on the front lawn.

They had just fought.

The sharp scent of spruce cuts through the spring air.

Chris kneels and plucks a dandelion. He blows the white, fluffy seeds, watching them drift and scatter like fragile dreams in the afternoon breeze

Everything falls silent.

Beth's chest tightens, heavy with guilt, pain, and loneliness. Tears gather at the edges of her eyes, stinging and relentless, threatening to spill.

She snapped back to the present. The memory was so vivid that, for a moment, she forgot where she was. Her cheeks were wet.

Renewed energy surged through Beth, and she rushed to the window, yelling, "I don't need your stupid gun! And I don't want a boyfriend!"

"Well, that's a shame."

She shrieked and spun towards the door. Jason stood frozen in the threshold, wearing a burgundy-collared shirt and dark blue jeans, concern glinting behind his glasses. An oversized backpack drooped against his back, another bag slung over his shoulder.

With a hand pressed to her mouth, Beth sucked in her breath. She looked and felt ridiculous standing there with a wet face.

"Sorry. Mom used to say I should work on my introductions." Jason shrugged. "My timing stinks."

"You're here," Beth said, her excitement sounding more like an accusation.

Jason's shoulders slumped, and he stared at the floor by his feet. "Sorry. Sounds stupid, really, but I had nowhere else to go."

51

THE BOY

"Damn!"

He'd forgotten his jacket and the bolt cutter. And the shotgun. Every part of him wanted to scream.

A stiff breeze picked up, tousling the canopy above. Chris looked up, hoping to capture a spec of the sun, but behind a curtain of trees, the sky was a patch of creamy white. The air smelled of rain. He cursed under his breath.

He decided he wouldn't go back to the cabin just because of the stupid rain. He'd rather risk catching a cold.

A voice echoed through the rustling behind him.

"Yo, Chris. Stop!"

Chris spun around. Dylan came barreling through a thicket of green, pushing through branches that snagged at him.

What the hell was he thinking? Was he out of his mind?

He fired a finger to his lips, shooting Dylan a look. "Sshhh!"

Dylan wore stained ashen jeans, the hem of a Godsmack concert t-shirt peeking from under a dark gray fleece hoodie. His long hair masked his eyes, like a comb missing teeth. Huffing, he raked a hand through his hair, revealing half-open, reddened eyes. His smile faded. "What's up, dude?"

Chris had left Beth furious and conflicted, but he couldn't deny the relief of seeing Dylan tear through the greenery. The boy was starting to grow on him. Ordinarily, they wouldn't give each other a second glance, in class or on the street. But now, like the massive beast from his nightmares, Chris felt epic whenever Dylan drew near, eyes wide with curiosity and awe. "Don't yell like that. It attracts attention."

Another gust feathered Dylan's hair back over his eyes. "Sure, dude. Whatever you say. Whatcha doing out here anyway?"

"Well," said Chris, "I was thinking about taking a leak."

Dylan threw his head back, laughing. He slapped a hand over his mouth with exaggerated flair. "Well, I ain't here to watch you do that, man."

Chris caught sight of a purple bruise and a crusted brown ring circling Dylan's left nostril. He stifled a smirk.

"Actually," Dylan continued, avoiding eye contact, "I'm worried about Jason. So I followed him here." He glanced over his shoulder. "I don't think he knows."

Chris kept silent, wincing at the faint smell of marijuana.

"He rode his bike here, but I couldn't take mine. That's what I get for trying to jump that stupid ramp this morning. Busted my front wheel. And my nuts. But Jason was careful. Couldn't even find where he parked his bike."

"If you didn't take your bike, how'd to get here so fast?"

A branch creaked nearby. Leaves fluttered on the forest floor, swirling around their feet.

"I talked my neighbor into dropping me off about a block away. He's cool. I told him I had to see a friend across town. I couldn't ask my mom. It's Friday, and she thinks I'm at school.."

Chris smirked. "Clever," he said.

Gratitude flashed across Dylan's face. He grinned, nodding.

"What's Jason doing here?" Chris took a small step forward, ready to charge back towards the shack.

"Oh, his dad, dude! He never came home!"

Chris swallowed. "Well, he must've left a note or something."

Dylan shook his head. "Don't think so. He's like, gone or somethin'. Jason said he's never been away this long. Not since his mom's been gone. I think it's startin' to mess him up."

There was no longer any doubt. Did Jason suspect anything? Was he back for revenge?

"So, why did he come back?"

Dylan stole another look over his shoulder. "Dunno. But he brought his pack with him."

"Uh, huh." Before he knew it, Chris was already moving through the trees. He pictured the revolver on the mattress and shuddered. What if Jason saw it? Would he freak out? Chris hadn't come all this way and lived through what he had just to let it blow up in his face because of some nerdy kid with a crush.

Dylan spun around, shadowing him.

Making sure he wasn't spotted, Chris crept along the edge of the clearing before approaching the shack. He pressed his ear against the splintered north wall and listened. Voices floated through, too muffled to understand. No signs of friction. He slipped back towards the trees, signaling Dylan to follow.

So, what's the plan, Stan?" said Dylan.

Leaving Jason inside with Beth left a sour taste in Chris' mouth, worse than the beach plums. But charging in like a madman and ordering Jason to leave would only make matters worse.

He remembered Dad: the way his cheeks flushed crimson, nostrils flaring at the slightest provocation. Dad was passionate and quick to anger, but there were times when he knew to pause and leave the room.

What would he be thinking now? What would he do?

Though it weighed on him, Chris forced himself to step away. "I have to catch breakfast."

He moved north, each step echoing in the quiet. After a few paces, the silence struck him. He turned around.

Dylan lingered behind, his expression unreadable.

Sighing, Chris tilted his head and said, "You coming or what?"

52

THE GIRL

Frantic, she shoved the revolver into Jason's jacket pocket.

Seeing him appear as he had stirred forgotten feelings of hope and delight she used to feel on Saturday mornings or when Mom would make spaghetti with garlic and olive oil.

The wind picked up. Jason shut the door and peeled off his chunky backpack, placing it on the mattress.

Beth turned away so her back faced him. She pulled her shirt against her face, soaking up the tears. Then she spun around, revealing bloodshot eyes.

The ceiling shuddered. Jason looked up. "Looks like rain. I should get out and check the roof. See if it holds through the storm."

Before Beth could react, Jason took off to the shed. She heard his footsteps above her head while he inspected Chris' handy work.

After a while, Jason pushed open the door, puffing wind into the room. Blankets fluttered, rags on the wall tore off the nails holding them. It took extra force to grip the door and push it shut.

"Everything okay?" asked Beth, hugging herself.

"Yeah. I think so," Jason panted, slapping the dust clinging to his clothes. "I'll say this—your brother did a good job. I just needed to secure a few things. I added some lumber and a few rocks to hold them. Not a permanent fix, but we should be okay tonight."

"Tonight?"

Not bothering to straighten the crooked glasses on his face, Jason drooped down onto the foot of the mattress. He rested his head against the wall, scuffed fingers laced across his chest, and closed his eyes with a pained sigh.

Beth remained standing, picking the dirt under her fingernails.

Jason said his dad hadn't come home. He kept his secret from friends and neighbors, unwilling to confess that his father had abandoned him. Memories of officers storming through his front door haunted him, sealing his lips about family matters forever.

He said reporting his dad missing would only turn his life into a headline again, and the police might ship him off to the state. Or worse, he could be sent to live with relatives he barely knew, somewhere on a farm in Oklahoma. He hated the idea of starting over in a strange town and at a new school. He needed time to decide his next move.

After a tight silence, he opened his eyes and looked over at Beth, grinning. "But you don't want to hear all of that. Besides, that's not the only reason I came."

Confusion crossed Beth's face as her friend pulled out a small bottle of soda, some easy-open canned foods, and a crusty loaf of bread. It offered a faint, comforting aroma in the room.

"Wow! Where'd you get that?"

Jason laughed. "It's just some food. I thought it could carry us for a day. You must be missing all kinds of stuff out here." He popped the tab on a can of black beans. Generic cans of white corn and peaches in light syrup sat beside him on the bed.

Over the years, Beth learned ways to avoid eating whatever cold meal sat on her plate. While Mom watched her soap opera in the living room, Beth would wrap food in a napkin, slip it into her pocket, stroll to the bathroom without being seen, and bury the soggy clump in the wastebasket under dirty tissues. Sometimes, she even flushed it down the toilet.

But now, Beth knew true hunger. She felt ashamed.

"You sure you want to stay here?" she asked. "I mean, there must be other places you could go."

Jason nodded and fell silent, gazing at the half-opened can. "But none of those places have you there."

Beth bit her lip, eyes fixed on the food spread across the bed.

Heat bloomed in her chest, uneasy and sharp. Few people, let alone a boy, had ever shown her such kindness. Why did gratitude feel like a fresh bruise beneath her skin?

Jason sliced off the lid and emptied the contents into two Styrofoam bowls. He fished out two plastic spoons, handing a hearty serving to Beth. "Sorry, it's not warm. I planned to heat this, but..." He gestured to the door.

"That's okay, Jason. This food looks great."

He stirred the beans in his bowl and gestured to her lap. Patiently, he waited for her to take the first bite. "Enjoy," he insisted.

Beth scooped up a spoonful, dipping it into her mouth. Her teeth squeezed down on the beans, releasing its salty, smoky flavors. Aside from the deer meat, she couldn't remember food tasting so good.

A grin formed across Jason's face as he watched her eat. He scooped up a spoonful and stabbed it into his mouth.

Rain pattered against the windowpane, steady and insistent.

Beth's gaze drifted to the window. The sun vanished behind a heavy, dark sky, casting a worrying shade of darkness. Her eyes glazed over as guilt crept in for driving Chris away. Because of her, he was stuck outside, alone in the rain. She hoped he still had the flashlight.

A strip of light caught the shack floor, caked in grime and muddied sneaker prints. Beth thought she saw the crusty outline of a boot print and nearly dropped her spoon.

Ignore it. It's just your imagination.

A shift on the mattress pulled her back. Jason had been talking, but not a single word registered.

THE BOY and DYLAN

"We got a problem, buddy."

The sky had faded from white to gray, dull as dusk. Thunder cracked like wooden bats against a hollow metal pipe. They wouldn't be seeing the sun again today.

Dylan shivered.

Chris had grown used to the biting chill and barely noticed. Then he frowned. Catching fish in the rain was close to impossible, even for an experienced fisherman.

He slipped off his pack and dropped it on the floor with a pained grunt, positioning it so the flatter end faced up. He perched on top, using it to keep his butt dry. His stomach rumbled.

Dylan followed and sat on a root as thick as a leg. He dug into his pants pocket and pulled out a plump joint. "Once it starts raining," he said, "I won't be able to light this."

Ogling the hand-rolled cigarette, Chris caught the faint smell of pot and shook his head. But who was he to judge? He held bourbon. And judging by the weight of the canteen, there was plenty.

"Damn. I'm tired, dude," said Dylan, thumbing the flint wheel on his lighter.

The stream's roar told them they were still on the right path.

"*You're* tired? Try lugging this thing around with you everywhere you go."

"No kidding." Dylan crooked his head, eyeing Chris' seat. "What you got in that thing anyway? Baseball cards?"

"Very funny."

Dylan slid the joint into the corner of his mouth. After several tries, he sparked a flame and lit the fun stick. A red light glowed from the tip like a mini torch. He inhaled sharply, held it in a few seconds, then coughed out a thick cloud of white smoke.

Plucking the joint from his mouth, he offered it to Chris.

"I told you. I need to focus on food. I'm just taking a break."

"I shoulda known," Dylan smirked. "Jocks don't do this kind of thing. Gotta stay fit and strong, right?" He took another puff and coughed, then pointed at the canteen slung over Chris' shoulder. "You mind, buddy? I could use some water."

Chris opened his mouth, then shut it. Grinning, he pulled the sling over his head and handed it over.

"Thanks, pal. Appreciate it."

"No problem." Chris turned his head like something had caught his eye, a grin struggling to break free.

Dylan unscrewed the cap and took a swig, then spit it out. Liquor fired out his mouth like a busted shower nozzle. He wiped his mouth with his hand, eyes burning on Chris. "Real funny, asshole."

Chris broke out in laughter, rocking back and forth on his beanbag. "I have my moments."

"First, your sister tries to dent my face in. Now you're trying to poison me." He shook his head. "Little shit."

It had been a while since he laughed, and it felt good.

Once again, it didn't matter that the joke was on him; Dylan joined in, unable to contain his amusement. His lips parted in a roar.

"Sorry. But you would have done the same thing."

It took a moment for Dylan's laughter to break. "What the hell are you doing with booze anyway? I thought jocks didn't put that stuff in their bodies."

"I don't." Chris' eyes grazed the area. "But it's getting cold. It's supposed to keep you warm. I had a few shots already. Unlike you, I can take it."

A middle finger fired in front of Chris' face. "Whatever, man. If you had told me what was in it, I wouldn't have flinched."

"Uh, huh."

"You know what? Screw you, man." Dylan held his joint high. "This is more my style. Drinking makes me pissed off anyway."

Grabbing the canteen from Dylan, Chris said, "I get it. You need a strong stomach to handle this stuff." He took two short shots, wincing after each one.

Dylan curled a hand over the joint to block the wind, then took another hit. "Hey, you have yours. I have mine. We'll leave it at that."

Chris nodded, keeping the peace.

Drops of rain patted dry leaves, filtering through the canopy. A flash of purple lightning lit up the sky, followed by a roar of thunder. Winds rocked the branches above, casting ominous, dancing shadows across Dylan's face. A damp smell filled the air.

"We headin' back or what?"

"What's the matter?" Chris knocked back his third shot, feeling his brain lighten and his toes tingle. "Scared of a little thunder?"

"Screw you, dude. I can handle whatever you can."

The pot and banter drew Dylan away from thoughts of Jason. He began to feel a surprising empathy for his new friend. "There's still hope for you and your sister, y'know," he said. "You think the cops will go easy on you?"

Everyone knew girls were nosy, always asking pointless questions. But not Dylan. Chris liked talking to him; he could tell Dylan enjoyed it, too. It must've been the excitement of spending time with a wanted kid.

Chris dropped his head, studying the damp earth.

You don't think you're going to get away with this, do you?

"So, what's your plan?"

Puzzled, Chris turned to Dylan.

"Ya' know, the next step? You're not staying out here forever."

Dylan was right, causing Chris to face the grim reality again.

"I mean," he added, "everyone's lookin' for you. They know you had something to do with that cop's—" he looked away— "murder and all."

"Yeah." Chris rubbed the back of his neck. "Figured that."

He glanced upward as the branches began to weep, blinking away the sharp sting of cold raindrops.

I live here now. I know every corner of you.

53

THE BOY

They lost track of time, absorbed in their chosen vices—swapping stories about embarrassing moments and the pretty girls they knew in school.

After Chris swilled his fourth swig of bourbon and Dylan fired up his second blunt, he fished out his Frank Eufemia baseball, tossing it to him. "C'mon, let's play. We can test each other's reflexes."

With every throw, the ball slapped their hands, leaving angry red marks that would soon bruise. But Chris had forgotten his troubles, and Dylan, whose hands stayed unscathed—having missed at least half of the pitches—took pleasure in the competition.

It took some convincing, but Chris agreed to return to the shack. He'd planned to spend the night by the stream and cowboy camp, like he and Beth had the night of the fire. But Dylan insisted, warning him about the dangers of getting sick in the rain. So they turned their toes south, casting off two roaches and crude baseball logos in the mud.

They arrived to find Jason and Beth sitting on the mattress, talking. Jason had refused to leave Beth alone, and with Chris back, it was too late for Dylan and Jason to head home.

Chris prowled the room, nerves raw as a hunted doe. His fingers searched his pants for a missing revolver, leaving muddy footprints in his restless wake. His eyes darted, hands twitching, every muscle coiled to lash out at whatever crossed his path. The itch to pick on something, to rip it apart, reminded him of Mom.

He announced the sleeping arrangements, leaving no room for argument. Jason would sleep on the loft, away from Beth, while Chris lay beside her on the mattress. Dylan had told his folks he was spending the night at Jason's, so no one worried when he passed out sideways at the foot of the bed.

The energy between him and Beth had thickened since the fight. Tension hung in the air, fierce and palpable. Icy, shaky stares zipped in all directions. Dylan, too stoned to notice, lay on the mattress with his eyes closed, humming rock lyrics. Jason tried to mollify the mood, offering food while Chris collected water from the pump.

Jason unearthed a small propane tank and a Jetboil buried among planks and stacks of firewood, then, with the cast-iron pan, heated up the vegetables. To everyone's surprise, fuel remained.

Jason's kindness set Chris on edge. Why wouldn't he just leave? What did he want? The thought that Jason's father had wrecked everything since storming in made Chris' stomach churn. No matter how he tried to ignore it, Jason carried that man's blood. How different could he really be?

The image of the hunter sprawled on the floor like an overstuffed scarecrow, underwear exposed like a secret Chris was never meant to see, flashed through his mind. A bitter burn shot up his throat; he felt an urge to rip into Jason, the offspring of something so cold-blooded.

He almost blurted out the truth about the hunters, but Beth's glare cut him off. He stumbled into the rain, dumping his meager dinner in the dirt.

Then he clambered up the ladder and collapsed on the loft, the sleeping arrangements forgotten.

THE GIRL

THE GIRL

The rain kept on. A fuzzy moon filtered through the window, the only light in the room.

Chris and Dylan slept while Beth and Jason stayed awake. She'd never shared a space with a boy—let alone a bed. Only dolls had ever perched in the chair beside her, their lifeless faces and black eyes catching the faint light as she fought to ignore them and sleep.

They sat cross-legged, two feet apart, facing each other. Beth remembered girls in the locker room bragging about their experiences with boys, about what it felt like to have someone's tongue in their mouths. Some of them had larger breasts than some older women and crowed with delight about what it felt like for boys to touch them.

In his sleep, Chris hugged the flashlight to his chest. The rifle, shotgun, canteen, and backpack lay by his legs.

The soft light offered Beth solace. Still, her fingers tapped her knees in nervous tension; she rocked back and forth, unable to find a comfortable position on the mattress.

"Don't worry about the roof," Jason assured her after catching her glance upward for the third time. "We'll be okay."

Beth nodded. "Sorry about Chris. He never drinks, you know? He's just been through a lot."

"You too."

Beth gave a tight smile. "And you."

Jason sighed. "Yeah, I'm sure my dad is fine. He's left before."

"Really?" The peculiarity of this statement fascinated Beth, much like the time she'd seen a homeless man in New York City snub a woman offering him food. Dad coming home each night had always been a given. Now, a sudden, sharp sense of love mingled with remorse and panic, coating her insides like honey.

"Yeah. When my mom was alive, they'd get into some bad fights. Sometimes my dad would leave and not return for days." He looked around the room. "I guess this is where he went."

"That's awful."

Jason said nothing.

"But I'm sure he'll be back soon."

Thunder rumbled in the distance, and a brief flash of purple bleached the room. Beth swallowed hard, blinking. She opened her mouth to speak, but all that came out was a yawn.

Are you nuts? What was that?

Jason laughed. "You're not like other girls, Beth. And what's even cooler, you don't try to be."

He suggested they sleep. Careful not to wake Dylan, Jason adjusted his knapsack into a makeshift pillow for Beth, then arranged the clothes and blankets on the mattress. He asked if she was comfortable sleeping next to him, and Beth attacked her fear with a resounding, "Yes."

As she positioned the pack where she'd rest her head, a soft breeze brushed the back of her neck.

"Beth?"

She stopped and turned.

"I've been thinking..."

The space between them shrank. A soft breath touched her face, and her skin warmed. Jason leaned in, using his hands for leverage, lips brushing her face before settling on her bottom lip.

Oh my God!

A moment later, Jason pulled back, his head cocked slightly, like an eager puppy awaiting approval.

Beth giggled, staring at her fingers. "Sorry. My lips are chapped."

THE BOY

THE BOY

He glided from sleep, the ceiling eighteen inches from his head drifting into focus. His first thought was of mummies enclosed in coffins.

The room was chilly and dark. Rain tapped against every corner of the shack. Chris could barely make out the faint outline of the window by his feet.

What day was it? How long had he slept?

Time in the woods melted into a haze. It crawled by like molasses through an hourglass, slow and sticky, as if the hours themselves resisted passing. Days blurred together in a wild, tangled rush Chris could barely hold onto before his mind slipped away. Memories from before the fire faded into mist, so distant they felt like fragments of someone else's dream. Mom and Dad's faces drifted out of reach, features dissolving the more he tried to remember.

Hunger gnawed at him, a sharp ache that twisted his stomach and made him dizzy. The past seemed to lose importance; anxieties were tossed aside by more pressing concerns. Survival demanded focus.

His head ached. His body burned, hands tight and sore. He'd kept his socks on last night, so at least his feet were snug. When he rubbed his eyes, he winced; bruises smeared both palms. He could barely flex them into fists without cringing.

Images of a spinning, wet fastball racing towards Dylan came to mind. Chris couldn't recall returning to the shack. He snorted, and an electric shock fired through his skull like a searing bullet. He blinked, shapes and outlines surfacing through the haze. Turning his heavy head to the left, he saw two lumps lying side by side, a foot apart. Beth was asleep, Jason's blanket pulled high over her head.

Chris shifted his weight on the unyielding bunk. His back ached for a soft surface. He inched down the ladder, mindful not to slip on the rungs. It groaned under his weight, but in the breathless silence of the room, he hardly noticed. Relief washed over him when his feet touched the floor without his legs collapsing underneath him.

His throat felt like sandpaper. He caught sight of the travel mug by Beth's buried head and grabbed it, guzzling the last lukewarm drops of water.

Nausea struck like a blow to the gut. Chris clamped a hand over his mouth to keep from hurling on the floor and darted out the door, draining his stomach of everything he'd eaten in the last few hours. His body quaked; then came the dry heaves. He couldn't remember ever feeling this awful.

All he wanted to do was die.

THE GIRL

THE GIRL

She lay on her back, eyes open, body taut from the icy air. It was still drizzling. Chris snored above her head; Jason and Dylan slept still as a pack of koalas, leaving Beth with only her imagination and inner voice for company.

Jason lay spread out on the far side of the mattress, and a pinch of resentment struck, knowing the boys were fast asleep, lost in their own worlds.

Her mind drifted back to the kiss. She felt ashamed for not liking it as much as she'd imagined. Why did it feel so weird? Other girls liked it, so why not her?

Don't worry. It's always better when it's a fantasy. Reality disappoints. Memories are fun. Give it time, you'll remember loving it.

Hard to say, since it had been Beth's first kiss.

"You think it was his first kiss?" she whispered.

She listened to the faraway winds, sounding like racecars on a freeway. Soon, cold whispers echoed in the shack, the walls shaking. Spring had come, but it didn't matter. Mother Nature ridiculed Beth's desperation. Every gust of wind laughed at her, biting into her insides, expanding like water bottles in a freezer. She imaged a higher force at work, mocking her. Thunder was its roar, lightning the blinding eyes winking down, the wind its breath puffing against her cold skin.

She'd learned to detest the dirt, the trees, every animal that scurried by. They were cold, impassive to her plight. They may not have been pampered indoors, but they had a way out. They were free. Beth used to squirm at insects; now, she shook with fury whenever they dared crawl on her skin and flick against her face. They teased her with their cruel little games.

She squeezed her fists against her prickly chest. She brought a hand to her face and nearly cried out; it felt void of blood. Pulling the blanket halfway over her face, she prayed for the wind to stop. Poking at a painful hangnail or her middle finger was all she could do to distract herself from worry.

Things were becoming too much to handle.

THE BOY

THE BOY

He closed the door behind him, drifting towards the mattress where Dylan lay curled up, snoring. He envied Dylan's simplicity—his ability to disconnect from a situation and slip into a world of indifference to the suffering around him.

A curdling ache twisted in Chris' empty stomach as he dropped to the floor beside his sister's head. Maybe being near her would offer some comfort, help set him at ease. But he felt shattered, drained after purging every ounce of energy outside. "I'm living a nightmare," he muttered.

In the moon's muted light, Chris stared at the crown of Beth's head sticking out of the blanket. He knew she wasn't as delicate as he made her out to be, not like those ceramic dolls Mom kept on her dresser. But as her brother, he had to protect her. Otherwise, what good was he?

Until now, Chris had stood unshakable, convinced that honor guided his every decision since the fire. The thought of abandoning Beth to the state felt like surrendering every other breath for the rest of his life. Without her, he was off-kilter and hollow, like a wolf whose mate had been ripped from its grip.. Losing everything was one thing, but letting Beth go was where he drew the line.

And now, he began doubting his decisions. And his motives.

Chris leaned against the wall, closing his eyes. In the inky void of his mind, he saw Beth's face, tousled hair veiling her tired, panicked eyes as the (now dead) driver's car shrank, then faded up the hill.

The pain in his head intensified with every move. The effort to reach for food in his pack felt beyond him, a task he couldn't execute. Besides, he was too sick to eat and would just throw it up again.

For the fourth time in his life, Chris wanted to cry. But the thought of Beth seeing him as a blubbering mess was unthinkable. He was the strong one, the dependable one. And now that he was the head of whatever family remained, it didn't always mean making easy choices—or even being liked.

On a desperate impulse, he stepped back on stage. Poised and ready, Richard stood behind the podium, grinning that proud, toothy grin. Chris spoke in a low voice, head rolling against the wall.

"Ladies and gentlemen, our returning champ is back for another round! First question: Before switching to number 23, what number did Don Mattingly wear?"

"46."

"Who was the longest-tenured Yankee captain?"

The name Chris had planned to give his son: "Derek Jeter."

"And who wore the number 2 before Mr. Jeter?"

"Mike Gallego."

A rustle on the bed stopped him, but he didn't open his eyes. Beth must have shifted in her sleep. He waited a minute before continuing.

"Where do the New York Islanders play their home games?"

"Uhhh…shit. Wait..."

A dark silence.

How could he forget something so simple?

Incensed, he huffed out short bursts of air through his nose. "…Levittown?"

Richard took a second, frowned, then turned his tan face to the audience. *"I'm sorry, Mr. Pacelli. But because you've been such an awesome contestant, how many Stanley Cup Finals did New York Islanders Mike Bossy play?"*

"Five."

"Last question for the bonus: Two Hall of Famers were Mike Bossy's linemates during the bulk of his NHL career. Name both."

"Bryan Trottier? It's him. I know it."

"Who else...?"

Chris drew another blank, and the room fell quiet again. What the hell was going on? Why couldn't he remember? It felt like a mind eraser swept away parts of his memory—pieces of his landscape, who he was. Memorizing dates and facts for school was not his specialty, but sports trivia came easy. It sank in without effort. He could've blamed the hangover, the fatigue, but he didn't want to lie to himself. He couldn't stand to keep embarrassing himself any longer.

He turned his back to the saddened crowd and shuffled offstage.

"I can't do this anymore, Beth," he panted, half-hoping she was awake. Maybe she was. It didn't matter anymore. The pain, guilt, and solitude were wearing him down. Like Dad used to say, *A man only has so much strength to give.*

"I'm sorry I pulled us out here..."

THE GIRL

She woke, distressed, fresh tears brimming at her eyelids.

Somehow, she'd managed to fall asleep. But for how long? A couple of hours, maybe. Long enough to dream.

Beth found herself strolling down a dark, rainy sidewalk, a shotgun slung over her shoulder, wind patting her skin. A young, foolishly happy couple approached a hundred feet away. The woman giggled, her face buried in the collar of the man's blue scarf that hung around his neck. Terrified of being seen, Beth dashed into a mass of bushes. Her finger hovered over the trigger. The couple strolled on, unaware of the panicked presence trembling in the underbrush.

Then something pulled her from her dream. Deep, muffled murmuring, like the wind curling through the trees. Had the ghosts of the hunters, or the man in the ravine, returned for vengeance? What about Mom and Dad? Maybe they were so disappointed they'd rather let her die in the woods than see her show her face in society again.

Beth's limbs tensed, then settled inside her cocoon of clothes and blankets. Her breathing held steady, and she avoided sudden moves. Chris sat inches away on the floor. Words like *"Pacelli,"*

"Yankees," and "Mike Bossy" were among the few words she caught. He sounded beaten, weathered.

"I can't do this anymore, Beth."

Did she hear him right? If Chris lost hope, where would that leave her? His change after Mom and Dad died had been inevitable. But it shook her. He'd grown distant, even hostile. But why?

"I'm sorry I pulled us out here..."

Beth felt her twin's certainty and strength fade like a dying flashlight beam. It distressed her, and it angered her.

Or did it?

Maybe the resentment was for Mom and Dad, for leaving them alone in this mess.

Or for the hunters, who'd made everything so much worse.

Perhaps for society, indifferent to their suffering.

What about Chris?

Or God?

Herself?

It was all of them—everything.

A torrent of unwelcome emotions rushed in, rattling her guts, stirring nausea.

Lying in dark silence, Beth couldn't bring herself to face her brother. She felt like a coward and loathed herself for it.

And yet, she felt a deeper sense of protectiveness towards him—stronger than anything she'd felt before, even when she picked up that shotgun.

A lone, silent tear slipped from the corner of her tired eye. It clung to her cheek, and for a moment Beth thought it had frozen there before it finally slid down to the mattress.

54

JASON

Tensing his muscles, he stepped into the duplex, his footsteps tapping across the chocolate-colored linoleum. The smell of rotten food filled the house, and Jason winced. "Dad?"

His eyes scanned the torn sofa and mismatched recliner against the far wall of the living room. A dusty television sat in the corner. Open magazines and several half-empty glasses of flat soda spread across the chipped walnut-colored coffee table.

Jason wandered into the kitchen and looked around. A green fruit bowl sat on the black-and-white checkered table, crammed with bullet shells, coins, and business cards. No pots or pans sat on the stove. No note.

The rooms were just how he'd left them.

A red blinking light on the cordless phone base caught his attention. He picked up the receiver and pressed play. Several messages played, all for his dad, none for Jason. One came from his dad's friend's wife. Her husband was missing too, and she asked if Jason's dad had seen him.

Grudgingly, he returned the woman's call. A sigh of relief came when her voicemail picked up. He left a message saying he didn't know where the men had gone and that he'd been staying with relatives in Rookwood until his father returned.

Jason gazed at the numbers scribbled on a small notepad next to the fridge and decided to call some of his dad's friends. He bit the inside of his cheek while waiting for them to answer. No one did. He hung up without leaving another message.

Hooking the cordless into the base on the wall, he decided that the woman's message was the last sign, convincing him to pack up and return to the shack.

He walked down the hall and stopped at the foot of his dad's bed. With the shades pulled down, the room was colorless, like light straw. Yesterday, he'd studied the folds in the comforter; they looked like accordion bellows. The pillows stayed in place, arranged in layers. It was no mystery dad was a rough sleeper. And it was clear he hadn't slept here last night.

Jason felt a sudden, violent anger ignite. He yanked the dresser drawers out, overturning them onto the bed. Like a hungry badger digging for food, he pushed through the pile, flinging shirts and underwear aside. He uncovered stacks of nude magazines with teen girls, squeezed between piles of hunting journals next to the bed.

A stack of cash sat inside a hollowed hardcover book in the top drawer of the end table. Jason fanned through the bills, counting two hundred dollars. Grinning, he folded them, stuffing them into his pants pocket. "Serves you right, Dad," he muttered.

Money was fine, but no sign led to his dad's whereabouts. It was as if the man had vanished, like air leaving a balloon.

Furious, Jason stormed into his bedroom and packed a pair of jeans and a few warm sweaters thin enough to fit in his overnight bag. Before leaving, he glowered at his single sofa bed. A folded photo on the dresser caught his eye and he picked it up, his sad grin reflected in the crimped picture. Sliding it into his back pocket, he hustled back to the kitchen and emptied the pantry of canned goods, shoving them into his backpack.

Bowing his knees, he lifted both bags and dropped them by the front door. They were heavier than expected. How the heck was he going to carry them into the woods?

Jason thought of calling Dylan but decided against it. If Dylan's mother was home, she'd recognize the caller ID. She might even pick up before Dylan had the chance. The last thing Jason wanted was to deal with another adult. He'd grown suspicious of grownups and no longer trusted them.

He scarfed down some cereal, then drank the rest of the juice in the fridge. Dumping the empty bowl into the sink among the dirty plates and silverware, he frowned at the flies whirling above them.

The news!

Knowing what the police were doing might ease the twins' doubts about where they stood.

Jason rushed back into the living room and tapped the power button on the remote. He scanned a string of channels before settling on the local news.

A crisp weatherman faced a regional map splashed with colorful arrows and stripes. He feigned concern over a possible thunderstorm hitting the county.

After a commercial break, a young anchor addressed the twins' story. Jason gasped as Beth and Chris's photos flashed on the screen.

The report implied doubt about the twins' case. The police had few leads, the operation turning secretive. Search parties continued, but fewer residents joined. Officers from other towns came aboard to help, and the FBI was also involved. The story lasted less than two minutes.

Jason switched off the television. Grunting, he lifted his backpack, sliding his arms into the straps. He slung the overnight bag across one shoulder to keep it from slipping. His knees buckled, and he steadied himself.

He stopped before twisting the front door knob, dropping the bags at his feet. Eager to leave, he hadn't noticed how fast the day had passed. It was too late to return to the woods. And he'd promised Mrs. Putridge, the kind widow across the street, that he'd help unload boxes from her attic. The woman planned to move next month and desperately needed help.

He would have to wait for Sunday.

55

SANDERS

SANDERS

An idea struck. Simple, but brilliant.

"Captain, my father's ill. Stomach cancer. The doctor says he has weeks to live. My mother's struggling and needs me to fly to New York." A sigh. Then, "I hate to do this. Especially with so much is going on." The detective even managed to spark a tear.

It wasn't a total lie. His father had died years ago of cirrhosis. Sanders was just recreating the memory.

"Take all the time you need," the captain said, placing a gentle hand on Sanders' shoulder. A moist glint in his eyes suggested he knew something about family discord. "We have plenty of help. We'll handle the load while you're away. Give your father my best." The dark crease in his brow showed he meant it.

Secrecy was an asset. Sanders had a talent for deception, spinning words with the finesse of a street magician or a seasoned actor playing emotions, slipping into new skin. For an undercover cop, unchecked emotion and loss of control spelled disaster. To sharpen his edge, the detective enrolled in a drama course at the New York community college, one that taught something called the Meisner Technique.

Most days, he lingered in the back of the room, arms folded across his barrel chest, sizing up the insecure, applause-chasing students who howled and wept as if under a spell.

But over time, Sanders stepped into the spotlight, feigning interest in the scripts, moving through scenes with his classmates. He learned fast that words were secondary; the real work was tuning into his partner. The relationship. The connection.

Sanders excelled at reflecting their falsehoods, absorbing their pain. Young actors, he found, carried a load of fears and tears.

After the meeting with the captain, the barriers lifted. No more obstacles. Nothing stood between Sanders and the twins.

With a bottle of whiskey loose in his shaky grip, the detective finished assembling his gear. He realized he could interrogate the twins for a long time. It all depended on how compliant the little brats were. But if events went the way he imagined, Sanders planned to take two long, fun-filled days. He doubted it would take longer. No child could withstand interrogation beyond forty-eight hours.

He eyed the supplies laid out on the bed, next to his neighbor's fishing gear.

1) A pack of 18" and 26" heavy-duty zip ties
2) Two bandanas (pink and blue)
3) Can of pepper spray
4) 9" ultra-sharp steel slicing knife
5) Serrated sheepshead blade with a solid lock-up
6) Pair of 8" ultra-sharp pruning shears
7) Lighter
8) Chloroform
9) 9mm Glock pistol, double-stack magazine, eleven rounds
10) Four-foot piece of plywood

And, of course, Sanders had his hands. He brought an open palm to his face, studying the lines and wrinkles like he would the ones around a suspect's eyes. His gaze landed on the thimble-sized scar at the base of his thumb. Jaw clenched, he flexed his fist.

Reflexively, he crossed the room—then stopped short, fist hovering inches from the wall.

"C'mon," he muttered. "Keep it together."

Crushing something nearby was all he could do to sooth his nerves. But he didn't need the hassle today. After his last outburst, a neighbor sharing the same living room wall had griped to management about the pounding.

People no longer had the balls to face their neighbors. They'd rather rush to those in charge whenever conflict arose, like a panicked child running to the principal.

Sanders stumbled to the closet, face-first into a jumble of pants and belts, trying to grab the handle of his overnight bag on the top shelf. Laughing at himself, he reached up again, yanked the bag, and dropped it onto the bed. He packed the supplies, leaving out the fishing pole and tackle.

Then he sprang to the living room and sprawled on the couch, fingers still wrapped around the neck of the bottle dangling by his side. Only a few drops remained but he was too drunk to care. With the remote, he clicked on the TV.

The plan was simple: watch the Yankees, hoping they'd take down the Cubs, then start fresh early tomorrow. Some spirited entertainment seemed a fitting reward for his effort.

Commercials.

Buy this, buy that.

All bullshit. Not an ounce of patience remained for another stupid, grinning fool hawking another product no one needed.

Sanders diverted his eyes and spotted something on the floor beside the couch. He shook his head.

But eagerness won.

Groaning, he coiled up and grabbed the book from the crusted carpet, falling back into the sofa. He flipped open to a random page.

October 13

I'm very sorry I haven't written in a long time, but I just didn't have the time. Yesterday, I went to Stacy's bowling birthday party. I scored a 40 - not so good. I kind of ruined the party. I picked up a bowling ball and accidentally dropped it on her friend's foot. She was crying. It hurt her real bad.

Today, I found out it was broken!! I feel so guilty. It's like everywhere I go, I cause trouble. I just hope she's all right. Everyone knows about it, that I did it, and she's carrying crutches.

Sanders thumbed to another page. The girl did a fine job acting clumsy and innocent.

July 18

Remember when I told you that I hated my mom and family a little bit? Well, ever since I came back from camp, my mom and I are very nice to each other. I ask her for something, she gives it to me – almost every time! When I pass her, I hug her and kiss her. My dad's kind too. He showed me something awesome on the computer. And my brother's very nice. I hope everything stays the same.

He slapped the book shut, flicking it onto the coffee table beside the TV.

Sanders couldn't imagine ever having kids. He and Linda had tried, but the universe stepped in like it always did and pulled the plug. A happy family wasn't just unlikely; it was laughable.

So really, why bother? Kids were a recipe for migraines, sky-high blood pressure, and a drain on your wallet. Sure, they started off adorable, all wide-eyed and trusting, but that sweetness was just a fleeting trick of nature. Before long, those little monsters would flip the script, declaring you the worst parent ever for skipping a carnival ride or refusing to shell out cash for the latest overpriced gadget.

"Fucking kids," he grumbled. "Who needs 'em?"

Sanders eyed the diary. Maybe he'd keep it as a prize for his work, leave it on the coffee table among the *Popular Mechanics* and *Guns & Ammo* magazines. On the right kind of day, the conspicuous book might even lift his mood. A reminder that he was a good man. A risk-taker. Someone willing to go the extra mile for the greater good.

A thought flashed in the detective's mind, curling the corner of his mouth. Tearing out pages and shoving them in the girl's mouth stirred a deep, rich laugh. What a surprise it would be to see her most prized possession in a stranger's hands.

Sanders made a mental note to pack the diary.

Satisfied, his eyes flicked to the TV, then strayed, snagging on a photograph.

His face fell.

There, captured in a battered wooden frame atop the scarred end table, David Powell and Sanders stood shoulder to shoulder. Sanders leaned in, elbow resting on Powell's shoulder, a cocky grin on his face. Powell, eyebrows arched in mock surprise, jabbed a thumb at Sanders, both caught mid-laugh. The snapshot was one of many from the captain's community picnic, a day meant to strengthen the bond between police and citizens.

Sanders grabbed the frame and rested it on his chest. As he stared, the image blurred. Not from drunken haze but tears. He missed his friend. He vowed to honor Powell and Bennett and uncover what happened to them.

"I'll find you," he mumbled.

With the bottle hanging from two fingers and a hand curled around the frame, Sanders sank into a blackout.

56

THE GIRL

She lifted herself on her elbows. The air hung cold, thick with musk. She tapped into every last scrap of energy before rolling off the mattress.

Chris lay curled up on the loft, sleeping soundly, his face buried in a pile of shirts. Jason and Dylan were gone. That made sense. Why would they stick around? Besides, Dylan must have hated waking up at the foot of the bed like a family dog.

Beth grappled with the doorknob, then pushed the door open. Outside, gray and white fog hung heavy. The forest stood quiet, dark with the smell of wood and mud.

The drizzle had eased into mist. The morning sun stayed hidden, dew painting the foliage. Blackbirds chirped, loud and bold, staking their claims and warning rivals away.

Beth tried to move quietly so Chris wouldn't wake, but the slick concrete betrayed her. She slipped and stumbled against the door, slamming it shut.

Chris snorted, then rolled over towards the back wall.

The ground was slick with mud; she kept to the slab to stay dry.

A breeze whispered in, laced with pine, filling Beth's senses like a wild, dizzying car freshener. Instantly, she was back in her kitchen at home, picturing the umber tiles, tawny cabinets, and the sharp evergreen-lemon scent that lingered after Mom mopped. She remembered Mom lining up the kitchen chairs across the dining room. She and Chris would scramble onto the ladder-back seats, steering their imaginations into a full-sized movie theater, their minds alive with scenes from whatever movie had captured their hearts that week.

But those days were long gone, even before the fire. Chris found his world in friends and sports; Beth retreated into her imagination, her TV, and her journal. She imagined her lavender book floating down a river, skimming along a curb, then slipping into a sewer in front of a stranger's house.

The chilly air seeped through her bones. Wrapped in Jason's jacket, she wrapped her arms around herself. It was the first time a boy had ever offered his jacket to her. How proud Jason's father must have felt, knowing he'd raised an intelligent, respectful, compassionate boy.

Her mind wandered to Mom and Dad. Would they look at her with pride or disappointment? Maybe she was just as heartless as the kids who tormented her at school. She started to wonder if Mom's drinking and Dad's anger were somehow her fault. Still, she ached for their return. She'd accept any cruelty or neglect they offered. She'd welcome the cigarette smoke into her lungs, swallow the bitter meals, endure the sting of hands against her cheek.

Squinting against the gray sky, Beth gazed above the trees, longing for the sun's warmth on her shoulders, and sobbed, "I miss you, Mom and Dad."

THE BOY

THE BOY

He sat with his head in bruised hands, legs limp over the edge, a sharp, acidic taste in his mouth. A scratch burned on his right cheek. The shack reeked of mold, the room laced with shadows. Splinters of ashen light bled through cracks under the door and window, signaling the dawn.

The bottles in Dad's bar rushed to mind, lined up like silent witnesses. Chris would study their levels but never touch them. Dad must have handled it well. Mom did too, slipping in a few drinks with her sleeping pill now and then.

Chris's mind raced to draw everything from last night, but all he could remember was puking outside the door and crawling across the floor like a blind turtle. He remembered playing with Dylan but couldn't remember how they got back to the shack.

Even sitting, he felt off-balance, like stepping off a long, rocky boat ride. Nausea churned. His head throbbed. His eyes begged to close as he patted around for his backpack. He was sure he'd dropped a water bottle in there yesterday. It took a minute, but when his neck could support the weight of his head, Chris opened his eyes. The knapsack sat way off in the far corner, by the door.

What the hell was it doing there? And where was everyone? Had Jason and Dylan taken Beth with them, leaving him for dead? What could he have done to deserve that?

His nostrils flared.

Curiosity drove Chris to shift his body inch by inch until unseen straps yanked him back. Pain shot through every muscle; each movement felt like a battle.

His body shrank back, curling into a fetal position. He listened for movement outside—chirps, hisses, soft crackling—and caught the edge of sobbing, murmured voices, none of it clear.

Chris strained to remember the hunter, how he'd pinned his sister like a cinder block smothering a kitten, her wide-eyed, frozen face pleading for help. It was all he could do just to move.

Adrenaline juiced his blood, and he sat up, leaping off the loft. He sensed Beth outside the shack but couldn't tell if Jason was with her.

By now, Jason had to know his father wasn't coming back. Chris had to tell her, convince her to cut her friend loose.

With an unyielding will, Chris unleashed the pain like a cord ripped from a tight outlet, freeing that familiar vigor. He hauled the backpack onto the mattress and dug out the pistol taken from the officer's duty bag. It weighed about two pounds, lighter than the revolver. He flicked his thumb against the release, but the magazine didn't drop.

Oh, right.

He'd stowed the clip in a separate pocket inside the knapsack.

He slid the magazine into the handle, snapping it in place.

Growth never came easy. Like it or not, Chris had shed his old skin. He'd built a solid mental barrier between himself and the murders; instinct and fire now guided him. The deaths of the officer and the hunter were not part of any plan, but they were part of his story. Shame no longer clung to him, nor did the voices that once held him back. He had torn free from every lesson hammered into him since childhood.

No longer a student boxed in by textbooks and fat, scowling teachers, Chris was a student of life—armed with free thought, instinct, and weapons.

He understood man's overwhelming longing for survival. Battling hostile conditions in the woods, he no longer felt like a boy but an animal, void of consequence or concerns other than to endure.

He slipped the weapon into the front of his jeans and stepped outside.

57

THE BOY

Fortunately for Chris, Beth was alone and took the news well.

But her reaction worried him. She'd pressed herself against a tree, lips moving without sound, as if speaking to herself, a glazed look coating her eyes.

Seeing those unblinking eyes, her body still and unpredictable like a praying mantis, Chris let a moment of softness take hold before brushing it off. Pushing Jason away was the right call. If he returned—and Chris knew he would—the nerd could snap, try to hurt Beth.

Chris had already decided to kill him if it came down to it. But if he could avoid it, he would.

He told her about the conversation with Dylan, and the hunter's tattoo. There was no doubt that vile man was Jason's dad. "It's gonna be okay, Beth," he said, voice lacking conviction. "It's not safe if he keeps coming back anyway."

As he spoke, images flashed before his eyes. Faces and places he might never see again. Rock tunes blasting from his bedroom stereo. Sliding towards home base, circled by crowds of zealous fans. Erica's smooth, glowing skin beneath his curious fingertips, her eyes gazing adoringly from the metal stands. Okay, she may never have attended any games, but he pictured her springing up from the bleachers in her checkered Vans, sand-colored pigtails bouncing low.

The hope of ever knowing what it felt like to kiss a girl like Erica shriveled inside him, brittle and useless like a dying kidney.

Worst of all, Beth liked Jason. When two people liked each other, the rest of the world disappeared. Chris felt left out. Why did she get to experience that with Jason? It wasn't fair.

He waited until Beth turned away, studying the branches of a towering pine, before he turned his back and reentered the shack.

Sometimes girls needed to be left alone.

THE GIRL

The air closed in around her. She struggled to breathe. Then came the image of the hunter's face after splitting open his head, the driver's terrible scream fading down the ravine.

Her mind fought to escape the woods and return to her old life. But the world felt blurry and distant, like running from the masked killer towards salvation, waist-deep in mud.

Stay calm.

That was what always worked when life turned vicious—Beth retreating into incredible fantasies and joyful memories locked inside her mind like precious metals in a dusty crate:

Playing Manhunt during warm summer nights with the neighborhood boys.

Listening to Dad's stories from childhood, like the time he slipped a running hose into a hole in the ground, only to get bit in the butt by a swarm of bees from another opening.

Writing on the front porch, protected beneath a sheath of stars.

A crushing urge to shriek at the sky tightened in her throat, but before she could, her legs bent like crooked straws and her butt smacked wet wood. She begged the forest to swallow her whole and take her from the torn wreckage of her life.

"How—how can Chris be so calm and just walk away?"

Don't lose it. Hold it together.

For the first time in a long while, Beth kicked the voice from her mind. What was the point of being rational? How could she be so naïve, letting herself feel happy with Jason? Mom had been right all along—stupid. So stupid!

A fat bunny with an oversized cotton tail peeked from behind a thick tree stump. Distrustful but curious, it studied the sad creature before it.

Beth's fingers curled around a rock at her foot, and she hurled it at the animal. The bunny scurried away as fast as it appeared.

She was alone again, just as it should be. But she refused to cry and swore she never would again.

She remained in that same position all morning and into the afternoon.

○   ○   ○

The twins avoided eye contact the rest of the day.

It didn't matter that Beth offered to share the remaining canned food and bread. Chris refused to eat a bite. His stomach protested— she heard it from across the room—and still he said no. He planned to head outside to trap and kill a squirrel or rabbit once he felt better. For now, he'd focus on staying hydrated.

"Please shut up and leave me alone," he said. "I need to sleep. For the last time, I don't want any of that crap your friend brought."

There was no right way to respond, and Beth lacked the will to push. "You don't have to be cruel," she said.

Chris shot up to a seated position. "Me? Are you serious?"

"Yes."

"Look at yourself, Beth. Call me cruel all you want. But I never wished my family dead."

Beth's mouth dropped.

"I'm going through this too," he said. "But I know how to handle it. Did you ever stop to think you're too sensitive? I'm doing what's best. I'm not interested in right or wrong anymore. I care about what's smart. I got us this far, yeah?"

Fragmented words jumbled in her mouth, but Beth couldn't speak. Was Chris right? Was she too sensitive? And what the heck did he mean about wishing family members dead?

Chris sighed, rubbing his temples. "This sucks for me too," he said, voice softening. "But you don't see me making out with a girl after shooting her dad in the face."

Beth shot a sickened look at her brother.

"I'm thinking about myself," he continued, "and you. That's it. You let things get too far, and other people can get hurt."

He's right. We both know he's—

Shut up, shut up, shut up!

There was nothing more to say.

Chris lay on the loft, trying to sleep,

Beth sat on the mattress, writing.

They remained in place, wrapped in a dull, aching silence too heavy to lift, one that stretched thin across the rest of the day.

58

SANDERS

He climbed out of sleep, dazed with heavy, bloodshot eyes. The frame still sat in his hand, Powell's boyish face the first vision of what promised to be a hair-raising day.

The room glared with an unnatural brightness. Sanders squeezed his eyes shut, tasting the cracked dryness on his lips, rough as a ditch digger's hands. He'd drowned in hard liquor for years, but yesterday was different; passion and excitement had glued the bottle to his mouth. Now, his skull throbbed, monstrous and swollen, as if a beast hammered at his temples with a two-ton mallet. He gave the beast Chris' face, letting it power his drive and shape the day before him.

That was all the detective needed to roll off the couch and stumble into the kitchen for his first cup of coffee. He'd swapped creamer for shots of whiskey, the best remedy for the pain. This morning was no different. Instead of fueling a long workday, this hair of the dog would supercharge his spirit.

After pouring the first cup, Sanders pulled open the pantry that doubled as the liquor cabinet, then froze.

"Fuck."

Two ounces remained in the twenty-five-ounce bottle, tucked among rice, pasta, and canned goods. The detective had been too drunk and busy picking up supplies yesterday to buy more. He made a mental note to stop by Lion's Lair later. Roger would take care of him.

Cursing himself, Sanders snatched the bottle and slogged to the counter. He poured the whiskey into a mug, then added the coffee. Taking a first sip, he watched the window across the room and frowned. For some reason, he'd left his blinds open last night.

A light drizzle tapped against the glass, oddly soothing. Sanders wouldn't let rain derail his plan.

The green clock on the microwave read 7:12 AM.

The detective was already behind schedule. The more time he gave the twins, the more chances they had to slip through his fingers. He needed time to stop by the bar, reach the hunter's lodge, get into character, and locate them. He knew it wouldn't require much effort to lure them in. But it had been a long time since the department shut down that building. He had to check it out first. What mattered was achieving the plan, not how he did it.

He took another sip.

Warmth spread through his veins, melting away the petty concerns of yesterday.

The memory of that young boy, shaking on his father's lap, had stirred something in Sanders he thought he'd left behind in New York. That day, he let instinct take the reins. Ordinarily, he would have waited, lured the man from his home, and confronted him with an ultimatum far from prying eyes. But the raw, burning urge to make things right had drowned out caution.

There was right, there was wrong. And when the law fell short, there was Sanders, finishing the job.

People could think what they wanted: corrupt, merciless.

He didn't care. He was neither. He just finished what needed finishing.

No more justifying; he made his decision.

Sanders downed the last sip and made for the shower. He scrubbed himself under the hot, rushing water, his excitement growing like a young boy approaching his first summer day.

He swung open the weather-beaten door of Lion's Lair. The thick scent of sawdust and rye greeted him as he stepped inside. Pale light spilled in, oddly sober for a Sunday. As always, the air felt thick, heavy. Steely Dan's "Dirty Work" buzzed from the corner speakers. At the far end of the bar, a middle-aged man hunched over a gin and tonic, long arms looped around the sweating glass.

I know that look, Sanders thought, then turned away and made for the bartender. Lion's Lair had a reputation for being the top watering hole for broken folks in town.

A nineteen-year-old dressed in a black shirt and jeans sat at a round table in the back, so focused on his food he didn't bother to look up. His dark hair fell over his eyes as he ate. Sanders recognized him as Alfred, the barback.

"Sanders, how are ya'!" The purple lights above the bar cast shadows over the bartender's face and shoulders. Beads of sweat dotted his forehead and nose. He slapped a dirty white rag on the bar, offering his hand to the detective.

"Morning, Roger." Sanders pulled out a stool at the end of the bar, across from the sad customer. Watching everyone from the best vantage point was second nature. He held out his arm, shaking the bartender's hand. "How're tricks?"

Roger grinned. "Not too bad. Just doing what I do."

Sanders nodded.

Roger examined Sanders' brown and green button-down shirt, dark jeans, and worn brown work boots. "Everything alright? Did you get a call?"

"No. I was in the area. Thought I'd stop by."

Roger pulled a lowball glass from under the bar. "Your usual?" He gripped a bottle of rye whiskey and unscrewed the cap.

"Hold off, Roger." Sanders raised a hand, browsing the tower of bottles behind the bar. "Let's go with Macallan 25 today."

The bartender cocked his bald, sweaty head. "Yeah? Celebrating something?"

"You could say that."

"Neat...?"

"On the rocks."

"You got it." Roger dropped a fat ice cube into the glass, then gently drizzled in the whiskey. He set it on a black square napkin in front of the detective. "There you are," he said, stretching his arms on the bar. "So, what's the occasion?"

Terry Reid's "To Be Treated Right" ticked on the jukebox, quelling the leftover sorrows in the room.

The glass felt heavy in Sanders' hand as he lifted it. His eyes glazed over, watching the smooth ice chunk chime with each shift of his wrist. A subtle balance of cinnamon and citrus drowned his mind, if only for a moment. Light caught the glossy amber, making it glow in the glass, tempting that first sip.

It had been years since Sanders drank Macallan 25. Linda had surprised him with the news she was pregnant. Twins. To celebrate, he'd picked up sparkling cider for her, Macallan 25 for himself, and two rattles, pink and blue, tucked inside two dozen sterling roses.

But she never got the flowers. And the bottles, drained after one hour, ended up in pieces inside the skull of a parasite.

Several minutes passed before Sanders brought the glass to his lips. He took a deep breath, then sipped.

"You know," said the bartender, "I saw you on television the other day. Lookin' sharp."

Sanders let the cold drink rest on his tongue before swallowing. Smoke and spice flooded his palate, trailing down to his toes. The warmth settled in, steady and welcome.

No one spoke for a while. The sad man shifted on his stool, emitting a muffled grunt, tugging the detective from his trance.

"Damn shame about what happened to that young officer," said Roger. "I think he was expecting his first kid, right?" He shook his head. "Did the police find out who did it?"

The muscles in Sanders' back tensed. "We have suspects. Just not in custody."

Roger took a moment, his bushy brows nearly touching. "You know, those photos on the news—the ones with the young kids..."

Sanders looked at his friend. "Yeah?"

"Maybe it wasn't him, but..."

"What are you saying?"

"Well, a while back...I dunno. It's been some time, but a kid came in alone. Polite, but out of place. He rushed into the bathroom and grabbed a pack of matches on his way out."

"Yeah...?"

"He looked like the boy in those photos. I didn't know what was happening at the time, you know?"

Sanders relaxed his face, but tension held in his body. "What did he look like?"

The bartender shrugged. "I dunno. All these kids look the same to me." After a pause, he said, "Kinda short. But then again, all kids are short to me. You know, the usual. Baseball hat, backpack, that sort of thing. Looked like he might've been heading to school, but he couldn't have been. It was so late in the day."

A fire ignited inside Sanders. The little bastard had been here. It made sense he'd taken matches. He knew Chris had been a Boy Scout; starting fires wasn't new for him. "A bit odd, but I'm sure it's nothing. Thanks, Roger."

The customer rattled his empty glass.

Roger excused himself, attended to the customer, then returned to Sanders.

"So, taking some time off?" he said, changing the subject.

"You could say that." Sanders took another sip. "Just a break."

"Yeah?" The bartender wiped down the dusty bottles behind the bar with a rag. "So, what's next? Starting a new venture?"

Lucky Roger was a good friend, or Sanders would have cut the man's curiosity short with just a look. He tilted his head back and poured the rest of the thick, syrupy liquor down his throat. It felt like liquid fire scorching his senses.

"I hope you're not thinking of leaving the force. Not having you on the street would be a disservice to this town."

Sanders forged a tight smile.

Roger produced two shot glasses from beneath the bar, setting each down in front of himself and the detective. "I know taking a shot like this is unusual. Normally, I'd grab some good vodka, but it's lucky for you my bar specializes in whiskey. And you're a valued customer." He pulled a bottle of 30-year-old Highland Park from behind the bar. He took his time pouring the shots. "Besides..." He handed a glass to Sanders. "Consider it a thank you for helping keep this town safe all these years."

The detective's eyes lit up. "Yeah...?"

"Here's to you." The bartender lifted his glass and waited for Sanders to follow. They clinked in a friendly toast.

Sanders wasted no time shooting it down. The whiskey offered a fruity, oaky finish that rolled effortlessly down his throat— severance pay for the bullshit he dealt with the last twenty years. "Thanks, Roger."

"Anytime. It's the least I can do for all those fights you helped me break up."

"Just doing my job."

"In fact..." The bartender dipped below the bar, presenting a long, metallic cylinder with "The Balvenie" printed on the label. "I'm giving this to you, my friend." He handed it to Sanders.

Sanders took the gift and read the label. "Single malt Scotch whisky," he muttered.

"Aged fourteen years. Offers a nice balance of fruit and vanilla. It's yours."

Sanders looked at his friend. "Thanks, Roger."

The second shot coursed through his veins. Sanders surged with the restless thrill of a young man on the brink of independence, his body alive with warmth, boldness, and a simmering hunger for payback.

It was time to move on.

He shot down the rest of the whiskey, then struck the glass against the bar.

"It's playtime," he whispered as he rose from his stool, kicking it out from behind.

Part 3

Part 3

Revenge is an act of passion; vengeance of justice.
Injuries are revenged; crimes are avenged.

-Samuel Johnson (1709-1784)

If revenge is sweet,
why does it leave such a bitter taste?

-Unknown

59

59

SANDERS

SANDERS

He pulled his pickup into the strip-mall parking lot. Theories of what had happened here sprang to mind as he braked into the last spot, facing the storefronts. He hadn't been here since the department collected Powell's body from the squad car.

A young boy, weighed down by a clumsy knapsack and another large bag, stood by the curb, gripping the handlebars of his bike. Glasses sat askew on his crinkled nose. Three older boys, wearing black jackets and bleached jeans, hung by the curb, blocking the entrance.

The blonde one smoked a cigarette, blowing puffs of smoke in the young boy's face. A shiny three-inch scar winked above his right eye. It might've looked like a knife wound to some, but Sanders knew better. The mark didn't make the boy look tough, but rather like he'd fallen face-first onto something sharp. His friend, a burly guy with a scraggly beard and a hairy gut peeking beneath his shirt, drank from a bottle wrapped in a plastic bag, leaning against the young boy's bike. The third, a stocky Latino kid, cackled at the boy's Spider-Man knapsack, jabbing the burly one in the ribs.

Sanders hated them already.

Scenes like this were nothing new. Habit and instinct nearly pushed him to question what underage boys were doing outside a convenience store, drinking. But then he remembered setting his police badge in the nightstand by the bed.

Today, Sanders was not an officer of the law but an ordinary citizen—a common man.

He pushed open the door and stepped out of the car. The boys smirked, then turned back to the boy on the bike.

"Stop being such a baby," said the blonde. "We'll watch it for you. You think we'll steal it or something?"

Sanders moved for the entrance. With the blonde and Latino blocking the door, he'd have to move them out of the way before entering.

The blonde dropped his hands onto the handgrip, and the boy gasped. "You seem slow, so I'll explain it again," he said. "You pick up a few supplies, and we watch your stuff. Simple."

The boy peeked at Sanders, mouth slightly parted, eyes wide with panic. Sanders softened for a moment before addressing the others. With a tight, pencil-thin grin, he regarded the blonde. "How are you, kid?"

The Latino snorted and smacked his friend on the back. "Hear that? The man just called you kid!"

The blonde nodded at his friend, his expression grave. He fired Sanders a look.

Sanders lingered in silence, eyes sharp and unblinking. Being just another face in the crowd, an ordinary guy, felt suffocating. More rules, fewer privileges. Navigating the blurred lines of undercover work, dipping into crime, never came naturally. In New York, the department had busted him running with his dealer crew before he even got the green light. A few lines of coke and a brutal swing of a lead pipe had been enough to exile him from the UC squad.

To quell his nerves, Sanders imagined the blonde's strawberry blood fanning out along the oatmeal walkway after crushing his nose with the heel of his boot. He turned to the shaky boy on the bike. "You okay?"

The young boy shrugged, then cleared his throat. His words spat out in a rush. "The guy won't let my bike inside, and I have nothing to chain it with."

"And these punks are giving you shit?"

The young boy dropped his jaw.

"Hey," called the blonde. "I don't see how any of this is your business, old man."

Unalarmed, Sanders held his gaze on the young boy. There was something about him, something Sanders couldn't quite place. He turned to the blonde, still addressing the boy. "I have an idea. Why don't you go inside and pick up what you need? Leave your bike and stuff here. I'll watch it for you."

The boy accepted Sanders' offer. When he wasn't wearing a badge, handgun, or nightstick, Sanders found that people, even kids, warmed up to him. They trusted him. He might have exuded cold indifference, but he was honest. Many found his blunt sincerity refreshing. Respectable.

Huffing hot air through their noses, the three boys stepped away from the glass doors. The young boy hesitated, then curled a shaky hand over the faded fingerprints coating the aluminum handle. He looked at Sanders again, doubtful.

"It's okay," Sanders reassured him. "I'll be here when you return."

JASON
JASON

With his knapsack knocking his back, he rushed through the aisles, hunting for a can opener. He grabbed a red basket and filled it with four 16-ounce bottles of soda, raw veggies and fruit in small containers, a bag of chips, candy bars, and a handful of tiny dessert cakes.

A door marked *Employees Only* creaked open in the back. A tired-looking man with a goatee, heavy feet, and a silver ponytail, stepped out. Jason thought of a genie drifting out of his cramped lamp.

Racing to the register, Jason slapped a crisp twenty-dollar bill on the pockmarked counter. The old man took his time sliding behind his workstation, then offered Jason a polite nod.

Close-lipped, Jason nodded back, wondering if the clerk

remembered him. It was hard to forget the old man, the only one working the store. His fuzzy, gray eyebrows and heartfelt eyes reminded Jason of his grandfather, and how he would also mumble sharp remarks about his destructive food choices. *You know, you shouldn't be eating stuff like this*, the clerk had once said, gesturing at what he labeled a bunch of addictive products made by shady corporations meant to control and harm. *Did you know they put artificial dye in these things? Red 2, Red 40..."* One of Jason's favorite remarks was when the old man bagged up a pint of skim milk, saying, *Why don't you buy the whole milk and then add water? That's what the companies do, you know.*

Jason collected his change and plastic bags and whirled towards the exit. After two steps, he stopped, his sneakers squeaking against the linoleum.

Hazy leaflets grouped among local business cards and flyers hung on a corkboard by the door. Among them was a page from the *Wanapatchee Trends* highlighting the Pacelli twins. Under their monochrome faces, bold print letters read: *Have You Seen Me?,* followed by their stats. Jason noted Beth's thin, straight mouth and browbeaten eyes.

"Police have been here a couple of times, looking for those two," said the clerk, his voice tense. He pointed to the board with an arm covered in gray curls. "You hear what they did? Pretty despicable if you ask me."

Jason nodded, his attention locked on the photos, trying to mask the unease in his eyes.

"The police are offering a reward for information leading to them, you know," the man added. "They're about your age, right?"

Eyes wide, Jason pressed his lips together and nodded once, ogling the cutting smirk on Chris' face.

"I've seen you before, yeah?" the clerk pressed. "You all go to the same school?"

Jason caught a glimpse of the clerk's face and shrugged. "Thanks," he said, raising the bags in his hands.

The clerk stared at him. "Be safe out there, kid."

Jason pushed open the door, his heart pounding, wondering what would come next.

SANDERS

SANDERS

He lifted the kid's bicycle and overnight bag into the back of his pickup. The three boys leaned against the brick wall, arms crossed, waiting for the prize Sanders promised them.

Whistling, he snaked around their rigid, drunken forms and swung open the passenger door. There, on the mushroom-colored leather, waited a six-pack of beer, warm from weeks of neglect. He had bought it a month ago, then left it behind, forgotten. The bottlenecks clinked together as he placed them on the hood. The boys stared, eyes sharp with curiosity.

Sanders fished his keys out of his pocket. "You know what's curious?" he asked. "The human body—amazing thing, but so fucking vulnerable. Looking at you three, I see nine pressure points that, if struck, can cause intense pain or even temporary paralysis." He paused, studying them for a moment. "And if someone struck any of you right at the base of your little pointy noses..." He set his bottle opener on a cap, flicked it off, and took a long, thirsty sip. "...it'll trigger brain shock, fracture your nasal bone, and—surprise—you'd die. Now..." Grinning, he uncapped a second bottle and placed it on the hood beside his leg. "Who wants to have a drink with me?"

The boys exchanged nervous glances. The blonde spoke first, voice wavering with forced bravado. "We don't want no drink with you, old man. How about you give us the beer and get lost?"

"That's not gonna happen," said Sanders, taking another sip. "Besides, I could use the company."

The burly one stepped forward. "Whatchu talkin' about, old man? We ain't interested in having no drink with you."

"Well, that's the only way you're getting it," Sanders said, scanning the area before brandishing his shiny Luger Semi-Auto

Handgun. He set it down beside the beer. "I'm not gonna bullshit you. You can have a beer with me, but after that, I decide what happens next." A long pause. "I loathe little pricks who bully kids smaller than them. So, you might want to think about your next move very carefully."

The boys froze. No one moved; no one took a beer.

The Latino and the blonde stepped back, then spun around. Footsteps pounded the blacktop, fading into the distance. Sanders had to stifle a laugh.

The burly one stayed. Maybe he was drawn to Sanders' audacity to drink in public with a handgun in full view. He reached out, grabbed a beer, and took a swig.

"Thank Christ," Sanders said with a mock sigh. "I thought I'd be drinking alone. You're one brave little bastard, aren't you?" He took another drink, then belched. He eyed the boy, from his greasy hair to his saggy XXXL jeans and bright yellow basketball shoes. "Okay, maybe not little. But brave. Or just stupid."

The boy, as if in a race to the bottom, slammed the beer in less than a minute.

But Sanders moved quicker, tipping his head back and draining his beer in a single, effortless gulp.

Later, he slouched behind the wheel, bruised fingers wrapped around another beer, and watched the fat kid shuffle off, head hanging low like a child learning to walk.

Then he waited for the kid to exit the store so he could offer his second proposal of the day.

60

SANDERS

"Going camping?"

The boy flinched.

Sanders glanced at his passenger. He knew to exercise caution. Slurred words came easy when drinking, and that would only spook the kid. A master at detaching from his inner demons, Sanders had perfected the art of playing the "trustworthy guy."

The boy gripped his knapsack, uncomfortable and sheepish. He exchanged a shy grin and rubbed his sore shoulders, his motions slow and restrained.

Sanders caught the change in his breathing and the subtle shift in his posture, tense as if he were preparing for something.

After thanking him, the boy asked Sanders to drop him off at Skyway Drive near Ramapo Mountain State Park, saying he wanted to explore Van Slyke's Castle ruins. Odd, since he looked more like a bookworm than the outdoors type.

Sanders pretended to focus on the road, offering the boy space to speak. But all the boy gave were shrugs, head shakes, and nods. Perhaps his parents taught him not to talk to strangers, though he accepted Sanders' offer with wary gratitude.

"Nice day for fishing," said Sanders, popping a stick of gum in his mouth. He offered the boy a piece.

The boy responded with a polite wave of his hand. "I-I'm fine. Thanks."

There's something about this kid...

Sanders had worked in the same county for years, met countless people, and seen even more faces. Could this kid be just another face in the community?

No one spoke for a while.

"You look like a kid on a mission. I brought my gear. Plan to catch some trout in that river." He could almost hear the boy's muscles stiffen.

"You're going out there too?"

Finally, the boy spoke more than one syllable.

Sanders grinned. "Absolutely."

He turned onto Skyway Drive, picking up speed. Thick, leafy trees blurred by like endless green smudges on canvas. Tiny droplets of rain hit the windshield, flicking the boy's face. Sanders squinted through the mud-spattered glass. A damp, earthy scent bathed the truck.

The boy freed up a tense grin, the corner of his mouth twitching. His hands gripped the knapsack like it might fly out the window. Gusts of air swept his hair, exposing a sweaty forehead.

Oh, shit. Could it be?

The name Reid zipped to the front of Sanders' mind, spotlighted in scarlet. Sanders favored using word association to retain facts, this time linking "Reid" with "seeing red." He knew this kid; his case was why the department had denoted Sanders to file coordinator in the first place.

He remembered the boy's jumpy eyes, knees pulled tight to his chest in the corner of a dim room. The father had watched their exchange in silence, glowering at his son, his stare growing darker by the minute until his eyes became two deep voids inside shallow sockets. "Are you alright, son?" Sanders had asked.

The boy's eyes had flicked to his father for permission. "I-I'm fine. Thanks."

There wasn't much the police could do. With the father held in an overnight cell and the mother allocated to rehab, relatives accepted responsibility for the boy before his folks petitioned the state to return custody, which they did. Once the state received favorable reports about the mother's progress, the police had to allow the child to return home. And, of course, having sidestepped police brutality charges, the department was grateful and took care of Mr. Reid for his generosity. This treatment only pissed Sanders off more.

He blinked his way back to the present. He wondered how he could use this incredible finding to his advantage. He relaxed, knowing he wouldn't be recognized. The boy had been much younger at the time—six years old, if Sanders remembered correctly. Even so, kids lacked the aptitude (or perhaps interest) to retain adults' faces and names. They had no focus, no concentration.

They drove on in silence, tension thick between them.

After turning onto the gravel lot at Ramapo Mountain State Park, Sanders parked the truck and grabbed the boy's bike and overnight bag. He asked if he needed help; the boy politely declined. Traffic splashed past several yards away.

"Take it easy, kid," Sanders called, lifting his bruised hand. "And enjoy your dinner!"

Pushing his bike onto the trail, the boy stopped and turned around. "Huh?"

"Well, it's Sunday, right?"

The tension in the boy's body relaxed. He emitted a nervous grin. "Thank you."

"Anytime, kid. Who knows, maybe our paths will cross again."

JASON
JASON

Skilled at spotting a drinker, he pushed through the brush to get out of sight and away from that heady scent. He scrambled along a disused trail too narrow for the man's truck. It soon faded into the tangled mess of the woods.

The lie about wanting to see the castle and water tower came out suddenly, and Jason felt proud when it did. No doubt the man believed him. He appeared harmless, but it was wise to keep as far away from people as possible—especially adults.

The man saved his butt from a beating and possible theft, yet, he foiled Jason's plan for a smoother trip to the shack. Something about that driver stirred suspicion. Still, Jason reminded himself to focus on his path and avoid injury.

After burying his bike in a sea of brush, using the heel of his shoe, Jason marked the nearest tree by chipping away bark the size of a fist. Weighted down by the knapsack on his back and the cumbersome overnight bag slung across his chest, he pulled himself up slopes and hills, avoiding ditches, roots, and large rocks with determined effort.

He paused at a clearing ringed by thickets of maples and pines beneath the muzzled sun. His legs burned, his hitched breathing and bone-weary muscles confirming how long it had been since he hiked these trails with his dad.

Jason fanned his fingers on his right hand, aiming his little finger towards the hazy yellow sphere. Visualizing a line down the middle of the angle between his pinky and the 12 o'clock mark, he surmised the line pointed south. At least, that's what his father had taught him years ago.

He altered his trajectory, heading southwest. Luckily, the terrain leveled out, and his tracks grew solid until he spotted his father's shack. It stood a few hundred feet away, the east end masked in a sea of foliage.

Neither Beth nor Chris was outside.

Jason stepped up to the door and knocked. A hollow gesture, like apologizing after someone's loved one died. "It's just me. You two in there?"

No response.

"You two okay?"

Silence.

He opened the door. It dipped on its hinges, the silence beyond thick and waiting.

61

SANDERS

Those drunken assholes had pushed him further behind schedule. Fine. He'd taught them a brutish, defensible lesson: think twice before picking the wrong mark. You never know who someone knows, or when they'll shed their wool and bare the wolf.

The discovery of who the kid was hit like a jolt. Sanders had considered leaving him back at the store, a rabbit tossed to a pack of seething boas. But something, call it a hunch, drove him to step in and offer a ride. And once again, his instincts proved right.

Could this kid be the wild card he'd been waiting for?

The bag and fishing rod shifted during the drive. Sanders reached deep into the aluminum diamond-plate tool chest inside the trunk. His soles slipped on the slick blacktop, and he tumbled backward into the driver's door to stop from falling on his ass.

Amused and relieved to have avoided such crude conduct before the boy, Sanders laughed. He tried again, pulling out his gear. He slung the bag over his shoulder, tucked the plywood under his arm, and tapped his jacket pocket, smiling.

The diary was there, where he'd left it.

First thing first: find and inspect the hunter's lodge.

It had been a couple of years since Sanders last dragged his prey there, and he needed to check for intruders and prowlers. He remembered the structure settling on a hill far north from the faceless entrance off Ditchburn Street, but off Skyway Drive, it stood a great deal closer. About a mile south of the lodge lay the castle ruins; to the east was the stream that seemed to run endlessly in both directions. Though his memory faded, Sanders had his compass and, above all, his instinct.

He planned to watch for clues along the way: footsteps and game trails, signs kids had passed through. Out-of-place cracked branches, trash, gear, or baggage were clear markers.

Anxious to get rolling, Sanders nearly forgot Roger's gift. He reached inside, snapped open the casing, and pulled out the bottle, studying it.

He looked around before unscrewing the cap. Cars whizzed along the road. He flicked the scotch towards himself and said, "Here's to you: unapologetic and unafraid."

He brought the bottle to his nose and drew in a breath. Rich notes of tropical fruit and spicy, creamy toffee drifted up his nostrils and through his body, comforting his guts. He took a sip, tasting sweet vanilla and hints of apple. He sealed the cap and packed the bottle inside his bag.

Sanders, fishing rod in hand, bag hanging over his shoulder, and plywood tucked under his arm, headed into the woods, shoving branches aside before entering. A gluey patch of clouds broke, allowing a shaft of light to punch through. The ground felt swampy beneath his boots. Surrounded on all sides by tress, the woods looked like dusk inside. Chickadees clamored overhead.

He'd thought to drive his truck down a service road or logging trail to save time, but that would only instill fear and distrust in the kids. It was wiser to walk on common ground as a harmless fisherman.

About forty-five minutes in, Sanders came to a gravel service road and trailed it. It was wide enough, showing signs of regular use. He knew hunters had bought land here before the state made it an official park, but before he came to see any, Sanders veered off the path, keeping a close eye on his compass. He soon realized he'd headed far enough east and aimed north.

Out in the woods, there were no rules. No hierarchy, no law. You had to play—or fight—on equal footing, or the dolt obeying principals lost every time. And kids never played by the rules, especially homicidal ones. Cheating came easy to them, done effortlessly, with smiles and wide eyes.

One time, the New York psychiatrist snagged Sanders' attention by claiming the brain's frontal lobe kept growing into your twenties. "So, kids," she said, "are dashing around with their reasoning centers and judgment still under construction."

Was that flimsy excuse really supposed to explain it all?

Sanders shrugged off the thought, refocusing on the trail ahead.

O   O   O

He reached the hunter's lodge.

Just as he remembered, the old-world shelter perched on its gentle hill, half a mile north of the dilapidated castle. The lodge, oddly enough, brought to Sanders' mind his squat, round geometry teacher from high school, built like a hulking triangle.

Its long sides soared upward, meeting at a crown twenty feet high. What remained of the brown and black shingles still cased the building. Behind the tall, two-paned window on the second floor, faded peach curtains drooped like tired eyelids. A thirty feet tall chimney jutted from the roof near the entrance; a circular decorative plate gleamed at the peak. The door, splintered and gray with age, held six shattered windowpanes patched with cardboard, flanked by two more cracked sheets of glass. Four rotting wooden steps, each one creaking and split, led up to the entrance of what was once a charming retreat.

In a brief, sentimental moment, Sanders wondered what this place must have been like during the height of its popularity. He imagined hunters and their families stopping by for juicy venison before carrying on with their sylvan excursions.

Then came its closing, and the meth gang had moved in, using the building as a factory to manufacture poison.

Visions of that arrest drowned Sanders' mind. Captain Ramsey had sent him and David Powell here after receiving a tip from locals living off the trail road. A stinking, sickly smoke had been rolling from the chimney and windows, flooding the sky with a gray haze. Powell suggested calling for backup. But Sanders refused.

"We can handle it," he'd said. "It's what we get paid for."

Powell nodded, but it wasn't long after Sanders kicked the door down that his partner called in backup, fouling the detective's plan to administer his brand of justice.

Careful not to slip through the splits in the wood, Sanders inched his way up the steps, mindful of putting unnecessary pressure on the cracked areas. A rusted padlock sealed the brass door handle.

He laughed.

He looked over his shoulder to ensure no one was nearby, then raised his foot before slamming the heel of his shoe into the wood. The door swung open, crashing against the wall behind it. The collision sounded like a blunt gunshot. Sanders' eyes widened with delight. He stepped inside, the floor creaking under his weight.

He found himself in a stale room washed in uneven, pale light and hit by the sharp stench of rot. Slanted, discolored walls surrounded the dusty plank floor, marked by jagged holes and a cathedral-style ceiling punctured with gaps. A rusted radiator and bent bands of sheet metal leaned against the wall behind a suede olive-green couch overlaid with grubby red pillows. Weathered picnic tables and benches filled the space, along with broken ceramic lamps and sagging cushioned chairs. A deer head, mounted inside a fractured frame, hung above the stone fireplace. In the far right corner, a staircase rose into the darkness above.

Sanders set the bag and rod on the couch and propped the plywood against the wall. He unpacked the zip ties and pepper spray, tucking them into his inside jacket pocket; the Glock, he clipped onto his belt. Then he buried the bag, with the rest of the tools, inside a two-foot crevice in the floor.

He pulled out the scotch and took a drink. The alcohol stirred his appetite. He tore open a pack of beef jerky with his back teeth, spat the wrapper on the floor, and popped a few pieces in his mouth.

He inspected both floors, noting where he might restrain the twins. The concrete pillars on the first floor, left of the stairs, looked best. How far could runts, strong as insects, go shackled to cement?

Sanders knew his actions were defensible. What he was about to do, he owed to the community. He owed it to himself. Most of all, he owed it to Linda.

He once read that people don't choose their destiny—destiny chooses them. He never disputed that.

Sanders grabbed the tackle box and fishing rod, then vanished into the trees, stepping beyond the edge of light into waiting silence.

62

THE GIRL

Jason stepped inside.

Chris lay on the loft, back to the door; Beth lay coiled on the mattress, burrowed in blankets up to her chin. Her neck crooked towards her brother, watching. She had been crying, eyes swollen and red.

She had heard someone approaching long before the door opened, and wondered if Chris had too. The visitor could have been another hostile hunter or even the police, but she refused to care.

Without a word, Jason set down his bags before sinking to the foot of the mattress, his motions neat and measured. Not even a fly stirred.

Time passed. Neither twin uttered a sound or moved.

Her mind swirled with clashing colors: red, pink, and purple aches, each shade deepening as she watched Chris unravel, reminding her of the boy who once puffed those dandelion seeds into the wind.

The growing distance between them seemed inevitable, fueled by Chris's hunger and isolation. Maybe he was slipping from reality altogether; his stories about Jason's father could be nothing but wild imaginations.

But who was she kidding?

"Beth?"

She blinked her way into focus. Wearing a rueful smile, she turned to Jason.

"You okay?"

She bobbed an unconvincing nod, pressing a finger to her lips. Jason nodded. "I have news," he whispered.

"Oh?" muttered a throaty voice from above.

Jason's eyes shot up at Chris' twitching feet. "Yeah," he said, a touch louder this time. "And food. Money."

"Good for you," said Chris after a while, "but we don't need your charity. And shouldn't you be home with your dad?" He lay motionless, save for his feet, his face a few inches from the wall.

Jason flinched.

Beth gasped, her head whipping upward. "Chris!"

"It's okay, Beth," said Jason. "I get it."

"Sorry. Chris is not feeling well."

"Don't make excuses for me, Beth!"

Her teeth clenched behind tight, trembling lips. Her eyes drowned in tears, but she refused to offer the satisfaction of seeing them fall. She dug uneven fingernails into her palms to distract herself from the pain scarring her insides. When that failed, she shot up from the mattress, threw off the blankets, and stormed outside.

"Yeah. Run off. See how brave you are out there alone. Cause your boyfriend won't be sticking around."

Beth hadn't even reached the fire pit before a surge of emotion burst through her, and she buried her reddened face in her hands. A crunch behind her drew her to look over her shoulder. Without a word, she turned back, wiping her eyes with the back of her hand.

"You okay?" Jason took a step closer. Mist coated the clearing, the air thick and murky from the storm. Fallen leaves and needles bristled across the sodden ground. Each step felt like treading through a marsh.

An unbearable silence passed before he turned to head inside.

"I just...needed to be outside."

Jason stopped and spun around. Once they were close enough to touch, his fingers grazed Beth's arm. She stood still, closing her eyes.

Like watching a loved one plunge into a ditch you dug yourself, looking into Jason's eyes felt excruciating. Beth's gaze drifted to his chest, her vision blurring until her friend became nothing more than a shimmering mirage before her.

"Hey, I get it," Jason said with a smile. "And don't worry about me being offended. I mean—" He flicked a thumb over his shoulder— "that's not my real home, you know."

Beth giggled.

"Okay, okay." He straightened his glasses. "It's a shithole."

With so many emotions bottled up, a roar broke from Beth's throat. She doubled over, clutching her knees, gasping for breath.

"See?" said Jason, nudging her. "Who says nerds are boring?"

Birdsong fluttered above, a gentle chorus of encouragement.

Jason's gaze grew tender as he moved in, gathering her up with practiced ease.

She pushed back, palms braced against his chest, but he held steady. After a few trembling tries to break free, Beth surrendered, hiding her face in the crook of his neck. His chest was a haven, warm and yielding against her wet cheeks, and he smelled faintly of soap.

Overhead, a goldfinch darted by, its chirp bright and clear.

Guilt crawled into every crevice of Beth's insides. Jason had returned, and it was no surprise why. His father was missing, and he had nowhere else to go. In her mind, she saw the body buried fifty feet deep inside a dry waterhole, bugs and urine covering the rotting corpse. Acid swirled along the walls of her stomach.

"I'm so sorry," she cried. "I'm so bad. And I miss everything. I'm scared for Chris. I don't understand what's happening. No one needed to die."

After a long and tearful moment that left Beth furious with herself, Jason suggested they hang outside so Chris could rest. He offered to cook something, but her body recoiled at the idea. Even eating felt wrong.

That's when Jason faded into the dusty shadows of the shed, emerging with the small Jetboil tank. Beth watched as he pulled a handful of white and Scotch pine needles from nearby trees and dropped them into the Jetboil cup with water from the pump. Then he snapped an orange three-legged stabilizer beneath the fuel tank. After screwing on another metal piece, he placed the cup on the stand, locking it into place.

"It's a solid unit," he grinned as he dragged the device along the forest floor, searching for stable ground. "My dad says you got to find your happy spot. Or else—*psshhh*! Hot water everywhere."

Beth flinched, then smiled.

Jason snapped the lid in place and switched on the regulator. He clicked the electric igniter, and a flame sparked. Moments later, water gurgled inside the cup. He discarded the needles and poured the water into a tin cup and travel mug, his movements slow and cautious.

Beth sat on the damp log, sniffing the mug in her hands. Steam drifted across her face, offering much-needed warmth to her stiff, chapped skin. She held the cup still in her lap to keep it from sloshing, then took a sip. The tea ran down her throat, dulling the ache in her belly. Thick traces of pine and sap clung to her tongue. Not wanting to offend Jason, she buried a grimace.

"Not a fan?" he asked, slurping his tea.

"No. It's fine. It's just..." Beth trailed off and took another sip, cradling the mug in her hands. "...why the needles?"

"I know," Jason laughed. "Odd, isn't it?"

"No," she said, gazing at her cup. She thought of Jason's kiss and smiled, remembering the faint taste of licorice gum on his tongue.

"I get it," he reassured her. "My dad made this for me once, too. I asked him the same question."

Beth's eyes traveled to Jason's feet, her stomach somersaulting. "Really?"

"Yup. He said the needles had vitamin C or something." Jason shrugged, his smile fading. "I wasn't paying much attention. I thought he was full of it. I mean, he had liquor in it and everything."

Beth scratched the side of her cup with a split thumbnail. Something inside pushed her to tell Jason the truth about his father.

But how could she betray her twin—and devastate her only friend? Her lips curved into a mournful smile. "Your dad drank too?"

Jason dipped his head and turned towards her.

Despite herself, Beth found her eyes wandering upward, locking with Jason's. A light breeze sifted through the trees, blowing hair across their faces. She looked away and nodded. "So did my parents," she said.

"Yeah." Silence stretched between them as they listened to the birds. "But did your dad ever hit your mom?"

Beth shook her head. "No! That would be awful."

She could see why some parents thought a slap was the answer when a kid talked back, dodged homework, or challenged the rules. Sometimes Mom would even land playful punches on Dad's arm or chest when he encouraged Chris' harmless pranks, like when Chris fished out mysterious blocks from the freezer, feathered with ice, laughing. But did fathers actually hit mothers?

Dad was a reserved man, emotionally distant and hard to approach. Strict but not abusive, except when Beth had been unresponsive to him about her homework, lit that match on their Long Island front lawn, and returned home late that summer night.

But he never struck Mom.

She remembered him opening doors for women in public and walking houseguests to their cars at night. Feeling a fresh, sad appreciation for Dad, her insides felt heavy, like blocks of lead.

"I know what happened to your folks was horrible," said Jason after another pause, "but it must have been nice they stayed together. That's rare."

It was rare. Like many homes, hers held tension and discord, yet Beth couldn't name a single kid whose parents stayed married. That had to mean something.

Were Mom and Dad just stubborn and old-fashioned? Did they love each other? If so, was it an unspoken love, one that didn't need soft words or earnest hugs?

63

SANDERS

SANDERS

His boots squelched in moist soil carpeted with pine needles and maple leaves. Sanders slapped aside branches and sidestepped scat, alert for footsteps and clues.

But because of the storm, there were none.

A milky white sky hung low over the trees. Red-winged blackbirds and goldfinches cheeped overhead. Sanders took recurrent breaks to catch his breath and regain balance. He was more out of shape than he'd thought.

A rushing sound rose from the east side of the woods. Two hundred feet later, he spotted a stream rushing north over a bank of rocks. Sanders set down the tackle box and pole. He kneeled and dipped his hands into the water, splashing his face. It was cold as hell but refreshing.

In front of him, a bluebird clamored, beating its wings.

Sanders snuck another sip from the flask, picked himself up, and walked on. If the twins stayed in the woods, they had to use the stream as a water source.

He clung to the west side of the water, keeping a close eye on the compass.

After a mile of slogging along uneven turf, twisting around fallen trunks and large rocks, Sanders reached a section void of trees or shrubs. It offered a glimpse of the open forest, and he was grateful not to have to watch his feet while he walked. Still, no prints. He blew out a breath, pausing to tighten a loose knot in his laces.

The stream narrowed into a brook, then a creek. The birds grew louder, more shrill. Then a faint trail of footprints surfaced on black soil.

"Bingo."

Recalling Chris Pacelli's shoe size, Sanders followed with renewed energy and vigor. Areas thick with needles and leaves offered the most struggle, making it impossible to walk a straight line. Several times, he retraced his steps and changed course.

He snaked around a rotting trunk, and the footprints vanished. His head jerked in all directions. "Where did you go, you little shit?"

THE BOY

THE BOY

"Ladies and gentlemen, our record-breaking and youngest contestant, Chris Pacelli, returns with a bank of one hundred thousand dollars! Does he have what it takes to head to the final round with the prize money tonight?"

Beams of light polished the stage, marking the returning champ. A mounting roar poured from the audience.

Richard, with his tan, polished face and dark blue starched suit, announced the first question: *"What led to the success of the New York Yankees in the late 1990s and early 2000s?"*

A proud laugh. Then, "Derek Jeter. And Mariano Rivera, and Jorge Posada."

"Who pitched a perfect game against the Minnesota Twins on May 17, 1998, at Yankee Stadium?"

"David Wells."

Richard looked down at the blue card pinched between his thumb and forefinger. The crowd rose to their feet, holding their breath, gripping one another.

The host's eyes traveled upward, grinning. *"You don't think you're going to get away with this, do you?"*

The crowd burst into evil laughter, pointing at Chris with knotted fingers the length of rose stems.

Something outside, a laugh, pulled him from sleep. Chris jolted awake and had to brace himself to avoid falling off the loft. He squeezed his eyes shut, cursing under his breath.

Ripples of pain shot through his head, and his belly felt like a deflated balloon. Strange, since it felt hard and heavy inside. He couldn't remember drifting off to sleep but must have soon after Beth stormed outside.

He groaned, covering his eyes with the crook of his arm. What little light leaked through the window slashed his face like a blade slicing open his forehead.

Focusing only on survival had affected his body and brain. Without restful sleep and a filling meal, Chris' thoughts and feelings expanded into a tangled maze, like cobwebs stretching across a forgotten attic. He could no longer keep track of time; it was a forgotten memory, days streaming into one another. He wondered if men in prison or war felt the same way.

Chris hated being alone. Beth could handle it—he couldn't. He missed school, the team, his friends. Even Dylan. But Dylan had turned his back on him, too.

What the hell had he done to deserve this? Since the fire, he'd taken charge, made the calls, stayed alert. So why was everything falling apart?

Alone in the forest, there was no choice but to relive your mistakes. You had to own them. That forced Chris to confront his relationships with his family. He thought of Aunt Margaret, Uncle Brian, and his cousins who lived in California and Florida. Italian and Irish families valued bonds and loyalty, but after Dad moved them to Jersey, the distance between relatives grew. Chris wondered if they resented Mom and Dad for leaving New York.

The unease of wrongdoing rushed back. Chris was too weak to fight the guilt. He'd committed crimes, some accidental, some not. He'd battled to avoid prison and stay with his sister. But in doing so, he'd created a stony rampart around himself. A kind of cell.

A sob escaped. Pangs of regret had hit when Beth walked out, but Chris lacked the strength and energy to follow her. She was all he had left. And now he felt her slipping away. The pain inside was like an abscess, worsening by the hour.

Whispers outside pulled him from his thoughts. Chris pushed himself to sit up, then climbed down the ladder, wincing as pain shot through his body when his feet hit the ground. He pressed an ear to the wall beside the window and listened.

"Why did you come back?"

Silence. Then words, too faint to make out.

"Hey, it's okay."

"No, no. It's not okay."

Had Beth told Jason the truth about his father? If she had, Chris would have no choice; he'd have to kill him.

Breathing through his nose, he whispered, "No, Beth. Don't..."

He shuffled across creaking boards towards the door, glaring at Jason's bags. But there was no time to check them now. He had to get outside, fast.

He adjusted the handgun tucked in his waistband and opened the door, wincing as light hit his eyes, stepping outside. Above the warble of birds came more whispering. He held his breath and narrowed his eyes, focusing.

Jason sat beside Beth, his left arm draped across her back. "What can I do? You want me to talk to your brother?"

A pause.

"Yeah, you can talk to me." Chris raised his arms, startled to feel them trembling. "I'm right here." His right hand drifted to his waist, waiting.

He took a step forward.

SANDERS

He examined the fallen tree and tangle of bare branches, a grim grin pulling at his lips. Could've been a coincidence. Maybe not. A single dry twig hung cracked and peeled, its fragile end crooked to the right. In these woods, nothing was random. Accidents, sure. But nothing random.

The branch hung three feet off the ground. Maybe a bear or deer had pushed it that way. But there were no tracks in the soil, and no animal would try to mask its prints. Sanders made a mental note of the area in case he needed to circle back and try a different path, then headed west.

Five minutes later, the thrill drained out of him. Could the kid have headed along a parallel path?

"Sonofabitch."

His shirt stuck to his back; his underwear bit into the crack of his ass. Scotch fueled a reckless courage in his veins. Patience thinning, he quickened his pace. Ignoring snags on his clothes and scratches on his face and arms, he barreled through the brush, dodging only trees and boulders.

Then came a cessation of solid ground beneath his feet, and his foot slipped on wet leaves, his ankle twisting beneath him. Before Sanders could catch himself, he was sliding down a cliff.

"Shit!"

Wet soil parted like water. A torrent of earth rained overhead. Sanders snatched a line of ivy and closed his eyes, blocking the rock-strewn hail. With the heel of his boot, he found a foothold along the cliff and steadied himself.

A swarm of birds shot from the treetops.

He heard the faint thud of the box and pole smacking the ravine floor and cursed.

Sliding against the rocky wall sent sharp pains shooting across his back. His sweaty grip slipped down the ivy. He needed to decide fast—climb back up or allowing himself control to slide down the nearly vertical crag. Before he could choose, Sanders lost his grip and skidded down further, his body pressed against the side. The pain was maddening, like blows from a blunt knife. Still, it slowed his fall and might let him reach the bottom unscathed.

A nasty smell fired up his nose, increasing the farther he sank. He dug his heels into the side, slowing the fall, eyes shut. Then a thump echoed off the ravine walls. It was his boots striking the floor, sending a shock up his body. His body ached, his backside damp from the wet wall of the ravine. He opened his eyes.

High above came a yelp, then rustling vegetation.

The floor stood gray, jagged, and rocky. A rill, swollen from the storm, streamed alongside his feet. Looking up, he saw that the edge of each side was no more than ten feet wide. A low-hanging sky peeked through a hood of trees and foliage stretching along both sides.

The stench was nauseating, like rotting animals under an angry sun. Sanders turned his head.

"Jesus Christ!"

Buried in dirt, leaves, and sand lay a human carcass. Some unsuspecting bastard must have fallen and broken his neck.

Inside the horrific scene, Sanders caught sight of his tackle box and fishing pole. They lay a few feet from the gray, bloodstained leg of the body, spattered in mud.

Sanders took in shallow breaths through his mouth and stumbled closer. He fell to his knees, mouth gaping. Eyes numb. Numb, yet taking in everything. He knew this body.

It was Bennett.

Tears pierced his eyes, his mouth tight and pale. Motionless, his eyes scanned the scene, absorbing the clues as he had at countless crime scenes before. He examined the body, the unnatural position in which it lay. Most murders had thirty seconds of planning, if that. Scuffs of mud and plant-life stains on the clothes told Sanders someone had pushed the body over the edge. And the son of a bitch tried to hide it.

The awareness hit like a pinprick in his brain. Someone dumped the body and didn't bother to bury it. An adult would have known better. He would have been terrified of being caught, digging a hole for the body until his knuckles bled.

But a kid would have been afraid to go near it. They'd want to forget, pretend like it never happened.

"Jesus Christ..."

It occurred to Sanders that he was dealing with a classic psychopath. Based on the information he'd gathered since the fire, the boy seemed logical, without a sense of right or wrong. Like a puppet master, he marveled at power and control. He lacked feelings for people, and remorse when hurting them. He refused to admit his actions were his fault, even though he knew they were wrong.

And Sanders knew many psychopaths begin their work by killing members of their own families.

The stench of death was intense. Sanders needed to get out of the ravine and send help fast. Bennett had been a husband, father, and pillar of the community. And a friend. He deserved better than being cast down a cliff like sewage.

Sanders stood and reached for his things, then stopped. Forget the damn tackle box. It would only weigh him down. He walked to the ravine edge, searching for a way up. Strands of ivy hung thick but looked flimsy. He grabbed a handful and tested it, tugging hard. Sure enough, the strand pulled free.

But the ivy wasn't the only thing to flutter out from the stones and dirt.

His eyes narrowed.

A crusty pink slip of paper drifted by his feet. He snatched it before it blew into the water.

Sanders pressed out it against his thigh. One side was blank; the other had typed lines with empty spaces for signatures. Rain had smudged most of the print. Two words remained clear.

It hit him like falling from a plane without a parachute. Breathless, Sanders fought to breathe, teeth grinding. Any hope of rational thought or following protocol vanished. His eyes darted over his shoulder at his dead friend.

He grabbed the fishing pole, wedging it down the back of his pants, then snatched a few tools from the box and slipped them into his jacket pockets. He crushed the paper into his fist, shoving it deep into his pocket.

Knotted around itself hung another strand of ivy. Sanders yanked. This one held. With both hands he hauled himself up the ravine.

The paper crackled against his hip. The pink slip with two words that stood out like a roach in a bag of white rice:

Chris Pacelli.

64

THE BOY

"So..." he took another step forward. "What is it?"

Jason flinched and spun towards Chris, glasses crooked on his nose. Beth shot up, the mug on her lap thumping against the dirt, spilling her drink.

Together, they stared, waiting for the other to speak.

No one said a word.

He reached for his waist, dark, chary eyes glaring at Jason.

"Chris..." said Beth, breaking the silence.

"Everything's okay," said Jason with a firm nod. "You two can talk. I'll wait inside." He ambled beside Chris and leaned in.

Chris tensed up, avoiding eye contact.

"Go easy," whispered Jason. "She's under a lot of stress."

The next few seconds passed by like minutes, Chris fighting the urge to sock Jason in the face. How dare this nerd tell him how to treat his sister? Before he could huff out a breath, Jason slipped away, reentering the shack. The door closed behind him.

He stared at Beth, waiting. "Well...?"

Beth's eyes dropped to a patch of wet dirt.

Just then, the sun's rays glinted across the clearing, a chorus of birdcalls echoing from every direction. Blake appeared, hovering near the pile of ash over Beth's shoulder. Chris hadn't noticed him.

"Did you tell him?" He took a step forward.

She shook her head. "No."

He studied his sister, squinting. "If you didn't tell him, what were you two doing?"

"We were just talking, Chris."

"Talking."

"Yes."

"In his arms?"

"Yes!" Beth's head shot up, meeting Chris' eyes. "I mean, no. We were having tea, that's all."

Neither twin spoke.

A rush of happy memories came flooding back, one after another. Chris wanted to share everything he'd kept inside, to say how sorry he was for being so much easier to love.

He missed the wild fun of their adventures after Independence Day, scavenging for scorched fireworks to add to their secret pile. The excitement of digging behind the shed, convinced they'd found the devil's hand when a big root popped out of the dirt. He remembered the weight of the coins in his pocket when they walked to the candy store, or the excitement of hiding under the dining table, pretending to drive their Batmobile. Shadows on the wall became their place for video game battles, and how he almost cried as they watched that old cartoon movie, *Dot and the Kangaroo,* together. He even missed the small things, like showing Beth how to tie her shoes and draw a star when Mom and Dad had run out of patience.

But the words dissolved on his tongue like aspirin. All that came out was, "You're stupid to be talking to him like this, Beth. Do you know what can happen if he finds out?"

"Stop calling me stupid," she snapped. "I'm not stupid!"

She pushed past him, storming inside the shack.

SANDERS

That rotten name, Chris Pacelli, echoed in his mind. But he turned the sting into something useful: fuel.

Since the fire, Sanders had managed brief flashes of sympathy for the twins. But as the investigation dragged on, even those faded; after today, they were gone for good. The stakes had risen. Sanders had crossed paths with hundreds, maybe thousands, of kids who'd survived tragedies far worse than losing their parents to a fire, yet had steered clear of the easy, lawless road. The twins, though, belonged to the lowest rung. The kind who broke into homes just to inflict pain, counting on crooked lawyers and gullible jurors to shield them from consequences.

Knowing this, Sanders had to summon a massive effort to transform into that "good guy" façade, and with the help of time and scotch, he managed.

The afternoon wore on, the air damp and warming but offering no relief. The sun glided across a hazy sky through patchy breaks in the clouds, casting the first hints of shadow.

A two-foot trail sprinkled with specks of fresh weeds stretched ahead, and Sanders followed it. A freestanding hut crept into view. It stood alone in shame, a forgotten memory. Then came voices rising beyond the trees.

He froze. Faint whispers, but he heard them. He walked on, eyes low, stepping over underbrush that could expose him.

A shout rang out from thirty feet away. Then came the sound of shuffling over dirt.

Sanders braced himself and rushed behind a small cluster of trees. After a minute, he peered around a trunk. It wasn't until the figure had gotten twenty feet beyond that Sanders saw who it was.

The boy moved closer, and Sanders knew he stood hidden. Shaking the tension from his muscles, he bent over and bowed his head, pretending to lace his boots. The footsteps drew closer, crunching over leaves.

A branch snapped. Then came a gasp. The boy reeled backward just as Sanders' head snapped up. "Whoa." He exhaled, then cracked a smile. "You nearly scared me half to death! Hey there, kid."

The boy stepped back, then froze. His tired eyes dark and glassy, as if seconds from tears.

"I assumed you were just a rabbit or something."

The boy's fists clenched into pale, scabbed balls, lips pressed tight. The kindhearted greeting had no effect on him. His left hand gripped a stick. His right hand relaxed, then drifted towards his waist.

Sanders followed the boy's eyes, then shifted attention to his hand. "You look a bit shaken. Sorry to have startled you."

"I'm not." The boy cleared his throat. "I was taking a leak, that's all."

Sanders let out a laugh. "Sorry, kid. Is this your tree?"

The boy's gaze locked on Sanders' hands, then flicked to the fishing pole resting in the grass.

"Well, I won't bother you." Sanders rose to his feet. He patted the dust from his thighs, then pulled a four-ounce water bottle from his jacket pocket. The boy watched as he took a sip. "Needed that." He offered the bottle, pretending not to notice the lump under the boy's shirt near his waistband. "You want a sip? You look like you could use it."

The boy kept still. His eyes radiated distrust. No warmth.

"If you want it, it's yours." Sanders gave the bottle a shake. "Go on, take it," he insisted, glancing skyward. "It's a muggy one today. You should have water if you're hiking out here."

The boy raised his right hand and seized the bottle, his voice low. "Thanks." He drank the water in one gulp.

"Good god, son," laughed Sanders. "You *were* thirsty!" A buzz of mosquitoes circled them as they faced each other. He looked away. "Anyway, it's no problem. We have to look out for each other out here." Then he picked up the fishing pole and turned around.

"What's that supposed to mean?"

Sanders turned back, smiling. "What's that?"

"Look out for what?"

"Well, we're out in the woods. Just be safe. Anything can jump out at you."

The boy's frown flattened into a straight line. "No shit," he grumbled.

Sanders pretended not to hear. Instead, he gestured to the stick in the boy's hand. "If you don't mind me saying, you've got a unique trekking pole. Never seen one like it."

"Huh?"

"The stick. I've never seen one that short."

"Oh." The boy's eyes glanced at his right hand, then back to Sanders. "Just something to, you know, swing at stuff in my way."

Sanders nodded. "Well, take care of yourself, son. And for God's sake, stay hydrated!"

"Thanks."

He turned on his heels and walked on. "And if you and your family are hungry or just want to relax, stop by my lodge anytime."

Seed planted. Let it take root.

After taking a dozen steps, the boy spoke again. "Lodge?"

Curiosity sparked. Good. Keep feeding it, slow and steady.

Sanders turned back again. He'd reeled the boy in. "Well, you must know about the castle, yeah? I own a lodge north of here, not far from the ruins. Just a humble place to park and relax."

The boy nodded once.

Still skittish, but listening. Push a little deeper.

Sanders grimaced. "Excuse me," he offered. "If you don't mind me saying, you don't look so good. Were you in a fight? Need something to eat?"

Leaves rustled from the trees as birds whirred overhead, squawking.

The boy gave a half-shrug.

"How about grabbing your folks and following me? I'm heading back there now."

Now, disarm him with clumsy charm. It works every time.

Sanders jiggled the pole in his hand. "Today was a bust anyway. I couldn't catch a fish if my life depended on it. I even used one of those water bottles to try to catch a small one—or at least bait. And stupid me lost my tackle box!"

The boy cocked his head, narrowing his eyes.

"I sawed off the top of the bottle, you see? Then shoved it in backward. The fish swim inside and are supposed to get confused and can't get out. I hear it's an effective channel. Only I must have done it wrong."

"Yeah, I heard that," said the boy, raising his empty bottle.

"Your bottles are too small. You need larger ones."

"Yeah?" Sanders snorted and slapped his forehead. "That's smart. I should have known. You must be one of those genius kids."

The boy shrugged, smirking.

"Listen, I don't mean to rush you, but I need to get back. My guys can use the help. I understand if you need time to collect your folks. Like I said, feel free to stop by—"

"I don't have any money. But thanks anyway."

Sanders grinned at the boy. "I'll tell you what, kid, no charge. For you and your family."

"Huh?" The boy's eyebrows rose behind an oily clump of hair. "Why free?"

"Consider it payment for your advice. And..."

The boy scowled at Sanders. "And, what?"

"Isn't it obvious?" There was a sudden silence. "You're an Islanders fan! That's enough reason for me."

The boy cast a shy look down at his soiled blue and orange shirt, grinning. "Yeah?"

Bingo! Pride. Something I could work with.

"You kidding? Who do you think was there in '80 when Tonelli fed Nystrom and scored in sudden death? He clinched their first Cup at the Coliseum that year."

The boy's eyes jolted wide, like he'd been hit by an electric shock. "You saw Nystrom score in overtime?"

"Hell, yes. It was epic. The crowd went mad. The Philly fans were whining like babies, but who cares, right?"

Entranced, the boy nodded. "Wish I'd caught that." Then suspicion crossed his face. "What was the score?" he asked after a moment.

Careful now. One slip and you blow the whole thing.

"For that game? Uh...let me think. If memory serves, 4 to 3."

The boy's face softened.

"Well, it's been good crossing paths with you, kid. Stay loyal!"

That'll stick. Now, wait for the next move.

"Hey!" called the boy, yanking Sanders back in.

"Yeah?"

"What kind of food you got up there?"

Sanders shrugged. "Whatever you want. We specialize in venison and chicken sandwiches, but I brag when I say our beef stew is our signature dish." He tapped his chest, grinning. "My recipe." He caught the faintest growl from the boy's stomach. Out of the corner of his eye, the unmistakable weapon tucked in the boy's jeans seemed to mock him. He tilted his head over his shoulder. "So...?"

"What?"

"You coming then? I've got to haul out before dark. Your family nearby?"

The boy's expression sagged.

Sanders glanced sideways. "Sorry, kid, did I say something?"

"No, uh...my folks said they'd meet me in about an hour. They're kind of out, doing their own thing."

"Oh."

"But I'm hungry."

There it is. A crack in the armor.

"Great! We've got a big-screen TV. You can catch the last of the Flyers and Penguins playoffs."

The boy stared.

Hook set. Keep the line loose.

"I know, I'm not a fan either." Sanders raised his hands in surrender. "I just thought, if you want to check out the rest of the game, you're welcome to."

"Oh, cool."

Just say yes, kid. Make this easy.

Sanders looked around. "You sure your family's okay with this?"

"Don't worry about them," the boy assured.

Got him.

"Okay, let's roll. Need a hand with your stuff?"

The boy looked over his shoulder, then shook his head. "No. I left my things with my folks."

He fell into step alongside Sanders. They trekked on, the sun's rays slanting through the green and brown forest, the air sweet and hopeful.

65

THE BOY

THE BOY

"You serious, kid?" The fisherman shook his head. "And you got away with that?"

"Sorta," said Chris. "My folks never found out."

He found himself at ease with the fisherman. Perhaps it was the man's crooked smile, or the way his bushy brows leapt up whenever he made a witty remark. Maybe it was the fisherman's endearing clumsiness that gave Chris an odd feeling of command. Engaging and disarming kids was easy; winning over adults was a different challenge altogether.

Still, Chris couldn't ignore that strange nagging sensation poking the back of his mind.

The fisherman had rambled on about his business, saying it had been around for three generations. He talked about the great reviews it got from local and national papers, even from famous people. People like Henry Morton Stanley, and some reporter-turned-explorer who used the famous Winchester Repeating Arms .45-75 lever-action rifle, which, according to the fisherman, was a link to Africa in the late 1800s.

After the man paused to sip from his water bottle, Chris jumped at the chance to share an amusing story, breaking the boredom.

He amused the fisherman with tales of the neighborhood kids, describing the moment they dared Jimmy, George's wild nine-year-old brother, to yank the fire alarm on a telephone pole. When a neighbor's house alarm blared, the kids thought it would be hilarious to outdo the racket with something even louder. Within minutes, gleaming fire trucks and two police cruisers thundered down the street. The kids, tickled by the uproar they'd unleashed, admitted their mischief. After collecting statements, the authorities released them with a stern warning.

"You had luck on your side that day," the fisherman said.

In reality, the man didn't know how lucky he'd been today. After seeing him behind that tree, Chris was seconds away from firing a round between his eyes. But the man seemed harmless enough, and the odds of running into another Islanders fan were extraordinary in Jersey.

Chris tried convincing himself he'd asked about the 1980 Stanley Cup game to test the man's sincerity. As it turned out, he'd forgotten the score. Like a dream that clings to you after waking up but fades with time, Chris' old life had slipped into the past.

The afternoon grew unexpectedly warm. Stomach grumbling and legs like two flimsy, thinning erasers, he thought about Beth, figuring time away from her would do them both good. Thoughts soon shifted to a hot meal of hot steak with a steaming pile of creamy potatoes. He'd even down Brussels sprouts if they sat on the plate.

"Mind if I ask you a personal question?"

The fisherman's shift in tone drew Chris from his thoughts.

"Why aren't you at school?"

Chris swallowed hard. "Huh?"

"School."

Chris, hands suddenly trembling, scrambled to devise a convincing excuse. His knees buckled, and he passed it off as a cramp. Did the man recognize him on the news, or maybe a headline? He reminded himself to keep calm and stay cool. He barely managed a word before the man cut him off.

"What am I thinking," he said. "It's a holiday!"

Chris' heart slowed, and he smiled.

The man shook his head. "As you get older, you tend to forget these things. Some folks stop recognizing certain holidays. Others forget them altogether."

They pushed up a sloping hill for a while before the fisherman spoke again. "You don't talk much, do you, kid?"

Chris shrugged.

"That's okay. I don't either."

"You could've fooled me."

The fisherman laughed. "I like you, kid! You're alright." He slapped away a branch, barely missing his face, his eyes widening. "Mind if I ask you something else?"

"Might as well. You've asked me everything else."

"What's with the marks on your neck? Looks like a mountain lion got at you or something."

He stayed silent.

"I don't mean to pry, kid, but has anyone been putting their hands on you?"

Chris touched his neck, feeling the sting from the marks. Outside the stream's fluid reflection, he hadn't had many chances to check the bruises. The man seemed concerned, but nosy—something Beth would call "inquisitive" whenever Mom labeled her as the opposite. "Nah," he muttered, shaking his head. "Happened while playing baseball."

The fisherman's boot stubbed a root, and the pole bounced on his shoulder. "Yeah? You a jock?"

"I guess."

"It probably explains those bruised hands," the man noted. "You should be more careful."

"Yeah," Chris muttered. "We played against a tough team. I dropped my glove right before catching a fly ball."

It wasn't a total lie. Dylan had tossed the ball, and Chris dove for it. It struck his hands like a stone.

The ground leveled into flat terrain, and Chris wondered how much further they had to go. He shot the man a glance and saw him wearing a strange grin. His eyes darted to the compass in the man's hand.

"Where is this place anyway?"

The fisherman turned to Chris, pointing ahead. "It's just beyond this hill. You must be starving."

They reached the high point of the next hill; the building emerged twenty yards ahead.

His first thought was, *What a dump!* But it hardly mattered. Fatigue and hunger kept him from stopping or turning back.

He paused fifty feet from the entrance, glaring at the crooked sign above the second-floor window that read, *The Lodge.* He shot the fisherman a distrustful look.

The man didn't seem to notice and kept walking. After a few steps, he turned around. "Oh, don't let the look scare you. We're doing some work on it."

"I'm not scared," Chris scoffed.

"Renovation. We've had this place for a long time. Finally getting around to fixing things up."

Chris nodded and marched forward.

They climbed the broken steps to the door. The fisherman stepped aside, sweeping his arm towards the entrance. "After you."

Chris nodded and turned the rusty knob, stepping inside. "What the—?"

He stepped into a dank, hollow room, the air thick with the smell of rot, like something torn from a nightmare. The floor gave way beneath him, and he sank into a pool of blackness.

THE GIRL

"Wow!" Beth's eyes shot open, disbelief flooding her face. She dropped to the bed, dust flying up in clouds. "Where'd you get all that?"

Jason tapped the bills against the zipper of his open knapsack. "Don't worry. It's mine, from my house."

She snapped her head up, meeting his eyes.

"Relax," he smiled. "It's just some food and a few bucks."

"Jason," she stammered. "This is...it's too much."

"It's not that much."

"But the money..."

"It's not much. I just thought it could hold us for a few weeks."

"Try a few months!"

Jason laughed, rubbing his glasses on his shirt. He spoke of his plans to capture small game for an early dinner.

Flushed, Beth chewed her lower lip, studying the open bags, clinging to the hope that Jason's dad had returned home. But he kept silent about it. She imagined herself in a dream where she could bend reality, like she had so many times before; she'd close her eyes and slip into invisibility, blending into the air around her.

She squeezed her eyes shut, imagining herself vanishing into the thick air of the room, fading like smoke from a match. Then Jason would be back at home, in school, happy with his father.

But when she opened her eyes, he was still there, and he could still see her.

"I figured you and your brother could use the help." He slid his glasses on, then raised his hands in mock surrender. "I know, I know. Killing a rabbit today of all days seems crazy."

Beth hesitated. "Why? What's today?"

Jason blinked. He adjusted his glasses, processing her question. "Why, it's Easter."

In the forest, you didn't think about holidays. Or days of the week or homework. Only survival.

Beth flashed a look at her friend, guilt weighing on her shoulders. Telling him the truth now would be like shoving him in front of an oncoming train after he'd just pulled her from the tracks. She cleared her throat to speak, but then a stark twinge pinched her chest. She needed air.

"You okay?"

Jason's voice grew distant, his presence fading. She stood and moved towards the window, hoping to see Chris resting on his log. But he wasn't there.

"Beth?"

She turned towards the door and stepped outside.

66

THE BOY

He jolted awake, shivering, chin knocking against his chest. His head throbbed with a fierce, relentless ache, his jaw pulsing with pain. The agony behind his eyelids was so sharp he dared not open them. When he tried to lift his hands, he found them bound behind him. Cold, unyielding restraints bit into his wrists and ankles.

He felt paralyzed, trapped in a fog of pain and bewilderment. Garbled sounds dribbled from his lips. His mind fought to recall what had happened moments before he blacked out. Had he fallen, slipped, and hit his head? He'd seen cartoons and heard stories about people seeing stars after a blow to the head. He never believed them. Now he found himself blinking through flashes of light.

Footsteps, heavy as rolling thunder, crossed the room.

"Wake up, you little shit," a brassy voice spoke inches from his right ear.

The sound shot a chill up his spine. His eyes fluttered before finding the strength to open. His head lolled on his jellylike neck.

The room smelled awful, a thick, suffocating odor. Pale light crept across the man's face, inches away, highlighting the hollows beneath his eyes.

Chris tried to draw a full breath but felt like he was snorting gravel. Pain burned in a deep place inside his skull, somewhere he hadn't known existed.

"It's about time. I was starting to get worried."

The man staggered across the room to one of the oversized chairs and dragged it across the floor. The boards groaned and cracked under the weight.

The sound tore through Chris' skull. He shut his eyes, a futile attempt to shield the pain.

The man parked the chair in front of him and sat down. Clouds of dust exploded from the cushion, hovering before dissolving into the air.

"I wasn't worried about you," he added. "I was getting bored, and when I get bored, I become unpredictable."

Chris froze, trying to convince himself it was all some twisted nightmare brought on by the worst days of his life. The man spoke again, his words slurred. He closed his eyes.

"Hey!" A boot kicked against Chris' chair, forcing his eyes open. "Don't even try to tune me out, kid."

Chris' eyelids drooped, as if weighted by cold metal coins. A sharp, metallic tang coated his tongue, conjuring memories of the day he sucked on a filthy penny to win a dare. Glancing down, he spotted a fresh bloom of blood on his shirt, its edges stiffening into a dark, brittle crust. Zip ties bit into his ankles, each twitch sending a jolt of pain through his skin.

Through a barely open slit in his eyes, an image of the fisherman came into view.

"You learn quickly. I like that."

The man slumped in a ratty chair, chewing a piece of beef jerky from a package in his lap. To his left, tools and other things were scattered on a table, implements Chris couldn't quite make out. Maybe his mind was playing tricks, but he swore he saw something purple.

"Wh-what's going on? Is Beth okay?"

A vague stretch of time passed as the man chewed in silence. Then he picked up a large bottle, half-filled with a dark liquid resembling iced tea, from the table.

"Well, kid," he said, "we're celebrating."

Chris squinted at the bottle before spitting out a gob of saliva. A pinkish blot landed on his left leg, a string of dribble dangling from his chin.

The man snickered.

Chris coughed, then flicked his head up, eyes dark and menacing.

The man took a swig from the bottle; a few drops missed his mouth and dripped down his chin. He gave off a different kind of energy. Shadows blackened his round face and full red cheekbones. His eyebrows, thick as fingers, bowed over large black eyes. His meaty lips shook when he spoke, and his bald head bared an ugly scar above his right ear.

He noticed Chris glaring at him and flashed a spicy grin. In one quick move he leaped from his chair; before Chris could react, he jerked his head back, pinched his nose, and poured scotch down his throat.

"You like that, kid? That's some good stuff."

Chris coughed, but the scotch still burned down into his hollow stomach. The room tilted; his head spun.

"You want to act like a man," the man clamped a hand on Chris' shoulder, "you drink like one. This is a celebration, right?"

"Wh-what…celebration?" Chris moaned, his speech slow and irregular. He could barely recognize his own voice.

"Well, for me. As for you, you're living the last day of your pathetic life."

Chris wanted to speak but couldn't find the words. He bit his tongue, waiting for the man to continue.

"Of course," the man added, "if you play your cards right, you may change my mind. But the best you can hope for is to limp away with fewer fingers and toes. After I'm done, you'll be begging for death. See, I'm giving you a choice. One I never had."

What was he saying? What had Chris done to him? He found his voice and, horrified, managed, "What did you do to me? Where's Beth?"

A breeze whizzed through the holes in the windows, stirring the threadbare curtains; Chris flinched. He saw the man's eyes spark at Beth's name.

The man turned left, surveying the items on the table, then sank back into the chair with a savage grin. "I fucked you up, kid. That's all you're getting from me. Now, your turn."

"My turn?"

"Well..." He leaned in, eyes seething with hatred. "It's simple. I'll ask you a few things. You answer them. Understood?"

Chris glared at what seemed like the devil himself, fighting the urge to blink.

A boot hammered into his ankle. The sound of steel striking flesh boomed inside the room, followed by a shriek of pain.

"I asked you a question."

This wasn't a dream. If it were, Chris would've woken long before the ties bit into his skin. For once, he welcomed the King Kong terrors—dangling off the Empire State Building—anything but this.

The man blew out a huff of hot air. "How about this? Keep up this little tough-guy act and I'll drag your sister in by her hair. Then you can watch while I torture her."

Chris' senses stirred; his stomach snaked into knots. This crazy sonofabitch kidnapped Beth. He must have her tied up in another room. He threw the man a pointed look, fixing on him; everything else blurred like the background in a portrait.

"So, what's it going to be, kid?"

Chris nodded, fighting to stay strong. "Yeah."

The man scoffed and shook his head.

"I mean—I'll cooperate."

"Good boy. I knew you would." The man swigged from his bottle. "Let's start with Bennett. Why don't you tell me about him?"

"What? Who's that?"

He stood, blowing air through clenched teeth, and picked up the pruning shears from the table. He stooped beside Chris. "See this, kid?" He snapped the glinting blades. "You think I'm screwing around? Ask yourself this: which could you stand to lose? A toe? A finger? How about your pencil-thin prick?"

Chris smelled hot alcohol on the man's breath as his mind raced for an answer. His throat closed as if he'd swallowed sandpaper. He thought of the young officer on Ditchburn Street. The two hunters. The driver at the bottom of the ravine.

The man trembled, his patience fading. Chris figured he must be a friend or family member of one of the dead men, and unless he somehow broke the restraints and escaped, he had to give the man what he wanted. He had to confess. "Which one was he?" he asked.

The man fumbled in his front pocket and pulled out a pink-and-brown ball of paper. He shoved it into Chris' mouth and slapped a heavy hand over his lips. "Does this ring a bell?"

Only after Chris stilled did the man let go. Eyes watering, he spat out the paper, gagging. Mud clung to his tongue. His gaze dropped to the sodden ball of brownish pink in his lap. The man pressed the paper flat and drove it into his groin. Agony shot through his crotch, electrifying every nerve. Blinding stars burst behind his eyes, white and hot across tears of pain, fury, and hopelessness.

"I didn't know such a small pecker could cause that much pain," the man grinned. "Now, look before I do it again."

Chris pried his eyes open and refocused.

He recognized the paper right away, and the man knew it. It came from his stash of pink slips. He'd run out of places to hide them; this one must've slipped from his pocket.

"Well...?"

His thoughts tangled as he tried to relive the instant he shot the police officer. The afternoon had been calm and cold. No wind. He could still see himself sweeping his gaze over the scene before tearing away in the cruiser. If the slip had fallen out, it must have happened elsewhere—the woods, maybe or swallowed by the ravine. Only then did he realize the man must have meant the driver, the one Beth had somehow tricked down the cliff.

"It was an accident," he said.

Their eyes locked for a long beat while the man weighed Chris' words. "Accident, huh?" he said. "Tell me then—how does a kid your size accidentally shove a grown man down a cliff, then climb down and shoot him in the leg?"

Doubt clawed at his gut. Had Beth lied about what happened?

Seeing the man's fists curl, Chris rushed into the story as he understood it: he had fired by mistake, hit the man in the leg, then jumped from the car, leading to the chase and the fall. But in his version, he'd climbed down the cliff to help, only climbing back up after seeing the man already dead.

The man listened, expression unreadable. But as Chris reached the end, something in his face twitched.

He stood, picked up a sheet of plywood, and leaned it against the chair. Then he stepped out of the cabin and returned with a boulder the size of a bowling ball. He dropped it a few feet from Chris' leg with a grunt. The impact made the floor tremble beneath him, sending vibrations up his legs and spine. Scowling, the man turned back, disappearing again. One by one, he brought five more boulders of equal size, lining them beside Chris.

"You know who Giles Corey is, kid?"

Frozen, Chris could only shake his head.

"I'm not surprised. You kids aren't being taught anything useful in school anymore. Mark my words, in a few years, you won't even be able to write your own name." He dropped into the chair, brushing dust from his thighs. "Anyway—Giles Corey. He was a man in 1692 who refused to enter a plea during the Salem witch trials. And because he wouldn't cooperate, the people introduced a new punishment. You know where this is going, kid?"

Fearing what might happen if he stayed silent, Chris shook his head.

"Yeah? I'm surprised your daddy never told you about it."

A flicker of rage sparked in Chris' eyes.

The man strolled over to the table and selected a knife. Humming under his breath, he seized Chris' wrists. He squeezed his eyes shut, trying to pray, but only got as far as "Dear God" before the words fell apart, lifeless in his mind.

How the hell do you pray? I don't know how to pray!

Then he saw himself with Beth and Grandpa, bundled up beside a kerosene heater in Queens. A snowstorm had knocked out the power. Grandpa sang a war song.

Praise the Lord and pass the ammunition! Praise the Lord—!

In one swift motion, the man sliced through the zip ties, freeing Chris' hands. But he kept still. The chair tipped, and his back slammed against the floor.

The man dragged him several yards, grabbed his wrists, and pulled them overhead. Then he fastened them to a concrete pillar with new zip ties.

Chris no longer sat slumped in a chair. He lay flat on the floor, arms stretched overhead.

"What are you doing?" he shouted. Pain blazed up his spine like fire. "I'm telling you the truth! I'm not lying!"

But the man didn't answer. He set the plywood on Chris' torso. Chris wheezed. His pale face twisted, reddening under the pressure. The plywood—half an inch thick, maybe twenty pounds—covered him from chest to knee.

"You think that's heavy, kid?" the man snorted. "I haven't even started." He squatted, lifting a stone. "I'm about to educate you on what pressing is all about."

THE GIRL

She paced the clearing, chewing her fingernails, nerves trembling like spider webs in a storm.

Keep it together. He'll be back. He's angry, that's all. Probably just walked off to cool down.

"You okay?" Jason's voice sliced through the silence.

Beth's heart raced. A wave of heat flushed through her, feverish and unsteady. A strange, hollow terror crept in, as if something had been carved out of her, a piece of her soul torn loose.

As time crawled, the afternoon chill crept in. Jason gathered wood and kindling from the shed and lit another fire. He brewed a fresh pot of tea while they waited. When Beth refused to drink it, he insisted.

"You won't feel better unless you drink and eat something."

She caved after a moment, sat down, sipped the tea, and picked at the canned vegetables, muttering half-formed thoughts under her breath.

"He'll be back." Jason rested a hand on her shoulder.

A surge of nervous energy tore through her, and she sprang to her feet, the empty can slipping from her hand and hitting the ground. "I have to go."

Jason opened his mouth to speak, but Beth was already rushing through the clearing, heading east towards the stream. "Wait!" he ducked into the shack and returned with a flashlight and his jacket. "We may need these."

Thirty minutes later, they reached the stream. It had been Jason's idea to follow the water north. The farther they walked, the faster Beth moved, her steps outpacing his. Jason lagged behind, struggling to keep up.

SANDERS

He dropped the third stone onto the plank. The kid's face flushed an even deeper shade of red.

Back in New York, Sanders had no trouble slipping into the bad cop role during interviews. His partners—guys with wives, kids, lives outside the department—were better suited for playing the good guy. Sanders never tried to be sympathetic. His strength lay in intimidation, control, force. A large man with a face that rarely shifted from its stone-set calm, he was built for the part.

When he drove up Skyway Drive with Jason, his mind churned through tactics for dealing with the twins. The options unfolded like a reel of scenes. First, the silent treatment—just stare at the boy, say nothing. But Chris was tough. The kind of kid who'd resist that kind of pressure. Sanders discarded the idea almost immediately.

Then came the calm approach: lead with compassion, not fury. Maybe the boy would open up in return. But it rang false. Sanders dismissed it at once.

Convincing Chris he knew everything was another option. If

the boy believed he had nothing to betray, he might crack. Sanders scoffed. He needed a harsher approach.

Next he considered praising Chris as a warrior, turning the boy's strength into a point of solidarity. But that idea felt thin.

The last option was the most primal: exploit Chris' love for his family, threaten harm to those he cared for if he refused to cooperate. That would get results.

But finding Bennett in the ravine shattered all plans.

Sanders knew boys felt as deeply as girls but masked those feelings with logic. Girls, meanwhile, often let emotion steer them, even when reason faltered. Here, Sanders had to improvise.

This kid was sharp. For a moment, Sanders almost bought the ravine story. But when Chris finished, he saw through the lie. If Bennett's death had been an accident, the twins—if they had any conscience—would have stopped and made an anonymous call. Instead, they left a man to rot, his body caked in mud. That wasn't remorse.

The boy lay wheezing, tears stinging swollen eyes. No sobs yet, just clenched teeth behind stretched lips.

Sanders loomed over the pitiful sight, a grin creeping across his sweat-slicked, weathered face. He couldn't fathom how the weight must feel on a seventy-pound kid. "Ready to talk, kid? The truth this time?"

The boy was stubborn, tough. Not once had he begged for mercy. His resolve stunned Sanders.

"I won't lie to you," he said, voice almost approving. "You've got heart. Must be some of your daddy's grit."

The boy flinched, a broken growl escaping his throat.

Sanders popped a piece of jerky into his mouth and downed a shot from the bottle. His hand grazed the tools on the table: knives, shears, a lighter, pepper spray. "No more playing around," he muttered.

He seized the lighter.

THE BOY

THE BOY

"No more playing around."

The sound of his sneakers scrabbling against the floor drowned out the crazy man's voice.

He fought like hell to stop the tears. Heat boiled in his skull, and he blinked until his eyes dried, forcing his vision to clear.

The weight pressed down on him—like King Kong crushing his chest. He had to sip shallow breaths to keep the board from rising and falling against his ribs.

Stay strong. You're a soldier. Soldiers get punished, sometimes tortured.

He saw the man flick his thumb across the spark wheel of a lighter, igniting a flame inches from his eye.

But instinct overpowered fear, and as his lungs strained, Chris blew out the flame with a shaky breath. Each time the man struck the wheel, he puffed again. The man's hands trembled, struggling to keep hold of the lighter. Even if he wanted to cover Chris' mouth, he couldn't.

But the flame held long enough to singe his bangs, burning them before they curled and vanished into the air. A thick, sulfurous stink flooded his nostrils, mingling with the room's stale, musty air.

The man tossed the lighter aside and glared at the tools on the table. He didn't seem to notice the faint, almost imperceptible lift at the corner of Chris' mouth.

He snatched the shears and squeezed the handles, his grin returning. The blades smacked against together with a piercing metal shriek, like a fork dragged across teeth.

Chris lay helpless, hands and feet twisting beneath the board.

Footsteps. The floorboards creaked beside his bound hands. Eyes half-closed, he strained to see what was coming.

"Now...which little piggy should I cut off first?"

A fist crushed Chris' heart, stopping it cold. He tried to swallow but couldn't.

"You always wanted to be a pitcher, right?"

A thousand pleas swirled inside him, but he said nothing. His eyes, wide as fifty-cent coins, spoke volumes. But he refused to beg.

"Well, kid," the man continued, "my buddy wanted to sail the world when he retired. That was his dream. And me...?" His voice trailed off, eyes glazing as if lost in some dark memory.

His eyes narrowed into slits. With a sudden, savage grip, he seized Chris' forefinger with violent precision, cold and merciless.

Before he could grasp what was happening, the man squeezed the blades. Blood gushed from the cut, raining red droplets on the boards. A spike of pain slashed through his hand. Chris unhinged his jaw, and screams leaked from his mouth like a swarm of squealing rats.

Seconds later, the blades clipped through the bone with ease, like kitchen shears through a chicken wing. A sharp snap split the air, and the finger popped off. It flew several feet, dropping by Chris' foot, leaving a red mark on the wooden planks.

The man lunged for the table, flung the bloody shears at the wall, and snatched the blue bandana. "Go ahead," he said, jamming it into Chris' mouth. "Scream until your throat rips for all I care."

His hands twisted against the crude ties, sweat soaking his skin. Pain tore through his hand like lightning; his body shook beneath the weight of the board.

The man danced towards the severed finger, crouching to examine it like a jeweler inspecting a diamond. "Guess you'll never be a pitcher no more, huh? Here..." He tossed the finger onto the plywood. "This'll come in handy if we need kindling for a fire."

His screams fought to push through the gag, but only muffled cries and groans escaped. Soon, silence swallowed him whole.

"This calls for a toast, what do you say?" The man grabbed the scotch, raised it to the hazy light, and scowled at how much was gone. "Damn." He sank back into his chair, ogling Chris in silence.

He stared at the ceiling, refusing to give the insane man the satisfaction of seeing him broken.

The man yanked the gag out of his mouth, whipping it back into his face. It landed on the board under his chin.

Chris gasped, coughing up tiny beads of saliva.

"Anything to say yet, kid?"

A snip of garden shears had sliced through his dreams. Just like that. Goose vanished in a heartbeat, along with any sense of being the best at everything. His ambitions lay as lifeless and numb as his severed finger. All he wanted was to shrink into the shadows and disappear.

But Beth was still out there, waiting in the silence. And Chris, broken and bleeding, lay paralyzed. He was no longer a soldier— just a husk of pain and dwindling hope, as helpless as a butterfly trapped between a lion's teeth.

Fragments of thoughts and shattered words flashed through his mind, each one broken and incoherent. All he managed to say was: "You took my finger."

SANDERS
SANDERS

The boy's limbs lay still and useless around him. Blood pooled beneath the disjointed finger, streaking broken lines of crimson across the floor.

He had to hide the boy somewhere the world would never look, somewhere those pitiful cries would vanish into nothing. The woodshed behind the lodge, thick with musk and mold, offered only a single boarded-up window. Inside, the darkness devoured everything, cold and silence pressing in until every breath felt stolen, until even your outstretched hand disappeared into the void.

Sanders gripped the boy's ankles, dragging him out the door around the building, and into the shed. Inside, he stumbled over a hardback chair and cursed. He yanked the boy into the far corner and lashed him to a steel pole that ran from floor to ceiling. Then, in one fluid motion, he grabbed the chair by its legs and smashed it against the wall until it shattered into splinters, sharp shards cutting the air.

A restless tension rattled him. As he placed the third stone on the plywood, a hollow sense of defeat crept in, as if victory had evaporated just out of reach. The boy refused to beg, clinging to his tale about Bennett. Even his tears dried up. Sanders knew pushing further would only drive the truth deeper underground. Time to change tactics.

Struggling to breathe, he pitched the stick across the room. It flew just over Chris' head, crashing into the wall behind him.

His eyes took a moment to adjust. Another chair and an oak desk came into focus, a lamp toppled and broken beside it. A shattered light fixture swayed from loose wires overhead. Dust coated the room, cobwebs stretched from corner to corner.

A sound ricocheted through the room. Sanders stiffened, breath caught. Only after a heartbeat did he recognize the laughter—his own, jagged and raw. In this place, a boy's mind could shatter. The darkness was not empty—it was waiting.

He added more ties to bind Chris' wrists to the pole, then gagged him. He slapped duct tape over the handkerchief.

"Don't try to take it off, kid," he warned. "You'll only tear your hands off in those ties. And if you try to escape, I'll use the knife next."

THE GIRL

The frantic search led nowhere.

She ignored the mud-soaked trails, the thorns, the burning legs. She chased every sound, certain one would lead to Chris. A snap of branches. A splash by the stream. Always something, but never him. A fox. A pair of rabbits. She passed them like trash tangled in weeds.

After a couple of miles, they stopped to rest. Beth stood only long enough to catch her breath before charging forward again.

"Beth!" Jason grabbed her arm, now streaked with scratches. "Shouldn't we head back? Your brother might be waiting for you there."

Panting, she turned to her friend and let his words register. Her throat burned, a fresh wound pulsed on her cheek. Sweat coated her skin, her hair limp across her forehead. She'd been chasing shadows, lost in pursuit. It hadn't struck her that Chris might already be home.

Home. That's what that place is now?

Their shadows stretched across the clearing as they stepped from the trees. The sun hovered low, ready to slip behind the hills. The air had cooled, painting a mask of gooseflesh over Beth's skin.

Jason scowled at the crackling by his feet. He'd forgotten to stamp out the fire before running off. He started kicking dirt over the embers but stopped. They would need it for warmth, for food.

Beth raced into the shack and pushed the door open.

Silence.

Jason took a minute before following. Nearing the entrance, he found the door open and peered inside.

Beth stood alone, her back rigid and unmoving.

"Beth?" Jason touched her arm. He circled the room, searching her face. "Hey." Only when he jiggled her arm did she turn, eyes sharp and hollow.

"He's not here."

"I know."

"He never came back."

Jason scanned the room, searching for any sign Chris had returned.

"We can't stay here," she said.

"What?"

She flew past Jason and out the door, then stopped short at the fire. A groan tore from her throat as she doubled over, clutching her stomach. She vomited, retching up the last of her breakfast, then collapsed beside the flames, sobbing.

Jason rushed after her and dropped beside her, nearly slipping in the mess.

"Something's wrong," she moaned, rocking back and forth. "Something's not right."

Calm down. Don't fall apart now. Chris needs you.

Beth shook her head and wiped her mouth with the back of her hand, scowling at the acid burning her tongue and throat. Her belly groaned. Her feet ached. "He needs me."

Jason stared, lost, then reached for her hand. "What is it?"

A gust of wind whipped through the trees, casting shadows across the clearing. Then silence fell, thick and heavy.

Beth lost track of time as her nerves unwound. She blinked up at the sky. Clouds wore streaks of blood orange and smoky gray, melting into ashy smears. Soon, the sun would dip low enough to blush the clouds pink, fading them into her favorite powder blue.

The colors called up memories of gentle comforts: stuffed penguins, clowns, and dogs that once crowded her bed with warmth. Comforts no longer near.

Jason stood and headed to the pump for water. "I'll make us something hot to eat."

A crunching sound punched through the trees.

Beth bounced up with newfound vigor. "Chris?"

"Beth..." Jason's voice was low, tense. "You shouldn't be making noise. We don't know what's out there."

The sound stopped. Then, silence.

Don't say, Hello. Don't say, Is someone there?

"Chris?"

"He's not out there. I don't think he's out there, Beth."

She stepped into the trees. Jason followed a few paces behind. She halted, straining for any trace of her brother.

"I don't think anything's out there."

"Chris may be," she snapped. "Waiting for me."

After a while, she let Jason guide her back to the shack.

Then a scream tore from inside.

67

DYLAN

He didn't think much of the man creeping into the shack. From where he stood, it vaguely resembled Jason's dad.

But Beth's scream changed everything.

He took five steps towards the hut, then froze. The door burst open, and Jason and Beth stumbled outside, heads down, followed by the large man with Chris' weapons slung across his shoulders.

Neither Jason nor Beth had arms by their sides; they walked with jackets draped over them like capes.

The man was not Jason's father. And he wasn't a cop—no uniform. Just an air of quiet menace.

Dylan regretted leaving early yesterday, but hunger and being stuck at the foot of that filthy mattress had pushed him to wake Jason and insist they go. He wondered if Chris resented him for it.

Still, he came back for Jason. And maybe, for the thrill and excitement of hanging with two fugitives in the woods. But the thrill Dylan felt vanished after seeing Jason and Beth march out with a man who looked ready to do some damage.

They slipped into the trees.

Dylan spotted his chance, crept to the shack, and eased the door open.

Empty—except for food on the bed, Jason's backpack slouched against the mattress, and Chris' knapsack wedged by the wall.

Rather than wait for Chris, Dylan decided to follow Jason and Beth. He rushed to slip on Chris' pack, the straps biting into his shoulders. The bolt cutter poked out, keeping the zipper from closing.

He cracked the door open; his stomach cartwheeled, half expecting the man to be outside waiting for him.

No one.

It took a moment for his gut to settle. He peeked around the building. Jason and Beth were fifty yards ahead. Oddly, they were being led through closed areas, not along any trail.

Dylan followed, keeping his distance, tracking their movement by rustling leaves and shifting shadows. If by some chance they were headed to a patrol car, there was nothing he could do.

But if that man wasn't a cop, Dylan swore he'd do whatever it took to help his friends.

THE GIRL

The zip ties bit into her wrists. Her hands grew numb, but she stayed silent. The man was drunk, unstable, and pissed off. Who the heck was he? What did he want? Did he know the hunters? The man in the ravine? Could he be some angry spirit, reborn in a new body?

He ordered Beth and Jason to walk ahead, warning them to stay quiet. Moving deeper into the dim woods with bound hands took everything Beth had. Any noise beyond her footsteps might earn a blow to the back of her head.

At first, she feared the man was leading them to the well, but he steered west, forcing them through thick underbrush. She thought of the beautiful castle with its cigarette-strewn floor and walls defaced with chilling Halloween-type scribble, and longed to curl up into the safe, dark place inside the red brick fireplace.

Were her reflections right? Was she meant to suffer in the ruins of a once-beautiful home, haunted by a cruel and selfish sorceress?

Earlier, while the man ordered Jason to tie her up, he had thanked him, even regarded Jason with unsettling approval.

What did that mean? Had Chris been right about Jason?

Guilt crept in as Beth silently cursed her brother. How could he leave her? He was a boy—Dad's son. He was supposed to protect her.

She glanced at Jason, wishing he'd do something heroic. But he just stumbled up the rises and drops in the floor beside her, glasses askew, head low, lips twitching. Maybe he was thinking. Planning an escape?

You've been watching too many movies.

The voice was right. All those hours Beth spent in her lavender cocoon reading dark novels and watching silly movies could've been used to learn real-world survival.

But after her first week in fourth grade, everything changed. A skinny boy in a baseball cap mocked her hair, her walks, her voice—called her a boy. His friends laughed, eager to join the teasing. The girls were worse, skilled in cruelty, sharp with spirit-crushing jabs.

That's when Beth accepted her clumsiness and boyishness as facts. That afternoon, she went home and decided being alone was better. Trying to make friends was a waste of time and only led to heartache. Books and TV became her world. They wouldn't laugh at her. They would carry her somewhere far—somewhere magical.

She needed to focus, think about what to do. Perhaps it was naive to expect Jason to take charge, and now it was on her.

By the time they arrived, the sun's arch slipped to the other end of the sky. Vegetation cast long shadows ahead—a menacing introduction to what awaited them.

Beth had no idea how long they'd walked when the building appeared like a brown behemoth before them. It stood alone. Trees and plants edged to its foundation and crept up its walls, nature reclaiming what was once hers. The house reminded Beth of the shack, and she shivered. It was only larger, on the other side of the forest. Another place to be trapped.

As they neared the rotting porch, she thought of *Hansel and Gretel* and froze, nearly tripping on a stone. "Sorry," she whispered.

"No talking," snapped the man. "Keep moving. Inside, now."

Beth and Jason traded a glance. Jason climbed up the creaking steps and stopped at the door.

"Turn the knob and open it," the man slurred, shotgun locked in a grip by his side.

Jason swallowed, nodded, and twisted the knob, slipping inside.

A gasp escaped Beth's lips as the man turned to face her, expectant. "You, too. Let's go."

Until then, Beth kept her fear in check. But as she pulled herself up the steps, she faced the blackest thoughts of her unhinged imagination. Were more men waiting inside, lined up in a wide semi-circle? Wearing mucky jumpsuits, snickering behind horrible masks, clutching rusty, sticky knives with talon-like hands? Her mind filled with gray, hollowed bodies swaying from hooks around dripping pipes in the ceiling. She tasted metal.

Nerves stinging, Beth stepped inside. The musty air hit her nose; dust stirred, and she sneezed. She could barely see ten feet in front of her.

The man shut the door. More dust puffed from the floorboards.

The large room looked empty—no bodies hanging. But shadows and ugly furniture left plenty of places for monsters to hide.

Her eyes found Jason, his expression unreadable.

The man yanked off their jackets and led them to a thick pillar. He ordered them to sit back-to-back. Beth could feel Jason's sweaty hand brush hers; the touch repelled her.

"What do you want from us?" asked Jason as the man tied his wrists to the column. His voice cracked with fear. If Beth weren't so terrified, she might have laughed.

The man circled them, boots thudding, then stopped in front of her. He crouched so that their faces were level. Sweat dotted his face, his breath reeking. Beth imagined it curling towards her, clenching herself against the urge to recoil.

For an instant, he met her gaze. Then she looked up, fixing on the man's flushed forehead. She feared trapping herself inside that awful place where the dead men lay, stuck in a spot faced only in dreams where killers tracked her down endless roads into chilling houses and tight bathrooms with windows the size of dinner plates.

Softly, the man spoke. "You like to read and write. You're

smarter than people think."

Beth gasped. "I…guess."

"You're smarter than your brother. You'll cooperate."

She pressed her lips together, an oath to avoid saying something stupid.

"That officer your brother left in that parking lot? A good man and friend. He destroyed my partner's family." The man stood up, crossing his arms. "I doubt you understand the damage that causes."

Wait—! This guy's a police officer?

Their eyes linked, and Beth fought for breath. She squinted as a trace of recognition sparked.

"You had your chance to turn yourselves in, and didn't. I thought about taking you in, but now that I've got you..." He scratched his chin, grinning. "Ever heard of forgivable justice?"

She shook her head.

"How about a man named Vladimir Jankelevitch?

The man's words grew fuzzier, making her focus harder. "No."

He inhaled sharply. "Since you've been ditching school, I'll educate you. Vladimir joined the French resistance against the Nazis. Ring a bell?"

Again, Beth shook her head.

"He said true forgiveness is personal, between the torturer and the victim. No governments. No state or outsiders. Sadly for you, that requires that the victim be alive. And since Powell and Bennett are gone, that door's shut. Your guilt? Useless."

Beth could hear Jason's breathing, shallow and uneven. It distracted her, like a persistent noise she couldn't escape.

Focus. He's saying something important. Play along.

"So I wonder," he continued. "What's the point of pretending to forgive if it doesn't help the dead? Even if *I* chose to forgive you, you'd still carry that guilt, wouldn't you?"

Their eyes met again, confusion and panic twisting inside her.

"Now, why don't you start from the beginning? And I don't mean that woman's house and her daughter that you scared half to death. I mean the fire."

Beth didn't realize she was shaking until the zip ties threatened to tear her flesh. But it wasn't just the man's words—it was the fresh pool of blood near her hip, leaking through the floorboards.

"You never liked your family much, did you?" the man said. "Being mocked, ignored—it hurts, right?"

Beth's jaw dropped.

The man grinned wider. "C'mon," he pushed, "you can tell me." He leaned in, lips brushing her ear. "It'll be our secret. I've done bad things too."

A shiver ran through her. "I-I…I'd never hurt my family."

He pulled back, eyes locking with hers. "Don't lie to me."

Beth opened her mouth, then stopped. *Don't ever say what you know,* Dad had warned. *Follow the rules, but keep your mouth shut.*

"What happened to my brother?"

Jason's hands stirred behind her, his hair brushing her neck. She could feel his panic rising.

The man's nostrils flared. He turned to Jason. "What about you, kid? Got anything to say before I lose patience?"

Beth could swear she heard Jason's heartbeat. Or maybe it was hers, hammering so loud it drowned everything else.

"I have tools I don't mind using. Just like I did to your brother."

He's bluffing. Don't believe him. Chris is probably at the shack, waiting for us. Wondering where we are.

The look on her face drove the man to reach inside his pocket. "You think I'm playing?" He pulled out a small, soft object and held it inches from her face, pinched between his fingers. "Look familiar?"

Beth shrieked and jerked back. Her head thumped against the pillar, drawing another cry.

A bloody finger.

"You know what this is?" he whispered.

A stubborn lump rose in her throat. She squeezed her eyes shut, turned her head, and found her voice. "Where is he? Where is Chris?"

The man nodded. "Stubborn, too, huh?" He leaned into her ear.

"Don't go anywhere. I've got a surprise." He stood, his shadow swallowing her. "And you," he said to Jason, "don't even think about playing hero while I'm gone."

His boots thudded across the boards. Beth couldn't see what he was doing, then came the heavy slam of the front door.

DYLAN

He watched the man steer his friends into the lodge.

For the first time, he appreciated the pot sharpening his senses. It allowed him to trail behind, listening intently and pinpointing Jason and Beth's location. Scents that once escaped him now filled the air. Juniper berries clung to the breeze.

But the drugs also heightened his fear; every flutter of wings, every buzzing insect, every snap of a twig made him catch his breath. He felt jittery, like an old lady, neurotic and lost in paranoia.

More than once, he stumbled, nearly falling flat on his face, tempted to turn back. Then he could sink into his frayed recliner, light a fresh joint, tap his calloused thumbs against the game controller, and pretend the day never happened.

But he'd seen too much. New resolve gripped him; newfound determination and purpose pushed him deeper into the woods. The forest felt alive, its presence suffocating, like it knew exactly where he was—and it didn't want him here.

A single beam of light slipped through the boarded-up windows, but Dylan couldn't see a thing. Whatever that man was planning, it was pure malice.

He crouched behind a tree, teeth sinking into his nails, deliberating his next move. A tickle crawled up his arm. Dylan twitched, smacking away a beetle the size of an almond. His arms burned from the brush, but he didn't care.

"Think, damn it," he muttered, shifting over a root.

It occurred to him that he was still wearing Chris' pack. He slipped it off and unzipped it. "Sorry, Chris. But I'm sure you get it," he whispered, digging through the clothes.

Beneath them, he uncovered shirts, binoculars, handcuffs, duct tape, pens, and the bolt cutter. The bizarre collection was odd and unsettling. But not panic-inducing. The bald man had already done a hell of a job with that.

The bolt cutter sat heavy in Dylan's hands, a poor defense against a madman with guns. But it was all he had.

Sweat coated his palms as he wondered what Chris would do in the same situation. For a short kid, Chris was gutsy. Would he charge in like a superhero to save his sister? Dylan, an only child, imagined he would be protective, maybe even heroic, to a younger sibling. But the truth hit hard: he was selfish, and the idea of risking his life for Jason and a strange girl made his knees buckle.

"Oh, screw it!" Just as he moved to rise, a noise fired from the front door.

He froze, catching his breath.

Shadows jumped from a bright, moving beam as the man descended the steps, flashlight in hand. Dylan thought about grabbing the binoculars for a closer look but feared relinquishing the bolt cutter, which he gripped so hard that his fingers ached.

Was the man coming for him? Was he like some rabid animal, scenting his fear, hungry for blood? Panic surged as Dylan whipped his head around the trunk, ready to strike with everything he had. But the man disappeared.

Then Dylan spotted the flashlight beam cutting through the trees, vanishing behind the building. Safe and undetected, a sigh of relief washed over him. But where was this man going? And what had he done with Jason and Beth?

Dylan never saw himself as a hero—he was the anti-hero, the villain. When designing game characters, he made them menacing with loud tattoos, bulging muscles, wild hair, and deadly weapons. He cheered for the criminals in movies, curious about their unfiltered thoughts and actions when no one was watching.

But he wasn't caught inside some video game; this was real. And the thought of being a hero electrified him.

"This is it," he whispered, sucking in a deep breath. "Prove you're worth something."

Leaving the pack behind, Dylan snaked around the tree, then crept up the stairs and through the door, the bolt cutter clamped in both hands.

THE GIRL

THE GIRL

Jason hissed behind her ear. "Beth, do you know him?"

She shook her head, too hopeless to speak. Numb from the tight knots, her wrists throbbed in the restraints.

"Why didn't you tell him what he wanted? This guy isn't bluffing. We're in deep trouble!"

Beth struggled to hold back tears, but felt a wet streak trickle down her cheek. It burned her more than fear. But she refused to break—not in front of the man demanding answers.

Hey. Remember summer camp? Those girls wouldn't leave you alone. What did you say to me then? What did you do?

"And what did he mean about the fire?" Jason pushed. "What's going on?"

"I'm not saying another word until he tells me what happened to Chris."

"This isn't a game, Beth!"

C'mon. You remember.

"I know," she said. "I've known that since the beginning."

Jason shook his head and snorted.

Silence followed, thick and tense. Wind rattled the boarded windows. The front door creaked open, and something groaned across the room.

A silhouette stood in the doorway, haloed by the sinking sun like a blinding apparition.

Beth held her breath.

Jason twisted towards the sound. "Who's that?"

The figure, holding something long, stood quietly.

"Chris?" Jason called out. "Is that you?"

Beth knew it wasn't. The figure stood a couple of inches taller.

"Jason?" a voice whispered. "Is that you?"

Jason exhaled. "Dylan! Yes, it's me! Get me out of here!"

"Sshhh!" Dylan dashed across the room, stumbling over debris on the floor. "Keep your voice down. He's close."

Jason writhed in his restraints. "C'mon! Hurry!"

Dylan dropped beside him and snapped through Jason's ties with the bolt cutter, freeing his wrists and ankles. After releasing Beth, he wasted no time running back to the door, his shoes slapping against the floor. "C'mon! Let's get the hell outta here!"

Relief sparked inside her, but faded fast. Misery weighed her down, leaving only apathy. The fire had destroyed everything: her home, her parents, and her sense of safety. Chris didn't even seem to want her around anymore. And yet, the thought of leaving without him left her immobilized.

Even her journal, a bored friend who'd grown tired of listening, was gone. With no food or water, she wouldn't last two days. And if she did, she'd be alone. Jason wouldn't stick around; he'd either uncover the truth or soon think Beth and her problems tiresome and decide she wasn't worth the trouble.

So what was the point of surviving unless it was with purpose? Leaving now would be like betraying herself and every belief she ever held. Screw those exhausting instincts. To hell with survival for survival's sake.

"C'mon, Beth," panted Jason by the door. "Let's go!"

Beth's head stayed bowed, hands limp at her sides.

So, you're really gonna stay here and wait to get dismembered?

Why not? She was guilty, wasn't she? It didn't matter her age or the reasons for doing what she did. She'd considered the families affected by the deaths she caused and realized the crazy man was right—a proper punishment was in order. She didn't deserve rescue. Or forgiveness. And reverting time was impossible. It was time to pay.

"What's the point?" she said, unsure if she was responding to Jason or herself.

Dylan left Jason by the open door and crouched before Beth, stepping into the puddle of blood. He studied her, eyes red and heavy with worry.

She turned away, closing her eyes.

"Hey," he whispered. "It's time to go."

The silence returned. Jason lingered by the door, outlined against the last block of fuzzy sunlight. He shifted his weight, rubbing the red marks across his wrists. He kept looking over his shoulder.

"Do you know where Chris is?" asked Dylan. "Is he here?"

Hearing Chris' name sent a charge through her, like static snapping down her spine. Her eyes shot open and she lifted her head, scanning the room. Chris wasn't in sight, but he was close. And if anyone was going to find him, it had to be her. Self-pity could wait. "He's here. And I'm not leaving without him."

A heavy thud echoed from the back of the lodge.

"What are you waiting for, Dylan?" urged Jason. "Just grab her. Let's go!"

"Screw this." Dylan scooped Beth over his shoulder. He fought to gain balance, muscles trembling, burning with effort. "Whatever you did," he said, "you don't deserve this shit."

Then he tore across the room towards Jason, who'd already slipped off the porch and vanished into the trees.

68

THE BOY and SANDERS

A stinging slap yanked Chris awake.

"Wake up, little shit." Sanders tossed away the crumpled duct tape. "You're not here to rest."

The first thing he felt was pain exploding in his right hand, racing up his arm and through his body. He tried to raise his hand to his eyes, then remembered the binds. What had happened was no nightmare—his finger was gone.

Blinking to clear his vision, Chris found himself sprawled on a cold floor in a dark room, his back pressed against a pole. Sanders loomed over him, his face hanging in the air like a ghost, rusty eyes above a twisted, blood-red mouth. The smell of wet timber, dried beef, and liquor filled Chris' nose.

Before passing out, Chris grappled with thoughts of ending his life. If he killed himself before the crazy nut cut off all his fingers and toes, at least he'd die on his own terms, dignity intact. And it would take away the man's pleasure in doing it himself.

Then, images of his sister flashed in his mind, stopping him. "Beth...where is she...?"

"He misses his sister." Sanders shifted his weight, straddling Chris' body. "Hurts, doesn't it? Missing someone you love."

His words sliced through Chris like a steel saw. The room stood silent around them, no sounds from outside.

Dizziness kicked in, and Chris turned his head. What was the point of sparring with this guy? The man held total control. What worked for Chris at Aldian Park didn't work here. At school, Chris could provoke his peers, challenge them to honor their threats. And half the time, they'd fail to show up for the fight. But this wasn't school. This man was intelligent and dangerous—two qualities most kids lacked. And he showed up, armed with everything that stripped Chris of any hope or victory. He was fish bait compared to this guy, a worm on a hook used to reel Beth into this nightmare.

"Please," Chris pushed, his throat so raw he felt it crack. "Just leave her alone."

Sanders pulled back a few inches. "Well, aren't you the brave one?" His eyes flickered, followed by a shocking tweak in his chest. Maybe it was all the bullshit sensitivity training from his years in New York. Or maybe the booze screwed with his mind. Either way, it didn't matter. Sanders had a plan.

He unhooked the pistol from his holster, his expression shifting from suspicion to curiosity. "Answer me something," he whispered. "Who's the kid with the glasses? Is he part of your little gang?"

THE GIRL and DYLAN
THE GIRL and DYLAN

The sharp crack of a gunshot, followed by a chilling cry, shook the woods to their foundation.

"Jesus Christ!" panted Dylan, stumbling over a fallen branch. Dusk had settled, and he crept around trees, barely able to see. "What the hell was that?" His shoulder dug into Beth's diaphragm, the pressure foiling her efforts to breathe, let alone protest.

Still, she strained to speak, stammering in between breaths. "N-No! S-Stop! Let m-me d-down!"

But Dylan marched on, pushing past splintered branches, rotting logs, and the cold slap of wet leaves. Before trailing Jason and Beth to the lodge, he never realized what he could endure. Ever since his talk with Chris, the idea of being a soldier—resilient, trustworthy, the one others counted on—had taken root in his mind. Now, just like in his games, he was the soldier, hauling a wounded companion through the muck. Only this time, his 'comrade' was a squirming, defiant twelve-year-old girl.

"L-Let me d-down!" Beth kicked and punched Dylan's back. Images of Chris hobbling in the front yard sliced through her mind, turning the world from dark to blood red.

She saw it again:

The boy crashing into Chris during a football game.

The sickening crack of his collarbone snapping like a chicken wing, overlapping on itself.

Chris clutching his arm, face wet with tears.

The excruciating pain she feels as she watches.

Beth had never seen Chris so helpless as when Mom wrapped her arm around his waist and guided him into the house. A storm of fury ignited in her, and all she could do was storm up to the boy, eye stinging with tears, shouting every nasty word that came to mind. She refused to believe it was an accident.

She could hear Dylan hissing for her to shut up, but didn't stop until he pulled her off his shoulder, dropping her to the forest floor. A sharp rock stabbed her back, triggering an involuntary yelp.

"Sshhh!" Dylan's weight pinned her down as he slapped a sweaty hand over her mouth. He whipped his head around, eyes darting. "You want him to find us?" he growled, gasping for air.

His grip stifled Beth's screams, but her body quaked under his weight, making him feel like he was riding a mechanical bull. He knew Beth could be tough, but the raw strength and fury beneath her fragile exterior took him by surprise.

Rage and frustration surged through her, the veins in her head pulsing. The more Beth fought, the harder Dylan pressed, his trembling hand firm against her nose, cutting off her breath.

Then it hit her—the revolver, tucked inside Jason's jacket pocket. She'd slipped it there yesterday. But the man had taken the jacket!

Dizziness crept in. Fear replaced the rage, and soon darkness greeted Beth in a world where thoughts and cares no longer existed.

THE BOY
THE BOY

He had often wondered what a gunshot felt like—morbid curiosity sparked by his studies of the Civil War. But he never imagined he'd experience it. Chris could only describe it as hot, searing pain, like a blister the size of a thumbnail exploding inside his body.

At first, shock drowned the pain, and for a moment, he wondered if the man had fired a pellet gun. But as the shock wore off, a burning sensation shot through him, creeping and bubbling under his skin like wildfire. When the sharp, sulfuric tang of gunpowder filled the air, followed by the metallic taste on his tongue, there was no denying the bullet's power.

Then came the screams.

Louder than Chris imagined possible—so thunderous the man had to cover his ears to drown out the noise. Before Chris could savor even a crumb of satisfaction, the man swung his leg back, punching the heel of his boot into his stomach. Breath exploded from his lungs, and Chris arched forward so hard he heard a crack. It felt like the man's foot tore through him, leaving another hole.

The screams twisted into strained gasps as hyperventilating pulled him back into the harsh world he'd just been ripped from.

69

BETH and CHRIS

Beth hated to shower, especially in winter.

Stepping back into the cold world beyond the misty glass doors, she found herself thinking about the womb. Sometimes, she even longed for it. How ruthless to be torn from a warm, protected place and thrust into an icy world that didn't seem to care about a baby's shock or pain. Funny how the first thing a person feels in life is suffering.

Despite being seven minutes older, Beth felt like the little sister, the Robin to Chris' Batman. Mom liked to tease that Chris booted Beth out of the womb to claim more space for himself. Beth never laughed at that. Sometimes, she even nursed a quiet grudge. Maybe if Chris had arrived first, he'd be the one with the fragile immune system, the one whose body struggled fend off every passing bug.

Beth's first few weeks in life may not have been the worst, but they were still rotten. Born into distance, and Chris born into touch, she didn't get to go home wrapped in a cotton cap and blanket. Instead, she'd been taken from Mom's arms and forced to spend her first weeks behind slanted glass in intensive care.

Doctors, fascinated by her rare condition, hovered in white coats and masks, prodded her endlessly in search of answers. While Chris snuggled at home, warm and held, Beth survived behind glass, her world humming with machines and fluorescent light. She was untouchable, except through thick rubber gloves.

The bond a baby instinctively reaches for—mother, skin, heartbeat—was replaced by latex and observation inside a clinical and sterile environment. Maybe that distance lingered, not just between Beth and her mother, but between Beth and everyone else.

Still, it could have been worse. Whenever life felt heavy, or a flicker of bitterness towards Mom began to bloom, Beth would think of the Chinese girls, and the weight would lift. Grandma, who died before the twins were born, used to tell the story of a young Chinese couple in the same maternity ward where she delivered Mom. When the father discovered they'd had twin girls, he was horrified. Disgusted and ashamed, he insisted he and his wife leave the babies for the nurses.

When that thought no longer eased her heart, Beth turned to books. Reading offered comfort and power. She found relief and control in creating worlds where pain had purpose and endings could be rewritten. She crafted characters who charged into adventure, bending to her will and dancing to her voice. On the page, she was a quiet god.

Sometimes, those stories slipped into her dreams. And though Beth hated to sleep, she loved to dream.

Once, Beth experienced the euphoria of a lucid dream. She was steering a two-hundred-ton bulldozer straight through the front door of her house. Walls crumbled, dirt rained over her head like sooty hail, and shattered glass crunched beneath the treads, grinding the foundation. Her family stood unhurt but horrified, their faces twisted in disbelief.

Beth hopped off the tractor with the same ease as stepping off a stool and beamed. *Don't worry, everyone! I'm dreaming—it's fine! I can do anything I want!*

Then she popped from her dream, sure she'd felt intangible bodies crowding her, waiting to pull her spirit into some mysterious abyss. She feared the elusive dream gods had discovered her trespass into their clandestine world and were reaching through the seams to silence her.

Dying in your sleep had always sounded peaceful. But the more Beth thought about it, the more unsettling it became. What if you died and didn't know it? No closure. No goodbye. An eternity of unawareness. That, she imagined, might be hell.

It seemed unthinkable to demolish her own home and hurt her family. So why had the man brought up the fire? Why did the accusation make something inside her twist? What if her subconscious has buried a plan so dark, so impulsive, she'd willed herself to forget it? Beth didn't fantasize about hurting anyone. But she'd read enough to know that the subconscious was powerful and controlling, capable of more than anyone dared to believe.

○   ○   ○

Aside from the occasional nightmare, Chris rarely gave dreams much thought. He didn't need the escape. He loved life—the clatter of skates on ice, the thrill of motion, the ease with which people gravitated to him. Friendship, coordination, and charm came easily. While Beth lay in bed on slow, gray Saturday mornings, he was already outside, skylarking across frozen lakes or asphalt courts with his buddies.

Still, he admired his sister's comfort in solitude. But her lack of need for praise or approval puzzled him. There was something unshakably self-contained about her. Something he couldn't name.

For Beth, time once bled like watercolors in a rainstorm—soft edges, no borders. Spending time sheathed among the walls of her shell, seasons blurred and months slipped past unnoticed. She'd often forget what time of year it was. When did spring begin? When did the air turn cold? How long was a day? A year? Did time move differently for everyone, shaped by perception, by age, by intelligence, by pain?

Sometimes she'd find herself stunned to witness the sun peeking up from the horizon, how easily gray surrendered to light, as if her thoughts alone could turn the earth and control time.

As the twins fell concurrently into unconsciousness, each thought was the other: wrapped in a thick blanket of warm blood, sharing the same fragile dream.

70

SANDERS

He underestimated the impact of his kick. The blow lurched the boy's body forward so hard that the ties snapped, unleashing him from the pole.

He slung the boy over his shoulder and stumbled to the lodge.

For a moment, Sanders stared, blinking as if the room had warped around him. Inside, the air folded around him, thick, stale, too quiet. He shook his head, a futile attempt to gain focus, then stiffened.

He dropped the boy like a rucksack of bricks and circled the pillar with manic energy, eyes dragging over every inch.

The broken ties lay on the floor. Shadows lurked everywhere, thick in the corners as if waiting to speak.

Sanders moved with swift, angular steps, carving through the room in sharp, diagonal lines. If the kids were close—watching, holding their breath in some crawlspace—he'd have caught that sour mix of sweat and sugar that clung to frightened children.

But there was nothing. Just the dark. And the slip of something unraveling inside his head.

His hand slipped to the Glock at his hip as he snatched the sheepshead knife from the table, snapping open the blade with a clean, metallic click. Without a second thought for the rotten staircase beneath him, Sanders charged up the steep stairs, his boots slamming against the steps like gunshots.

He tore through each room, overturning tables, splitting desks in a furious rage. Dust and debris hung in the air like ash after a fire, thick and grimy, clinging to his sweat-slick skin.

"Where are you, you little bitch?"

He picked up a hardback chair and hurled it at the boarded window. The leg caught and punched through what was left of the glass, popping a board free and exposing the bottom section of the three-by-two-foot window. The loose plank fell, thudding against the dirt below.

Sanders shoved his head through the opening, his hard-boiled, twitching eyes raking the treeline for movement.

THE GIRL
THE GIRL

She woke shivering, her back stiff, head throbbing. Every time her neck gave out and her head dipped, she jolted up again, fighting sleep with what little strength she had left. As usual, her body always won.

The dusty moon vanished behind a sea of dense clouds, turning the sky from pale sapphire to bottomless black. The woods stood still. The only sounds were invisible crickets chanting in the grass and trees—and someone breathing. And it wasn't her.

Beth lay on the rocky forest floor, cheek pressed against two jagged lumps, the heartless airs of the forest curling around her. Her throat felt dry and raw. The last thing she remembered was Jason vanishing from the lodge—and Dylan, dragging her away.

It felt like waking inside a nightmare—a horror film. A girl wakes up alone in the woods, voiceless, the air cold and creeping under her skin.

Back home, Beth would plan heroic escapes from hair-raising scenarios like this. But here, outside her bedroom, her body lay frozen. One wrong step—one root, one stone—and she'd smash her head open in the dark.

And even with the sun shining, the woods wouldn't let her off that easily. Freedom, if it still existed, stayed out of reach. She wasn't going anywhere yet.

A jacket lay across her chest, cold and stiff with dew. She

rubbed her eyes and turned towards her pillow, expecting Jason's legs and finding Dylan's instead.

Slowly, she pushed herself onto her elbows. Dylan lay slumped against the base of a wide tree, head bent to one side, asleep. Dark hair veiled his eyes, his mouth forming an O. Beside him sat Chris' knapsack; beneath his right hand was the bolt cutter.

Hesitantly, she reached out and shook his shoulder. "Dylan, wake up."

Heavy breathing stopped as he shivered awake. "What is it?" he slurred, his eyes fastened shut, voice thick with sleep. "What's wrong?"

"I don't know." Beth clutched the jacket against her chest. "You tell me."

It took Dylan a minute to peel open his eyes and gather focus. Guarded, he looked at her. "Did you see or hear anything?"

Beth bit her lower lip, shaking her head.

A deep breath, then, "Thank God."

Beth kept her eyes on Dylan.

The corners of his mouth flattened. "What?"

She sniffed. "I...I'm scared."

A pause. The lines on Dylan's face disappeared. "I know," he said. "Me too."

"Who is that man? What does he want? Why is he doing this?" But even as she spoke, Beth could not deny a feeling of recognition for the man. A shadow of familiarity she couldn't place.

Dylan shrugged. "I don't know. But he's pissed off at you for something. And now Jason's caught in it."

She turned away, chest heavy. "You too."

Dylan sighed, opened his mouth, then stopped. He looked like he might snap back, but shrugged instead.

A breeze stirred the branches, carrying the scent of pine. Beth curled tighter under the jacket, trying to resist the cold creeping into her bones. Something small scurried through the nearby brush, the rustling spiking her pulse.

"What now?" Dylan rubbed his eyes with the back of his hands.

She thought long and hard about what to do. Chris was still out there, trapped with that man. She had to find him.

But she'd left the revolver inside Jason's jacket.

Was violence justified—maybe even forgiven—when it was the only option?

She thought of Dad.

In moments like these, Beth often imagined what he'd do. Maybe Chris did the same. But she lacked the courage to ask. Instead, she'd grown used to relying on her own voice, hoping it echoed her father's. "I'm going to get my brother," she said.

Dylan, eyes masked by the darkness surrounding them, stiffened his back and studied her face. "Listen," he said, his voice quiet, "I want to help. I'd even go back to Jason's hut and check for your brother. But..." He nodded at the bolt cutter. "I can't. Everything has gotten crazy. It's gone too far."

"I never asked you to help. You and Jason already did enough."

Throughout her short life, Beth learned battlegrounds weren't just for men and boys, nor bravery to those who rushed in first.

"Now it's my turn."

THE BOY

He woke to the sound of his own crooked breathing. Streaks of moonlight slipped through the window behind him, brushing the room in shades of ash. Everything was still. A silence so complete it pressed against his eardrums.

A window reflected against the wall before him, and his eyes drifted to his small, shrunken shadow. Shame crawled through him, and he looked away.

After a minute, the room began to take shape. The hard angles of a desk. The warped curve of a broken analog clock, dangling like a fractured eye on the wall.

For a minute, Chris hoped he was trapped inside a dream. But pain pulsed through him, raw and relentless, burning his hand, leg, throat, and chest.

People didn't feel pain like this in dreams. No, he was awake.

"I'm not dead." The words rose from his throat by surprise. The gag was gone, but he could barely speak. The screams had stripped his throat bare.

Chris was in a different room. Good thing, too, because the shed felt ten degrees colder and smelled of shit. He sat on a hard, rickety chair, wrists and ankles bound to the arms and front legs.

He shook his wrists, and something rattled.

Handcuffs.

The crazy bastard had abandoned the ties for metal shackles. Now, he couldn't move without metal dragging against the raw skin along his wrists. Lacking the resolve to withstand new pain, he kept still.

Did the man think he'd turned into some contortionist? That he would chew through the plastic like a starved rat?

Head bowed, Chris took in shallow breaths. "Screw my life."

Like Dad, the man had a talent for sniffing out lies. Chris had thought long and hard about telling him everything—the truth about the hunters and what Beth had done. But the man didn't seem to want answers anymore; he wanted retribution.

So why hand Beth over, too? Of course, the man could have her trapped and hurting right now. Still, Chris held onto that splinter of hope that she remained uninjured and well.

Only an old friend could calm his nerves now.

A familiar voice coiled out of the silence. *"Welcome back, Christopher Pacelli."*

The glamorous host stepped out from the corners of Chris' mind and emerged into a wonderfully burnished presence before him. He wore a black tuxedo, a white carnation pinned to the lapel, and silvery hair combed across his forehead.

Chris gave a crooked smile. "Please...call me Chris."

"You got it, Chris." Hope and concern filled the host's bright blue eyes. *"I came here to say, we're all rooting for you, pal."*

He stepped back, outstretching his arms.

Then the far wall, once lined with broken, rusty nails, vanished. A long line of eager fans emerged, packing the space under lights brighter than the sun. Girls whispered to one another, motionless, pressing their hands in front of tight mouths. A boy who looked oddly like someone on Chris' baseball team punched the air with his fist. Adults in jerseys and bright hats gave a thumbs up, arms raised in a wave of desperate hope. Chris' name stretched across their backs in bold, stitched letters: PACELLI.

He scanned the crowd for Mom and Dad, aching to see them. But he failed to sketch their faces in his mind and saw only empty outlines. "Thanks, Richard."

"Anything for Chris Pacelli."

Chris tried to smile before a breeze whipped against the brittle window. It brushed against the back of his neck, snuffing the lights, peeling the crowd and glamor away, erasing Richard's grin.

Everything fell quiet as Richard knelt before him. His stage-show charm softened; the lines around his eyes grew small, focused. *"I have someone here who wants to speak with you,"* he said gently.

Chris shrugged. He shut his eyes and dropped his head. He expected God—fluffy white eyebrows and beard, finger raised in wrath.

Instead came a shuffle on the floor.

Then a voice. Rich. Calm. Familiar. "Hello, Chris."

Chris raised his head, then froze. Standing before him was Dad, taller than he remembered. He wore a crisp, blue Navy uniform, his white round cap and black shoes gleaming under the spotlight aglow above him. "Dad...?"

He gave a slow, sure nod.

Chris couldn't believe it. His eyes had to be playing tricks. Maybe, in this half-conscious haze of nausea and dread, his mind conjured the vision. But after blinking several times, Dad was still standing there. Solid. Watching him.

"That can't be you."

Another nod.

"I must be going crazy. I am, aren't I?"

Dad shrugged. "Perhaps. But unlikely."

"What are you doing here?"

Dad breathed in a deep sigh. He circled behind the chair and placed a gentle hand on Chris' shoulder. Chris felt a heat bloom, strange and real, tingling all the way down to his toes. A river of tears rained from his eyes down trembling, flushed cheeks. His heart swelled, threatening to tear him in two.

"I'm s-sorry, Dad." Chains rattled as Chris attempted to wipe his eyes. "Is that why you're here? To tell me I screwed up? That I failed you? That you hate me?"

"No. I wouldn't have come for that."

Chris shook his head, choking on breath. "But it's all my fault, Dad. Everything. I ruined everything."

He sat quietly for a while, waiting for Dad to respond.

"You did the best you could. You could never disappoint me."

Chris looked down. "But it was me, right?" It was the first time Chris said it aloud—the confession shaped with breath and voice.

Dad gave a soft nod. "More or less."

"I'm a terrible person."

Dad shook his head. "I know why you did it—emptying the liquor cabinet. You didn't know I'd fall asleep. Or that my cigarette would start a fire."

At some point, Chris had pieced it together: the spilled alcohol feeding the flames, the house catching fire while Mom lay unconscious upstairs, silenced by her nightly sleep aid.

Anticipating a blow against the face, Chris flinched. But nothing came. "I knew you'd get mad about the stolen music. I thought if I dumped everything before you could use it...I just wanted—"

"To protect Beth." Dad's voice softened. "You didn't want her getting in trouble once you ran off to your friend's house."

Chris nodded. "A stupid idea, I know." He paused. "Guess I didn't empty them all, huh?"

Dad said nothing at first. Then, "I was hard on you. And now you know why."

"Yes, Dad."

Chris opened his eyes and raised his head. At last, the memory came clear: Dad's hazel eyes. The flushed cheeks and fleshy nose. The way one eyebrow would rise and the corner of his mouth would curl up when something amused him. How he'd rest his head on a thumb and two fingers when deep into a book. The quiet shrug he gave when asked a question he didn't know the answer to. And that scent—that faint, leathery musk that followed him home from work and settled into the room like a presence.

Chris was further away from home than ever. Yet as his gaze drifted, clarity returned, and he remembered more things. Fragments of childhood surfaced with startling vividness. Old feelings and sensations became clear. He remembered.

The pride swelling his chest when he brought home an A in History for the model World War II ship he and Dad built from popsicle sticks and string. Nearly falling off his seat laughing when Dad, hands caked in glue, cursed at the stubborn frame that refused to hold together.

The satisfaction of smacking down the final piece of their jigsaw puzzles, bonding them inside wooden frames in the family room. Puzzles that Chris promised to hang inside his own house one day.

Tensing as Dad scowled at the phone whenever it rang during dinner.

The quiet comfort of being carried in his arms after late-night drives home from New York, pretending to be asleep just to feel that warmth a little longer. Like a baby, bundled close and safe from the world.

He blinked. "Why are you here, Dad?"

They studied each other, the silence hanging between them.

"The bird failed to work. This seemed the only way you'd let me in now. I came to tell you: no matter what happened, your mother and I love you. You're a good boy. Get out of this mess. Look after Beth—she needs you."

The words pierced. Chris searched his memory but found no

trace of Dad ever saying he loved him. Funny how kids cared more about what adults than what they did. But Chris was starting to see that he and Dad had always shared the same feelings; they just spoke in different languages.

"Now give 'em hell, kid."

He shut his eyes, clenching every muscle to resist the ache in his heart that seemed to pump liquid fire instead of blood. It seared through him, regretful and longing. "I love you too, Dad," he whispered. "You and Mom. I always have. And I know Beth does too."

Silence.

"I just wanna go home," he murmured. "But I'm gonna die here, aren't I?"

More silence.

He opened his eyes. "Dad?"

But Dad was gone. Just like that, Chris was alone again.

THE GIRL and DYLAN

THE GIRL and DYLAN

Despite Dylan's insistence, waiting for the sunrise was not an option. Every passing moment offered another chance for that crazy bastard to hurt Chris—and Beth knew her odds of getting out alive were better if she marked him before he marked her.

Reluctantly, Dylan agreed to stay by her side until they reached the lodge. He'd come this far, and surprisingly, a gnawing sense of guilt compelled him to keep going. If not for himself, then for Jason. Besides, he couldn't bring himself to abandon a frightened twelve-year-old girl in the woods, in the dead of night.

The forest closed in around them, the darkness thick as wet wool. The air had turned sharper, colder. They followed a winding trail, slipping between knotted trunks and crouching low beneath branches like soldiers in war. Above them, no stars. No moon. Just an endless smothering dark.

They avoided open patches of earth, too exposed to feel safe. Crickets pulsed in rhythmic chants, unconcerned about the unraveling world below.

Beth's fingers brushed the flashlight, but Dylan stopped her.

"Don't. You flip that on, and he'll see us coming like we mailed him a goddamn invitation." Then he whispered, "Jesus...he could be behind us right now."

Memories of playing Manhunt crept into Beth's mind—the thrill of hiding in dark corners of the neighborhood during hot summer nights, slipping through shrubs and neighbors' yards, evading the hunter and the sentence on the porch steps. She even found a perverse pleasure combing the area for the boys whenever she was the hunter. Oddly, though, she preferred being hunted. Doing so offered more control. She could run as fast as she wanted, feet unshackled by hesitation, never welded to asphalt or drowning in dream-slowed panic.

But this wasn't a game. And it, sure as hell, was no dream.

Having Dylan near dulled the edges of her fear, but Beth didn't trust her ability to master her actions once he chose to take off. The only way to summon the grit she needed was to lean into the illusion, re-enter the game. Her brother was imprisoned, locked in a hunter's lair masked as a lodge. He was awaiting release, for home, for a warm dinner, and hockey on television. All that had changed was the topography: no concrete bordered by two-story homes, no porch lights. Only miles of dirt packed with trees and plants that seemed to lean in and listen.

To lighten the load, Dylan had dumped Chris' pack under a sprawling oak several yards southwest of the lodge. But he kept the bolt cutter.

He offered Beth some of Jason's snacks; she devoured them in silence, her hunger more primal than polite. But when they finally spotted the blackened chimney peeking out through the trees, her stomach coiled in knots again.

A grassy track, slightly uphill, reached the lodge. It loomed through the thicket like a haunted house. All it lacked was fog rolling from its broken windows and chimney.

Beth yanked Dylan down behind a pine tree, nodding towards

the faint glow from a ground-floor window. "There it is."

They listened.

No sounds, no footsteps.

Dylan turned to Beth. "You sure you wanna do this?"

Beth's eyes locked on the shadowy outline of the lodge. She ran on fumes, pumped with fear and rage. Hesitation, she reminded herself, was no longer an option once she launched the rescue. Uncertainty resulted in worse disasters.

Alexis' face flashed in her mind, determined and unshaken.

Okay. If Chris and Jason are inside, you'll get them out. Remember, this isn't about right and wrong anymore. It's about what's smart. It's about survival. Chris would agree.

Trembling, Beth closed her eyes and took a deep breath. Just as she started to rise, Dylan touched her forearm. She turned to him.

And try not to lose yourself. Don't forget what you'd said back at camp: anger and fear are heavy, temporary. Let love guide you. It's lighter. It lasts.

"Before you go," said Dylan, "I wanna say..."

Now, give 'em hell, kid.

Beth felt her life narrow down to this moment. Soon she would be on her own, apart from Dylan and the world. And not just physically. The kind of alone that lives inside you. The kind Alexis understood better than anyone.

"I just wanna say that..."

Beth's patience wore thin. Every second was another chance for the man to hurt Chris and Jason. "What is it, Dylan?" she asked, her voice tight.

Dylan exhaled, running a hand through his hair. "You're the bravest chick I've ever known. Really. Just wanted to say that."

He looked like he had more to say, but didn't. Beth focused on the shadows outlining his face, nose, lips. Back in school, she'd have kept her distance. Dylan seemed the typical insecure brute, offering snide comments and grating laughs in halls and classrooms. But here, in the thicket of panic and pine, he was raw and unsure like her, sharing an intimate yet poorly timed moment in the dark woods.

A grin tugged at Beth's lips; she leaned forward and brushed them against Dylan's cheek.

Then came the crackling of sticks underfoot, ten feet away.

"Isn't that sweet?"

Before either could react, meaty hands seized the back of their necks. Dylan cried out, a handkerchief muffling his scream. Beth twisted, slipped free.

No time to think.

She ran.

71

SANDERS

SANDERS

What a bunch of twits. Did they really think they could outmaneuver a seasoned detective?

Sanders made a living getting inside people's heads—including those who could barely locate their dicks. He could map their next move before they even thought of it. It was like being a psychic, only without the silk robes, tarot cards, or crystal balls. His tools were sharper. Lethal.

He intended to grab the girl before she made her move on the lodge. But Sanders had misjudged two things: Beth slipped in from the west, not the east—and with her came a fourth addition to her gang. The one who must have clipped the ties and set her loose.

Sanders hated surprises. They disrupted order, threatened control.

The chloroform had been meant for Beth, not her head-banging buddy. That's why she got away—squirmed out of reach like an eel in grease. For someone so shy and squirrelly, the girl sure seemed to have a following among the boys.

But Sanders knew she'd be back for her brother.

Still, these snags were taxing his energy and patience, bleeding him dry. These extra players had nothing to do with the fire or the murders. So what the hell were they doing out here? Smuggling food and weapons like they were on some self-righteous mission?

Time to get the twins together. Play them against each other. Just get it done before they multiply again, like those freaky Gremlins.

With a weary grunt, Sanders dropped the new kid onto the floor beside the couch. He flicked on a flashlight, sweeping it across the boy's face. The kid held a distinct skunk-like smell of pot, wore ratty clothes, and looked like he hadn't seen a barber in months.

After a spell of cold contemplation, he zip-tied the kid's wrists and ankles, hogtying him like he did that foul-mouthed prostitute back in Times Square. Then he dumped him on the couch.

He stepped outside, scanning the blanket of black trees, his movements slow and deliberate. No need for a flashlight. If the girl were out there, she'd see him and know what he was about to do. It was impressive that she'd lasted this long. But Sanders didn't believe for a second she could get past him unseen.

Back inside, he scooped up splinters of jagged glass from the shattered window, scattering the shards along the porch steps. He stood back and surveyed his work with a grim nod. He cleared his throat, slipping back into the lodge.

He dragged a chair across the room and settled into a shadowed corner, pondering the last few hours. A moment of bitter reflection crept in. Would crushing that bastard from Tribeca with rocks or slicing off the fingers he used to play "house" with his daughter have stopped what came next? Sanders had seen horrors he never wanted to revisit. Still, he kicked himself for letting that man live.

That was when Sanders shifted his tactics from brute force to psychological torment. Pain faded. But the mind, once splintered, never healed the same way. It was a cut you couldn't see but felt forever.

The police may have left that apartment defeated, but Sanders made sure to return. He'd coerced the man into his squad car and drove out to a secluded place off the island. In Westchester, Sanders introduced the pedophile to forced nudity and sensory deprivation—blindfolds, plugs, and other restraints cutting off every sense.

Twelve hours later, the man stood frozen and broken—unsure if he was alive or dead—tears streaming down his face.

"If you refuse to be a good boy, or if we receive another call, you're mine," warned Sanders.

Two days later, the man choked his daughter before shoving a .38 caliber revolver into his mouth.

With the 12-gauge resting across his lap, Sanders took one last swig of scotch, the burn tracing a familiar path down his throat. He leaned back into the shadows and listened for the lone wolf to start climbing.

72

THE GIRL

She whirled through thickets, thorns slicing skin, shoulders slapping trees. Her stomach knotted, mucus caking her mouth.

Breath gone, lungs on fire, Beth collapsed against a tree. The world spun; her head throbbed with blood. Nausea rose from her gut.

Bent over, panting, she wondered why she ever liked horror stories in the first place. They'd never scared her, not like they did other kids. They'd amused her. Watching clueless boys and shrieking girls stumble through shadows offered a strange comfort. Beth had always believed she was smarter than that. Smarter than them.

But here she was.

And there were no actors, no cameras, no make-up artists, no scripts. No one to yell "cut" and hand her a water bottle or fix her hair. This was real. The kind of story where the good guys didn't always make it. Where endings were as reliable as campaign promises.

But who were the good guys?

What was she afraid of?

For days, Beth had tried to decide whether she was one of the good ones or if that title belonged to someone else. Every time she'd figured it out, something awful happened. Something that forced her to act in ways she didn't recognize.

And now, another man down.

It was like everyone close to her was vanishing, one by one, like bubbles popping in the air.

The sorrow Beth felt at home and school forced her to reject the world. She grew furious because she didn't fit in—a misfit trapped among cool, likable people. It took time, but she found her place. When Alexis burst into that cabin and freed Beth from grief and embarrassment, the angry thoughts eased.

For as long as she could remember, Beth had prayed for something to erase nagging parents, cruel peers, and harassing teachers. The fire was the universe's brutal gift: it wiped them from Beth's world—and Beth from theirs.

Now, she felt like a machine missing a vital part. Every longing and regret in her short life hit her like a sucker punch. She missed Jason—his eyes, smile; he made her feel intelligent. She even missed Dylan's sneer and sarcasm. She longed for Mom and Dad, to hear Dad's stories at dinner, Mom's scratchy voice calling her from across the house. Most of all, she missed Chris. She couldn't function without him. She didn't know how.

To her amazement, Beth found herself holding the bolt cutter. She must have grabbed it after the man tried to snatch her like he did Dylan. But instead of fighting back, she chickened out and ran.

After a long stretch of cursing herself for her cowardice, Beth stood. Her shoulders and arms ached from carrying the heavy tool. Punishment for letting down everyone.

The idea of playing Manhunt fed her vigor, even lightened her legs, but it didn't last.

After what felt like an hour hiking through emptiness—maybe it was imagining Chris hurt, or the branches raking her face, ripping her skin—Beth slipped back into that burning place in her mind. The chamber where she'd attacked the boy who bullied Chris that winter, where she knocked Chris down on the kitchen tile after he called her a boy. The familiar space where she hurled objects at the wall dividing their bedrooms.

It was no different from the day Dad burst through a closed screen door and straddled a man at a neighborhood party, pounding his fists into the guy's head after he slapped Mom in a drunken daze.

Maybe Chris was right—she carried Dad's anger in her eyes.

Then came an image of Chris crushed beneath that beastly

hunter, the man's filthy fingers digging into his neck. It shoved the old memories aside. Suddenly, it was easy to let fury settle into her bones.

Sweat clung to her skin, but still Beth trembled. Raw emotions surged. She felt her grip on self-restraint slipping, terrified she might not find her old self again after tonight.

But the time for holding back had passed. Her survival voice had urged caution, love. Still, the moment called for Beth to let everything inside her ignite.

Beth was a girl born behind glass. And now, she had to break through.

The only way forward was through the shards.

$$\text{O} \qquad \text{O} \qquad \text{O}$$

The lodge came into view.

She crouched behind a thick trunk, studying the building's outline. Everything was dark, except for a dim light spilling from the first-floor window.

A damaged window sat on the side of the building on the second floor. The lower half was open, and there was no screen.

Could she fit through?

A tangle of trees flanked the lodge, but only one caught her eye. It rose high above the roof; branches had grown wild, some coiling against the siding and thinning near the back. A shard of moonlight broke through the top of the tree, seeming to signal an omen.

Beth hooked the bolt cutter's blades into her waistband. The weight pulled her jeans low on one side, cutting into her hip. She crept towards the lodge, eyes glued only to the tree, holding her breath.

All she had to do was make it up and through the window. Rescue Chris from jail. Escape.

"Yeah, right."

The darkness felt suffocating. A breeze rippled through the brush, and Beth shivered. It was as if the crazy man whispered in her ear, breathing on her skin. With every step, she expected hands to lunge from the darkness and grab her.

Her eyes shifted back to the side of the lodge. The broken window—did it lead to a bathroom? Like in her nightmares?

At the base of the tree, she drew a deep breath and held it. The lowest limbs were thick and reachable, but the trunk thinned as it climbed, and she wondered if the taller branches would hold her weight.

No more time to think.

Beth planted one foot on the lowest branch, reached up, and pulled herself off the ground. Her shoes scraped and shredded bark. Her sore hands clutched each limb. The higher she climbed, the thinner and shakier the limbs became.

"Don't look down."

She imagined herself a machine—always moving, unstoppable. Fuel pumped through her veins, feeding her core. Pain sparked in her leg, but she ignored it. Something strange was happening. She felt lifted, rising above the sour weight of her old life, of everything she had carried. Progress drove her to keep going.

Beth picked up her speed, and before she knew it, she'd reached the height of the second-story window. The climb had taken less than four minutes. The branch she settled on hung no more than three inches thick and bowed under her weight. She held her breath and kept still, the bolt cutter sagging at her hip.

"Wow," she breathed, praying the limb wouldn't splinter beneath her. "Good job."

She eyed the window. Crawling on all fours was the only option. Time was short, but not worth a broken neck. If she fell, game over. Crazy man wins.

Like a cat stalking prey, Beth slinked down the branch, freezing with each inch forward. Her legs trembled, rattling the leaves.

Three feet from the window, she hesitated. Headfirst or feet? The gap was tall enough, maybe wider than a ceiling vent. If she angled right, she could fit. The concern was avoiding slicing her skin on the bits of broken glass lining the frame.

Beth licked her lips. "Okay," she whispered. "Face first."

A cast iron lantern glowed in the far corner of the room, throwing a soft, yellow light. But not enough to see if anyone was waiting on the other side.

Beth drew the bolt cutter from her waistband and slipped her head inside, her heart pounding with anticipation of what she might find.

Darkness.

She eased in further.

Glass snagged the cuff of her shirt, and she gasped, yanking it free.

The window sat five feet above the floor. One wrong move and she'd fall and break a bone. She already knew how much that hurt.

"What is that?" a gruff voice said.

Beth jerked back, then froze.

"What's going on?" the voice asked again.

"Chris?" she whispered. "Is that you? Please say it's you!"

73

THE BOY

He sat in the dark, dazed by the exchange with Dad, unsure if he could untangle delusion from reality. Then came rustling outside.

It must be the wind.

A shadow fell across the wall, then moved.

Had Richard returned? Dad? That crazy bastard?

Chris shot a glance over his shoulder and spotted a silhouette, one he'd know anywhere. A thin, limber frame. Wisps of hair poked out around her head.

Beth.

He couldn't believe it. His sister was here to rescue him.

Great! But how?

"Beth!" he whispered. "It's you!"

THE GIRL

The voice sounded odd, hushed and sickly, but it was Chris! "Sshhh! Yeah, it's me."

"I think he's here. Downstairs. Don't make a sound!"

She nodded, her eyes taking their time adjusting to the darkness in the room. "I need something to break my fall."

A pause.

"Chris? Can you help me?"

"No, I can't," he said, rattling the steel constraints. "I'm chained to this chair."

424 | NANCY P. CORBO

Damn. If she jumped and hit the floor hard, the man would hear and come running. She called to her inner voice, but nothing came. Fine. She'd figure it out herself. "You sound close. Can you slide back a few feet? Help break my fall."

"Are you serious?"

Beth bit her lip. She tugged off her sneakers, untied them, and held them by the tips of their mud-caked laces. She dangled them a foot above the ground, then let go. They hit the floor with a soft thud.

"Whatever you're up to, Beth," said Chris, "be careful."

She eased the rest of the way through the window, hanging by her hands, then dropped. Her socks slipped on the slick floor, and she stumbled backward, landing on her butt. Fortunately, she held close to the bolt cutter before it could smack the ground.

"Beth, what are you doing?"

"I fell. I'm fine," she snapped, rubbing her tailbone.

The room was dusty and stank like a wet hamper. Fighting a sneeze, Beth scrambled up, circling the chair before her. The light in the corner dropped narrow gray shadows across Chris' face, highlighting bruises along his jaw and a cut running from his eye to his cheek.

She held up the bolt cutter. "Look what I have. Tell me what to do with it. Tell me how to get you out."

Before Chris could answer, she rushed across the room, snatching the lantern in the corner. Warm, yellow light spilled across his right hand, gripping a wet handkerchief, trembling on the arm of the chair. Blood had streaked down the side of his thigh.

"My God, Chris. What did he do to you?"

Chris squinted, turning away his tear-streaked face.

He was bruised all over.

Nine fingers.

A bleeding leg.

Shoving every emotion aside but fury, Beth set down the lantern and focused on the bolt cutter. The jaws weren't angled. She twisted them, hooked one blade beneath the chain binding Chris' right hand, and squeezed.

Nothing.

She tried again, with more pressure. The grips dug into her palms, carving red welts. Pain shot up her arms.

It felt like lighter fluid pouring over the embers inside her chest. Her breath quickened, her body tense with fury.

Screw the noise.

Beth unclasped the blades and slammed them against the chain, disgusted by her weakness. Tears pricked her eyes. "C'mon...!"

Chris watched her in silence, the edge of his mouth curling as if trying not to laugh.

"What's that look for?" she snapped, wrestling with the tool.

"You don't have the patience for this." His smirk grew. "Remember when Mom brushed your hair? The bristles got stuck in a knot."

"That wasn't funny," she hissed.

"Mom tried to yank the brush through to detangle it, and you screamed like the house was on fire. You grabbed the brush and smashed it on the bathroom counter so hard, a chunk of it flew off."

Beth grunted, squeezing the cutter again. "And I got two weeks with no TV. Thanks for the reminder."

Chris shook his head. "Beth, it's no use. You should go. Before he hears you."

She stopped and turned to face her brother, breathing heavy, her face slick with sweat. Her look said it all: *I'm not going anywhere.*

After a moment of stillness, the pain in her palms dulled. She repositioned the cutters and tried again. The blades bit the chain with another sharp clatter, like bicycle chains slapping the spokes.

"Sshhh, wait!"

Beth froze. "What?"

Chris lifted his head. "I heard something."

Silence.

Then, "Beth...?" A voice, faint and trembling, drifted up from downstairs. "It's Jason. I'm here."

Chris fired her a look, shaking his head. "No, Beth. Don't trust him."

426 | NANCY P. CORBO

Jason had ditched her and Dylan earlier, yes. But he was terrified, just like she was. And with that charming, wide-eyed innocence, staying mad felt like smacking someone who'd just handed you the first dandelion of summer.

"I found the key. To release Chris."

She hesitated, then leaned the bolt cutter in the corner behind the chair. She slipped her feet into her sneakers, tightened the laces, and crept towards the doorway. A faint glow spilled up the stairs, casting a thick amber beam across the hallway.

She stepped into the hall, the floor creaking under her weight. Chris whispered something, too soft to hear.

Beth crouched behind the wide oak newel at the top of the stairs. Eight steps sloped to a landing, then curved out of sight to the left. She couldn't see anything past the bend.

"Jason?" she whispered.

"I'm still here."

"You have the key to the handcuffs?"

"Yeah."

"Can you bring it up? I can't see anything from up here."

A long pause.

"I-I can't get up there," he said. "I fell outside and bruised my ankle. It's bleeding. I can't climb the stairs."

"Where's Dylan?"

Silence.

"Jason?"

"Yeah. No—Dylan isn't here," he said, voice unsteady. "It's just me. Come down and let's get outta here."

Beth rose, a clammy hand gripping the handrail. "I'm coming..."

74

THE GIRL

THE GIRL

"Jason, you still there?"

Submitting to fear and doubt had grown effortless, mechanical, like swatting away a fly from your plate. At school, Beth would take great pains to avoid eye contact, hoping the bully would vanish like fog. When that failed, she slipped away, jeers fading at her foot heels.

But things were different now.

She would not retreat, not from anyone—not even the crazy man standing between her and her family.

"I'm still here," called Jason from downstairs.

She took a breath and stepped off the landing, making sure both feet hit the tread before moving down the next step. Four steps down, she paused at the winder. Each tread squeaked louder than the last.

Eight steps left.

Anxiety crept in, but a surge of adrenaline drowned it. Beth felt alive, sharp. A toy juiced up with fresh batteries, her senses on fire. She even felt the dust coating the ceiling pepper her hair.

A tingling ran up her spine when taking the final step into the room the man had bound her a short time ago. "Where are you?"

"Over here."

Her eyes took a moment to adjust.

Jason stood tall against the same pillar, a single key dangling from his forefinger. His face looked oddly exposed without his glasses.

"Jason!" A surge of elation rushed through her, proof she hadn't imagined the voice. He was here, ready to help. She sprinted to him and threw her arms around his neck. "Chris got shot," she cried. "That man cut off his finger! We have to get him out of here now!"

But Jason didn't move. His expression stayed flat. Aside from the shaking in his raised hand, he kept still as stone.

Beth snatched the key and raced upstairs. She didn't slow down until the key slipped into the first lock on Chris' injured hand. After a few rushed attempts, the cuff snapped open. "It worked!"

She freed his arms and dropped to her knees to work on his legs. Her hands trembled, her face hot and sweaty. "We're getting you out of here, Chris."

The final cuff cracked open.

All they had to do was walk downstairs and out the door.

THE BOY

THE BOY

He pushed himself up, left leg tingling, right leg screaming.

The motion winded him, like sprinting the bases after cracking a home run. Only now, there were no teammates, no fanfare, no parents hollering at blind umpires. Just pain, fog, and the sound of his sister breathing hard beside him.

"Can you walk? We need to move before he comes back."

Beth's voice pulled him back, and he felt some of his balance return. But unless he could leap from the window and scale down a tree, the only way was through the hall—downstairs.

He looked up, drew a long breath, then nodded.

Beth collected the lantern, wrapping her right arm around his waist, guiding him into the hallway. Groaning, Chris kept his bleeding hand cradled to his chest, biting his cheek to avoid crying out. Luckily, that pain had already started to numb.

They paused at the top of the stairs.

He tilted his head, listening for movements or voices.

Nothing.

Silence roared through the cabin. He felt the blood rushing

between his ears.

"C'mon!" Beth held the out the lantern, gulping between every step. "Let's keep moving. You got this, Chris."

He felt useless, a wet rag slung across her shoulder. He offered eager nods and cheerless smiles, hoping her fortitude could carry them both through the front door.

He wanted to tell her about his talk with Dad, but time was short. And Beth's eyes were distant and focused, locked on escape. He even tried cracking a joke, something to ease the air or grab her attention, but the words tripped and died on his tongue. He had so much to say, but her relentless determination, her fierce loyalty left him speechless.

Aside from the lantern, darkness swallowed the staircase, so Beth told Chris to hold the railing with his good hand. He obeyed, though hundreds of thoughts packed his mouth, dizzying his mind. Who knew what waited for them below?

He thought of nights they used to lie side by side in his bed, hand shadows dancing across the wall, the babysitter downstairs waiting for Mom and Dad to return. The memory was swallowed by flashes of threadbare towels, blue and pink safety pins, and climbing the wooden spindles of their staircase in Long Island. Suddenly, Chris understood what it felt like to be Robin—the wingman, not the captain.

Step by step, they reached the landing. The floor shifted under their weight, groaning.

After what felt like hours, they stumbled upon the first floor.

A dim light glowed in the far corner. Cracks in the boarded windows struck thin streaks of gray, just enough for them to escape.

Lumbering across the room, Chris spotted Jason standing beside the pillar and gave him a subtle nod.

Pale and stunned, Jason kept still.

A voice cut through the dark. "You're not going anywhere."

Chris felt Beth's muscles tense beside him. She stopped short, colliding with him.

In a flash, a shadow lunged from below the stairs and snatched him from Beth's grip before he could hit the floor.

"Chris!"

Beth stumbled, dropping hard onto one knee. The man locked a thick arm around Chris' neck, dragging him like a hostage across the floor.

Chris panted faint, tangled words, his shoes scraping madly against the planks. He twisted, thrashed, but the pressure on his throat locked him in place.

Beth's voice broke free before her mind could stop it. "Let him go, *you fucker*!"

Jason gasped.

The man froze, then laughed. "Listen to little Miss Potty Mouth!" He flung Chris onto the couch beside Dylan's lifeless body, eyes glued to her. "No longer the shy little girl anymore, huh?"

He stepped closer.

"Get outta here, Beth!" cried Chris.

Her eyes swept the room, as if searching for direction.

What was she waiting for? If she didn't run, she'd be caged here, too. And the man would take her apart slowly, one finger at a time, like daisy petals.

"Run!"

The man closed in, and Beth switched focus.

75

SANDERS

"I knew you'd be back."

He'd been crouched behind the stairs for nearly half an hour, listening to the whispers and footsteps on the second floor—an idea offered by his new partner-in-crime, whom Sanders kept locked in the corner of his right eye.

Just like he predicted, the girl returned. The porch glass had done its job, steering her towards the tree. The tree that climbed all the way to her brother's window, just far enough from the stairs, tempting her with false safety.

The girl was resourceful. Sanders gave her that.

"Your leaving broke my heart." This power, manipulating them like dolls without strings, felt intoxicating.

"Go!" the boy shouted behind him.

But the girl didn't move. She stood frozen, eyes locked on Sanders. Then slowly, she shook her head.

Even drunk, he saw the shift in her eyes. Something clicked inside her. She stiffened, her eyes turned cold, steady, unblinking. Radiating courage and clarity, she gave the look of someone who'd made a decision.

Intrigued by her pluck, Sanders stilled. He watched, fascinated.

With the shotgun slung over his shoulder, he inched forward, closing the gap to five feet. Why she hadn't tried to escape was extraordinary but logical. Kids were stupid, always thinking of themselves as indestructible.

"I have a proposal for you, Beth."

Sanders saw her jaw ease, but imagined her insides pulsing harder than his with every step he took. "You and your brother. I'm offering you a choice. How's that sound?"

The air between them thickened. Distinct smells of fear and guilt ripened, scents Sanders could read like headlines. Years on the force had taught him to sniff them out, even if those skills had dulled after getting kicked to a desk.

His head grew dizzy, insides shaking. At first, he thought it was nerves, then remembered having fantasized about a moment like this for twenty years. Only the encounter took place where everything began—inside a charming, two-bedroom home on the cliffs of Sleepy Hollow, before the final act unfolded at the quarry, where he left what remained of the man's body.

These tremors were not stress-induced but excitement. The buzz of triumph. Sanders was finally getting what he earned.

Only something else crept in. Something unsettling. Something cold.

76

THE BOY
THE BOY

Flopped on the couch with Dylan's head against his side, he watched the man's eyes lock on Beth's every move.

"Go get help, Beth!"

But his wheezing commands failed to deter the man. Restless and mystified, Chris shivered, witnessing this strange connection between them. He avoided sudden movements, the man standing two steps away from his sister.

Jason cleared his throat, and Chris snapped his head at him, shooting him a look. Since laying eyes on him in the annex, Chris never trusted Jason, and for good reason. The kid—son of a deranged asshole—had proven his falsity by leading the crazy man here. He must have learned what had happened to his father and was out for revenge. There was no other explanation.

"Hey, asshole!" he called, voice strained. "Leave her alone. It's me you want!"

The man smirked, eyes fixed on Beth. "How does that sound?" he asked again.

"A choice...?" echoed Beth.

"Unless you want to pick up where I left off. You think mutilating your brother's pitching hand ends this?"

"Leave him alone. Don't hurt him anymore."

The man nodded—not in agreement, but understanding. "Sympathy for your family now. How noble."

Beth twitched.

"I see you. No one understands you. You resent them all for it."

She shook her head.

"You've wished them dead." The man smiled, nodding again as if confirming his words for her.

Chris saw the tremor roll through his sister's body. Her fingers twitched by her sides, but didn't lift. "Don't listen to him!"

—and Chris (sometimes).

He shifted against Dylan's limp weight, sucking in shallow breaths. At some point, pain had turned to fear. Soon, fear sowed rage and an irresistible impulse to leap from the couch, slam the man into the floorboards, and drive rusty nails through each eye. But with an injured leg and an empty gut, the lust for revenge was a utopia— an impossible fantasy.

Then the man withdrew a pistol from his belt, cutting off Chris' thoughts.

Everyone held their breath as he traced his fingers over the weapon. "Feels good." A beat. "You want it?"

Unfazed, Beth glared at the man towering before her, eyes steady.

"Since you've played with these before," the man said, stepping in, "how about this...?" He reached out for her hand, catching the tips of her fingers. He drew them forward, setting the pistol in her grip. "One bullet. Use it wisely."

The pistol looked huge in her hand. Beth stared past it as if it were nothing more than a plastic water pistol.

"Don't get any ideas," the man said, hinting at the shotgun slung over his back. "I'm quicker than you."

Beth's voice cracked. "Wh-Why...?"

"Because you're not as guiltless as you look." The man's face turned grave. "And it's time you learned what it feels like to watch someone you love die."

77

THE GIRL

THE GIRL

"Your boyfriend or your brother?"

The shotgun barrel leveled at her chest, the same weapon that had split the hunter's skull.

Beth's fingers traced the Glock in her hand, but her eyes stayed on the shotgun's dark barrel—a hole that promised a clean, justifiable end. Death felt distant, yet she welcomed it. The end felt like a dream. The nightmare was real and close. And she couldn't close her eyes and disappear when awake.

Fear gave way to wonder and speculation as she faced the danger before her: a man, unmasked. It took a moment to recognize him—dark, sour eyes, lumbering gait, scars marking his bald head, and deep lines cutting through his face. A heartbroken man stood before her, hollowed by grief, his feelings buried beneath a searing, unstoppable rage. And it gripped her. Beth knew this man.

Or, knew of him.

"Jason!" snarled Chris from across the room.

Jason flicked his head to Chris, eyes agape.

"Do it, Beth. Jason brought him here! We were fine until he showed up!"

The revelation hit her hard, switching her focus from the man to Jason. Her fingers tightened around the pistol.

"That's not true," snapped Jason, pointing at Chris. "He's lying."

"Don't listen to him, Beth. He knows about what we did to his dad. He led this guy to us. For revenge!"

Jason's face changed. Consternated, he looked at Chris but only got a cutting stare in return. His eyes shifted to Beth. "What is he talking about?" His voice wavered between alarm and distrust.

In came images of the hunter's broken head, the urine-soaked corpse. Beth's hand trembled on the pistol.

Jason's face seemed so exposed and unprotected without his glasses. The purity in his eyes delivered a forgotten image of a little girl offering soda in her kitchen. The biting memory of innocence was like a blow to the stomach. Beth saw the boy she had tried hard to avoid at school, how she'd sneak peeks over her stack of books. Campfire talks, that clumsy kiss, and Jason's way of making everything she said and believed feel important.

But the chaos and confusion of the moment stifled the desire to fall apart for Jason and his loss.

"You know what I'm talking about," said Chris.

Silence returned as the kids exchanged uneasy glances.

"She shot your father in the head, that's what. And he freaking deserved it."

Jason flinched. "What?"

"Then we dropped his body in the well he dug for himself."

"Sounds like your cue," interjected the man. "Show them."

Everyone turned as Jason drew a pistol from behind his back.

78

JASON

"Beth, tell me he's lying."

The next few minutes passed by in slow motion.

The uncertainty and silence were unbearable. Like when his father made him stand in the shower, lice cream dripping down his scalp, threatening to blind him if he moved. That had been the scariest moment in his life.

Until now.

Gripping the pistol, Jason swallowed hard, blood draining from his fingers. He stared at Beth through eyes misty with tears.

She mirrored his gaze, a cauldron of alarm, concern, and pain.

O   O   O

Minutes earlier...

Jason learned that when cold and hunkered in the dark, the best way to calm his mind was to think of TV show songs. He hummed them in his head, recalling the kiss with Beth—her dry, trembling lips and how they felt like roasted clay. Her eyes held that canny skill for avoiding connection, the way she stiffened whenever he drew near.

He even caught himself running through multiplication tables—anything to block out the panic.

Huddled behind the staircase, gnawing on two pruned fingers, Jason listened to the bangs and whispers upstairs. From across the room, the man's breathing echoed. Sharp, exasperated puffs fading to deep, fitful snorts. Jason dared not peek to see if the man had passed out; he'd already pressed his luck sneaking back inside the lodge.

Panic had seized Jason, driving him to abandon his friends in a desperate bid for survival. After Dylan sliced through his restraints, Jason tore into the woods, blind to everything but escape. Only when a gnarled root sent him sprawling did the weight of his betrayal crash over him.

Running away was something a coward would do. *But not you,* as Dylan once said.

So, he found his way back to the lodge, searching the first floor but finding no one. Upstairs, he came across Chris tied to a chair, lifeless, chin resting on his chest. He had to stop himself from screaming before rushing downstairs, desperate for the handcuff key.

He heard thumping on the stairs, then raced behind the winding staircase, unseen. The door slammed open. The man hobbled in, Dylan limp across his shoulder. He thought about grabbing the knife and demanding Dylan's release, but then remembered the man's shotgun. No knife could stand up to that.

The next option was to escape. But outside was dark and dangerous, especially without a flashlight. And each time Jason considered rushing for the front door, his muscles locked up, paralyzed, as if an electrical shock seared his nerves.

His choices were bleak: slip upstairs and find some way to rescue Chris and escape through the second-floor window, or wait for dawn, then flee and get help.

The floor groaned, freezing his thoughts. There was no time to scream. The man slapped a hand over Jason's mouth, yanking him off the ground.

79

THE BOY

"See, I told you they were together!"

"Beth." Jason's fingers twitched around the pistol at his side. "Is this true?"

Beth sobbed, struggling for words.

"Don't think that you're at a disadvantage," the man said, pulling a second handgun from the back of his jeans.

Everyone froze.

The man moved to the couch, shotgun still trained on him.

Jason backed into the pillar as the man brushed past, his finger grazing the trigger guard.

"Same rules," the man said, his teeth showing in a mocking grin. He placed the Glock on the arm of the couch, taking his time.

Chris tried to writhe away, pressing against Dylan's weight.

"One bullet, use it wisely. And don't even think about pointing it at me. You know what I can do." He backed up, positioning himself against the fireplace, eyes sweeping over the three of them.

Chris took his eyes off the man long enough to glance at the gun in Jason's hand, regret lacing his thoughts. How did he know Jason was holding a pistol? He knew Jason would do anything the man said to stay alive. And now he had more reason than ever to retaliate.

"Beth," Jason pushed. "Did you do it?"

A long moment, then, "It's true."

Jason's jaw dropped.

The man grinned.

Chris froze, watching Beth use the weapon in her hand as an excuse to avoid eye contact with Jason.

"I wouldn't be too surprised, kid," said the man. "She's done this before." He turned to Beth, frowning. "Haven't you?"

Jason's armed hand rose to his waist as if pulled by some invisible thread. "What is he talking about?"

"She killed her mommy and daddy. Burned her house down."

Chris held his breath. He didn't make a move for the Glock.

Beth's head shot up. "I didn't kill my parents."

"We already know you're capable of murder. So why not put arson on your list of crimes?"

"This can't be true," said Jason.

"It wasn't faulty wiring or a gas leak."

Jason cocked his head, offering the man a glassy stare.

"What, you're not going to trust the man who tried to save you from your father six years ago?"

The man marched to the table and picked up a small purple book covered in tiny white hearts.

Beth gasped.

He tossed the diary at Jason; it slapped against the floorboards, dust puffing around his ankles. Jason recoiled, like a snake had leapt at him.

"Have a read. It's all there." The man dragged a hand into his front pocket, pulling out a crimped photo of thirty students from a sixth-grade class, two of whom were Beth and Jason. He waved it in front of Jason. "Must've slipped out of your pocket while planning your revenge," he sneered. "Still want it?"

Chris knew what the man was doing. He had to pull attention away from Beth. "I did it!"

All eyes snapped to Chris.

"It was me, okay?" His gaze met Beth's. "I was the reason for the fire. It was *me*. I did it to try and help you. I knew Mom and Dad would blame you for what happened at the store."

Beth held her breath.

"And all I wanted was—remember how we used to joke about

dumping Mom and Dad's drinks, then slipping Mom a sleeping pill so we could run off and do something fun?"

Beth nodded once.

Out in the corner of his left eye stood Jason, raising his weapon to chest level as if taking a cue from the man.

Chris switched his focus to Jason. "Don't point that gun at her, fucker!" He seized the Glock off the couch and aimed it at Jason's chest with his shaky left hand. "Your father was a piece of shit. He deserved it."

Jason, still aiming at Beth, jerked his head to Chris. "You two...my father...?"

Beth straightened her arms, and Chris saw her handgun pointing just above his head. "Chris...you didn't."

He kept his eyes on Jason. "It was an accident, Beth. I was looking after you."

Jason, still fixated on Beth, didn't register the threat. "Why...?"

"Your dad was a sick pervert! Now, drop the fucking gun!"

"Chris, no more," pleaded Beth. "Stop pointing that at him."

Jason blinked the wetness from his eyes. His hands shook, his finger hovering over the trigger.

"Stop pointing that at her!"

Seconds later, the blast of gunfire, followed by another, roared inside the lodge, dropping one kid to the floor.

80

THE GIRL

Explosions rocked the lodge. A familiar, acrid stench of gunpowder assailed her nose. For a moment, she could hear nothing but the blood rushing in her ears.

The jolt forced her finger to the trigger. The sound of the shot tore through her skull; her wrist throbbed where the pistol kicked back.

From the darkness came a sharp clink of metal, followed by Jason's strangled howl as he crashed to the floor. The force of the shot slammed Chris against the couch, his body jerking forward before colliding with the armrest.

"Chris! Jason!" Despite herself, she dropped her weapon and rushed to Jason, falling to her knees.

The bullet struck his chest. Blood oozed out of the wound, his body quaking. Tears streaked his cheeks, blood leaking from his mouth. He stared up at her, eyes wide, fighting to breathe.

"I…w-wouldn't…have sh-shot…" he choked. "The gun…I knew—I wanted to f-fool him, m-make him think…I thought…" His voice faltered, breaking apart as it left him. The life in his eyes dimmed, slipping away like mist. His eyelids fluttered, a ragged breath caught in his chest, and then…nothing.

Silence hung in the air, dense and suffocating.

The man's voice broke through, thick with satisfaction. "Finally, one out of the way." He picked at his teeth with a dirty fingernail.

The true enemy revealed himself, standing tall and drunk in a worn chambray shirt, shabby service boots, and a menacing grin. Chris had been wrong for destroying Mom and Dad's bottles, and for shooting the officer—but he wasn't the enemy. Beth understood that his actions, driven by good intentions since the fire, didn't make him deserving of this punishment. Neither did she. Jason and Dylan were harmless, caught in the crossfire. They were all on the same side.

The irredeemable damage she and Chris had caused surged through her, a weight of shame crushing her chest. She knew what it felt like to renounce the world, to withdraw from society. And it had its advantages. But the shame, the gnawing disgrace, was worse than any prison. You could escape a cell. But how do you escape wounds hooked like tumors in your guts? Emotions, she learned, were as addictive as sugar and television.

Although she felt free of guilt from the house fire, she wasn't entirely innocent. If she hadn't walked into Chris' room that day—her sorrowful, desperate eyes pleading—he might not have felt compelled to take her with him. He'd have walked to George's and returned home after a day or two once things cooled down.

And Mom and Dad would still be alive.

Without a second thought, Beth dashed across the floor, stealing the handgun that flew from Jason's hand. She jumped up and took aim.

The man flinched, then stiffened. He made no move to lift the shotgun. He gave her a twisted smile and stood taller, his sureness more terrifying than opposing fire.

If she wanted her brother and Dylan to live, surrender was not an option. She had to do the smart thing—remove the obstacle, so the kids left standing could survive. Screaming, she pulled the trigger. The gun fired and bucked in her hand.

The shot grazed the man's shoulder. He grunted, stumbling back. No blood.

"BB's, kid. You think I'd give him a real gun?" He laughed, tapping his shoulder. "Na, I wouldn't take the fire away from you two." He looked over at Chris, slumped over the couch, his weapon forgotten. "Thanks for the pellet gun, kid."

What the hell happened? Beth had fired over Chris' head, deliberately missing him, hadn't she? But he fell forward, not backward, his head and chest unharmed. Why had he dropped his weapon?

"Chris!"

"Enough!" The man advanced, forcing her towards the couch.

Standing before Chris, her body shook with fury. Then, an alarm screamed inside her head.

The jacket!

The revolver, tucked inside the jacket, hung over the edge of a two-foot-high metal radiator. Chris' head had fallen next to it.

Beth saw an opening. She could signal him without the man noticing. If Chris managed to seize the revolver, he could take a shot before the man interfered. But if she went for the weapon, the man would react fast, marking the end for both of them.

Before she could act, a groan rose from beside Chris. Dylan shifted, and his eyes fluttered open.

In seconds, all eyes shifted to Dylan. The distraction gave Beth just enough time to meet Chris' gaze. He looked up, face stripped of color, marked with red scratches and soot. She directed him with a firm glance to the jacket.

Drained but with unyielding spirit, he nodded. A desperate, painful cry tore from his throat as he moved for the jacket, pulling out the revolver in one motion. He aimed upward at the man, his right hand shaking against his chest. The wound looked awful, a grim testament to the pain he fought to control.

The man caught sight of the revolver, but five feet away, there was no time to knock it from Chris' hand. He rushed for cover behind a padded chair by the stairwell.

Chris pulled the trigger, screaming against the gunfire. The revolver roared and jumped in his hand, the bullet tearing through the air. A second scream ripped from his throat, raw and desperate.

Beth shrieked and fell to the ground, guarding her head with her arms.

The bullet missed, splintering the wall. The man ducked, zigzagging towards the chair.

"No!" Chris fired again. The bullet hit the man's left shin with a sickening crack of bone and bursting flesh.

The man roared unfamiliar curse words. The shotgun flew from his grip and punched the floor, skidding away. As he hit the ground, his foot kicked the lantern, busting the glass. Flames erupted, engulfing the armchair in seconds, then spreading across the overturned, desiccated picnic table. They surged towards the window, drinking the curtains as heat and smoke flooded the room.

Chris pulled the trigger again and again, but only hollow clicks answered. "Beth!"

The cry pulled Beth back from her stunned state, her brother's intentions clear. She shot to her feet and raced for the shotgun before the man could react. Fighting to catch her breath, she aimed the barrel at his head, five feet away. Her hands quaked around the sweaty, cold steel. Fear charged through her bones, but it failed to faze her the same way. The feeling was dull and lifeless, like an old scar.

The man scowled at her, clutching his wound. Bits of bone lay scattered around him, and blood leaked from his leg. His eyes, once full of rage, now shrank in fear, exhuming a fragility Beth knew too well.

His lips parted, exposing clenched teeth. "You think you got me, kid? You think you've got what it takes to kill another officer?"

"Don't listen to him," gasped Chris from across the room. "He's no cop! Do it!"

Demands brimmed her mind: *what was smart? What was right? Eye for an eye? Kill or spare?* She seized on Dylan's moment of clarity, a flicker of hope that Chris might survive. "Dylan!"

"Wh-What's going on...?" His panicked gaze darted around the room before locking onto her.

The fire mounted the far wall, splitting furniture just three yards from her. Keeping the shotgun on the man, Beth grabbed the knife and slid it to Chris. After several failed attempts, he cut Dylan free.

"Get Chris out of here."

"What is going on—?"

"No questions, Dylan. Just go!"

He rose, legs unsteady.

"No, Beth," said Chris. "You're coming with us."

She kept her eyes on the man. "Chris, stop being stubborn and get the hell out of here! Go!" Her voice felt foreign, as if someone else was speaking.

Dylan flinched. He reached out, his hand resting on Chris' arm, then hooked an arm around his waist. Despite Chris' protests, Dylan pulled him up, his legs uncooperative, and guided him to the front door.

"Beth!" shouted Chris. "We're not leaving without you!"

The fire swelled, crackling and hissing, the room growing hotter by the second.

"Dylan, take him out of here. Get him help. I'll hold him off."

"Beth..."

She stepped aside, keeping the man in her line of sight. Her gaze flicked to the boys by the open door. Her right eye drifted to Chris, and the silence between them spoke louder than words.

A storm of emotions swirled inside her. He was an apparition, blurry through her tears—one she wanted to hold and tell she regretted ever wishing dead. Standing there, she willed him to understand.

"Chris," she sobbed, voice breaking. "It's okay."

BETH and CHRIS

Chris held her gaze. In that look, years of memories and unspoken words passed between them, bridging years of distance. A quiet mix of joy and sorrow stirred. His mouth twitched as though he might speak, but no words came. None were needed.

Beth felt it deep in her bones, her lips trembling. She bit her bottom lip to hold herself together. A tear slid down her cheek, free of anger or shame. For a moment, she almost smiled. He nearly did, too.

"Watch the glass outside," she said, her voice low. "Dylan, use your flashlight."

Dylan nodded, guiding Chris through the door.

Beth sniffed, and Chris turned back, grief in his eyes—echoing the same sorrow he'd held when blowing that dandelion years ago.

He stood there, chest tight with something between regret and longing. It was as if the years, the distance, and all the things left unsaid were suddenly too much to carry.

Beth's insides twisted, a silent echo of the pain shifting between them.

There are marked times in life when you wish time would stretch—either to savor a perfect moment or avoid what's ahead. The twins found themselves in one of those moments.

After a moment, Dylan nudged Chris on. The two started down the stairs, disappearing into darkness.

Beth kept an eye on the door, half-expecting, half-hoping her brother would turn back again. "W-Wait, Dylan!" she cried, her focus on the man.

Two faces emerged at the threshold.

"Where's your car?" she demanded.

The man searched her eyes. After a long pause, he revealed the location of his truck and slid his keys to Dylan.

"Dylan, Chris knows that entrance. We've used it before. Take him to the truck and get help. Be careful. I'll be right behind you."

Chris shook his head. "Beth, you don't know—"

"*Go!*"

Dylan urged Chris outside.

Beth was left alone with her worst nightmare: a man who challenged her nature, who sparked every nerve in her body. One who hurt her brother and killed her friend.

A man, unmasked.

81

SANDERS

"Just you and me, kid," he snorted, his half-hearted George Burns joke falling flat at the girl's feet.

He'd thought of strapping Jason to the pillar before dragging the twins downstairs. But the idea of turning them against each other was far more tempting. Genius. The worst punishment than seeing someone you love in pain was to have to do the hurting yourself. With proper manipulation, the twins could destroy each other.

But that didn't happen.

Now he sat slumped on the floor, injured, awaiting the girl's next move. Heat ripped through his leg, but the scotch dulled the pain. The boy's escape with his revived accomplice only strengthened the urge to leap to his feet, knock the girl into a coma, and limp outside to finish the job.

But something in her gaze sabotaged his efforts to move, locking his joints. It was as if she held up a mirror, forcing him to see something he'd kept hidden since Linda died. Something he thought he'd never see again. Something he'd forgotten existed.

He saw himself.

THE GIRL

There was no voice in her head, no guidance telling her what to think or do. All she had was instinct. She looked at Sanders, a barrage of emotions she couldn't decipher, building inside her.

To her left sat a lighter, handcuffs, and bloodied pruning shears. A glance at them pulled Jason's body into view, and Beth shuddered. She fought to steady her eyes, focusing on the tools, knowing what she had to do.

"Well...?" taunted Sanders. "If you're gonna do something, do it. Otherwise, I'll make a move, and we'll see who's faster."

Standing two yards away, shotgun aimed, Beth shuffled back, gripping the forestock. She punched it forward and back, the brassy click echoing over the crackling fire. Her shoulder protested, but she needed the man to know she meant business. When he flinched, she knew he understood.

She patted the table with her left hand, finding what she needed.

"Crawl over to my journal and slide it here."

Beth watched as Sanders slid the book across the floor, his grip tightening before he released it.

She stopped it with her foot and crouched down, scooping it up. The book looked shabby and strangely dog-eared. She slipped it into her back pocket, patting it once.

Losing loved ones was agonizing. Beth knew. She saw Mom and Dad, covered on stretchers, pushed into the white van. The crude sound of the doors thumping shut before the vehicle raced away with its shrilling sirens and flashing lights. She wouldn't wish that on anyone.

Then the glint of Sanders' wedding band caught her eye. "You're an officer," she said.

Sanders pursed his lips. "I was many things."

She nodded at the pillar. "Crawl over there."

The corners of Sanders' mouth rose. Slow and clumsy, he moved across the floor, smoke swirling around him. He coughed. "Now what?"

Beth tossed him the handcuffs. They clattered beside him. "Grab them."

"What?" Sanders sneered. "You wanna play a game?"

"Hurry. You know what to do."

Sanders slapped one cuff onto his wrist, locking it. Pressing his back against the pillar, he fumbled for the second, cursing through a few failed attempts before securing it. He lay on the floor, just as he had left Beth hours ago.

"Jiggle your wrists."

He did, then looked up at her. "If you're gonna kill me, do it now. I don't give a damn anymore."

Beth lowered the shotgun. "You're a smart officer. You'll get out of this."

"I'm not Houdini, kid," said Sanders. "You can't leave me here. And the fire's gonna destroy the forest. You know that, right? You want to kill all the cute animals?"

"I'll get help." The heat of the flames warmed her skin. Sweat beaded her forehead. "But I'm not leaving you here unchained."

She set the shotgun on the table and stepped towards Sanders, keeping enough distance so he couldn't slide out a leg and knock her down.

He grimaced, then coughed.

Beth crouched down, meeting his gaze.

SANDERS and THE GIRL

The world stilled. Even the fire seemed to pause its relentless advance.

A mass of emotions stirred between them.

Intrigued, Beth studied the man's face, shrouded in shadow, the flames flickering shards of light against his sweaty, red skin. Sanders was a towering, frightening figure, the kind that could scare off a bear. But his eyes betrayed him, revealing heartsick emotions long buried behind walls too thick to break. Emotions Beth knew well.

Sanders studied the girl in turn. She stood small, dirty, her lips pale, face marred with cuts. Her eyes—deep and hollow—nearly spilled onto the floor. She was no fearless criminal; she was a broken creature, filled with a rage so familiar that Sanders felt his blood turn cold.

Some merciless, ethereal force had pulled him here and refused to let go. He felt trapped, forced to face things he didn't want to see. Cold sweat broke out, his head spinning, his body numb. Nothing felt real. He could no longer feel his face or fingers, and sounds muffled around him—just like that night, twenty years ago.

"Why should *you* get to live?" he asked.

Beth understood the question. Mrs. Calmin, an avid storyteller, often shared tales about her late husband's work. For an old lady, she had a fondness for macabre stories, and Beth found them a welcome distraction from her own troubles. Stuart Calmin had known Sanders and even helped with his transfer to Wanapatchee. He often shared work stories with his wife, including one about the detective. After Beth pointed out a funny photo of the two officers force-feeding each other beer in the Calmin's backyard, Mrs. Calmin opened up about his past.

"Both officers were accidents," Beth said. "On the street and in the woods. And Chris and I stole that food to keep from starving."

Sanders' eyes dropped. "There's no excuse for what you've done. Those men were police officers. Cops don't take that lightly."

Despite himself, he looked up and saw the child those men had stolen from him years ago. He'd managed to avoid this image while interrogating the boy—but the girl was different. She unnerved him, disarming him with her raw vulnerability and unflinching rage. Chained to a pillar in a burning, empty lodge, Sanders cursed his curiosity, wishing he'd never picked up that damn purple book.

His eyes glazed over.

82

January, 20 years ago...

SANDERS

"She's not inside, Stephen," a voice echoes, faint, like a whisper across an airplane.

Shiny blacktop and police lights reflect off damp concrete. Officers block him from entering the house. "It's too gruesome," they say. The ambulance had already taken Linda to the hospital.

"Where is she?!" Sanders demands, struggling against the officer's grip. "What happened to my wife?!"

Dawn turns the shadows outside from charcoal to a silvery gray when he reaches the morgue. He can't stop shaking. The intruder stabbed Linda's swollen stomach twenty-two times. The diener urges Sanders not to see her face. "The damage would shock you," he says.

Haggard and hunched, Sanders demands to kiss his wife's face one last time. The gashes and lesions reveal how hard she fought.

For months, Sanders stays locked inside his mind, trapped in a psychogenic stupor. Years of sickening guilt follow, laced with an unyielding desire for death.

He'd insisted on leaving that night. Fresh out of the academy, Sanders was working weekends as a barback, trying to save for one last vacation with Linda before the twins arrived. She grabbed his arm, blocking the door. She begged him not to go, said something felt 'off.'

Denying her was a fuckup Sanders would carry to the grave. It smeared every second since, leaving a stain in his mind that no *amount of time could erase.*

Two months pass. No arrests. No leads.

Sanders spends his days at local coffee shops and fast-food joints, eager for any word on Linda's case.

Four weeks pass.

He overhears two men talking about a string of drug overdoses in town. Sanders knows the dealer's name. Seizing the chance, he tracks down one of the dead girl's family members and learns her father works as a detective's clerk.

He befriends the man, then proposes a deal: He will take care of the drug runner responsible for pushing dope on the man's daughter in exchange for information about Linda's case. To his surprise, the man agrees.

Sanders knocks on the dealer's door. He punches him cold, using a pillow to avoid bruising, then smothers him. He shoots him up with 40 cc's of heroin and a load of borax.

The police ruled the death a mistaken overdose.

Later, Sanders and the smiling clerk sit in a coffee house. The clerk slides him a document detailing witnesses and observations about Linda's case. All three offenders, including the driver, are named. But the police won't prosecute—one of the intruders' fathers is a high-ranking bureaucrat.

It is sunset.

The first man is under a rusted car in his driveway, fixing something near the front axle. The vehicle is angled, and his body is sprawled beneath it. Sanders kicks out the brace, crushing the asshole like the insect that he is.

No scream.

The driver from that brutal night is a pain in the ass. He lives with his parents and spends his time in the woods buying and dealing drugs. Sanders tracks him for weeks before scoring his chance. Along a secluded road, he strolls up to the driver's window and shoots two rounds into the man's chest. Then fires wildly into the vehicle, so it looks like a drug deal gone wrong. Sanders tosses the maggot's cash into the car, pocketing a cut—asshole tax.

No scream.

Switch to a limestone quarry fifteen miles from everything. Next to a river, underneath an abandoned trailer propped up on cinder blocks, Sanders takes his time with the third and last man—the savage with the knife.

Sanders slaps him once, twice, three times. Hard. The prick is trying to wake up.

He cuffs the guy's legs, spreads his arms, and chains them to the steel rebar. He runs a feeding tube through the tank lid, avoiding the prick's gaze as he feeds him soup and dog chow. The tube mutes the man's screams. Sanders refuses to let the asshole die from hunger.

Inside a seven-foot-high septic tank wedged in rock, the prick stands helpless, shit reaching his knees. A prisoner chained inside a dark and stinking dungeon. Using a knife, Sanders slices the skin along the prick's legs, letting the shit water leach through.

"You will die alone here," he growls. "No one will be coming for you, and no one will ever know what's happened to you."

The poison oozes into the prick's bloodstream for weeks. Outside, Sanders hears the chains hammering against the rebar and smiles. But the infection kills him too soon, leaving Sanders restless, hollow.

It isn't enough. Not even close. Maybe if he heard at least one scream. Just like the scream exploding from him that night on the blacktop—

○   ○   ○

Nausea hit in thick waves, leaving him drenched in heartache. He refocused on the girl stooped before him. "Was it worth it?"

Beth's eyes drifted to the fire before meeting his. "I was going to ask you that."

"No one gets out alive, kid," he said. "You know that, right?"

Her silence said she did.

Sanders closed his mouth. For the first time in twenty years, a string of tears broke free, drowning the silence that had suffocated him for so long—a dam splitting apart, drowning in regret.

83

DYLAN and THE BOY

DYLAN and THE BOY

"We found it, Chris!" The flashlight shimmered, its beam bouncing off the trees. "The guy's truck!"

An hour passed before they made it out of the forest. Dylan had no idea how he managed, but he did.

He knew not to expect an easy trek—thick brush, dark woods, only the flicker of drooping plants and glints of black bark. Branches scraped his face; his feet slipped over roots and stones. He spoke to Chris to keep him going, repeating that his sister would be fine, that Chris would be fine, that he would take care of him. Sometimes, the reassurance pulled Chris from his daze.

The landscape was fixed in Chris' mind, and in a low voice, he guided Dylan through familiar hills and dense patches of bush.

When Chris first regained consciousness, he found Dylan leaning against a tree, hair matted to his face, hands resting on his thighs, drawing deep breaths. The second time, Chris found himself draped over Dylan's shoulder, rust-red blood from his swollen finger staining Dylan's jacket, his leg leaving streaks of red across his Volbeat shirt. Each time Chris woke, nausea spiked, and every breath tore at his chest. He couldn't tell whether the sickness came from Dylan's bony shoulder pressing into his gut or the effort it took to inhale.

When they happened upon the truck, Dylan was drenched in sweat, legs and back burning with exhaustion. Grief over Jason's death clawed at him, but there was no time to feel anything. The twins needed him, and he couldn't let them down the way he'd let

Jason down. Failing them would mean failing himself.

And Dylan had already done that by allowing his friends to convince him to host that stupid house party while his folks were in Las Vegas.

Nervous energy had driven Dylan to clean before the guests arrived that night. He decided to dust the chandelier in the foyer, but slipped off the second-floor railing, crashing onto the tile and bruising his back. There was no time to tell his friends, and soon a swarm of kids arrived, stuck outside on the street, guzzling whatever alcohol they could sneak away from their parents.

Embarrassed, Dylan stepped outside to face them. Endless teasing drove him to grab a plastic vodka bottle and down what was left. Drunk, he stumbled, proclaiming his attraction to a classmate— a boy.

Rumors flooded the school. The whispers faded when months of anger and embarrassment exploded that afternoon in the hallway, after Dylan pummeled the kid harassing Jason.

Then a friend offered him a joint to ease the back pain.

Dylan often wondered how he'd react under duress on a battlefield. It wasn't until he carried his injured friend through a dark forest, lumbering over hills and erratic trails, that he learned the extent of his limits.

And the mission was far from over. Dylan still had to get Chris to a hospital and Beth to safety. She made it clear that she would find her way out on her own, but Dylan was not about to abandon her either.

Their bodies burst from the woods, lungs gasping for air. Dylan dropped to his knees, settling Chris onto the tarmac before moving him into the truck. Chris wheezed as his body met the cold ground.

Skyway Drive stood quiet, untouched by the world in the early hours before dawn.

Dylan swung open the door, easing Chris into the passenger

seat. A long, strained sigh escaped Chris as his body sank into the cushion, the softness feeling like a distant luxury. His leg and hand had gone numb; he shook uncontrollably, though a warm front made the air feel like summer had arrived early.

While Dylan rummaged through the glove compartment and trunk for rags and a first aid kit, Chris turned his head towards the forest, offering a weak smile.

Inside a breeze, branches and foliage waved at him through the gap in the trees, as if tempting him to return. It felt as though the forest was trying to lure him back, pretending it was a benevolent creation welcoming him. But Chris knew better. Turning back would drain every ounce of life he had left. The forest, he learned, was harsh and unrelenting, the most dangerous thing he'd ever faced or challenged. Even more than Dad.

A sliver of the moon hung low in the east, lucent over the trees. A thick and comforting scent of pine filled the air. Chris had no idea how much time had passed since they'd left the lodge, but pre-dawn light was starting to break between the towering trunks. It bathed the woods in a soft amber glow, offering a quiet relief. Beth would have an easier time finding her way out.

"Beth," he slurred. "You need to get Beth." But all that came out was "Beengeeth."

"It's okay, pal." Dylan wrapped his arms loosely around Chris, rubbing his arms to warm them. He stopped, shook his head, then shrugged off his jacket and draped it around Chris' shoulders. "C'mon, get warm."

Chris' gaze stayed fixed on the trees, eyes going faint.

"Listen, buddy. I'm gonna leave you here, but just for a little while, okay?"

He turned to face Dylan, kneeling beside the open door.

"The sun's coming up. I can get back fast. I'm getting your sister and your pack. Then we're getting the hell out of here."

"…my pack…"

Dylan nodded, the motion sharp and decisive.

The pack was the last thing on Chris' mind. He didn't care if he ever saw it again. But to conserve energy, he kept silent, dipping his head in one slow nod.

Dylan stood and turned, ready to sprint into the trees.

Then Chris spoke. "Dylan," he choked out.

Dylan looked over his shoulder, anxiety flashing in his eyes. Ashen light filtered through the green behind him, dappling the tarmac beneath his feet.

"Make sure sh-she gets out...safe. It wasn't her fault..."

Seeing the once-sharp Little League hero helpless only fueled Dylan's urgency to get moving. He had to look away, choking back the words he couldn't let Chris hear. Eyes tearing, he nodded.

"Would you d-do that...for me...?"

Dylan's expression shifted, his mouth hardening. He nodded. "Of course, buddy. I promise." He paused, then turned back to Chris. "Oh. And happy Easter, dude."

He turned again, disappearing into the trees.

84

THE GIRL

She pressed the journal to her chest, watching the flames consume the lodge, just as they had her house.

Until that moment, Beth had battled the haunting image of her parents' final moments in the fire. To soothe herself, she'd pictured Dad dozing peacefully in his chair, Mom drifting in gentle sleep, both untouched by the fire's merciless grip.

A weight pressed on her chest as she remembered Mom boiling spaghetti for "Italian Night" with the Girl Scouts. A crash, a splash, then a shriek. Beth whipped around to see her troop leader guiding Mom out of the room, skin peeling from her forearm like shredded cheese. Mom was crying. Beth stood still, eyes vacant, watching.

Her mind snapped to Jason, pulling her back to the present.

She stepped towards the lodge, then froze, overcome by memories of her friend. A shudder ran through her at the thought of his body desiccating to ash. In their brief time together, Jason had given her companionship, humor, hope—and oddly, love. He showed her that good, forgiving people existed. People who were willing to risk everything for others.

"Goodbye, Jason," she whispered.

A warm surge of energy swept through her.

Then came images of the detective. Countless horror flicks had prepared her for Sanders to burst through the door, screaming in terror, face dissolving in red and blue flames. Fireballs for eyes, whirling like pinballs; flames boiling his skin and face, arms outstretched in agony.

The detective said nothing as she turned to leave. His silence chilled her blood, more unnerving than any desperate plea or guttural scream. He'd even insisted she end it.

"Just put me out of my misery, kid."

Haunted by his actions towards Chris and Jason, Beth still refused the man's wish. She craved justice, not vengeance—and not by her hand. Instead, she pinned her hopes that the fire would summon help before it was too late.

Strangely, the distress and angst Beth felt faded in the forest; what remained was flushed out inside the lodge. Even in the dark, the woods felt and smelled different. After a grueling battery of tests, she felt herself changing, wondering if the beast she'd unleashed to save Chris would yield to the fragile courage, hope, and love stirring within her.

For years, she'd welcomed anger, fear, and disgust, building her character around the absence of companionship and affection. Aloof by defiance, Beth found amusement rebelling against her peers, convinced there was nothing to love beyond those lavender walls.

She'd kept her warmth hidden behind impenetrable barriers, shared only during rare moments with Chris, Alexis, and Jason— like the night she and Chris shared the stolen food and whiskey.

But Jason had cracked open a part of her she'd long forgotten, and now the haze staining her life seemed to lift. With Jason gone, could she find the courage to let herself be seen again?

Beth wondered if she'd passed the tests. Was she ready to face a world without Mom and Dad? She questioned whether society would accept her, or label her by what they had read, watched, and heard, forgetting she was only twelve.

A breeze kicked in, breaking her reverie. With a sharpened sense of purpose, she knew it was time to hurry out and contact the fire department. But first, she needed to take care of her brother.

Beth turned southwest, hitching up her jeans as they threatened to fall. Fresh winds swept through the trees beyond the hills of the forest. She cried out, pleading with the woods to release her from their unyielding grip. Soon, familiar patches of her surroundings emerged—rotting trunks, fallen trees she'd stepped over and used as benches.

Half a mile from the lodge, the undergrowth came to life with movement and sound. Her name echoed from all directions. Dylan appeared, his flashlight a lone star shining against the dark greenery. "Chris is inside the truck!" he panted.

He led Beth to where the trees gave way to the parking lot on Skyway Drive. Her sneakers tapped on the concrete, and she paused, the firm terrain feeling strange against her feet.

She didn't need to see the space on the tarmac to know Chris had taken off without her.

85

THE BOY

He swallowed the words he longed for Dylan to deliver to Beth, exhaustion clouding his mind. Too tired to speak, the ache pulsed between his shoulder blades, draining him.

Despite their constant bickering and differences, he felt an unshakable connection with Beth. They were one, a single unit. He believed twins could sense when the other was in danger or reaching out. And like dandelion seeds carried by the wind, he trusted his spirit would find its way to her.

The sun poked above the horizon, a patient, insistent glow piercing the glassy black of the woods, streaking the ground with cinnamon light.

A truck zipped past, pulling his attention over his left shoulder. He caught the hum and ticking of the car. Dylan had left the engine running, forgetting to open the vents. The turn signal blinked, its steady rhythm a metronome counting down to something inevitable.

Dylan had slipped up. He'd left the key in the ignition.

Chris pulled himself into the driver's seat, his wounds staining the leather. The truck reeked of stale beer and mud-soaked socks.

The engine roared to life. He shifted into drive, slumped down, and pressed the accelerator with a sore foot. A fierce sense of purpose dulled the pain. He had a new mission. No matter the cost, he'd see it through.

Blood-smeared hands greased the steering wheel. Morning commuters eyed him with wrinkled foreheads and sideways glances.

Halfway to his destination, he spotted a boy, nine or ten,

crossing Rookwood Avenue. He wore a green Jets cap and held what must have been his father's hand, kicking pebbles along the street. As if by divine force, their eyes met for a moment. The boy offered a tight smile, sparking the same fleeting, yet intense warmth Chris felt leaving Beth at the lodge.

He returned the smile, then hit the accelerator.

After a while, Chris pulled the truck over.

He set the gear shift in park, crawled out, and leaned against the truck, sipping breaths of air. His body felt like lead, and the shivering kept on. He looked up, mesmerized by what he saw.

The sky stretched clear above gray hills, a canvas of orange and gold bursting over the grassland, bleeding into electric blue. The horizon shimmered like heated grass, calling to him like a child for his mother.

He stepped onto the grass, then sank to his knees.

He longed to close his eyes, to escape the sting of shame and loneliness, until he touched home and found peace. His tongue, a dry, withered slug, searched for spit. His brain, once a plump grape, now shriveled to a raisin. His stomach clenched.

With each shallow breath, Chris felt the life bleeding out of him. His lost finger and leg wound, irritants compared to the searing pain in his shoulder. And it hadn't stopped bleeding.

When Chris shot Jason, the shock triggered Beth to fire her weapon. The bullet rebounded off the sheet metal behind the couch, puncturing his back. The impact pitched him over the arm, pain exploding in his chest. It was no intentional flesh wound like the shot to his leg.

"C'mon, Goose," he huffed. "You got this. You can make it."

Chris lacked the strength to stand, but he refused to give up. Not now, with Mom and Dad—distant yet steadfast—safeguarding him. He crawled on hands and knees, crimson trails tailing him until he reached the rise in the dirt. He lay his face against the white rubber slab and sighed.

His mind raced through the high points of his short life: his first kiss and how the girl tasted like bubble gum. Kelly Channing, six years old, the cutest girl in the neighborhood. Her short, blond hair felt like rose petals, silky and soft. Brandishing a trophy after the town proudly crowned him the only Little League batter in history to play every inning without striking out. Then came the sting of losing the New Jersey Little League State Championship.

He missed music.

Friends. The competition between them.

The joy of whacking a ball with a bat, square.

Cocoa Pebbles cereal.

The lazy Sundays, tangled in blankets on the couch with Dad.

Vivid memories of Beth rushed to the front of his mind: fantasies of being superheroes, flying through the house. In the backyard, churning invisible treats, like ice cream machines, with the pedals of their upturned bicycles. Shouting for Mom, urgency in their voices, demanding she drop everything to read the words on the TV screen during their favorite PBS show.

"Beth..." His voice scraped out, raw. "Where are you? Is anyone here?" With his eyes shut, Chris raised his head. Beth once told him a human head weighs the same as a bowling ball. He had no idea if that was true, but his felt like a fifty-pound medicine ball.

"Dad? Mom...?" He cut himself off before the tears could spill. A dull ache bloomed in his chest, spreading like a storm behind glass.

He could press on.

And in motion, memories were left alone, denied the chance to break him.

He opened his eyes and gazed at the pentagon-shaped slab.

Could he make it sixty feet?

A breeze brushed his skin. Chris became aware of the tweeting birds and thought of Blake, how his feathers matched the sky.

He lumbered on, praying for clemency from whoever might be listening. Time seemed to stretch—one minute, maybe thirty—until his hands found what he sought. Blood, warm and red against his cold, chalky skin, slicked his palms as he rested his head against the rubber block, his fingers tracing its surface. Sweat stung the cuts on his face and neck. The air buzzed, like a broken speaker hissing out a tune.

As Chris sank into the moment, the world around him transformed. Lights blurred into bright streaks and floating orbs, slashed by slits of blackness. His body grew lighter, almost weightless; the hum of distant traffic faded away. He realized his eyes had closed when the rumble of fanfare echoed against his eardrums, silencing the birds' morning melodies.

Richard pumped a fist in the air.

Mom and Dad stood before him, wearing proud grins.

Lights encased him, shining brighter than he'd ever imagined. Fierce and warm. They drew him in, gentle yet infinite, cradling him without hurting his eyes.

And there were no hard gods.

Chris exhaled his final breath, a smile curving his lips, his mind floating towards his twin.

The boy made it home.

Epilogue

It's easier to leave than to be left behind.

-"Leaving New York," REM

THE GIRL

They tore across streets and sidewalks, lungs and legs burning, pushing aside the fear of being recognized by the news.

In less than two hours, they reached Schicara Drive. What they saw stopped Beth cold: a charred skeleton of columns, heaps of debris, drifting ash.

Chris wasn't there.

Knowing her brother would never return, Beth, disconsolate and starving, sent Dylan home before dragging herself up her neighbor's front porch.

At first glance, Mrs. Calmin didn't recognize her. Then something clicked, and her eyes widened. "Oh!" she cried inside a hard-hitting embrace. "I'm so glad to see you, baby! I was so worried!"

The old lady's gentle smile broke Beth's last bit of strength, and she collapsed into her arms as if her bones had turned to dust. Mrs. Calmin wrapped her in a blanket, gave her warm food, and held her while she cried.

She poured out every moment since the fire. Mrs. Calmin, steady and composed, urged her to talk to the police.

When Beth stood before the authorities, she protected Jason

and Dylan, downplaying their roles. The boys had sacrificed so much for her and Chris, and she was determined to protect their names. She wanted the world to remember Jason for his gentle nature and selfless spirit.

The twins' case made national news, drawing attention to the towns of Wanapatchee, Rookwood, and Hollis. The public criticized the departments' "casual" attitude towards the case. The idea of murdering police officers and burning down buildings stunned the towns, and people were horrified to learn the truth about Deputy Powell and Detective Bennett.

After Beth confessed where she buried Jason's father and his friend, police uncovered the bodies from the well, sparking further waves of outrage.

The departments sent Beth's case to court. At the sentencing, the district attorney referred her to a juvenile review board. The judge agreed, provided she undergo psychological counseling. She complied, and the board sent her to a detention center for evaluation.

There, Beth was searched, showered, and issued a baggy uniform. The staff maintained a polite tone, always asking how she felt and whether she'd received drugs or alcohol from the other girls. They needed to assess if she was a danger to herself or others. They even took her shoelaces as a precaution.

For months, Beth passed the days in silence, drifting through time with a heavy heart, robbed of the chance to say goodbye to Chris. She wondered what might have happened if she hadn't convinced him to let her come that day. In time, she let go of the fantasy of a happy ending. The past, she learned, was seductive, impossible to ignore. It shaped her, added texture, marking her in ways she couldn't hide.

Lacking the will for connection, Beth trudged the halls, avoiding eye contact, praying she'd dissolve into nonexistence.

Mrs. Calmin visited each week with letters, cookies, and paperback books suited for a young girl. Aside from polite nods and forced smiles, Beth stayed silent. The only person she spoke to was her therapist, Dr. Ledger.

At first, she sat quiet in the woman's office, listening to the clock tick. Soon she found meaning in the doctor's name and began sharing her thoughts. Later, she learned Dr. Ledger's first name was Alexandra.

The talks helped Beth realize that clinging to the past neither eased her pain nor improved what lay ahead. For Chris' sake, she had stayed loyal to the past; in doing so, she forgot how to live. With Dr. Ledger's help, she eventually found peace with herself—and with Mom.

Beth realized she wasn't rebelling against Mom. She just wanted to show she could succeed without following the usual expectations for girls. Sometimes she wondered if her defiance had scared Mom, and if that fear had turned into sadness behind a short fuse.

Beth longed for Dad and Chris, but the emptiness left by the mother she never knew ran deeper—a pain she couldn't quiet. Drifting around the house, drunk on Mom's sad songs, like Brenda Lee's "I Want to Be Loved" and Barry Manilow's "Jenny," bleeding into her room, Beth ached for a bond filled with intimate talks, shared secrets, and laughter. She wondered if Mom had felt the same sorrow waiting for Dad to come home at night.

Six months later, her case returned to court. The judge, citing her sincerity and cooperation, released her into Mrs. Calmin's custody under probation, with regular therapy sessions.

It took time, but Beth forgave herself. She owed her family a life, and herself the freedom to move forward. Living became essential; the desire to experience the world grew stronger.

When she stepped out of the detention center, she was stunned to see Dylan waiting beside Mrs. Calmin. He turned, a wide smile spreading across his face, arms open, his short hair combed flat.

"We've been through too much to forget each other," he said. "And besides, I promised your brother."

O   O   O

No one knew what became of Sanders. When authorities arrived, the lodge stood empty. Near the concrete pillar lay a pair of unlocked handcuffs, discarded like a confession left to rot. The air hung heavy with absence, and the walls seemed to remember everything that had passed through them—every scream, every choice, every moment that could never be undone.

The fire department contained the blaze before it could consume the lodge and recovered Jason's body, giving him a proper funeral.

The detective was broken, scarred in ways Beth understood. She recognized his loss, and after years of wrestling with her own grief, she forgave him.

She stepped through the opening, a light breeze carrying the scent of pine and flowers.

The day was warm, the air thick with pine and flowering dogwood. Spring had come early, a season she'd shunned for five years. It felt more like late May than April.

A BB gun hid in her jacket pocket, a silent companion sharper than any photograph, known only to Beth. A solid echo of her missing half. In her other pocket sat a journal, its cork cover and double wire-bound pages whispering promises of secrets waiting to be written.

For years, visions of the woods and the shack haunted Beth. Now, the forest felt strangely forbearing; it welcomed her with delicate whispers and birds circling above fresh spring leaves. Blue jays jeered; magpies and robins sang high in the trees. The air hung dry and light across her face.

Dylan waited by his car, watching traffic fight for speed along the blacktop. Beth had refused to come, but he insisted, saying it was important that she find closure.

The clearing opened through the brush. Beth gasped as a shiver ran up her spine. The logs lay where the twins had left them, still stained a dark cherry.

She studied the shack. It stood alone and shadowed despite the afternoon sun cutting the clearing with streaks of light like a spiderweb. Greenery had carried on its takeover along the east wall, swallowing the structure like a florid flytrap. The siding looked weathered and scarred by years of neglect, with nests of twigs and leaves clinging to rusted nails. The window no longer held glass.

Beth drew a breath, tapped the BB gun in her pocket, and stepped onto the concrete slab. She paused at the door. The hinges barely held it upright.

She knocked, the sound thudding across the wood floors. Then she laughed and reached for the knob. A spark bit her hand, but she didn't flinch.

She opened the door and froze. The room stood still. The familiar scents of wood and mold filled the cabin, the air stale, dust prickling her nose and skin. Soft light filtered through a hole to her left and graffiti scarred the walls, exposing torn insulation. Gaps split the warped floorboards, softened by years of rain. The police had stripped the place bare. Even the mattress was gone.

The space felt haunted, and yet, Beth stood firm. The shack, small and ugly, was no ferocious, four-walled monster. It scorned, reproached, hypnotized—but it no longer hurt her.

"You don't scare me."

Warmth washed through her as her eyes sailed up to the loft. She could almost see Chris there, legs dangling over the edge, hat tilted low, tinkering with the radio, a faint smile on his face. Beside him she sensed Jason, the ghost of a grin lighting the silver frame of his glasses.

"Chris? Are you with Mom and Dad? Are you happy?"

A heartbeat later, a blue jay swooped through the hole in the wall. It danced above her before settling on the shelf to her left, head flicking, feathers bright against the gloom, its chirps sharp and clear.

Beth drew a soft breath.

Memories crashed over her.

Endless, shivering nights on the cold, urine-stained mattress;

the suffocating press of the hunter's body; Dylan curled at the bed's edge; the sharp tang of pine needle tea; Jason's uncertain arms; the electric jolt of their kiss; raw fish slick and briny on her tongue; the beautiful, looming castle; whiskey burning a path down her throat. Every moment blazed in her mind.

Beth let her gaze linger, drawing in the air, then gave a slow, resolute nod.

Mission accomplished.

She turned on her heels and stepped outside.

In the convenience store parking lot, Dylan sat in his used black Dodge Shadow, fingers tapping the wheel to the music in his head. He glanced at the orange can in Beth's firm grip. "You came all this way to buy a can of soda?" he asked as she slid into the passenger seat. "I thought you didn't even drink that stuff?"

Beth said nothing, her attention drawn to the trees, their branches unfurling fresh buds in the spring sunlight.

He slid the gearshift into drive. The tires thumped over speed bumps as they turned a corner onto Rearwood Avenue. "Thanks, but I don't drink that stuff anymore," he laughed. "My coach would kill me. Says it's poison."

Beth turned to her friend and smiled, his freshly oiled baseball mitt resting in the backseat sliding into her sightline. "Who says it's for you?" She tapped the power switch on her armrest. The window slid down, a warm breeze brushing her face.

The road stretched ahead, empty. Beth's stomach tightened as she imagined their next and final stop.

Dylan glanced at her. "So, what's next for us?"

She closed her eyes, letting the scents of spring fill her lungs. The voice that once soothed her with comfort and certainty had faded into silence.

Now, when the wind brushes her skin or the leaves whisper around her, she holds steady.

And in those quiet moments, her twin's words linger, just as they had glistened in his eyes the day he turned away from her for good:

You're freaking brave as hell.

Author's Note

Author's Note

When I was eleven, I loved stories like *First Blood* and *Red Dawn*. Around that time, the idea for this story struck me. One day, a classmate's house caught fire. I left my home, eager to offer support, but as I watched the chaos from across the street, fear and hesitation held me back. Feeling helpless, I went home, powered up my dad's IBM computer, and started writing. That novella still sits on my bookshelf today.

This story is based on real events. While the heart of the narrative reflects my own experiences and memories, I changed some details and characters, adding a few new ones to help shape the story. I turned to my first diary, which begins on July 10, 1986, along with relationships and conversations with family and friends.

I promised my eleven-year-old self I would share this story with the world, and I'm thrilled to finally share it with you.

Thank you for taking the time to read my book. I appreciate your reviews and promise to read each one. If you'd like to stay in touch or follow my future writings and musings, feel free to visit my author page on Instagram at @nancypcorbo or my website at nancypcorbo.com

From the bottom of my heart,
Thank you,
Nancy P. Corbo

Acknowledgements

Acknowledgements

A brilliant author once wrote: "Any writer worth their salt has inside them at least one good book about their childhood."

This is mine.

Writing a book is a lonely business. One can go mad without the support and encouragement of others. I am sincerely grateful to the following:

Thank you to author Tina Carreiro for taking the time and offering your wonderful guidance. You saved me mountains of time and stress!

Thank you to my editor, Chanel Mullins at *Revised Ink*, for helping me tighten Part I of this novel. I'm grateful for your insight and for catching the errors I'd missed.

And thank you to Sarah Binger for taking me camping at Mount Charleston and teaching me the ways of the woods.

Thank you to my parents, Richard and Diane, for raising me to be the strong and resourceful woman I've become—so that I never had to rely on anyone to support me in this life.

Many thanks to my twin brother Jeff, who helped shape this story. You taught me about baseball and shared some of the most intimate truths about your childhood. As the first to read this book, your contribution means more to me than you'll ever know.

My sister Barbara, thank you for being the second person to read this book and for your valuable feedback. I'm grateful for your gentle nudge that helped me move to the next stage.

Aunt Nancy, my second mother and dear friend, thank you for listening to my endless stories and for grilling those unforgettable rib eyes. Your generosity knows no bounds and touches my heart every day.

There are many loyal and loving friends I wish to thank; among them, the following were especially helpful as I wrote this book:

My patient and generous friend, Paj Crank, thank you for your friendship and invaluable feedback on this story before I wrote the first word.

Robert Cruz, for your love, support, and encouragement to keep living as an artist.

My friend Leon Kellar, for your unwavering support and for lending your talents to the cover design of this book. Thank you for dropping off late-night Chinese food when I refused to leave my desk to eat.

Special thanks to Val Stigers for your courage and for opening your heart and trusting me with your delicate story.

James Tabeek, Lisa P. Karpowich (Pieretti), Claudia Caramiello, and Jason Romas—thank you for being among the first to accept me as I am. I don't know how I would have survived high school without you!

And to Rob Neighbors, friend and author. You once reminded me, "No risk, no reward." That phrase stayed with me, inspiring me take this leap. By sending me your first published book, you nudged me to get off my butt and finish my own.

About The Author

About The Author

Nancy P. Corbo was born in Queens, New York, and raised in Wanaque, New Jersey. With a background in broadcasting and as a longtime member of SAG-AFTRA, she combines media experience and performance with creative writing. Now based in Henderson, Nevada, Nancy writes with passion and purpose while balancing her career as a nationally board-certified health and wellness coach. *Brave* is her first novel.

www.ingramcontent.com/pod-product-compliance
Lightning Source LLC
Chambersburg PA
CBHW021118260626
47169CB00005B/1330